Requiem for a Birder

Other Crooked Lake Mysteries by Robert W. Gregg

A Death on Crooked Lake

The Man Who Wasn't Beckham

Setting the Stage for Murder

The Scarecrow in the Vineyard

The Cottage with Too Many Keys

The Haunting of Hawk's Nest

In the Chill of the Night

Death Comes on Silver Wings

Tragedy at Welcome Inn

Requiem for a Birder

Robert W. Gregg

ISBN 978-1-4958-0572-1

This is a work of fiction. Names, characters, places, and incidents either are the product of the author's imagination or are used fictitiously. Any resemblance to actual events or locales or persons, living or dead, is entirely coincidental.

Published June 2015

INFINITY PUBLISHING
1094 New DeHaven Street, Suite 100
West Conshohocken, PA 19428-2713
Toll-free (877) BUY BOOK
Local Phone (610) 941-9999
Fax (610) 941-9959
Info@buybooksontheweb.com
www.buybooksontheweb.com

I would like to express my thanks for their help with a variety of issues I faced in producing this book to Dr. Melissa Brassell, Chuck Dinger, Lois Gregg, Brett Steeves, and most important of all, to my wife, Barbara, both for her many thoughtful suggestions and for her infinite patience.

I am delighted to dedicate this book to the many writers of detective fiction who have inspired me and challenged me to try my hand at proving that murder is both a fascinating subject and a crime that doesn't pay.

PROLOGUE

Few Crooked Lake residents or vacationers were familiar with Anson's Grove. For the driver or hiker who ventured onto the poorly maintained old farm road high above the lake's western shore, it was simply a patch of woods in the middle of a long abandoned vineyard that stretched for roughly half a mile and covered a great many acres. But few drivers or hikers had reason to find themselves on this road. It led only to a derelict house and had a dirt and gravel surface which had not been improved in ages. It also lacked a view of the lake, thereby depriving many, especially tourists, of a reason for venturing onto such a back country road to nowhere. Those who knew that these woods went by the name of Anson's Grove rarely knew who Anson was or why the woods bore his name. One of those who did was Agnes McKendrick, and that was because she was an inveterate birder, always on the lookout for places where bird watchers were likely to have a good day. In fact it was in considerable part due to her 'discovery' of Anson's Grove that she had been elected leader of the Crooked Lake Birders Club.

It was on a cool Saturday morning late in the month of June that Agnes and her fellow birders had driven over those last few miles of rough hilltop roads to see how many vertebrates of the Aves class they might find in Anson's Grove. On this particular day, seventeen members of the club had made the trip, driving in nine cars, all of which had been parked on what passed for the shoulder of the rutted road that wound its way down past the Grove to the remnants of that derelict house. These seventeen birders were a mixed lot: nine women and eight men, four married couples among them; those who lived on the lake the year around and those who called it their summer home; equal numbers of Baby Boomers and Gen Xers, and even a Millennial still in high school. If one were to employ terms common to serious birders, most of the seventeen were 'dudes' or novices, although two thought of themselves as 'twitchers' because they had taken trips abroad with the specific purpose of adding rare birds to their 'collection.'

Not surprisingly, some of those accompanying Agnes McKendrick were tromping through Anson's Grove for the sheer pleasure of sharing a beautiful morning out of doors with friends and fellow birders. For others, in more cases than they might wish to admit, such outings were a way to escape, albeit briefly, from unwelcome tasks at home or even from family members who had a way of getting under their skin. But one member of Agnes's group had a different agenda that day. This participant in the bird hike had never dreamed of killing a bird. But to kill a member of the human race was something else altogether, and a hike through Anson's Grove might provide a perfect opportunity to do just that.

CHAPTER 1

The quiet of that Saturday morning in June was broken by the sound of a gunshot. It was loud and it came so unexpectedly that the birders stopped in their tracks, momentarily shocked into immobility. And fear.

"There's somebody up here," one of them said, sotto voce, as if anxious that she not be heard by whoever had fired the gun.

"It's not even hunting season," another said.

"I think it came from back that way." The speaker gestured towards the woods behind them, and almost immediately a small argument broke out as to the probable location of the shooter.

"Now let's all calm down. I'll have to get his attention, let him know that he could hurt people if he isn't careful."

It was Agnes McKendrick, their leader.

"Hello, out there, whoever you are," she shouted. "Hold your fire. There's a group of bird watchers up here in the Grove, and we don't want anyone to get hurt."

Silence followed, as everybody strained to hear an acknowledgement from the shooter.

"Do you hear me?" Agnes once again raised her voice. Silence. And then a distant voice could be heard.

"Agnes, where are you? Come quick!"

In spite of the fact that the voice was barely audible, Agnes McKendrick recognized it. Mel Cone was calling. He, like some other members of the Crooked Lake Birders Club, was something of a law unto himself. She tried to keep them together, but they had a tendency to scatter, each anxious to end the hike with a longer list of birds spotted and identified than their fellow birders. Mel's voice was sure to scare off the birds that nested and fed in the Grove. But so was her own voice, not to mention the gun shot, and spotting birds in the woods was suddenly not anyone's first priority.

Reluctantly, Agnes urged the members of the Club who had stayed with her that morning to remain where they were. If the shooter were a hunter, they'd be safer staying put than crashing through the woods in response to Mel Cone's call. In any event, she had seen an oriole, or thought she had, and wanted her colleagues to keep searching the treetops in that particular corner of the Grove. She set off in the direction from which Mel's voice had come. As she worked her way through the woods, she found herself regretting that she had chosen to spend the morning in Anson's Grove rather than arrange for her birders to load canoes onto their cars and gather at the inlet at the north end of the lake. It was always easier to keep them all together when they were on the water.

When Agnes came out of the woods and into the field which had once been a vineyard, she could see no sign of Mel Cone.

"Over here," he called out.

Mel was standing next to a long abandoned pile of fence posts below the Grove and further down the hill towards the road.

"What on earth's going on?" Agnes asked as she picked her way across the stubble of the old vineyard. "We're supposed to be on a bird hike."

"It's not the birds I'm worried about. It's Vivian."

"Vivian?" The only Vivian Agnes knew was Vivian Neuberger and she was nowhere in sight.

"Yes, Vivian, and she's been shot."

Agnes hurried across the last several dozen yards to where Mel was standing. The ground was uneven, and she almost stumbled over one of the Crooked Lake Birders Club's newest members, sprawled in the tall grass beside the fence posts, before she saw her.

"Oh, my God. You shot her?" Agnes could not believe what she saw or imagine why it had happened.

"Of course I didn't shoot her, Agnes. Don't be stupid. There's a hunter somewhere up in the woods. You know that. You must have heard the shot - I heard you trying to get his attention. But he must have hit Vivian. I think she's dead."

"That can't be. She hasn't even tuned fifty."

What that had to do with the situation facing the two birders wasn't clear. Agnes backed away from the woman, obviously uncomfortable with the prospect of confirming for herself that Vivian Neuberger had taken her last bird hike. Cone had said only that he thought she was dead, but he knew for a fact that she was.

"I heard the gunshot, just like you did except I was back up there." He pointed in the general direction of a cluster of dead oak trees at the edge of the Grove. "I'd just caught sight of Vivian when I came out of the woods and was wondering what she was doing down here. It all happened so fast. There was the shot, and then she was down. My first thought was that she'd tripped over those damned fence posts. But it didn't take more than a second or two to realize that she could have been shot. I got here as fast as I could, but I think she died instantly." He knelt down beside the woman's body and gently rotated it so the leader of their club could better see where and how Vivian had been shot. Blood could be seen on her blue windbreaker where the bullet had penetrated.

"This is simply terrible," she said. "What's a hunter doing up here in June? Deer season's months away."

"Maybe it's open season on raccoons or something." Mel Cone was a gun collector, but he had never been much of a hunter. It suddenly occurred to him that if one of the club's members had been hit by a hunter's errant shot, they, too, might be in danger. "I think we should get out of here."

"We can't leave Vivian, Mel." No longer concerned with the bird hike, she turned back towards where she had left those who were watching for an oriole and called out to them in a surprisingly loud voice. "We're down here, everybody, down toward the Benson Road. Come along, and make some noise. There are hunters in the woods."

"Now," Agnes said to Mel, "what were you doing down here in the vineyard?"

"I was looking for one of those migrating chestnut-sided warblers I was sure I'd seen."

"That's crazy. Warblers aren't still migrating through here this late."

"You can't ever be sure, Agnes. That's what it looked like."

This pointless conversation came to an abrupt halt when one of the other birders, obviously well ahead of the group, came crashing through the underbrush above them in the Grove.

"What's this all about?" he shouted.

"It's Mrs. Neuberger," Agnes called out. "She's been shot."

The man who joined her and Mel Cone beside the fence posts was not a member of the Crooked Lake Birders Club. But he was a summer resident who had long been interested in birds; upon hearing of the organization, and having time on his hands, he had inquired as to whether he might go along on the club's next hike. It would give him something to do on a day when his wife, the sheriff of Cumberland County, was at work preserving law and order in this part of the Finger Lakes. Unknown to Agnes and Mel and the other members of the local birders club, he was also someone who had involved himself, informally of course, in the sheriff's recent efforts to solve a rash of murders on and about Crooked Lake.

"I figured something out of the ordinary must have happened," Kevin Whitman, now out of breath, said. "Probably that damned hunter."

"She's dead," Mel said.

"Dead?" Kevin was instantly on his knees beside the woman's body, still on its side, the blood on her jacket still damp. "That makes no sense. She's right out in the open. How could a hunter mistake her for a deer?"

"What's more it's not even deer season, and it's certainly not open season on innocent birders." Agnes McKendrick sounded almost hysterical.

Kevin didn't need to be told that it wasn't hunting season. But somebody had put a bullet into the back of this woman, this stranger he had met for the first time not much more than an hour earlier. Someone had killed her. It was probably some careless kid out in the woods having himself a lark. Or perhaps a hunter who was no respecter of New York state's regulations. In any case, in spite of the fact that he had no authority, he was the person best positioned to take charge. And taking charge included contacting his wife, who would either set off for Anson's Grove post haste or send one or more of her officers. What had begun as a pleasant hike in the woods on this otherwise beautiful late June morning had ended tragically. And inexplicably.

CHAPTER 2

"Sheriff's Department, Ms. Franks speaking. What can I -"

When she continued, her voice was more distant, more agitated. It was obvious that she was speaking to someone else.

"Excuse me, sir, where are you going?"

The voice which answered that question was even more distant.

"I'm going to talk with the sheriff."

"Please, I need to talk with you. The sheriff isn't -"

At this point Kevin heard the sound of what sounded like a chair moving, then voices, now unintelligible. Ms. Franks had apparently gotten up and followed whomever she was speaking to.

Kevin wondered what was going on, although he was more concerned that his effort to reach his wife had temporarily been put on hold. Whatever was going on lasted for all of two minutes, after which the sheriff's assistant was back on the line.

She started to apologize for what had happened, but Kevin cut her off.

"It's Kevin, JoAnne. I need to talk to the sheriff." Why hadn't he said my wife? Perhaps he had unconsciously thought that 'the sheriff' would make his call sound more urgent, less personal, than 'my wife.'

"This has been so embarrassing," JoAnne said. Her tone of voice made it clear that she was in fact embarrassed. "But like I told the man, Carol isn't here right now. Do you want me to take a message for her?"

"Is Sam there?" Kevin had to alert the officers that a woman had been shot and killed in Anson's Grove.

"I'll check. I'm pretty sure he hasn't left yet."

Once again Kevin was put on hold. It was Deputy Sheriff Bridges who next picked up the phone.

"Hello, Whitman, this is Bridges. What's the problem?"

"A woman named Vivian Neuberger has been shot while taking a hike to look for birds. She's dead. I think someone from the department needs to get over to Anson's Grove."

"How do you know this?"

"I'm standing right next to her body."

Sam knew that this was not the time to discuss what Carol's husband was doing on a bird hike, although he was both surprised and curious.

"Do you know who shot this Neuberger woman?"

"No idea. The odds are it was somebody who was hunting deer out of season. We're roughly at the southwest corner of that abandoned vineyard, just below the Grove. You'll spot the birders' cars on the shoulder of that wretched road down below the Grove."

"Who's in charge of these bird lovers?"

"Name's Agnes McKendrick." Kevin chose not to say that he had arrogated to himself the task of trying to keep the group together. Nor did he mention the fact that several members of the Crooked Lake Birders Club had wandered away from their leader and were not among the group awaiting the arrival of county law and order personnel.

"Okay, I'll grab one of the men and we'll be on our way. Do me a favor. Don't let any of your birders leave. Tell them I said they were to stay put until I get there."

"Whatever you say, Sam."

Ten minutes later Bridges and Officer Byrnes had left Cumberland and were well on their way to Anson's Grove.

"Who's Anson?" Byrnes asked.

"One of those old timers who seems to have made himself at home up here back in the day before cars and telephones. Truth is I don't know anything about him, other than he must not have liked company. What you'd call a hermit, I suppose."

"You ever wish you had a place back up here in the woods?"

"Not really. Why do you ask?"

"I can't afford a cottage on the lake, and sometimes I figure the next best thing might be a home with a view of the lake from one of these upper roads."

"I guess it could be nice, but not in Anson's Grove. You can't see the lake from there. It's about as close as you can get to nowhere in this whole area. You'll see."

Tommy changed the subject.

"So this is about people looking for birds?"

"That's what I'm told. Crazy hobby, if you ask me. Louise, she keeps a hummingbird feeder off the back porch in summer, but that's completely different. Why go running around in places like Anson's Grove, looking for rare warblers and woodpeckers?"

"Reminds me," Tommy said, "I was out on patrol with Parsons last week and we saw a loon. Don't see many of them around here. Bill says they stay up in the Adirondacks where it's colder."

"So I've heard." Sam didn't seem interested in loons. "You know, it's a good thing the boss was out when word came in about this business up in the Grove. She'll be fit to be tied when she hears about another shooting. Better it's us who get to check it out than her."

"And a good thing it was an accident. I think she's worried she'll get blamed for all the murders we've been having."

"Carol's a born worrier," Sam said. "But she has as much to do with our murders as you and I do with snow in January. And by the way, we don't know that what happened was an accident. Probably was, but who knows - maybe one of the birders had a grudge he thought he'd settle."

"You don't believe that, do you?" Byrnes sounded shocked by Sam's suggestion.

"All I know is what Whitman told me. A woman's dead, and there's nothing that points to who might have fired the shot that killed her."

The two officers broke off their conversation and except for a brief exchange on the terrible condition of the road, they drove the last few miles of their trip to Anson's Grove in silence.

CHAPTER 3

Deputy Sheriff Bridges had not bothered to park where the Crooked Lake Birders Club had parked earlier that morning. He had found a place quite some distance down the road where the ditch was not an insurmountable obstacle and had driven his car a punishing quarter of a mile across the old vineyard to where a dozen people were gathered.

"That's what I call quick turn around time," Kevin said as he greeted Bridges and Officer Byrnes as they got out of the squad car.

"Hello, Kevin," the deputy sheriff said. "Carol wasn't in the office, so I got the short straw. What have we got, a hunting accident in June?"

The birders had moved way from Vivian Neuberger's body, as if uncomfortable to be too close to the presence of death. Most of them had taken seats on the ground a few yards away from the fence posts. The lone exceptions were a tall, thin man with a mane of white hair and a stocky woman who was wearing what looked like an Alpine hiker's outfit, minus the alpenstock. They stood somewhat closer to the body, but their backs were to it and they appeared to be having an argument.

"That's what it looks like. According to the people here, none of them saw anything. I've got a list of who was on this bird hike. They're all right here except for several people who seemed to have wandered off. You should talk with Mrs. McKendrick here. She's in charge of the group, and she knows all of them better than I do."

"You say some of the group have wandered off." The deputy sheriff turned his attention to the leader of the Crooked Lake Birders Club. There was just a hint of criticism in his voice. "How did that happen?"

"I don't know where they went." Agnes was anxious to explain that keeping her fellow birders together was something like herding cats. "They weren't with me, up in the Grove, when Mel found Vivian, and I don't think I'd seen any of them for the better part of half an hour."

"You have their names?" Sam looked at Kevin.

"I do. I know it's important that you see all of them, but it's especially important because one of them is the husband of the woman who's been shot."

While this who's who and who's where conversation was going on, Officer Byrnes was on his knees beside the late Vivian Neuberger.

"I don't know what he thought he was aiming at," he said, raising his voice to get Bridges' attention, "but he couldn't have done it any better. Right smack in the middle of the back."

"You'd think whoever fired the shot would have wanted to see if he'd scored," Sam said.

"Maybe he did." Kevin offered an opinion. "If he was a hunter, he figured he'd got himself a deer but realized he'd killed a woman instead. The guy'd have been scared out of his wits. Deer hunting out of season and he finds himself facing a big fine *and* a murder charge. I'll bet he took off in one helluva hurry."

"Who found her?" Bridges asked.

"I did. I'm Mel Cone." He stood up from his seat on the edge of the vineyard.

"You see anyone else?" Sam looked skeptically at Cone.

"No, I didn't. I was looking for a chestnut-sided warbler."

Officer Byrnes found this amusing. Bridges did not.

"You must have heard the shot," he said.

Mel Cone looked and sounded defensive.

"I did. I'd just spotted Mrs. Neuberger and she went down almost immediately," he said. "It was obvious she'd been shot."

"Where were you when this happened?" Bridges didn't say so, but it occurred to him that Cone himself might have been the shooter.

"See those dead trees up there?" Once again Mel pointed to the edge of the Grove above and behind them.

The Grove was pretty big, but not so big that all of the birders wouldn't have heard the shot that killed the Neuberger woman. Not that is unless they had been making an awful lot of noise. Sam had never been a birder, but common sense said that birders wouldn't be making a lot of noise. He was well aware that every member of the Crooked Lake Birders Club who'd been on the hike that day would have to be quizzed as to just where they'd been, what they'd seen, what they'd heard, from the time they parked their cars until Mrs. Neuberger's body had been found.

"About those members of your group who've disappeared," Sam said to Mrs. McKendrick. "It's really important that you try to remember when you saw them last, where they were going."

"Oh, dear, I don't really know. Paul is always taking off. He's a loner, if you know what I mean. I don't like to be critical, but to be honest he thinks he knows more about where we're going to find them - the birds, I mean - than I do."

"Who's this Paul person?"

"Raymore. Paul Raymore. Like Mr. Whitman said, one of the other missing birders is Bill Neuberger. He's Vivian's husband. He's new in the club, like his wife, but I don't remember him ever wandering off from the group. The others who did are Sallie Finch and Michael Nagle. Plus Mr. Cone, of course."

"So neither of the Neubergers stayed with you this morning." Sam seemed to find that fact interesting. "You're what - the one in charge of these bird hikes? The one who's supposed to keep everybody together?"

Agnes McKendrick suddenly reached out and grabbed Kevin by the arm.

"I've got to sit down," she said. She didn't look well.

She's held up pretty well, Kevin thought, but it's finally dawned on her just how serious a matter this is. Bridges had as much as told her she didn't handle things well that morning.

"It's not her fault, Sam," he said. "Birders are an independent lot."

Sam's face reflected the fact that he didn't need the sheriff's spouse to tell him how it was in bird land.

"Look, we've got to take care of Mrs. Neuberger. There's nothing to be gained by Officer Byrnes and me running around through the woods looking for a hunter who mistook a woman for a deer. If that's what happened, he could be miles away by now."

He turned to the members of the Crooked Lake Birders Club and explained that the sheriff's department would be in touch with each of them in the very near future. He then posed several final questions for everyone.

"Did any one of you see another car when you arrived this morning? A car that didn't belong to other members of the club, a car parked somewhere around here?"

No one spoke up. Sam's face registered frustration.

"Okay. Now about a gun being fired. You all heard it, right?"

Heads shook yes in unison.

"Did any one of you catch a glimpse of someone who could have been a hunter while you were on your hike?"

This time heads shook no. One of the women said something to the effect that they'd all been concentrating on their search for birds.

"One final question, and I'm sure you'll understand why it's important. While it's likely that a hunter shot Mrs. Neuberger, it's also possible that one of the birders on the hike did. I'm going -"

"Excuse me, officer," Peter Hornaday interrupted, "but I hope you aren't insinuating that one of us killed a fellow birder."

Sam looked at the tall thin, white haired man.

"I'm not insinuating anything," he said. "But who could have shot Mrs. Neuberger if it wasn't a hunter? It seems to me that hypothetically any one of you *could* had done it. Which is why I'd be grateful if everyone who was on the hike would consent to being searched for a gun. Don't you think that would be a good way of proving that the one who shot her was a hunter?"

"But wouldn't you need a search warrant for that?" It was the white haired man again.

"Look," an exasperated Sam said, "I'm not interested in making a big thing out of this. I'm assuming that none of you had anything to do with killing Mrs. Neuberger, and that you'll all be as anxious as I am to prove it. The best way to do that is to agree to a quick search."

Sam knew what the birders presumably didn't, that in the circumstances he was within his rights to proceed without a warrant. The time taken to obtain one would only risk the loss of critical evidence.

There was some mumbling, but in the end no one objected, especially when Clara Olcott, a registered nurse, volunteered to assist when a couple of the women expressed reservations about having the male officers frisk them. The search was essentially perfunctory, and not surprisingly turned up nothing that looked remotely like a gun.

"Okay. You're all free to go. Just don't leave the area until you've talked to the sheriff or one of her officers."

"But we're leaving for our daughter's place in Tennessee this weekend, my husband and I." It was the woman in the Alpine hiking outfit.

"We aren't trying to ruin your plans, but the sheriff is going to want to talk with everybody, and she can't do that if you're in Tennessee. What's your name?"

"Emily Nugent."

"Okay, Tommy, make a note beside Nugent on Whitman's list that she should be seen right away. Any other problems?"

There didn't seem to be any, and within a few minutes everyone except Kevin, Agnes, and the two officers had started the trek to their cars.

Sam would have liked to put the late Vivian Neuberger's body in the back seat of the squad car and take her to the nearest hospital. But that's not how things were done in Cumberland County; he'd have to place a call to the coroner and leave a message for Carol with Ms. Franks. It was obvious that Kevin intended to hang around to see what happened, and there was nothing he could do about that. Mrs. McKendrick was another story.

"I assume that you'd like to let Mr. Neuberger know about his wife," he said to her.

"It would be the decent thing to do," she said. "I hope that it won't be a problem."

"Somebody has to tell him, that's for sure. I'd like to do it myself, but I'm needed around here for a bit longer. Chances are news of it'll be all around the lake by nightfall anyway. Don't start speculating about what happened, but go ahead and talk with him if he's at home." As soon as he'd said it, Sam saw the problem. "Wait a minute. Did the Neubergers come together this morning?"

"I assume so," Agnes said, "but I arrived early and I can't be sure."

"So there's a good chance Mr. Neuberger's still somewhere up in the Grove." It was then that Sam had another thought. "Mrs. McKendrick, was there a time when everyone was supposed to reassemble somewhere? You know, when the bird hike was officially over?"

"Sightings are best early, so we usually wrap up around nine. I'd told everybody that we'd meet back at our cars at nine o'clock."

Sam looked at his watch. It was now almost a quarter past nine. If Mr. Neuberger and the other wanderers had done what their leader had asked them to do, they might now be at their cars, waiting for the rest of the group.

"Tommy, why don't you high-tail it back to where these people left their cars. See if Neuberger is there. The others, too. That would be this man Raymore and - who'd you say the others were?"

Agnes supplied the names: Sallie Finch and Michael Nagle.

"Wait for them if they aren't there yet," Sam said to Officer Byrnes, "and get them to tell you where they've been, what they've heard and seen. They might know more about this than the ones that stayed with Mrs. McKendrick. And see if any one of them has a gun tucked away somewhere."

A real possibility, Kevin thought. After all, he couldn't see how the obedient birders who'd stayed with Agnes could possibly have killed Vivian Neuberger. But while it was highly unlikely that any of those who had wandered off had killed her, one of them might have.

Officer Byrnes set off at a trot for the cars, leaving the late Mrs. Neuberger with Kevin, Sam, and Mrs. McKendrick.

"By the way, how well do you know the Neubergers? I think you said she was new to the group."

"I hardly know them," Agnes said. "This was only the third time they'd joined one of our hikes."

"And yet both of them set off on their own today. Did either of them say why? What they were doing?"

Once again Agnes look uncomfortable.

"I'm sorry. I'm afraid I didn't even see her leave the group. To tell you the truth, I thought maybe Mr. Neuberger might have been just going off to take a pee somewhere and was embarrassed to say so."

"Yeah, that's possible," Sam said. He didn't bother to comment that such a mission needn't have kept him away from the rest of the group for more than a few minutes. "If I were you, I'd go on home now and stay there until the sheriff calls. I'm sure you'll be the first person she'll want to speak to. Officer Byrnes will probably be the one to let Mr. Neuberger know what happened to his wife, so I suspect you can forget about giving him the bad news. You can go ahead and give him your condolences if you want to, just don't get into a conversation about who might have done it. That's our business. And by the way, I really am sorry about what happened here this morning. I hope the Birders Club survives to hike another day."

"Vivian would have wanted us to carry on, and I shall make sure that we do."

It had been a terrible day for the woman who had 'discovered' Anson's Grove, but as she headed for her car she made a conscious effort to straighten her shoulders and walk confidently. Kevin and Sam watched her until she dropped out of sight over a hummock in the distance. Then the deputy sheriff placed his calls to the coroner and the sheriff's office, and they settled down to wait for Officer Byrnes' return.

CHAPTER 4

Kevin would have liked to be the first to talk with Carol about the tragic ending of the Crooked Lake Birders Club hike in Anson's Grove. It was not to be. She had been detained longer than she had expected at a county budget meeting, and when she got back to the office Sam Bridges was impatiently waiting for her.

"I'd love this job if it weren't for the fact that budget issues raise my blood pressure." She hung her jacket up on the coat tree and collapsed into her chair.

"I'm afraid I have other news that's going to raise your blood pressure even further," Sam said.

"I already know about it. JoAnne's all upset, and I don't blame her. There's no excuse for such thin skin."

"What are you talking about?" Sam looked and sounded puzzled.

"It's that town clerk who came in here this morning ready to chew me out. JoAnne was close to tears about the way he treated her."

"You're talking about the fracking business?"

"Yes. Aren't you?"

"No. I'm afraid my news is somewhat more important than that."

"Good grief, all I do is step out of the office for a few hours and everything goes to hell," Carol said, a smile threatening to break out. "What's your problem?"

"Somebody got shot this morning, up in Anson's Grove. Seems the Crooked Lake Birders Club was taking a hike and -"

Carol sat up abruptly in her chair.

"The bird club? What happened?" Carol sounded anxious, as well she might.

"Oh, sorry, I wasn't thinking about your husband. He was there - I guess you knew he would be. He was the one who called and told us about it. One of the birders was shot. No idea who did it, but -"

Carol interrupted.

"What's his condition?" She asked. "I don't mean Kevin, I mean the man who was shot."

"It's a her, name's Vivian Neuberger, and she's dead."

"Oh, my God. Here we go again."

"I'm sure you're thinking murder, but we don't know. It was probably somebody hunting out of season."

"Go ahead, make my day. Tell me all about it."

For the next twenty minutes Sam gave Carol a detailed account of what, to the best of his knowledge, had happened at Anson's Grove that morning. It was soon apparent that much of what he knew was the result of what Kevin, Agnes McKendrick, and a few of their fellow birders had told him and Officer Byrnes. There were no discrepancies in their stories, but there were enormous gaps which could be attributed to a preoccupation with birds and the fact that several of the birders, including the victim of the shooting, had left the group during the course of the hike.

"You say that eventually you accounted for all of the birders," she said. "Or that Byrnes did. Do you have their names? I'm especially interested in the ones who didn't stick with the group."

"Here's the list." He handed her the list which Kevin had prepared. Those who had wandered away from the group were underlined. Sam was regretting that he hadn't asked Tommy to detain the missing people who had not stayed with McKendrick throughout the morning. Bill Neuberger, quite understandably, had insisted on going back to see his wife. But Michael Nagle, Sallie Finch, and Paul Raymore, the other missing 'wanderers,' had all gone home after answering Byrnes' questions and submitting to a search. Nagle had come with the Taggarts and didn't want to keep them waiting any longer. Finch had promised to drive a distraught and crying Jeanne Lerner home. And Raymore, who had come alone, had excused himself on the grounds of urgent business.

"The only one I talked with," Sam said, "was Neuberger, the victim's husband, and he wasn't much help. He was obviously terribly upset, but what would you expect from a guy who'd just learned that his wife had been shot? He did say he couldn't stand McKendrick. Said she talked too much, moved the group along at a snail's pace. Claims he had to get away from her. But just where he went he doesn't know. He'd never been in the Grove before. Frankly, I don't think any of them had been in the Grove before. For what it's worth, Neuberger's not consistent. He went wandering off on his own, but he's angry with McKendrick because she didn't keep his wife with the group. He didn't exactly blame her for his wife's death, but it was clear he thinks she'd never have been shot if she'd stayed with the others."

"Which is almost certainly true," Carol said. "No hunter is going to confuse a bunch of birders for a deer. And if whoever killed her wasn't a hunter, he'd still never have taken a shot at her if she was with all those other people. Ergo, she's dead because, like her husband, she went off on her own."

"What's your opinion of the hunter as killer thesis?" Sam asked.

"I know no more than you do, probably less because I've never been in the Grove. But from the way you describe things, he'd have to have been somewhere up in the woods and out of sight from where Mrs. Neuberger was when she was hit."

"I'd be just as ready to assume it was one of the birders who shot her," Sam said, "except none of them had a gun."

"That's hardly surprising," Carol said. "A gun could have been ditched just about anywhere, especially by a birder who left the group. What does Tommy have to say about his conversations with the ones who took off on their own during the hike?"

"They all had pretty much the same story - nobody had anything in particular in mind. They just preferred to be alone, not forced to stop at every third tree to listen to McKendrick. My impression is that some of these birders take this stuff seriously while others can take it or leave it."

"That's probably true of stamp collecting and every other hobby. But you're right, we're going to have to sit down with all of them and get a sense of who they are and how they relate to each other. There's always a chance that somebody saw something or heard something that will help."

"So how do we proceed?" Sam asked.

"This may sound like I'm planning a wasted day, but I'd like to take a good hard look at Anson's Grove tomorrow morning. I've never been there, and it might help if I could get a feel for its size, how easy or how hard it is to see things from the Grove. Unlikely, but I just might see something that would give us a clue as to what happened."

"You planning on giving it a look around by yourself?"

"Actually, no. I need to have someone along who went birding yesterday, and that would have to be Kevin. He'll have a fair idea of their path through the woods, where those who left the group peeled off."

Sam was well aware that Kevin liked to involve himself in his wife's investigations, and it made him uncomfortable. But in the circumstances he could hardly object to the sheriff scouting the Grove with her husband.

"Sounds like a good idea," Sam said, although he doubted that she'd learn anything he hadn't already told her. "What's next?"

"Right now I think I should be calling the Neuberger residence to let him know how sorry I am about his wife. And to tell him we won't be leaving any stone unturned until we find out who killed her. Turning over stones begins with you and me making appointments to ask questions of everyone who was in the Grove this morning. Why don't you take that list down to JoAnne and get her started calling people. These won't be ten minute interrogations either. Make sure we have plenty of time to size these birders up."

"Shall we see them here or at their homes?"

"Let's make it here. Let them do the running around."

CHAPTER 5

Kevin was waiting at the back door when Carol got home. For all she knew he had been there ever since he'd returned from the aborted bird hike, eager to share with her his impressions of events at Anson's Grove.

"I understand you had an interesting morning," she said.

"You might say so, and I'm sure you already know what happened."

"Sam filled me in, but I'm anxious to hear your report. Not sure why, but I have a hunch that you'll have a slightly different take on it."

"That may or may not be true. But I was on the hike and he wasn't. Go ahead and change clothes, and I'll uncork the Chardonnay and give you my version of our latest Crooked Lake murder."

"Murder?" Carol sounded surprised and looked doubtful. "You don't know it was murder. It sounds suspiciously like a hunting accident to me."

"I'm not saying you've got a murder on your hands, just that I don't believe some crazy hunter brought that Neuberger woman down. But once you've eliminated a hunter, it's hard to picture the cause of her death as other than a deliberate shooting by a fellow member of the Crooked Lake Birders Club. And believe me, I'm not just looking for another opportunity to play sleuth."

"I certainly hope not. Go ahead and open the Chardonnay while I get into something more comfortable."

The sun had gone behind a large and ominous looking cloud, but they always looked forward to having 'cocktail hour' on the deck or the dock if possible, so Kevin poured two glasses of wine and carried them out to the Adirondack chairs at the end of the dock. Ten minuted later Carol reappeared in slacks and a windbreaker.

"Are you sure you want to become a birder?" she asked as she took a seat.

"I've always been a birder. Maybe I should say a birder of sorts. I have to confess to giving other interests priority when I'm down in the city. The only birds you see down there are pigeons - hundreds, probably thousands of them. Anyway, we were off to a good start this morning until the shooting."

"Why don't you step back and walk me through it from the beginning. I mean everything that you did and observed - getting to the woods, assembling for the hike, looking for birds, finding or not finding them, right up to when you learned that one of the birders had been shot."

Kevin smiled. He had been sure that Carol would want all the details he could remember, and he had devoted the afternoon to thinking about those details.

So he began with the arrival of the birders' cars on the poorly maintained road that provided access to Anson's Grove. There were two cars parked on the shoulder when he got there. One belonged to their leader, Agnes McKendrick, the other to a couple whose name, he had learned, was Taggart. They had brought with them a boy named Michael Nagle. Kevin went on to reel off the names of the other birders, accounting for a total of seventeen people who had come in nine cars.

Carol nodded knowingly at some of the names, but drew a blank on most of them. She didn't know the Neubergers, who had apparently lived on the lake for only a year or two, but she did know McKendrick, the mother hen of the club, and had a nodding acquaintance with half a dozen of the others. Kevin repeated Sam's instructions to the birders that Carol would be making appointments to talk with all of them.

"Tell me," Carol said, "what goes on in bird hikes? I've never been on one."

"I suspect it varies. Agnes McKendrick may not be your typical leader. She talks a lot, mostly about what birds you're most likely to see and where to look for them. She seems knowledgeable, and she doesn't like to be challenged. We identified, or rather she and a couple of the other veterans did, about a dozen different birds before we heard a gun shot and a man named Mel Cone raised a hue and cry about Mrs. Neuberger being shot."

"Hold up a minute," Carol said. "Sam says several people left the group before you all knew she'd been shot, including her husband. How'd that happen? Did they tell McKendrick, or just wander off? In other words, did she - did *you* - know they'd gone, and if so where they were going?"

"I wish I could tell you just when and where they left the group. If I'd known what was going to happen, I'd have paid more attention. For what it's worth though, I'm pretty sure none of them told Agnes they were going off on their own."

"Did you actually see any of them leave?"

"Only young Nagle. He sort of drifted over to one side and took off when Agnes was pointing out some bird high up in a cottonwood. Poor kid was probably bored."

"Sam mentioned that four of the birders dropped out during the hike. What about the others?"

"Actually it wasn't four but six. The extra two were Mrs. Neubeger and the guy who discovered her body, Mel Cone. Sam was talking about four because that's how many were still missing when we all got together where Neuberger had been shot. At the time I didn't know everybody's name, but the ones who were missing turned out to be Mr. Neuberger, a chap named Paul Raymore, Sallie Finch, and, of course, the Nagle kid."

"So you have no idea when the rest of them gave up on the hike?"

"I'm not sure they all gave up on the hike. Some of them like Raymore and Cone were apparently among the most seasoned birders. They probably just weren't interested in following Agnes. She herself made it clear that she didn't like their independent streak, especially Raymore's. I don't know about Neuberger or Finch. As to when any of them left, it's impossible to tell. I'd guess that both the Neubergers and Cone and Raymore left fairly early in the hike."

Carol was disappointed that Kevin wasn't more helpful, but she knew that there was no reason why he should have been paying closer attention to the whereabouts of sixteen other birders. Who would have thought that an innocent walk in the woods would have such a tragic ending.

"How far away from McKendrick's group would you say the gun shot came from?"

"No idea. I've never fired a gun, and the only ones I ever heard fired were when a former friend of mine was buried at Arlington National Cemetery. And that was right next to us, not off in the woods someplace. Somebody said it might have been a hundred yards away, but I'm sure he was just guessing."

"Who said that?"

"Somebody named Taggart. I haven't a clue whether he knows anything about guns."

"We'll be talking to him. I was going to ask if you had any idea what kind of a gun you'd heard, but you're no expert. So let's talk about the birders. Any impressions you'd like to share? I'm thinking about individuals, not the group as a whole."

"Like I said, some of them have been doing this for years and know a lot. Raymore, for example, let's you know that he knows a lot. Then there are those who wouldn't know a blue jay from a swallow. I'd put Nagle in that category. He's just a high school kid who came along because the Taggart couple are neighbors and asked him. But if you're wondering if any of the birders acted suspiciously or said something that caught my attention, the answer is no. Most of them didn't say much of anything. The most voluble one's named Pearl Hornaday, but she's just what you'd might call a motor mouth. Didn't say anything interesting. I'm sure McKendrick wished she'd shut up."

"How about after the shooting, when they all knew Mrs. Neuberger was dead? Anything interesting in any of their reactions?"

"Not that I'm aware of. Nothing except a couple of them were having an argument. At least that's what it looked like."

"Who was arguing?" Carol asked."

"A woman named Nugent. She stood out because she was dressed like a Swiss or Austrian mountain climber. The man - I'd guess he was the oldest of the birders, and Agnes says he's the husband of the woman I called a motor mouth."

By the time they headed back to the cottage for supper, Carol was even more certain than she had been when talking with Sam that she needed to see the Grove for herself. She explained to Kevin what she wanted to do the next morning, and that she wanted him to come along. It was not until after supper, when it was getting dark, that she brought up the other matter that was worrying her.

"If it hadn't been for what happened up in Anson's Grove, I'd have been sharing another bad news story. You ready for another downer?"

"Nothing as bad as Mrs. Neuberger's death, I hope?" Kevin asked.

"No, but it's not good. If I hadn't been tied up at that county budget meeting, I might have been able to head off trouble. But it was JoAnne who had to deal with him."

"Him?"

"The town clerk over in Somerset, Jasper Eglin. He came barging into the department and stormed right past JoAnne's desk and into my office. Never asked if he could see me. Anyway JoAnne explained that I was tied up elsewhere and finally got him to leave a message after a few minutes of unpleasantness. It seems that he was angry with Officer Barrett because he'd been overheard criticizing Eglin for his efforts in support of fracking."

"Oh, oh, the fracking fight." Kevin, like everybody else in the Finger Lakes region, was aware of the conflict between supporters and opponents of the hydraulic fracturing of rock to obtain natural gas from shale. Its supporters see it as the answer to energy independence. Its opponents argue that it is a major threat to drinking water and the local environment. For better or worse, the governor had recently decided the issue, at least for the time being, by banning fracking in New York state.

"It looks like it may be getting personal. You don't really know Jim, but he's become a hard core environmentalist. He's a good officer, but somehow he's also an ardent anti-fracking guy. Anyhow, it seems he said some things about Eglin recently at *The Cedar Post* that the town clerk found offensive. According to JoAnne, he claims Jim's language was downright nasty and that I should fire him. "

"Is criticizing pro-frackers a firing offense?"

"Not to my knowledge," Carol said. "There's a little matter of the first amendment. But I don't want my officers poor mouthing county or town officials. No need to antagonize people we have to work with, some of them in a position to trim our budget. I'll have to hear Eglin out and talk with Barrett."

"Along with a handful of birders," Kevin reminded her.

"I know, and that'll take a few days. Just when I thought the pressure had eased up."

CHAPTER 6

It was at 9:25 the next morning that the Cumberland County patrol car pulled over onto the narrow shoulder of the road at the east end of the abandoned vineyard. Anson's Grove could be seen off to their left some distance up the hill. There was no sign of human activity anywhere in the vicinity. A flock of crows took flight from the Grove, flew noisily for several dozen yards, and settled down again high in a cluster of white pines.

"It's up there that we began our hike yesterday," Kevin said to Carol as they got out of the car. He pointed up the hill to where the old vineyard suddenly gave way to a stand of tall trees which continued for as far as they could see to the north. "Parking and walking are somewhat easier around the bend up ahead of us, but this will do if you don't mind getting dirty."

"Mine is a dirty job, Kevin. Lead the way."

They climbed the hill to the point where the woods began.

"It was about here," Kevin said when he and Carol reached the spot where the Crooked Lake Birders Club had entered the woods the previous morning. "I remember that red oak that looks as if had been split by lightning. I'll do my best to follow the route we took, but after awhile every tree looks like every other one. Especially when you're looking up for birds."

It was a relatively easy walk. The trees blocked out most of the morning sunlight and the floor of the Grove was cushioned by pine needles in most places. Had it not been for the more somber purpose for their visit to Anson's Grove, they would have enjoyed what they were doing.

"Have you seen anything that reminds you of where Neuberger and the others might have left the group?" Carol asked.

"I'm afraid not. In retrospect, my biggest mistake was staying with Agnes at the head of the pack. The ones who dropped out were always behind me, and they weren't announcing their intentions. Mrs. McKendrick said something once about sticking together, but she must have figured that she was simply wasting her breath.

Anyway, she stopped nagging and it was only later that I realized that the Neubergers and Cone and Raymore weren't with us. I do know that Finch and the high school student stayed with the group quite a bit longer."

It was more than a half an hour into their hike when Kevin spotted a large ring of some kind of toadstools at the base of a large tree.

"I remember this," he said, suddenly more alert. "The Finch woman made some kind of remark about how dangerous they were, how stupid it was to assume they were edible mushrooms."

Kevin bent down and picked one of toadstools and sniffed it.

"What do you think you're doing?" Carol asked.

"Just seeing if they smell funny. They don't. Finch said something about a friend who had almost died from eating the wrong kind of mushrooms, but what I remember best is that she went over to a nearby tree and sat down, told us she'd catch up with us in a few minutes."

"And you're going to tell me that she never caught up with the group."

"Right. It wasn't until we'd all come down to where Cone had found Mrs. Neuberger's body that I realized that Finch wasn't with us. The high school kid, Nagle, I know he left not much more than ten minutes before we heard that shot ring out and Cone raised the hue and cry. Nagle's the only one of our group that I saw leave."

They continued their walk in the Grove for nearly another half hour. For the most part Kevin didn't have a difficult time recalling the path the group had taken the day before. It was usually a broken limb, a tree with unusual bark, a cluster of trillium, or some other marker that pointed the way. There were a few false starts, but they finally found themselves at the place where the birders had been when they'd heard Mel Cone calling them.

"I'm glad I came," Carol said, "but we really don't know anything we didn't know yesterday. Anson's Grove is a nice place, and we might consider coming back some time for a picnic. But I have the distinct impression that it isn't going to be easy to figure out who shot Mrs. Neuberger. Maybe when they dig the bullet out we'll know more, and it's always possible that somebody will say something that is helpful, but from what I've seen these woods look like they'd make a pretty effective hiding place."

"And we've only seen a small fraction of it. For all we know there are a few killers running loose in the Grove as we speak."

"That isn't the least bit funny, Kevin."

"I know," he apologized. "I was just thinking about how easy it would have been for whoever shot Mrs. Neuberger to have done it without anybody ever knowing he was anywhere around."

They worked their way out of the woods and set off down through the vineyard in the direction of the road, which looked as if it could be a mile away, although they knew it was closer.

"There are some old rotting fence posts where Cone found her. I think we're going to have to bear off to the right. Just watch where you step. This is awfully rough ground. It's a wonder none of us took a fall hurrying down to find out what Cone's problem was."

"I wonder how long it's been since grapes grew here?"

"No idea. Maybe the Historical Society will know," Kevin said. Two cautious steps later he heard the car.

"Looks like somebody else is visiting the Grove today." He pointed to where a car had come into view far below them.

"I thought you said it's a road to nowhere."

"It is, just an abandoned - hey, look at that."

The car had come to an abrupt stop not far from Carol's parked patrol car, backed up on the shoulder, turned around, and set off in the direction from which it had come.

"It looks like he's had a change of plans," Kevin said.

"A very sudden change of plans, and I'll bet it's because he saw my car. Not just any car, but a cop car."

"Maybe somebody else thought he'd like to take a walk in the woods."

"Either that or the derelict house at the end of the road is the old family homestead. No, I'm sure you're right. But why would the sight of a patrol car scare him off like that?"

"I wish we were closer to the road. At this distance it was just a car, any car. Black, maybe dark blue. I wonder if he saw us?"

"If he did, he wouldn't have recognized us. But he'd have figured that whoever came in the car was an officer of the law, and he wasn't interested in explaining his presence at the Grove to an officer of the law."

They had resumed their walk, still wondering just what might have accounted for the behavior of the driver of the car on the road to nowhere.

They stopped briefly at the spot where Vivian Neuberger's body had been discovered.

"Unless her body was moved after she was hit," Carol said, "the idea that she was killed by a hunter who mistook her for a deer makes no sense. It was broad daylight and this is an open field. You'd have to be blind to think the Neuberger woman was a deer. Which means she wasn't killed by a hunter. Right?"

"You're saying she was killed by one of the birders," Kevin said. "Well, that's my theory, too. But it's still a puzzle. I'd assume the person who shot her was back up in the Grove among the trees. It'd be a pretty brazen guy who'd stand somewhere in plain sight to take his shot. Cone would have been sure to see him. But he'd have to be a damn good shooter to hit her in the middle of the back if he fired from up in the Grove. The nearest trees must be at least fifty yards away."

"So how about Cone as the killer?" Carol suggested. "The way you and Sam tell it, he was fairly close to Neuberger. He admits he saw her go down, and he's the guy who yelled for the rest of you to come running. How convenient!"

"Maybe," Kevin said, "but I'm not willing to abandon the idea that whoever shot Neuberger did it from the woods. Suppose he wasn't an excellent marksman. Maybe he was extremely lucky."

"Luck wouldn't have had anything to do with it." Carol wasn't buying Kevin's suggestion. "Somebody who wanted to kill Neuberger wouldn't have counted on a lucky shot to do the trick. You know what, Kevin? We're just mindlessly speculating. Let's call it a day. There's just too much we don't know. Agreed?"

"Yes, but it's fun to speculate. Informed speculation is what I call it."

"Your speculation is no more informed than mine."

"How do you know? Have I ever told you about my safari trip and the rhino I bagged?" Kevin asked facetiousy.

"Come on, you're an environmentalist, not a big game hunter."

They were half way back to the cottage, where Carol would be dropping Kevin off before going back to the office, when he began speculating again.

"I've got a hunch I know what that car driver was doing. He'll turn out to be one of my fellow birders, and he left something in the Grove - his gun! We know none of them had one when they were searched, so it had to have been buried somewhere in the woods. He was coming back to get it, but saw the patrol car and decided he didn't want to run the risk of running into one of your men. It would make him look suspicious. And what if he had a good reason for worrying about looking suspicious? Like what if he was the killer?"

"I thought we'd agreed we weren't going to do this," Carol objected.

"But what if it *was* Mrs. Neuberger's killer, right down there just a few car lengths from your car?"

"Okay. You go right ahead and fantasize about it. I'm going to spend my afternoon quizzing your fellow birders, trying to find out what they saw and heard yesterday, what they know that might give our thoughts a little more focus. Who knows, one of them may confess to being the driver who decided not to take a walk in the woods today."

CHAPTER 7

The driver of the old Volvo kept his speed as close to the speed limit as he could, considering how anxious he was to get as far away from the Grove as he could as fast as he could. It was unlikely that the police car would follow him but what if it did? Or what if he were pulled over by some other officer of the law? He cursed at what he thought of as the ridiculously modest speed limits which the county had posted on these lightly traveled back roads. If he didn't dare drive any faster, he could at least change direction frequently. As a result, the Volvo followed a decidedly circuitous route back to his home in Yates Center. A left turn at the first intersection, a right at the next, a lengthy detour past West Branch. Eventually he pulled into the open garage on Hollyberry Street.

He sat for several minutes before leaving the car, closing the garage door, and going into the house. He had not panicked, but on reflection perhaps he had been unnecessarily anxious. The Sheriff's department did not know who had killed Vivian Neuberger. But would his presence by the Grove have raised suspicions? Why was he there? Why had he felt it necessary to go back to the scene of the crime? He must stop thinking of it as the scene of the crime. It could have been a hunter who mistook the Neuberger woman for a deer. A tragedy, no doubt, but not a crime in any conventional sense of the word. But his imagination was in overdrive, and he knew why.

For the truth of the matter was that he was not only a birder. Yes, he was someone who was interested in adding to the already long list of birds he had seen and positively identified and in learning all he could about their mating and nesting habits. But he was also interested in homo sapiens, especially those of the species who were neighbors or belonged to the Crooked Lake Birders Club. And he had paid enough attention to some of them that he knew, or thought he knew, a lot about *their* mating and nesting habits. If officers of the sheriff's department were to find him back in Anson's Grove, they would be curious and they would ask him questions. Hard questions, pointed questions. What then would he do? Pretend to know nothing about any of his fellow birders? That is what he knew he should do. If he reported what he knew he could damage the reputations of several people who were entirely innocent of Vivian Nuberger's death. On the other hand, this might not be his best strategy. He might become a local hero if he shared what he knew with the sheriff. But his better judgment told him to act as if he barely knew his fellow birders. That would not be difficult if and when the sheriff came calling to ask questions about the fatal bird hike, as he knew she would. But it would have been much more difficult if she or one of her officers had apprehended him in the Grove this morning. Or were to do so on some other morning.

Unfortunately, he faced a problem. He had been intent on looking for something in the woods this morning, something he had carelessly left there yesterday. But the sheriff or one of her officers, perhaps the one who had taken charge after the shooting, had gotten there before him. It was doubtful that the driver of the patrol car he had seen at the Grove knew that he had left something in the woods. But whoever it was must have gone into the woods, which meant that his little notebook might accidentally have been found. The thought was very upsetting, but there was nothing he could do about it. He would simply have to hope that the driver of the patrol car had taken a different path through the Grove than he had.

He opened the fridge and took out a beer. It was too early in the day to start drinking, and he had no intention of having more than one. But he needed something to calm his nerves. Thank goodness Penny was not at home. She had gone up to Rochester to do some shopping, and, knowing her, she wouldn't be back until late afternoon. Not that it mattered. He had no intention of sharing with her his anxiety about his close encounter with a member of the sheriff's department. What is more, she knew nothing about his little notebook, and it was going to remain that way.

But he couldn't stop worrying about his carelessness. In the first place, he had been foolish to use the notebook he maintained for recording bird sightings to jot down things which had nothing to do with birding. That he had done so was understandable. After all, the notebook was always with him because he never knew when he would see an unfamiliar bird. The problem, however, was that the notebook was frequently at hand when things that pertained to his interest in the habits of his two-legged acquaintances came to mind. And some of those acquaintances had been on the bird hike in the Grove.

More important, however, was his decision to carry this important notebook in the pocket of his windbreaker instead of in his backpack. He knew it was an old windbreaker, and that the pocket's lining was frayed. But it was easier to reach it when he needed it, and he had needed it to record that he had seen a small flock of cedar waxwings. Exactly when the notebook had fallen out he didn't know, but he knew where he had been in the Grove when he had seen the waxwings. He remembered thinking he might have spotted a chestnut-sided warbler just before he saw Vivian's body ahead of him. Had she not been there, he would surely have reached for the notebook, discovered it was missing, and headed back to the Grove.

What was it a high school teacher had once told his class? No point crying over spilt milk; there's enough water in it already. He'd thought it was very clever at the time. Not today. He'd simply have to hold his breath and see what happens. He went to the kitchen and got himself another beer.

CHAPTER 8

Carol was aware that she hadn't learned much during her visit to the Grove. The one thing that she couldn't get out of her mind when she got back to the office, however, was the behavior of the driver who had executed a quick 180 the minute he saw her car parked on the shoulder of the road to nowhere. Kevin's suggestion that the driver had left a gun in the woods and had returned to look for it made as much sense as any other explanation for his presence. The fact that he had abandoned his plan so precipitously certainly suggested that he didn't want the authorities to question him about what he was doing there.

But she had no idea whether the driver of the dark car had been one of the birders on the hike through Anson's Grove. If he had not been among the birders, Kevin's thesis that he was looking for the gun he'd used to kill Vivian Neuberger made no sense at all. Maybe he was simply uncomfortable around law enforcement officials. Nevertheless, she decided it would be prudent to put some of her officers to work scouring the woods. For a gun? She wasn't even sure whether there was *anything* up there that they should be looking for.

With JoAnne's help she located three of her men who could abandon their patrol of county roads and institute a search of the Grove. None of the three were excited by the change in their day's agenda. It meant that they would have to leave the comfort of their cars and spend the day on foot, looking for a gun or heaven knows what in an area that covered a great many acres. Carol had anticipated their questions about the object of the search, and had done her best to emphasize its potential importance. She and Officer Damoth had actually had an amusing discussion about whether what he'd be looking for was bigger or smaller than a bread box. She had settled on smaller, inasmuch as it was doubtful that what the stranger had been carrying and then managed to leave behind would be as large as a bread box. More likely, she thought, that he'd left nothing in the woods and that the search would be a colossal waste of time.

Carol knew that a really thorough search would require more men than worked for the sheriff's department and more of the time of her limited team than she could spare. On the other hand, as she had discovered on her walk with Kevin that morning, there were fairly obvious paths through the woods, paths which the birders had clearly followed. There would be no need for her officers to investigate every square inch of the forest floor. She sent them off with a cheerful 'good luck' and little expectation that they would find anything that was not mother nature's doing.

Once that had been done, she sat down with Bridges and went through the list of birders which Kevin had prepared the day before. JoAnne, in consultation with Sam, had already made a number of calls and scheduled several appointments. The members of the Crooked Lake Birders Club who had been on the hike in the Grove all knew that they would be meeting with the sheriff, and many of them had apparently stayed at home, waiting to be summoned. The Nugents, as promised, had been given one of the first appointments in order that they would not have to alter their plans to go to Tennessee. Otherwise, those who were to be called first were the people Sam had thought it most important to speak with, notably those who had left Agnes McKendrick's group and gone wandering off through the woods.

Unfortunately, two members of Sam's 'urgent - see first' list were not scheduled for visits to the sheriff's office that afternoon. They were Bill Neuberger, husband of the shooting victim, and Paul Raymore, who had a client he had to see. Neuberger was given a one day reprieve to let him deal with his grief. So it was agreed that Sam would talk with the Nugents and Sallie Finch, while Carol would question Mel Cone and the high school student, Michael Nagle. Meanwhile, JoAnne would flesh out the schedule of appointments for the next day. With luck, they would have seen all of those who had been on the bird hike in no more than two days.

———

The first of the birders to visit the sheriff's department in Cumberland were Emily and Gerald Nugent. Sam could think of no reason why their ages were important, but from force of habit he guessed that they were about fifty, give or take a few years either way. Both of them had dressed up, whether to make a good impression or because this is what they did when they weren't on a bird hike, he didn't know. Sam couldn't remember what Gerald had been wearing the day before, but he had no trouble recalling Emily's misguided attempt to look like a character from 'The Sound of Music.' Without the faux Alpine attire, she was a reasonably attractive woman.

Sam asked about what they did, about family, about the forthcoming trip to Tennessee. It was an attempt to put them at ease, but it didn't look as if it was succeeding. It was Gerald who seemed least comfortable.

"Are you long time birders?" Sam asked.

"Not really," the husband answered. "Emily longer than me. She's an expert. Well, sort of. I suppose next to Mr. Raymore and Mr. Cone, we're both amateurs. I suppose I do it for the exercise."

"But I take it you both enjoy it."

"Until yesterday, we did," Emily said. "I'm not so sure I'll have the stomach for going on Agnes's next hike."

Sam wondered if it might be quite some time before there would be another hike. But it was time to get down to business.

"Mrs. Nugent, when I arrived yesterday you and one of the others, I think it was Mr. Hornaday, were talking. Actually, I thought you might be arguing. What seemed to be the trouble?"

The woman blushed.

"It wasn't an argument, just a disagreement. Peter was blaming Agnes for taking us up to the Grove, and I was insisting that what had happened was no cause to criticize her. She gets too much criticism anyway."

"Why is that?"

"I don't know. Maybe it's just that she's the one that runs these affairs, and some of the group don't like to be ordered about." Emily shook her head. "I didn't mean that. She doesn't order us about. It's just that somebody has to be in charge, and it's Agnes."

The conversation went from there to questions about their fellow birders, with emphasis on who among them left the group and when, and whether they had said anything about where they were going. The Nugents weren't very helpful.

"I think most of us were paying more attention to Agnes and to the birds she thought she'd seen or whose call she recognized," Emily said. "I'm pretty sure Vivian left fairly early in the hike and that her husband probably followed her, maybe five minutes later. But I don't think they said anything about their intentions. And Sallie Finch, it was later and we'd come across some funny looking toadstools. She said to go on, she'd catch up. As I remember it, she never did. Maybe she felt sick."

"One final question," Sam said. "Do either of you own a gun?"

"Oh, goodness, no." Mr. Nugent made it sound as if the very idea was repellent.

"Gerald has never been a hunter," his wife added. "I can't understand why people want to shoot those innocent deer."

Those innocent deer are the cause of too many highway fatalities, Sam thought, but didn't say so.

All in all, his conversation with the Nugents struck Sam as inconsequential. Two people who were paying attention to birds, not their fellow birders. It would probably be the same with the others. After half an hour he thanked them for their time and wished them a pleasant trip to Tennessee.

———

Sam had a fifteen minute wait before Sallie Finch arrived. He had no idea what to expect. She had not been a part of the group who had gathered near Vivian Neuberger's body until he and Byrnes got there. Tommy had seen her and questioned her briefly when he met what they were now calling 'the wanderers' down by the parked cars. She had apparently stayed behind when the group had discovered some toadstools; in any event he had never seen her, and Tommy's report had been brief and uninformative.

The woman who walked into his office reminded Sam of a bird. She was short and slight, and was wearing a light brown suit over a cream colored blouse. But it was less her size and outfit that suggested the resemblance to a bird. It was her head, and more particularly her face. Her chestnut colored hair fit her head like a cap. Her eyes were small but sharp. It was certainly his imagination, but he thought her nose looked like a beak.

"Officer Bridges, this is a pleasure. I'm sorry to have missed you yesterday."

Her grip when they shook hands was surprisingly firm. Sam wondered at her choice of words. He could think of no reason why she would find it a pleasure to be meeting him.

"I'm also sorry we didn't meet yesterday at the Grove. I'm sure you know why you're here. The death of one of your colleagues is both a serious and a totally unexpected matter. We are in the process of talking with everyone who was on the bird hike, trying to form a picture of just what happened. Please have a seat."

"Of course. I don't know anything about Vivian's death, but I shall do my best to help you in your investigation. I've thought a lot about it, and from my perspective - that of a layman, of course - I can only imagine that some irresponsible hunter is responsible."

It was obvious that Sallie Finch intended to take the initiative in their discussion of the shooting death of Vivian Neuberger. Sam felt an urge to comment on her observation that a hunter was both irresponsible and responsible, but he left it alone.

"I have the impression that the Crooked Lake Birders Club is something of a mixture of people who know their birds and are amateurs. Where would you put yourself?"

"Do I look like an expert?" she asked.

"I'm sorry," Sam said, "but I'm not sure what an expert looks like."

"Well, I'm not one of them. Ask Paul Raymore. He runs circles around the rest of us. And enjoys doing it."

There was just a hint of animosity in her voice. It seemed that Sallie Finch didn't like Paul Raymore.

"Anyway, you've been part of this club for how long?"

"It's not the sort of thing one remembers to the month or the day, sheriff. But I joined about a year ago, maybe closer to two."

Sam usually corrected people who called him sheriff, but not this time.

"I didn't get to meet you yesterday because it seems you had left the group who came running when Mr. Cone discovered Mrs. Neuberger's body. Was there some reason why you didn't stay with Mrs. McKendrick and the rest of the birders?"

Sallie smiled.

"You probably don't know Agnes very well. I don't mean to sound critical, but she's a cross many of us have to bear. I wasn't the only one who set off on our own, as I'm sure you know or will discover before you have finished interrogating everyone. In any event, I'd had enough of her hectoring, and when we all got involved in a conversation about poisonous mushrooms I took advantage of the situation to cut out. I enjoyed the peace and quiet, even saw a few interesting birds without her help."

"What did you do when you left the group?"

"I sat awhile, then took a walk."

"Took a walk?"

"Our leader said to meet back at the cars at nine, and it was getting close to nine. So I set off in the direction of where we had parked. That's where I met officer - Byrnes, isn't it? - and heard that Vivian had been shot. A horrible ending to an otherwise boring hike. It would never have happened if we'd taken canoes as we'd originally planned to."

Bridges was surprised by this information.

"You're saying that the original plan was to look for birds on the lake instead of in Anson's Grove?"

"That's right. Water birds are more fun, don't you think?"

"Why the change?" Sam asked.

"Agnes. She's been touting the Grove for months. She thinks of it like it's her private preserve."

Until a relatively few minutes ago, Sam had never met Sallie Finch or heard anything about her other than Byrnes' brief report. It had quickly become clear, however, that the bird-like Finch woman didn't much care for some of her fellow birders. Why, he wondered, had she joined the club? And then remained a member?

"Do you own a gun?" he asked. It was a question he and Carol would be posing to everyone who had been in the Grove the day Vivian Neuberger had been shot.

"You are wondering if I might have killed her. Is that it?" Sallie gave Sam a smile of self satisfaction.

"Inasmuch as Mrs. Neuberger was killed by a gun, its seems like a logical question, don't you think?"

"Unfortunately, I can't help you. Your Officer Byrnes searched me and came up empty handed. I neither own a gun nor belong to the NRA."

Sam had decided he didn't much care for Sallie Finch. He wondered if others shared his opinion.

"Did you, by chance, see anyone else after you left Mrs. McKendrick's group and before you got back to your car?" Sam was sure the answer would be no. It was.

"No, I never saw the shooter. Perhaps I'd have been more alert if I'd known that someone had it in for Vivian. Poor woman. And Bill. You have to feel sorry for the one who's left, don't you?"

Three down, five if you count the ones Carol is talking to. Which leaves ten more for tomorrow. Sam had the feeling that discovering who had killed Vivian Neuberger was going to be a difficult task that would take a long time.

CHAPTER 9

Down the corridor and across from the squad room the sheriff was doing what Sam was doing, albeit with different members of the Crooked Lake Birders Club. Her first appointment was with Mel Cone, the man who had discovered Mrs. Neuberger's body. Carol was looking forward to meeting several of the birders, but Cone promised to be among the few most likely to know something important about the shooting. That was not the case with Michael Nagle. He was just a high school student and was along on the hike only because neighbors had invited him. It was unlikely that he knew many of the other birders, and in spite of the fact that he had been identified as one of 'the wanderers,' she could think of no reason why he should be considered a suspect in the shooting.

It was shortly after 2:30 when JoAnne ushered Cone into Carol's office. As with the other birders, she had no mental picture of what he would look like. Nonetheless, she was surprised. The man looked like what she imagined ferrets looked like. She had never seen a ferret, but she had read novels in which a certain kind of shady character had been compared to a ferret. Of course she had no idea whether Mel Cone was a shady character. She did her best to forget everything she thought she knew about ferrets.

"Mr. Cone, let me thank you taking time to see me. As you know, we're meeting with everyone who was on your bird hike yesterday, trying to get a better picture of just what happened to Mrs. Neuberger. I understand that you are the one who found her. It must have been a shock."

"It certainly was. Like I told your deputy, I heard a gun shot but it never occurred to me that somebody'd been hit. When I saw Mrs. Neuberger, my first thought was that she'd stumbled over some old fence posts and fallen down. But when I got to her I saw the blood on her back."

"I'd like you to tell me how you happened to be so close to her when she was hit. Had the two of you arranged to meet?"

"Oh, goodness no. It was just coincidence."

Carol had never been much of a believer in coincidences.

"So you just happened to be nearby, is that it? What were you doing in the vineyard? I thought the bird hike was up in the Grove."

"It was, but I frequently do better when I'm off on my own. Some of the others will tell you the same. Anyway, I was looking for an unusual warbler I thought I'd seen. When that shot rang out, I was startled and looked around me to see if I could tell where it might have come from. That's when I first saw her."

"About how far away from you would you say she was?"

"I'm not a very good judge of distance, but I'd say no more than thirty, forty yards."

Carol filed this bit of information away for future reference. It had occurred to her that maybe the fatal shot had been intended for Cone, not Neuberger. If they had been as many as forty yards apart, however, that was extremely unlikely. On the other hand, had Cone himself been the shooter, thirty or forty yards wouldn't have been much of a challenge in an open field. He may have been the one who had discovered the victim, but Carol knew it didn't mean he had not also fired the shot that killed her.

She was about to ask Cone whether he was by avocation a hunter when he chose to strengthen his case for having left the Grove and thus been in a position to discover Mrs. Neuberger's body.

"Are you a birder?"

"I'm afraid not," Carol said. "Why do you ask?"

"I'm sure you find it suspicious that I'm the one who found Vivian. Agnes McKendrick is a nice lady, and she's probably a good leader for those of us who are novices. But if you really know your birds you don't want to be tied down with a bunch of people who get excited if they see a robin. Does that make sense?"

Carol smiled.

"You aren't a novice, is that what you're telling me?"

"I don't like to brag, but I've been doing this for years and I've seen just about every bird known to the Finger Lakes."

"I've heard that quite a few others broke away from Mrs. McKendrick's group, including Mrs. Neuberger. Is she a knowledgeable birder?"

"I think you could call her that. At least she was interested in nature generally. She taught biology at the school in Southport."

Carol had not known this.

"How about her husband? And Mr. Raymore and Mrs. Finch?"

Cone seemed puzzled, but only momentarily.

"Oh, you're talking about the others who didn't stick with Agnes. At least Paul and Sallie know their birds. I'm not sure about Bill Neuberger. I've assumed he joined the club because of Vivian, but you'd have to ask him."

"Did you run into any of these people after you set off on your own?"

Again there was a moment's hesitation.

"No, only Mrs. Neuberger, and that wasn't until somebody fired a shotgun."

Time to make another mental note, Carol thought. We don't know yet what kind of gun was used to kill Vivian Neuberger. Does Mel Cone know it was a shotgun, or is he only guessing?

"By the way," Carol asked, "I assume that you know these people pretty well, all of you belonging to the birders club. I'm talking about Raymore, Sallie Finch, the Neubergers. Friends, any of them?"

No hesitation, but Carol noticed that Cone suddenly looked wary.

"No, we're not what you'd call close. The people you mentioned are all relatively new members of the club. Anyway, Connie - that's my wife - she's not very outgoing." He decided to retract that characterization of his wife. "No, that's not fair. I guess it's a couples thing."

Carol thought she knew what he meant, but chose not to pursue it. She asked several more questions, none of which elicited answers that were helpful. It was time to talk a bit more about guns.

"Do you own a gun?"

Cone had no trouble interpreting this question.

"I think I've been answering all of your questions with a 'no.' But I do have a gun. Several, in fact. However, I never take any of them on bird hikes. They tend to scare off the birds."

He seemed to think that this was a funny line. At least he laughed. Carol allowed herself a small smile.

She also allowed herself to ask a question which was nothing short of an invitation to Cone to share his opinions of his fellow birders.

"Tell me about the members of the bird club. Are there people who don't get along? People who strike you or others as some kind of a problem?"

Carol had expected another 'no,' but Cone thought about the question and offered a cautious 'yes' with specifics.

"Like I said, Agnes McKendrick, she's a problem for many of us. She's really a decent sort, but you're never allowed to forget that she's in charge. Then there's Sallie Finch. She's got a waspish tongue. Not that she uses it on anyone in particular, but I'm careful not to cross her. I suppose I ought to mention Paul. Raymore, that is. He has to be number one. You claim you've seen a Kirtland's warbler and he'll give you a smug look and tell you about the ivory billed woodpecker that he's spotted."

"You have to be kidding. I'm no birder, and even I know that those woodpeckers are extinct."

"Okay, I'm exaggerating. But you get my point. When it comes to birds, trying to top Paul is like trying to get the NFL to relocate one of its teams to Southport."

"What you're saying is that birders are a competitive species."

"Yes indeed. We call the really competitive ones twitchers."

The birder who showed up at the sheriff's door late that afternoon was the youngest of those who had been hiking in the Grove and he was most definitely not a twitcher. To Carol's surprise, he arrived accompanied by his mother. He was close to six feet tall and looked younger than she had expected him to. He also looked bored. His mother looked worried.

Carol welcomed them, offered coffee or a coke, and apologized for taking them away from more pleasant pursuits. Michael shook hands at his mother's urging, but declined to say anything. Mrs. Nagle, who introduced herself as Fran, did her best to cover her son's silence with a torrent of words which did less to explain that silence than it did to underscore her own anxiety.

"I probably should have left word that I would be coming along with Michael today," she said. "I hope you don't mind. Michael has never been in a situation like this before. I mean somebody getting killed like that. It's a terrible thing for someone so young to be suspected of shooting that woman. But you have to understand that Michael had nothing to do with it. He only went on that bird hike because -"

Carol had to interrupt this rambling monologue.

"Mrs. Nagle, please. Let me assure you that Michael is not here today because we suspect him of having anything to do with Mrs.

Neuberger's death. Because of what happened yesterday, I must talk with everyone who was on that bird hike, not just Michael. Why don't you just let me ask him a few questions. Because he was there, he's in a position to help my investigation. I'm sure you understand, don't you, Michael?"

"But Jenny told me that it's because Michael didn't stay with the rest of the hikers that -"

Carol again cut Mrs. Nagle off.

"Forgive me for interrupting again, Mrs. Nagle, but I don't know who Jenny is, and she knows nothing about why I need to talk with Michael. I would appreciate it if you would let your son answer my questions."

"Well, of course, but you need to know that he is a very sensitive young man and he -" She paused, then reached out to take her son's hand. He promptly pulled it away from her.

"What is it you want to know?" Michael asked. His voice was flat.

"Let's go back to the beginning, Michael. I know that you aren't a member of Mrs. McKendrick's bird watching club. How does it happen that you went on the hike?"

"The Taggarts asked me. They thought they were being nice and I figured I should say yes."

"The Taggarts are good friends," Mrs. Nagle said. "That's Jenny and Bob. They're nice people, and Michael mows their lawn and helps them with odd jobs."

"She doesn't care about the Taggarts, mother. And I don't do odd jobs for them."

It was becoming obvious that Michael Nagle would have preferred it had his mother stayed home. Which prompted a question.

"How old are you, Michael?"

"Fifteen, which is why I didn't come alone this morning. The dumb law says I can't drive yet."

"I see," Carol said. It was as she had figured.

"It's like he says," his mother said, "but I had to support him."

"I don't need your support!" The silent young man was now angry, and sounded very much like a typical adolescent, challenging parental authority.

Carol thought that Mrs. Nagle actually looked frightened.

"You went along with your neighbors yesterday," Carol said. "Are you yourself interested in birds?"

"No. Why should I be? If you'd heard them talking about a two thousand mile migration and winter and summer plumage or dumb stuff like that you'd know what I mean."

"That must be why you left the group during the hike, right? It just wasn't your thing. When you left the others, where did you go?"

"Nowhere. I just wandered around. There's no law against that."

"No, there isn't. But I wondered if you saw or heard anything that might help me understand how it happened that Mrs. Neuberger was shot."

"I wasn't looking for her, that's for sure, so the answer is no."

Why 'that's for sure?' Carol wondered. Was Michael simply indifferent to Mrs. Neuberger, like he was to birds? Or was there a hint of disrespect in his voice?

"You didn't know Mrs. Neuberger." Carol wasn't sure whether she was making a statement or asking a question.

"Of course I knew her. Had her for two semesters of biology. She's one of those evolution freaks."

Well, well.

"I don't think I understand," Carol said. "She's an evolution freak?"

"The text book spends a whole lot of pages on Darwin and evolution. But Mrs. Neuberger, she's a true believer. You want to get a good grade from her and you've got to treat evolution as the greatest thing since we kicked the Brits out of the United States."

"I'm sorry." Mrs. Nagle had decided to explain things. "We don't go along with some of these science theories. Michael doesn't mean any disrespect. It's just that in our home we take the Bible more seriously than what they teach in our schools."

The conversation had taken a decidedly interesting turn. But Carol thought it best not to follow the subject down the road toward which it was heading.

"I need to let you get back to whatever you need to do," she said. "I've just got one more question, one I'm asking every one who was on the bird hike. Do you have guns in your home?"

"What's wrong with that?" Michael was again angry.

"I'm not saying there's anything wrong with owning a gun, Michael. I'm only asking if there are guns in the Nagle household."

Once again, Mrs. Nagle came to the rescue.

"Hank's a hunter. So's Michael and his brother." Fran said it in a way that was a testament to how proud she was of her men.

Carol would like to know whether those guns were kept under lock and key, but she was sure that the answer would be 'of course.'

"If you think of anything that you forgot to tell me today, Michael, I wish you'd give me a call. It's been nice meeting you. Thanks for coming in."

Actually, it had been a tense meeting. She had initially been unhappy that Michael's mother had been present. By the end of their meeting, however, she realized that the mother's presence had been a plus. There had been an understandable generational conflict on display, but Carol had a sneaking feeling that there was something else going on in the relationship between Michael and his parents. At least in his mother's case. Finding out more about them might not be easy, but she knew that she would be devoting more time to the Nagles than she had expected to when she first learned about the death in Anson's Grove.

CHAPTER 10

When Carol got home that evening, little did she know that her next twenty-four hours were to be dominated by one of her most experienced officers, Jim Barrett. He had set off with Officers Byrnes and Damoth earlier in the day to canvass the Grove for something someone had left there. Assuming, of course, that something had been left there, a rather big assumption.

The task facing the men was a large one, inasmuch as the Grove covered quite a few acres and they had no idea what they were looking for. Tommy Byrnes had made the task somewhat easier because he had been at the Grove the previous day and therefore knew something about the area in which the birders had spent most of their time. But it was still a daunting assignment, and Carol had no great expectations for their success. It was not until 5:55, when it was already past quitting time and the three of them were heading back to their cars, that Barrett spotted something that looked out of place. It was a small notebook, and its cover was a dark beige, much like the color of the carpet of pine needles which covered the floor of the woods.

He doubted whether it was what Carol wanted, but it was the first thing he had seen other than a couple of cigarette butts which suggested that someone had been in the Grove. The cigarettes had worried him, inasmuch as they had been known to start many forest fires and Jim abhorred forest fires. The notebook posed no danger to the safety of the woods, although its presence was bothersome for someone who didn't like it whenever careless humans defiled the beauty of nature.

He picked it up and turned to the first page. It contained a long list of bird names which had been entered in no apparent order. They occupied several pages. No question, he thought, this belongs to a bird watcher. Bird watchers had been in the woods yesterday, and one of them had somehow lost the book in which he had entered the name of each new sighting. He wasn't sure whether Carol would be interested.

Byrnes and Damoth headed home. Officer Barrett could have done the same. But he didn't. If what the sheriff was looking for was so important that she'd put three of her officers on it, she would want to know immediately if they had found something. Jim turned the car around and headed for her Crooked Lake cottage.

Carol had been home for no more than twenty minutes, during which time she had changed into her bathing suit for a quick dip in the lake with Kevin. They were just coming back to the cottage when Officer Barrett appeared at the door.

"Hi, Jim." Carol would normally be uncomfortable welcoming someone at her door in her bathing suit. But the very fact that he was there was enough to convince her that something important had happened. Kevin, who was right behind his wife, found himself deriving no little satisfaction from the fact that one of Carol's underlings was having a good look at more of his boss than he was used to seeing.

"I'm sorry to come barging in at a moment like this," Jim said, "but I have something I'd like you to see."

"No problem. Kevin and I are very informal, aren't we, dear?" She didn't expect an answer. "Come on in. Like to join us in a beer or a glass of wine out on the deck?"

"Are you sure you wouldn't mind?"

"Absolutely not. If you like, you can call your wife and tell her your boss has detained you. What will it be, beer or wine?"

"I guess I'll have a beer, thanks."

Carol pushed the screen open and ushered him in and on through the cottage and onto the deck. Officer Barrett seemed to be overcoming his initial embarrassment. If the sheriff didn't mind that he was seeing her in a brief bathing suit, why should he feel awkward.

"You have news for me," Carol said. "And something in your hand. I doubt that you'd be here unless you have something you found in Anson's Grove. I must say, I'm surprised. But I'm also dying of curiosity. Tell me."

"Here," he said, handing her a notebook. "I didn't stumble on it until we were about ready to call it a day. It looks like somebody's list of birds he'd seen, plus some stuff I don't think I understand."

"That's great. It probably means it was left in the Grove just yesterday during that bird hike. Where did you find it?"

Barrett explained where it was relative to the place where Byrnes had said Mrs. Neuberger's body had been found. Not all that far away, Carol thought. She hoped the notebook would contain the owner's name.

It didn't. She scanned it briefly, immediately aware that the list of birds would be of much less interest than the notes which appeared pages later towards the back of the notebook. She was anxious to spend some time trying to make sense of those final entries. But she could not do that with Jim Barrett sipping his beer beside her.

"Jim, you are a miracle worker." She leaned across and gave her surprised officer a peck on the cheek. "Oh, please forgive me for taking liberties like that. I tend to forget myself when I unwind at home. But I must confess, I never thought you guys would find anything. I was even feeling guilty that I'd asked you to spend the day in the woods."

"It was no trouble, really. I'm just glad we found something. Do you think it solves the shooting?"

"I wish it did, but I'm afraid not. I don't even know what it means. But I think we're making progress."

Kevin, who'd said nothing since Barrett had arrived, spoke up.

"In Carol's experience, a notebook in the hand is worth two birds in the bush. You must remember that priest who ended up a scarecrow a few years ago. He kept a notebook, and without it you might still be trying to figure out who killed him. And there was the Swedish exchange student. She, too, kept a notebook. Or maybe you'd call it a diary. You ever keep a diary?"

"Not me. My sisters did. I think they still do." Officer Barrett was surprised at Kevin's recall of old cases. Carol wasn't, and changed the subject.

"You'll have to ignore Kevin," she said. "But how about birds? The notebook tells us this guy keeps a record of birds he's seen. Did you ever do that?"

"I never thought much about it as a kid. The only birds I knew anything about were the geese that Dad would shoot. These days I guess I pay more attention because there's so much talk that some species are disappearing. Not the geese, of course."

"No, you're right about that. When I was growing up here you didn't see geese except when they were migrating. Used to be big flocks of them. You'd hear them flying over, honking, making a lot of racket. Now people complain about the fact they can't get rid of them."

"Look, this reminds me I've got something I need to talk about with you. But the family'll be holding supper. Can we talk tomorrow?"

"Of course. My door is always open."

"Thanks. Maybe we could talk after squad meeting."

"Sounds good to me. But I'm the one who owes you a word of thanks. I mean the notebook."

"Like I said, it was no trouble."

When Barrett had left, Kevin turned his attention to the stove.

"Will supper hold?" Carol asked. "I want you to look at something."

"Sure. What's the problem?"

"It's this notebook Jim brought in. I was hoping for a gun, but I think the notebook may be just as interesting. Here, take a look at it. Most of it simply lists birds. Presumably the ones the person whose book it is had seen and identified. The last pages are another story. I haven't had a chance to study it carefully, of course, but it's not about birds. Just look at the end of it and tell me what you think. You seem to remember the priest and the exchange student. How about this birder?"

CHAPTER 11

The small beige notebook contained a list of 57 birds that covered seven pages. The first one on the list was the ubiquitous robin, the last the almost equally familiar goldfinch. But the list, while consisting mostly of birds of forest and open country, also included a number of water birds, which meant that it had not been compiled the previous day in Anson's Grove. It was Kevin's guess that not more than a dozen birds on the list had been added on the recent hike.

"But that's pretty self evident," Carol said. "What about the entries at the end of the notebook? They don't have anything to do with birds, or if they do it must be in some kind of code."

Kevin turned to the end of the notebook and read what he found there.

'I'm wrong. Can't be him.'

Then, a page later, two more entries:

'It's going to be Elvis!'

'Wrong again. It's Daddy Bird.'

"Well, there is a reference to a bird," Kevin said.

"So what? I'm no bird watcher, but I'm pretty sure there's no species named daddy."

"I'm just kidding. Whoever wrote this drivel wasn't talking about birds. Daddy Bird sounds like something from a children's book. And what about Elvis?"

"It's obviously a reference to Elvis Presley, which tells us absolutely nothing."

"Maybe it's Elvis Costello," Kevin suggested. "Why didn't he choose The Byrds?"

"That's ridiculous, Kevin. I think he - or how about she? - was thinking about somebody named Elvis. And if that's true, I'll bet Daddy Bird is also a person."

"The first line, the one on a page by itself, doesn't use a name. Just that he's wrong. He twice says he's wrong. But about what?"

"I feel a headache coming on," Carol said. "All I think I know is that this stuff at the end has nothing to do with being a bird watcher.

Whoever it was was just using a notebook with a list of birds he'd seen to jot down random thoughts about something else."

"And that something else includes someone named Elvis and Daddy Bird. It seems to me the best strategy would be for you to ask all those birders you're interviewing if they've lost a notebook. Their reaction to that should tell you what all this mumbo jumbo is about."

"I don't think that's a good idea. I'd rather keep on brainstorming what you call mumbo jumbo. We've only spent about fifteen minutes trying to make sense of it. Why don't you make it your order of business for the day tomorrow to come up with some possible explanations? Like maybe somebody's writing a novel and is talking about characters or plot developments. What if the novel is a bodice ripper, and the rippers are Elvis somebody and Daddy Bird? You see what I mean?"

"I hope I could do better than turn Elvis into a bodice ripper, but I'm willing to give it a try. For what it's worth, I very much doubt that this birder is also a novelist. If he is, he's well on his way to producing a real flop."

"Let's eat. What are we having? Not crow, I hope."

"I'm glad yesterday's shooting hasn't cost you your sense of humor. No, not crow. Stew. And I'm speaking of the noun, not the verb."

Squad meeting had ended the next morning and Carol had retired to her office to review the appointments JoAnne had scheduled for her with the members of the Crooked Lake Birders Club. She and Sam were to have four 'interrogations' apiece, Carol having decided that there was no reason not to see the Taggarts, the Hornadays, and the two single women, Smith and Olcott, together. It was while she was scanning the brief notes in front of her that Jim Barrett appeared in the doorway.

"Hi, Carol. Can we have our talk now?"

"That's why I'm here. Come on in and shut the door."

Barrett looked uneasy. Carol wasn't surprised.

"Coffee?"

"I've had too much already. If I look nervous it's because I am."

"No need to be. I know all about it, Jim. And I've already had a conversation with Jason Eglin. He's angry with you, but he's overreacting, and I told him so. What's more, I know you, and I'm one hundred percent sure you didn't use the language he claims you did. If it helps, I'm with you on the fracking business. We don't know enough about the risks to the lake, to our ground water - oh, why am I telling you this? You know more about it than I do."

"That's good to hear. I really mean it, Carol, but that's not what I wanted to talk about." Jim took a deep breath. "Well, I suppose in a way it is. It's hard to say this, but I have to give notice because I'll be leaving the force."

Carol was more than surprised. She was shocked, and she was sure Jim knew it.

"I think I just heard you say you're going to be leaving us. Tell me I heard wrong."

"I'm afraid not." he said. "It's related to the fracking argument, actually. You may know that there's an organization here in the Finger Lakes that's been actively working on some important environmental issues. Fracking is one of them. I've been talking with people, and it sounds like something I'd really enjoy doing. They offered me a job, and - well - I said I'd take it. I told them I'd have to give you plenty of notice, so you'll have to tell me what's fair."

Officer Barrett visibly relaxed in his chair. Telling her what he was going to be doing had obviously been difficult, but to his credit he'd come right to the point.

"Jim, let me offer my congratulations." She stood up, leaned across the desk, and shook his hand. "I'm not going to pretend that we won't miss you, but all of us have to do what's right for us. And you'll be doing this in a good cause, maybe several good causes. Will the family have to be moving?"

"I don't think I'd have done it if we had to move. But there's what they call the western lakes office, and it's just over in Canandaigua, so, no, we're staying put. The money's not quite as good as it is here, but it's not bad. And would you believe it, I'll still be on the road a lot."

He said it with a smile.

"Only you'll be doing good," Carol said, reciprocating the smile.

"I like to think I've always been doing good working for you."

"You have, and it won't be easy to fill your shoes."

"Which brings up the subject of when I should let them know I'll be available."

Carol had no idea how long it would be before she could hire a replacement. She knew she couldn't make Jim's departure date conditional.

"How about a month? Unless, that is, you'd like to stick around until we catch whoever shot that woman over in Anson's Grove."

"A month sounds more than fair. Did that notebook make it likely you'd wrap the case up faster?"

"I wish I could say it did, but the honest answer is no. The wheels of justice grind slowly around here."

Jim stood up, then sat down again.

"These have been good years," he said. "You've been a great boss. All the guys say so. You aren't planning on leaving, are you? I mean something like going back into law?"

"I appreciate the compliment, Jim, and no, I'm not leaving. Now I'd suggest you get out of here before I start crying."

CHAPTER 12

Carol's report of Officer Barrett's announcement that he was leaving had put Kevin in a pensive mood. He had witnessed the departure from the Madison College faculty of several friends in the last few years, and they had all left him with mixed feelings: he'd really miss them but he understood that what they were doing made good sense for them as career moves. Whether Barrett's decision was wise, he didn't know. Non-profit organizations, even those with good causes to support, could be unstable. Like Barrett, he believed in the mission of environmental organizations, and he hoped that this one and its opposition to fracking would succeed. He'd be crossing his fingers.

To his surprise he found himself more worried about Barrett, whom he hardly knew, than he was about his wife, with whom he was deeply in love. Perhaps it was because he knew Carol so much better, knew how resilient she was, knew that she'd find a good officer to take Barrett's place. Or would she? Pay being what it was, she'd have to hire someone with limited or even no experience. He had served on faculty recruitment committees at the college, but he had no idea what the ground rules were for hiring people who'd be wearing uniforms and carrying guns for a sheriff's department.

They had talked about it at some length. It wasn't until daylight had given way to the total darkness of a moonless night that Carol had surprised him with what was less an idea than an announcement of her intentions.

"We need a woman," she said. "I'm going to hire a woman."

"How can you possibly know that? There may not be a single applicant."

"Really? What you're implying is that law enforcement is just too tough for the fairer sex, that there isn't anybody out there who'd risk life and limb when she could be a teacher in a safe little classroom."

Kevin could see where this discussion was going, and he didn't want to find himself in a losing argument.

"I know. I'm in a classroom and you're on law and order's front lines. I was only thinking of the odds."

"Maybe it won't be easy, but if I start the process with a smart, tough woman in mind, I bet I'll find one. Unless, that is, you think you might give some thought to abandoning opera and applying for the job yourself."

"It's tempting, but I can't quite picture having to say 'yes sir' every time you give me an order."

"Good. Because I really do want a woman for Jim's position. And now that that's settled, any more advice?"

"I think I should just let whatever happens, happen. So good luck."

Feeling better now that she had dealt with her sadness over Jim Barrett's news with a decision to double the number of women in the department, Carol approached the upcoming sessions with the rest of the birders in a more optimistic frame of mind. It was not that she now expected to learn more from these meetings, only that she was somehow more confident that the puzzling shooting of Vivian Neuberger would prove to have a reasonably simple explanation.

Agnes McKendrick was already seated in the office, drinking a cup of coffee which JoAnne had provided, when Carol emerged from the squad meeting.

"Good morning, Mrs. McKendrick. My morning squad meeting lasted a bit longer than usual. Sorry to keep you waiting."

"That's perfectly all right, sheriff. Waiting for a few minutes is the least of my worries."

"Yes, of course. The trouble in the Grove the other day isn't something we get over quickly. It had to be a terrible shock to you, and to your other birders."

"I don't really know about all of them, but I've never had an experience like that in my life, and I doubt if most of the others have either. We were lucky to have your husband along."

Other than the fact that he had been the one to call the sheriff's department, it wasn't clear just why the birders had been lucky to have Kevin with them.

"It was kind of you to let Kevin join you. In other circumstances I'm sure he would have enjoyed the outing."

"You know, of course, that I didn't know he was your husband. He never mentioned it. But when the officers arrived, it soon became obvious. He seems to be quite a good birder."

"We haven't talked about it a lot. I think it went back to when he was a boy scout. But I don't want to take a lot of your time, and I do have a few questions if you don't mind."

"No, no, of course not. That is why I'm here. Anything you want to ask."

"About Mrs. Neuberger, bless her soul. I understand that she hadn't been with you long."

"No, she hadn't moved to the lake until recently. Just over two years ago, I think. But we were so glad to welcome them - she and her husband, that is - into the club. Most of the birders are dudes. Perhaps you don't know the lingo. Dudes. I mean novices. And what with her being a biology teacher, she naturally knows more about the natural world." Mrs. McKendrick made a production of taking a kleenex out of her purse. "We're going to miss her."

Carol let her blow her nose and put the kleenex in the pocket of a casual jacket which looked much too upscale for hikes in the woods.

"I know, and it's harder considering how she left us. Do you expect to resume birding soon, or would the club think of that as unseemly?"

"I really don't know. I haven't talked to anyone except Mr. Neuberger, and that was to express my sympathy. Poor man. He was in terrible shape. We throw around words like broken hearted, but I think he really is broken hearted. Oh, I forgot. I did talk with one of the others, Mrs. Finch. That's Sallie. She called me that night, and you might say she's still in a state of shock, too."

"Considering that Mrs. Neuberger was killed by a gun, you can perhaps understand my next question. Are you aware of any of your birders carrying a gun when you hike?"

"I've never asked. For that matter, I've never told them they couldn't. Of course I'd prefer they didn't, but there are a few of them who probably would take offense if I asked them to leave their guns at home. I've never talked about it, but I think there may be some who think the second amendment is practically scripture. But none of my people shot poor Vivian. It had to be some fool hunter."

"You say a hunter probably shot Mrs. Neuberger." Carol tried to phrase her next question very carefully. "I have no reason to doubt that

that's what happened, but from what you know about your birders, does it strike you as possible that one of them might have done it?"

"That's a terrible thought, sheriff." The look that had come across Mrs. McKendrick's face left no doubt about it. "You can't be serious."

"I agree. It is a terrible thought, but I'm not in a position to dismiss any possibility. Perhaps a better way to put my question is to ask if you are aware of any strained relationships among members of the Crooked Lake Birders Club? I'm not talking about the occasional disagreement over what bird had just been spotted. I'm thinking of unpleasantness that may have had its origins outside of birding."

"Goodness, that's - well, it's kind of sensitive, don't you think? I've never been one to gossip." Agnes paused, uncertain what to say next.

"When you're in my business, you find yourself asking sensitive questions all the time. Let me be very clear. I have no reason to believe that any of your birders shot Mrs. Neuberger. But somebody did. I will be greatly relieved if it turns out to be a hunter. Unfortunately, I cannot dismiss the possibility - a hypothetical possibility, you understand - that one of the people who was with you on the hike in the Grove is the guilty party. It may be highly unlikely, but it's not impossible. Hence my question."

"Oh, dear. This is so difficult. Frankly, I'll have to confess that I don't get along with all of my birders. Or they with me. I don't think it's anything personal, but sometimes it can be a little awkward, if you know what I mean. But other than that, I can't think -"

Mrs. McKendrick has thought of an exception, Carol thought.

"Maybe there is one case," the leader of the club said. "I trust that you won't tell her I said this."

"Of course not," Carol said, mentally crossing her fingers.

"Well, there's Mrs. Finch. She's a perfectly decent woman, and she knows her birds. But she has a way of annoying people. I'm not talking about any one person, just people in general. She's sort of snappish, and sometimes it's hurtful."

"Can you recall an occasion when she's said something snappish and someone else seems to have felt hurt by it?"

"Please don't say I said this, but yes, there have been times like that. Sallie and Paul Raymore, they have their innings from time to time. I don't know whether what she says hurts Paul, but he doesn't hesitate to let her know he's annoyed. And then there's the Neubergers. For some reason they get under Sallie's skin. Or maybe it's the other way around. Anyway, you asked about strained relationships, and I think you could say that their relationship might be strained. Of course, that's over, what with Vivian being dead. Knowing Sallie, she might start picking on someone else."

It suddenly occurred to Agnes that she might have said too much.

"I'm sorry, but I have no business talking about my people like this. I sound like an awful gossip, and I hate gossips."

"You aren't a gossip, Mrs. McKendrick. I asked you a question and you've been trying to answer it to the best of your ability. All you are doing is helping me better understand the members of the Crooked Lake Birders Club. You must remember that before this week I barely knew any of them, including you."

When Agnes McKendrick had left, both to ponder whether she had been too indiscrete and to worry about the future of her birders club, Carol had but a few minutes remaining before the Taggarts were due. From what Kevin and Sam had told her, they seemed likely to be minor players in the investigation of Vivian Neuberger's death. For some reason, however, she found herself increasingly inclined to treat all of the birders as persons of interest in this unusual case.

CHAPTER 13

Carol's intuitive sense that she should not lightly dismiss the members of the Crooked Lake Birders Club who had stayed with Agnes McKendrick during the hike in Anson's Grove was to prove prescient. It would have been impossible for any of them to shoot Vivian Neuberger, of course. Or would it? She was reminded of all the locked room mysteries she had read, mysteries in which murder is committed under what seem to be impossible circumstances. Anson's Grove could hardly be called a locked room, but might there have been some way, however improbable, that one of the birders had somehow managed to shoot Neuberger while surrounded by a dozen other birders.

But that wasn't the reason Carol was determined not to conduct merely pro forma interviews with many of the birders. They may not have killed Vivian Neuberger, but they might have information which would lead her to the person who did. She spoke briefly with Bridges while she was waiting for the Taggarts.

"I know you'll treat Raymore as the possible shooter," she said, "but don't give any of the others a pass. They might know something that will help us. I think I leaned that from my chat with McKendrick just a few minutes ago. If most of these people have been taking bird hikes together for any considerable length of time, they'll have formed relationships and opinions about each other which might be important."

Sam smiled.

"I'll get everyone to confess to something," he promised.

"Let's not overdo it." At that moment JoAnne stuck her head out of her door and signaled to the sheriff that she had a call.

Carol mouthed a quiet 'who.' The answer was somebody named Taggart.

"Good morning. This is the sheriff. I believe I'm going to be seeing you shortly. Are you having trouble finding us?"

It was a woman who answered, and it was immediately apparent that there was a problem.

"I'm afraid we're going to have to cancel our meeting. We can't make it."

"I'm sorry. I've been looking forward to meeting you. I hope the two of you are all right, no crisis at home."

"Yes, we are having a crisis, Bob and me. We aren't sick, anything like that. But - how should I put something like this? - we're not on the same page about our meeting with you. Neither one of us has any idea who shot Mrs. Neuberger. It's not that. It's just that we need more time. Could we reschedule for maybe next week sometime?"

"I don't quite understand, Mrs. Taggart. What is it about needing more time?"

"Bob has something he wants to tell you, and I don't agree with him. That's all."

That's all? All of a sudden, Carol wanted very much to talk with the Taggarts. Especially Mr. Taggart. She'd been right about treating every one of the birders as a potentially important witness to what happened in the Grove.

"Mrs. Taggart, I obviously have no idea what it is that you and your husband disagree about. But I can tell that if we are going to solve Mrs. Neuberger's death it's important that everyone who was on the bird hike share everything that may be relevant, and then let us decide whether in fact it is relevant. So I'd very much like it if you and your husband would come on over to the office this morning. If you'd rather, I can come to your house. But we do need to talk, all three of us, and better to do it now than next week."

"But this is very personal, sheriff. I just can't do it, at least not now. I promise to call you back."

The phone connection went dead.

Whatever was bothering Jennifer Taggart might turn out to be unimportant, simply a matter of a minor disagreement between the Taggarts which had escalated to the point where compromise was impossible. But Carol was unwilling to concede its lack of importance.

"Sam, I've got a problem," she said as once more she cornered him, this time at the coffee machine. "The Taggarts don't want to see me, at least not today. Which makes me more determined to see them. I'm going to drive over to their place, so I may not be here for Jeanne Lerner. She's due at 11:45. Can you talk with her?"

"Don't see why not, but what is it with the Taggarts?"

"I wish I knew, and I intend to find out. Just a reminder about Ms. Lerner. She was driven to the Grove by Mrs. Finch. I have no idea whether they're close. But you've talked with Finch, and I understand that she's not a particularly pleasant person. So try to get the Lerner woman to open up about her. Okay?"

"Can do. By the way, is Jim really going to quit?"

"He is, but I'm trying to see it not as quitting but as trying something else. We'll miss him, but I hope he's happy."

"It's the fracking thing, isn't it?"

"That's a part of it. Look, I want to get over to the Taggarts a.s.a.p. We'll talk about Jim later."

She let JoAnne know what she was up to, and, checking the master list her assistant had prepared, made a note of the Taggarts' Southport address.

"Sam will see Lerner," she said, and was off.

It was half an hour later that she pulled up around the corner in the block next to the Taggart house. There was no point in giving the neighbors something to gossip about. She rang the bell and stood to one side where she wouldn't be seen until the door opened.

"Hello, Mrs. Taggart," she said, stepping into the foyer without being invited. "I'm sorry to pop in unannounced like this, but I must talk with you. Your husband, is he home?"

"No, he's at work. But I told you we couldn't meet with you today."

"I know, but while you may be able to wait, I'm not."

Mrs. Taggart backed away from the door and followed the sheriff into the living room. Carol hoped that her very presence in their house would change the woman's mind about discussing the issue which was causing so much disagreement between her and her husband.

"I know that you don't want to talk with me," she said, helping herself to a seat on the couch. "Unfortunately, I am investigating a serious crime. Somebody shot and killed Vivian Neuberger, and it is my job to find out who that somebody is. If you - or anybody else - is in possession of information which could help me, it is your responsibility to share that information with me. Otherwise, you put yourself in danger of being charged with obstruction of justice."

Carol knew that in practice it was more complicated than that, especially at this stage of her investigation when she didn't know whether what the Taggarts knew was in any way relevant to Mrs.

Neuberger's death. Nonetheless, she wanted Mrs. Taggart to talk, and it might be easier if her husband was not there to argue with her.

The two women stared at each other, Carol patiently waiting for a reply to her veiled threat, Jennifer Taggart unsuccessfully trying to find a way to finesse a delicate situation.

Carol won the standoff.

"I don't think you understand how awkward this is," Mrs. Taggart said. "Have you ever known something about a - let's say a friend - that the friend is desperately anxious to keep a secret?"

"I don't believe so, but I think I can imagine such a situation." Carol had tried to adopt a tone that said she was sympathetic to the woman's problem. "We are talking about a neighbor of yours, is that correct?"

It took a few seconds before the question was answered with a slight nod of the head.

When making a note of the Taggarts' address, Carol had quickly scanned the list of the birders who had been in Anson's Grove. She knew that they came from various places on and around the lake, with only four of them from Southport itself. Two of the four were the Taggarts. One of the others was Michael Nagle. She hadn't remembered the Nagle address, but now it had come to her so clearly that it was as if a flash bulb had gone off in her brain. It was the house next door. The Taggarts and the Nagles were neighbors.

She recalled the feeling she'd had after her meeting with Michael and his mother that something wasn't quite right. She also knew that Michael had been invited to go on the bird hike by the Taggarts, and that they had driven him to Anson's Grove. What it was that had produced the argument between Mr. and Mrs. Taggart she still did not know, but it was now obvious that it almost certainly had something to do with Michael Nagle, the testy teenager whose mother had clearly been very worried about him.

Carol had a sudden change of heart. She would not press Jennifer Taggart to unburden herself of whatever it was that she and her husband disagreed about. She would make it a point to speak with Mrs. Nagle. Her first impulse was just to get up and walk over to the neighboring house and confront the helicopter mother. However, a still small voice told her that that was not a good idea.

"Perhaps I'm being a bit too impatient, Mrs. Taggart," she said, getting up from her seat on the couch. "On reflection, next week should be soon enough. Why don't you and your husband give it some more thought and then get in touch with me. I really should apologize for surprising you like this."

The look of relief which came over the Taggart woman's face made a thank you unnecessary, but she said it anyway.

"Oh, thank you, sheriff. I promise to get back to you soon."

Carol wasn't optimistic that soon meant in a matter of just a few days.

CHAPTER 14

Kevin knew that his role in the Vivian Neuberger case, which had been unexpectedly important on day one, was now marginal at best. As a result, he had nothing important to do except concentrate on his annual effort to produce a paper on some aspect of opera. If past were prologue, such a paper might see the light of day every second or third year. At the moment he was not highly motivated.

Carol had left early for the office, where she expected to interrogate several of the birders who had been on the hike when Mrs. Neuberger had been killed. Kevin had taken his own sweet time over breakfast and the morning paper, and was actually debating doing something useful when he experienced a mild brainstorm. The focus of the brainstorm was the name Elvis. The notebook which Officer Barrett had found in the Grove had contained references to lots of birds and several comments which meant nothing to either Carol or him. Those comments, none consisting of more than a few words, were interesting only because they contained references to Elvis and Daddy Bird. But because they had no idea what the owner of the notebook had in mind when he scrawled those names in the back of it, they had dismissed them and turned their attention to other matters. But today, at an hour which was already embarrassingly late, Kevin's thoughts returned to the notebook and to Elvis.

Daddy Bird sounded like a term of endearment, but it meant nothing to someone other than the writer. Elvis, on the other hand, was a given name, if not a common one, best known as the moniker of a certain Mr. Presley. It should be easier to search for someone named Elvis than for someone who is affectionately called Daddy Bird. Kevin spent some of his otherwise wasted morning considering how he might go about turning the notebook's Elvis into a real live human being. Preferably one who lived on or near Crooked Lake.

Inevitably his ruminations on the matter led him to the telephone directory, or rather to the several directories which together covered Cumberland County. Kevin knew that an ever larger number of people were dispensing with land lines in favor of cell phones. He also knew that this Elvis might live far from Cumberland County. It was even possible that he was a dog or a horse, but one had to start somewhere.

His penchant for sleuthing aroused, Kevin showered and dressed and set about the business of seeing if there might be an Elvis Somebody living near Crooked Lake. Looking for a given name is obviously more difficult than looking for a surname, but Kevin had nothing better to do with his time, so he set himself the task of running down every page, line by line, in each of the areas' directories. It was a boring task, but so was researching and writing another paper on forgotten Handel operas or the relative importance of Verdi and Wagner. Once launched into the project, he kept at it with a perseverance which rarely came to his aid in his own professional labors.

Inevitably, his attention had wandered as he worked his way through the phone directories, so it was possible that he had missed an Elvis or two. But he definitely located three of them. One, in Corning, he set aside for the time being, concentrating instead on the two that lived near the lake. One actually lived on the lake, at the south end of Yates Center. The other had an address on a country road south of Cumberland. Kevin concentrated on the Yates Center Elvis. Hassett was his name, 16 Hollyberry Way his address. It was located at a point where the grid pattern of the village streets began to give way to an area of lake front roads.

Kevin no longer possessed the list of names and addresses of the people who had been on the bird hike. It had become the property of the sheriff's office. But he had a fairly good memory, and he remembered that one of the birders lived on Hollyberry Way. His problem was that he couldn't remember which of the birders lived there.

With nothing better to do with his time, he had a quick lunch and then set off for Yates Center and Hollyberry Way. He knew that it made more sense to call Carol and ask her which of the birders lived on that street. But then he'd have to explain what he was up to, and he wasn't sure she would be pleased to hear that he was insinuating himself into her investigation. Better to discuss it over a glass of wine at the end of the day.

When he reached Yates Center, it occurred to him that it might not be a good idea to be seen by a member of the Crooked Lake Birders Club. He didn't know which of the club's members lived in the area, but whoever it was would certainly remember him from the hike in the Grove. More importantly, it would by now be well known that he was the sheriff's husband. But he had come this far, and was in no mood to turn around and return to the cottage. He turned off the east lake road and drove cautiously down toward the lake, looking for a sign post announcing Hollyberry Way. He passed Gloxinina, Primrose, and several streets with floral names, and it was not until he was almost at the lake that he saw a sign that told him he was actually on Hollyberry. He had no idea whether he had passed number 16.

Kevin slowed to a crawl and continued to the bottom of the street, looking for numbers on the houses. No 16. He made a U turn in front of a large rambler whose front porch could not have been more than 35 feet from the lake itself. He had passed no more than three houses when he spotted number 16, a house too large for its location with weathered grey shingles and black shutters. He also spotted a man coming toward him on the side of the road. There were no sidewalks on Hollyberry Way, so the man had to step onto the grass verge to get out of the way. Kevin recognized him as Mel Cone. Cone's recognition of the driver came barely an instant later. Kevin had no choice but to stop.

Mel came around the car and rapped on the car window. Kevin rolled it down and managed a smile. He hoped it didn't look artificial.

"Well, if it isn't our novice birder," Cone said. "What brings you over to my side of the lake?"

Kevin had had no time to invent an answer to that question.

"Mr. Cone." His voice said he was surprised to see the fellow birder on Hollyberry Way, and indeed he was. "You must be the last person I expected to see today. How are you?"

"I'm fine, but you shouldn't be surprised to see me. I live here. Right up there at number 22."

Kevin was thinking fast, but he hoped Cone wouldn't repeat his question.

"You taking some vacation time?" It seemed like a safe issue.

"In fact I am. No plans, though, just being lazy. You're surprised to see me, I'm surprised to see you. You know somebody here on our point?"

"I'm afraid not," Kevin said. He hoped the story he'd been fabricating wouldn't sound too unlikely. "Truth is I meant to stop at *Dieffenbach's* back up the road, and got busy changing the channel and zipped right past it. I'm just turning around."

At least the last part was true. Kevin had no idea what he might need at *Dieffenbach's*. He didn't think he'd ever shopped there. If Cone doubted his story, though, he didn't say so.

"What's the word on Mrs. Neuberger's death?" he asked.

"No idea. The sheriff's been too busy to say much more than hello and good-bye to me."

They exchanged small talk for a minute or two, and then Kevin took off. He wanted to ask if Mel Cone knew Elvis Hassett, but thought better of it. His trip to Hollyberry Way had told him nothing other than that it was where Mel Cone lived. He could have learned that in a thirty second conversation with Carol or her major domo, JoAnne Franks.

CHAPTER 15

When Carol got back to the office after her visit to Jennifer Taggart, Sam was just in the process of saying good-bye to two women who, in spite of their white hair, looked as if they walked a couple of miles or more daily. One could have been close to five foot ten inches in height, the other more than a half a foot shorter, but both were attired in tailored slacks and colorful blouses and wore bright smiles.

"This is our sheriff, Carol Kelleher," Sam said as he made introductions. "I've just had a nice conversation with these ladies. Phyllis Smith" - he gestured to the tall one - "and Clara Olcott."

"Pleased to meet you," Carol said. "I'm sorry we're meeting you and your friends under such sad circumstances. I've just come from the Taggarts."

"Oh, yes," Clara said. "Jennifer is having a difficult time. I don't suppose I've ever known anybody who's been killed like this. It's more what you see in a movie than real life."

Sam seemed anxious to let the women be on their way.

"You've been very helpful," he said to them. "We'll stay in touch."

When they had gone, Sam explained to Carol that neither of them had been at all helpful.

"Neither of them really knows the Neubergers, they don't own guns, they saw and heard nothing. And I doubt they are serious bird watchers. But so it goes. Did you learn anything over at the Taggarts?"

"Nothing except that she's determined not to tell me what's bothering her. And something is *really* bothering her. Like these other birders, I don't think she saw or heard anything on the hike that's relevant. But she and her husband know something that he wants to share with me and she doesn't."

"Is it time to resort to strong arm tactics?"

"Absolutely not. That's not how we operate, Sam. But I think I'm ready to try an end run around her and go straight to the source of her problem."

"Want to tell me who that source might be?"

"I'm betting that it's the Nagle boy's mother and that it has something to do with him. Of course she may stone wall me, too. That's when we use strong arm tactics."

"What's next?"

"I think you've still got a few people to see, and I get to talk to the victim's husband." Carol looked at her watch. "He should be here in just under two hours. Frankly, I'm dreading it."

"Want me to tackle him?"

"No, thanks. You can't do all the heavy lifting."

———

Bill Neuberger didn't look at all like the man Carol had imagined. She'd heard that he was a stock broker who had moved to Crooked Lake fairly recently but still traveled down to the city regularly. That brief bio had caused her to expect a tall, slender, well coiffed man in a dark blue business suit, French cuffed shirt, and foulard tie, probably because that's what they looked like on television. She was dead wrong. Neuberger was no more than 5' 7", his head was completely bald, and he was wearing levis and a brown leather jacket. He also looked tired.

"Good afternoon, Mr. Neuberger," Carol said. "I wish we might be meeting under different circumstances." These were words she had used far too often in recent years, even in recent days.

"I agree. But we don't have to turn this meeting into a requiem for Vivian. You will be wanting to hear what I have to say about what happened on the bird hike, not my musings on the death of my spouse."

He was right, of course, but she was still surprised to hear him put it that way.

"The most difficult thing I do is discuss death with the recently bereaved. Unfortunately, most of those deaths are the result of accidents or foul play. Please have a chair, and if you'd like coffee Ms. Franks will take care of you."

"No thanks. Coffee and I do not agree." He settled into the chair across from Carol, started to extract a cigarette from his jacket pocket, and thought better of it. "I don't detect the smell of tobacco, so I assume that smoking is verboten here."

"It is office policy, but if you will be more comfortable if you have a cigarette, I think we can make an exception."

Carol hoped Mr. Neuberger would refuse her offer. He did.

"You aren't going to want me sitting here, looking glum, so please, go ahead and ask your questions. I have gone over everything in my mind that you could possibly want to ask, so we might as well get started. Why don't we make the first question the obvious one: did I kill my wife?"

Just as she hadn't expected Mr. Neuberger to look like the man across the desk from her, neither had she expected him to be so shockingly blunt.

"That is hardly my first question. In fact, I'm not sure it was even on my list. But I assume that you asked because you want to talk about it. Please go ahead."

"If I were in your shoes, the first thing I would think about in a case like this is who are the logical suspects. Let's forget about deer hunters with poor eyesight. I'm sure you do not believe Vivian was killed by a hunter, and neither do I. Therefore, you must believe that she was killed by one of the members of the Crooked Lake Birders Club. I agree with you. Moreover, she could hardly have been killed by one of the members of that club who remained dutifully with our leader, Agnes McKendrick. You, I am sure, would concur. Which means that the killer was one of those who decided that another minute with McKendrick would have been intolerable and therefore left her little coterie of friends to go off on their own. I think I know who all of those people were, but of course I cannot be sure, inasmuch as I assume that some of them left after I did. Ergo, I am not going to be able to tell you who killed Vivian. All I can do is tell you that it was not I."

Most interrogations in Carol's experience had not begun this way. At first it had surprised her. And then it amused her. He could easily have made a brief and thoroughly predictable statement that he had not killed his wife. Instead he had first to show off. He had wanted to demonstrate how clever he is, and that he wants me to know that he's a few steps ahead of me. And that he intends to stay there. She wanted to stand up and say 'Bravo.'

"I think you are right: our minds *are* pretty much on the same page. Except that I do not have the luxury of dismissing any possibility at such an early stage of an investigation. In any event, I had not intended to ask if you had killed your wife. But inasmuch as you have decided to cut to the chase, let me ask whom you believe to be the most likely killer?"

"It's as I said, sheriff, I do not know who all the people are who fall into my group of most likely suspects. That being the case, it's rather difficult - let us say premature - for me to hazard a guess as to the killer."

"You must realize that I do not know the members of the birders club nearly as well as you do. I do not know some of them at all. I assume, however, that at this point, even after a short time as a birder here on Crooked Lake, you would know something about these people, and especially about whether any of them seemed not to care for your wife. Or she for them."

"The last thing I want to do is to harm the reputation of an innocent person, and in view of the fact that I would be guessing, I don't think I should be pointing a finger at anybody."

"Fair enough. But I'm not asking you to accuse any of your fellow birders of murder. Or even to speculate that some of them might have had a reason to kill your wife. All I am asking is that you help me to understand the personal relationships among the birders. You seem to be a very observant man. How did your wife - may I call her Vivian? - get along with these people you went birding with?"

Neuberger smiled the smile of a man who was not going to answer that question.

"It's a funny thing, but we didn't really talk much about that. Viv was a serious bird lover. She might actually have ended up as a research scholar in some university's ornithology department if my career hadn't stood in the way. I'm a stock broker who is not in her league when it comes to the natural world. She has been my teacher. So our conversations weren't about people. They were about birds."

"Were you and Vivian friends with any of the other birders?" Carol asked, changing the subject ever so slightly.

"You will remember that we haven't been here all that long. Barely two years, in fact. And I was down in the city a lot, which made it difficult to establish friendships as a couple. Viv may have been a good acquaintance of a few of them, but hardly a good friend. But no, we didn't socialize with any of them."

"What was your reaction to these people? You've said you didn't much care for Mrs. McKendrick. What about the others? Anybody you thought might have become a friend if you hadn't been away so much? Or, like McKendrick, somebody you could do without?"

"I never gave it any thought. The Crooked Lake Birders Club was really never one of my priorities."

"You left Mrs. McKendrick and the bulk of the group fairly early in the hike," Carol said. "Where did you go?"

"Nowhere in particular. Like I said, I didn't cut out to go somewhere, just to get away from the boring stuff they were talking about. I was looking for some peace and quiet."

"And you found it?"

"I did."

"Did you run into any of the others who had also 'cut out?'"

"Never saw anybody until I got back to the cars at nine o'clock."

Carol decided to name those who, like Neuberger had gone wandering.

"There were six of you in all who decided to leave the group. Besides you, there was your wife, Mel Cone, Paul Raymore, Sallie Finch, and Michael Nagle. You didn't see any of them?"

"No. Why should I have? It's a big woods."

"Do you care to comment on any of them? Raymore, for example? Cone? The Finch woman? The young man, Nagle?"

"What's to say? Raymore, he's so into birds he probably never even watches the Super Bowl. Cone and Finch, too. Nagle, I'd never seen him before."

"You didn't by any chance, leave a notebook in the woods?"

It was a shot in the dark. It didn't score.

"No. What makes you think I did?"

"Are you a gun owner?"

"My, my, are you doubting my innocence?"

"No, I'm just touching all the bases. I've asked that question of everyone who was on the hike. How about you?"

"The answer in no. I'm not a hunter. I may be living up here in the boondocks, but I'm really a city boy. And I'll repeat myself: I did not kill my wife."

The interrogation of Bill Neuberger came to an end as a stand-off. Neuberger had said nothing incriminating. But his performance was not what Carol had expected. He had displayed no hint of sorrow at the death of his wife. He had treated their interview as a contest of wills, and it was clear that he had enjoyed jousting with the sheriff.

CHAPTER 16

By the end of that afternoon, Carol and Sam had talked with everyone who had been on the Anson's Grove bird hike except for the late Vivian Neuberger and Bob Taggart. Carol liked to think that they had interviewed them all. Sam preferred to refer to what had taken place as interrogation. In either case, they had asked many questions, received many answers, and, by common consent, come no closer to knowing who had killed Mrs. Neuberger than was the case when Mel Cone had stumbled upon her body.

Before they left at the end of the day, they sat down in the squad room and reviewed their impressions of the birders and what they had learned. It did not take long to set aside as inconsequential a fair number of people. Without exception, everyone in the group who had stayed with Agnes McKendrick throughout the hike ended up in that category. And to the surprise of neither Carol or Sam, everyone who had wandered away from the group found themselves in what the sheriff, somewhat hesitantly, found herself calling persons of interest.

Inasmuch as Sam had questioned most of those who had remained with McKendrick, Carol pressed him to defend his feeling that the time spent with them was largely wasted.

"I know it was impossible for any of them to have shot Neuberger, but I followed your instructions to take what they had to say seriously. No matter, none of them came across as interesting. Oh, some of them might be good conversationalists, but I heard nothing which sounded like a red flag."

Carol tried to imagine what a red flag would sound like.

"The one thing which stood out," Sam continued, "is that none of them knew Mrs. Neuberger. Other than as a birder, that is, and she apparently hadn't been with the club that long. I don't think they were just pretending not to be her friend. After all, they'd know we could check on it and catch them out if they were lying."

"The one exception to your generalization is especially interesting. I haven't met Mr. Taggart, but he and his wife stayed with McKendrick and most of the other birders. Yet they are definitely persons of interest. Not because they knew Mrs. Neuberger well; I never got around to asking her about that. But they know something about one of the people who didn't stick with the group, and that's Michael Nagle. Just the fact that the Taggarts are having an argument about whether to share what they know with me makes it interesting and possibly important."

"Where would you classify McKendrick?" Sam asked.

"She couldn't have killed Mrs. Neuberger, of course, but I'd trust her impressions of the birders - well, most of them anyway. She concentrates on the birds they're looking for, but she seems to have opinions of just about all of them. She may be wrong, but she pays attention to the club. Sort of like a mother hen."

"So we're agreed on the others, right?"

"Are we?" Carol asked. "Let's run down the list. Why don't you go first with the ones you talked to. Beginning with your last interrogation. Raymore, right.? Rumor has it that he's the most knowledgeable birder in the bunch."

"He certainly thinks so. I'm not sure I can figure him out. If he ever took time out to give some thought to Mrs. Neuberger, I'd be surprised. Birds are his life. No, that's not fair. But when we talked, all he could talk about was birds. And I mean rare birds. He actually spends his vacations traveling the world to add some exotic species to his list of 'gets.' That's his word, not mine. He spent a month in Madagascar last year, just to pad his list. He's been to Costa Rica more times than I've been to the bathroom."

"But what did he do when he left McKendrick's little cluster of amateurs?"

"Looked for more birds," Sam said derisively. "He wasn't optimistic, said that the best he could hope for was something that was migrating and got blown way off course."

"Did he have any luck?"

"No, and he blames McKendrick. In fact, he said that Crooked Lake is a lost cause where he's concerned. I have the feeling that he'd rather pack up and move to some place like Tanzania."

"So why is he on our watch list?"

"Only because he could have shot the Neuberger woman. We can't prove he didn't, so I guess we have to leave him there. But he's the longest of long shots."

"Okay, let's talk about Mrs. Finch," Carol said. "I've never met her, know nothing about her."

"You haven't missed much. She's the nearest thing to a bird herself. All you'd have to do is squint and you'd think you'd just had a close encounter with a sparrow. I'm not quite sure why she rubs me the wrong way, but she does. She isn't exactly unpleasant, but she manages to take little jabs at people when she talks. Mrs. McKendrick in particular."

"It has been my impression," Carol said, "that a fair number of the birders aren't particularly enthusiastic about McKendrick."

"I know, but the really critical ones are the ones who know their birds best. Mrs. Finch insists she's no expert, but she still enjoys sniping at McKendrick. The bottom line, I suppose, is that she's on your 'persons of interest' list because she's among those who didn't stay with the group. Otherwise, she's just a somewhat unpleasant woman. I can't see her as a killer."

Carol had the feeling that for some reason Sam didn't like Sallie Finch because she reminded him of a bird.

"Okay, it looks like I interviewed the others who abandoned Agnes McKendrick during the hike. That includes the victim's husband. And I'll have to say my interview with him was something of a surprise. I had assumed that he'd be the picture of a sad widower. But he never uttered a word that sounded as if he was in mourning. He actually started our little talk by telling me how he'd arrived at a list of promising suspects for his wife's death. Of course, he wasn't one of them. When I pushed him, however, he declined to speculate on who might have had it in for her. There was a moment when I thought he might be having fun at my expense. Bill Neuberger is not a likable man, but I have to be careful not to let annoyance with his style get to me. If I'd have been in his shoes, however, I'd at least have made more of an effort to look devastated by the loss of my spouse."

"That's interesting," Sam said. "I met him only briefly after Tommy told him what had happened. He came hurrying back to see his wife, and his pain looked genuine to me. He hugged her body for several minutes, seemed to be crying."

"Maybe he's by nature a stoic who'd managed to pull himself together by the time I talked with him. But I'm still not sure it wasn't an act. We'll see."

"What about Cone, the man who found Mrs. Neuberger?"

Carol managed a wry smile.

"I suppose I'm always inclined to harbor some suspicion of people who find a body. Reporting a dead body must seem like an easy way to look innocent. You're a good guy, helping the police. But most people who do what Cone did really are innocent. And he probably is, too. He was pretty straight forward, didn't say anything that suggested he was covering up his own wrong doing. Still, it'll be interesting to see what we learn about the shot that killed Mrs. Neuberger. If there's no evidence it came from a longer distance, Cone's ranking on my suspects list will move up toward the top."

"When I first spoke to him out near the Grove, he started talking about chestnut-sided warblers. My first thought was that he was showing off, but I guess he's just among the more serious birders."

"I have the same impression. He and Raymore are apparently the bird watcher pros. Which leaves young Nagle, and as of this moment I'd say he's the most interesting person of interest."

"You think he did it?" Sam sounded surprised.

"I don't know who did it. It may still turn out to be a crazy hunter. But like I told you, the Taggarts know something and it pertains to Michael. At least I'm ninety percent certain that it does. I initially thought he was just a sullen, contrary adolescent. But it was his mother that bothers me. Why is she so defensive? Most parents whose fifteen year old son goes on a simple bird hike don't worry that he killed someone before he got home. And Mrs. Taggart, her unwillingness to talk about the Nagles' problem only makes mommy's protection of Michael more curious."

"Do you have any idea what the family secret is going to be?"

"None whatsoever. But keep in mind that Michael's biology teacher was Vivian Neuberger, and he was quite frank that he didn't like her. I think the Nagle family takes a negative view of science when it contradicts their interpretation of the Bible. At least Michael does, and that's probably because he hears it at home. He was surprisingly up front about his hostility to evolution, and that's what Mrs. Neuberger was teaching. After all, New York state's textbooks emphasize evolution, which is hardly unusual in this day and age."

"So we're left with five suspects, right?"

"If you don't mind, Sam, I'd prefer that we not talk about suspects just yet. You and I don't know much at all about those five. Until the last two days I'd never met any of them, and even now I've not met Raymore and Finch. Persons of interest, that's the phrase. And I'd rather that we keep that one under wraps. too. This promises to be a long slog from Anson's Grove to the truth."

CHAPTER 17

"I hope you had a productive day," Kevin said as Carol ducked into the bedroom to change into something more comfortable than her uniform. "I ask only because I don't want to get too far ahead of you."

"You sound as if you've been up to something," she said as she reappeared in the kitchen.

"Not one something, but two. Let's go out on the deck and I'll enlighten you."

Kevin uncorked the Chardonnay and followed her to their favorite deck chairs.

"You always have more to report than I do, so why don't you go first," he said.

"It was just another uneventful day at the office, so I'll defer to you." Actually, in view of her problem with the Taggarts, and hence the Nagles, it had not been an uneventful day. But she was more interested in Kevin's cryptic comment that he had been up to something.

"Well, first off I finally got the dock in. As always, with a little help from my friends. Mike Snyder did most of the hard work. What's more, his daughter actually lent us a hand. But the important news - at least I think it is - is that I'm almost certain who Elvis is."

"Elvis?"

"Yes, the Elvis in the little brown notebook."

"Oh, yes, of course. But how do you know who he is, other than the man from Graceland?"

"It took a lot of work, mostly going through telephone directories, line by line. A very painstaking job."

"Nobody asked you to do it, Kevin. What prompted you to tackle this 'painstaking job?' And how do you know that you found the notebook's Elvis?"

"What prompted me is what has prompted every detective since Sherlock Holmes: a need to know and a willingness to use my head. I didn't think that an Elvis mentioned in a notebook found in Anson's Grove was going to be someone from some faraway place. How about right here, on or near Crooked Lake? Well, I made a line by line search in phone books and there he was, over in Yates Center."

"Let me repeat my question. How do you know that he's the right Elvis?"

"Because we have a scarcity of Elvises in the area. But you haven't heard the best part yet. I made a mental note of his street address and went looking for it. Turns out, it's on the southern edge of Yates Center, not more than a block from the lake. And guess who I ran into taking a stroll down that same street?"

"One of Agnes McKendrick's birders?"

"Bulls eye! Like to guess which one?"

"I wouldn't want to spoil your fun, so you tell me."

"Mel Cone. He's a neighbor of Elvis. And Elvis's name is Hassett."

Carol looked hard at her husband, trying to anticipate the rest of the story.

"You're going to tell me that you introduced yourself to Elvis Hassett. Right?"

"Wrong. I try to remember that this is your investigation."

"Okay, so what did you do? You grilled Cone, and he confessed to having left a brown notebook in the Grove."

"Like I said, it's your investigation. Besides, it's a fairly big leap from finding that Cone is a neighbor of Elvis's to the conclusion that the notebook is Cone's."

Carol knew that Kevin was right, but her intuition had gone into overdrive with his report that someone named Elvis is a neighbor of Cone's.

"I appreciate it that you didn't decide to take over my investigation - not all of it, anyway. But there's a chance that we learned something important today."

"Not to quibble, but how about *you* learned something important today. Meaning me.'"

"I'll be happy to give credit where credit is due," Carol said. "I'll prove it by refilling our glasses."

Which she proceeded to do.

"I wonder if there might be some way we could track down Daddy Bird like you've tracked down Elvis. Assuming, of course, Hassett is the right Elvis."

"Hassett *is* the right Elvis. I know it. It's a detective's intuition. But Daddy Bird strikes me as a lot more complicated."

Carol didn't say anything. In fact, she had closed her eyes and appeared to be either falling asleep or entering some kind of a trance.

"Are you okay?" he asked.

"Shh. I'm thinking."

The trance, if that what it was, lasted for about ten seconds and then Carol sat bolt upright in her chair.

"Daddy Bird. What might that mean?"

"Who knows? Figuring it out isn't going to be nearly as easy as finding Elvis Hassett."

"I know, but what does Daddy Bird sound like to you?"

"Like a character in a children's book," Kevin said.

"I don't think so. Whatever else he is, Daddy is going to be a man. Probably somebody's father, and assuming that the kid wasn't born out of wedlock, somebody's husband. Now how about Bird. Forget about a children's book for a minute. What do you think of when you think of a bird?"

Kevin tried to play Carol's game.

"The obvious answer is a little creature with wings that lays eggs. I assume, however, that you want me to come up with something less obvious. Right? How about bird as the Brits used it when they were talking about an attractive young girl. At least they did for awhile about the same time as Beatles mania broke out back in the 60s."

"Okay. A girl could be a bird, although not many people on Crooked Lake would be familiar with that usage. Anything else?"

"I've known bird brains and I may even have told someone he eats like a bird. But I'm not sure where you're going."

"How about simply referring to somebody as a bird?" Carol asked. "How about Sallie Finch?"

"Very funny, Carol. A Finch is a bird, ergo Ms. Finch is a bird. What's that got to do with Daddy Bird?"

"I'm not trying to be funny," Carol insisted. "But just today, when Sam and I were trying to decide who might be a person of interest in the Neuberger case, he said that Ms. Finch looks for all the world like a bird. More specifically, a sparrow. I've never met her, so I'm in no position to comment on his impression. How about you? You went hiking with her. Anything about her that reminds you of a bird?"

Kevin spent a thoughtful minute thinking about it.

"Well, for one thing she's tiny. And come to think of it, she's got a nose that's sort of - I'm not sure this doesn't overdo the bird business, but once you start thinking about it, her nose is a bit like a beak. So it's possible that somebody might think of her as a bird."

"Exactly what I've been thinking," Carol said.

"But we're looking for a Daddy Bird. Maybe somebody sees Sallie Finch as a bird, but certainly not a Daddy Bird."

"You're going to think I've gone off the deep end here, but please bear with me. All of the members of the Crooked Lake Birders Club know Sallie. If she's married, some of the birders probably know who her husband is. Let's say some of her fellow birders are accustomed to thinking of her, even referring to her, as a bird. Would it be that much of a stretch, if she's married, for them to think of her husband as Daddy Bird?"

"Whoa!" Kevin had been listening attentively to his wife, but it was now clear that he thought she had gone too far. "I'm prepared to believe that some people look at Sallie Finch and think she looks a bit like a bird. I'm not sure I agree, but what do I know. But you lose me when it comes to Daddy Bird. That's the kind of moniker you'd only use for a close friend, and according to you and Sam it's unlikely that Finch has very many close friends. What's more, we don't even know if she's married."

"You discovered an Elvis living in Yates Center," Carol said. "It shouldn't be hard to find out whether Sallie Finch is married."

"If you like, I'll do it. But the more I think about it, the more I'm wondering whether what we're doing isn't just a waste of time. I know, I got all excited when I had that Elvis brainstorm. But maybe Daddy Bird really is just a children's book. Wouldn't it be simpler just to ask around among the birders until you found the one who left a notebook in the Grove?"

"Yes, it's possible that Daddy Bird is a children's book, just like it's possible that Hassett happens to have a famous first name and Mel Cone as a neighbor. And by the way, why don't you take a look at children's literature on the internet and see how many Daddy Birds you can find."

"I'll do it tonight. First, though, how about supper? I'll check in the oven and see if the bird is done."

CHAPTER 18

The days on which Jim Barrett would still be attending squad meetings and taking to the roads for patrol duty were dwindling down to a precious few. Everyone knew they would miss him, and had told him so. A farewell party had been scheduled for a Saturday evening, and Carol had purchased what she considered to be an unusually handsome sweater with suede elbow patches. As it happened, she was dealing with issues having to do with finding his replacement when he stopped by her office the following morning.

"Do you have a few minutes to talk?" he asked.

"I shall always have time to talk with you, Jim," she said. "How about another coffee for the road?"

"Of course. Let me get it."

"You've brought me my coffee often enough. Now it's my turn." She beat him to the door and down the hall to the coffee maker.

"How's the transition going?" she asked when they had taken their seats.

"I should be asking you that question. How long do you think it will take to hire someone?"

"Considering the shoes we're filling, it may take a while. But I was thinking about your new routines."

"I think they expect me to hit the ground running. But it will probably be a few weeks before I find my groove. Actually I'm a bit nervous. You know how it is, you want to make a good impression."

"I'm sure you already have, which is why they wanted you."

Jim took another sip of his coffee and asked a question.

"Have you been to any of those public meetings where they discuss the fracking issue?"

"One or two," Carol said. "I assume they're not as contentious as they were before the governor announced the ban on fracking."

"I'm not so sure. The funny thing is that both sides have a good point. Fracking, it's the key to energy independence. But it's also an invitation to serious environmental damage. Where I have a problem is that so many of the pro-fracking folks think it'll be a bonanza for us locals. All gain and no pain. Have you ever been down to Pennsylvania to see what's happening? It isn't just what fracking is doing to groundwater, or what it can do to our lake. It's the truck traffic and the access roads, those huge well pads, the pipelines, the holding ponds for the stuff they use to get at the gas."

Jim paused to catch his breath.

"I haven't actually been on a fracking site," Carol said. "But I've studied it on the internet and I've seen all those roadside signs. You can probably see hundreds of them just driving around the lake. What is it that you'll be doing?"

"Mostly organizing protests, arranging meetings, things like that. I don't think they'll trust me to write speeches or editorials - I always got Cs in English class. When I was in high school, nobody had ever heard of fracking. And that's another thing."

"What do you mean?"

"That woman who was killed up by Anson's Grove, did you know she's a science teacher?"

"Yes, I know. What a terrible shame, her being gunned down like that."

"I wish I had had her as one of my teachers. She taught two kids who live down my street. They know how I feel about fracking, and they tell me she taught her students all about the dangers of doing it. I don't know it for a fact, but I think she got herself in trouble for talking about it in class."

Carol found this more than a little interesting. It led to her next question.

"You say she got into trouble for talking about fracking. Trouble with whom? Her students, the school board - whom?"

"It may just be a rumor, but word has it that some big moneybags in the county raised a stink, wanted her fired."

"You don't happen to know who these big moneybags might be, do you?"

"No. Like I said, it's just rumor. But what I do know is that there are some people around here who own property they'd like to see developed by one of the natural gas outfits. That guy who got mad because I criticized him out at *The Cedar Post* - the town clerk over in Somerset - he's probably one of them. Frank Grandi is reportedly another."

Carol didn't know Grandi, but she remembered her conversation with Jasper Eglin. He hadn't mentioned Vivian Neuberger, but he had made it clear that he thought it improper for a member of the sheriff's department to become an advocate for a cause that had nothing to do with maintaining law and order in the county. He might also believe that it was improper for a school teacher to talk about things that had nothing to do with the courses she was teaching. The thought occurred to Carol that had Mrs. Neuberger lived she might have run into trouble with the school board.

"It's a common problem, isn't it? Science teachers are always getting into trouble these days. Sometimes it's because they bring in creationism when they're teaching evolution, sometimes because they don't. Fracking's different, but it's also controversial."

"I hate to be leaving you guys. It's been a great job. But at least I'll be able to talk about the environment without some greedy town official telling me I'm out of order."

"And that's how it should be, Jim. I wish you luck. You're always welcome to drop in and let us know how it's going."

"Thanks. I've got to be shoving off or you'll fire me for dereliction of duty. There. Dereliction of duty - I've always wanted to say that."

"Come on, get out of here before I change my mind and refuse to sign your termination papers."

After Jim left, Carol got herself another cup of coffee and considered what she had heard about Vivian Neuberger's classroom attacks on fracking. Were any of her fellow birders strong supporters of fracking in the Crooked Lake area? Might any of them have taken advantage of the hike in Anson's Grove to get rid of one of its outspoken opponents? It seemed highly unlikely. After all, people don't go around killing those who hold different views on a public policy issue. Unless, perhaps, they have a personal stake in that issue.

When she finally turned her attention to other issues, it was only after she had decided that she'd have to find out more about some of these birders than she and Sam had learned in their recent interviews.

CHAPTER 19

For the most part, Jennifer Taggart had lived a worry free life. She and Bob had never had serious problems in their relationship, which had begun way back in high school. Their kids were navigating the teen age years without the problems so common among their peers. They were financially comfortable, thanks to Bob's stable job at the Silver Leaf vineyard and the fact that they had always budgeted carefully. Their tastes had never run to luxury goods and expensive travel. Had it not been for the recent difficulties next door at the Nagles, both of them could have described their lives as close to ideal.

They had felt sorry for their neighbors and for their son Michael. They had frequently thanked their lucky stars, to use Jennifer's expression, that Timmy and Lisa had never given them the trouble that Michael gave his parents, not only occasionally but practically every day. Their invitation to take Michael on the bird hike had been intended to give his mother, Fran, a break. Unfortunately it had resulted in the first real argument between the Taggarts in many years.

The argument was about whether they should tell the sheriff what they knew about Michael Nagle and why they thought it was relevant to the shooting death of Vivian Neuberger. Bob believed that they had an obligation to let her know because he was sure that the Nagles would never do so. Jennifer disagreed. To talk with the sheriff about Michael was tantamount to saying that they suspected that Michael was the killer.

"But that's the whole point," Bob insisted. "He could have shot the Neuberger woman. If the sheriff doesn't know about Michael's problems, it will only make it harder for her to investigate the tragedy up in the Grove."

"You are convinced, aren't you, that Michael killed her."

"We've been over this a zillion times," Bob said. "Let's not do it again."

The Taggarts were sitting in the living room of their modest but functional home. Dinner table conversation had skirted the issue of Michael Nagle, focussing instead on a movie that both of the parents thought was inappropriate for their offspring. Lisa had argued that they should see it before judging it, while Timmy put forward the fact that at least half of his class mates had seen it and didn't seem to have been harmed by doing so. As was to be expected, the younger generation won the debate and after dinner headed for their rooms to call friends and plan their evening.

"I don't care how many times, Bob. The point is that the Nagles told us about Michael because they needed to share their problem with someone. They expected us to be understanding, to stand by them. They certainly didn't expect us to turn around and tell everybody else."

"The sheriff isn't everybody else, Jen. Considering what happened on the bird hike, she should know that one of the people on that hike is a mentally disturbed teenager. Not only is he disturbed, he has done things which suggest that he had an unhealthy fixation on Mrs. Neuberger."

"But there are probably a lot of kids who dislike some teacher because she gives them poor grades or something. They don't kill the teacher they don't like."

"Please, Jen, let's get serious. Michael hasn't just disliked Mrs. Neuberger. He's drawn pictures of her being attacked by birds. Being shot. Even on a cross, being crucified. For God's sake, that's a helluva lot more than dislike. It was those pictures the Nagles discovered that led them to talk with us. They wanted our help."

"Yes," Jennifer said. "And we suggested that Michael needed psychiatric help, not that he should be reported to the authorities."

"True enough, but why did we tell them that he needed professional help? It was because his problems sounded like those of the troubled young men who shot up the Newtown school and the theater in Colorado. It's a long list, Jen - that congresswoman in Tucson, Columbine, Virginia Tech, Santa Barbara. It goes on and on. Why not here? Why not Michael?"

"Because it's not the same. In all those other cases, the shooter killed people at random, people he didn't even know."

"Yes, but surely you don't think Michael's innocent of killing the Neuberger woman just because he didn't mow down more people up in the Grove."

"Of course not." Jennifer sounded angry. "All I'm saying is that it's extremely unlikely that a 15 year old boy who dislikes his science teacher is going to kill her."

Bob Taggart found his wife's unwillingness to imagine that Michael Nagle could have killed Vivian Neuberger frustrating.

"Look, I don't want Michael to turn out to be the killer. I'm saying he could have been, and that the sheriff ought to know why. After all, how many 15 year olds are fanatically committed to the proposition that the Bible trumps evolution and make an issue of it in class? Who rudely challenges his teacher on the subject?"

"All he's doing is reflecting his parents' views. Do I agree with them? No. And I wish that Michael were more like Timmy and Lisa. But he's not our child, and the fact that we don't like some of the things he says and does doesn't give us the right to make it our business."

"Even if he lives in a house full of guns?"

"Please, Bob, you know as well as I do that Mr. Nagle keeps them under lock and key. He's told us so. You really do believe that Michael killed the Neuberger woman, don't you?"

"I'll say it one more time. Michael might have killed her. And it's because he could have that I want the sheriff to know what we know about him. His parents are worried about him, as well they should be. I'm no fan of home schooling, but Michael's the perfect example of someone who should be home schooled."

"But you know that Fran isn't up to doing something like that," Jennifer said.

"I do, but that's not the point. Look, why can't we find a way to talk with the sheriff without sounding like we're blaming Michael for the Neuberger woman's death. I'll be glad to leave out all the stuff about the Bible and concentrate on those God-awful pictures of Neuberger that Michael drew. All I want to do is urge the sheriff to talk to the Nagles."

"I'm sure she's already interviewed Michael. She's been talking to everyone who was on that bird hike."

"Well, she hasn't talked to me yet, and I don't believe that talking with Michael was much help."

"I doubt that she'll learn much more from his parents. If we were in their shoes, would we be willing to talk frankly about our son and his problems?"

Bob Taggart looked as if he were thinking about it.

"See?" Jennifer said. "Parents want to protect their children."

"Which proves my point, doesn't it? If we don't step up and say something, no one will. It's like we're participating in a cover-up. Can you live with that?"

"But we wouldn't be covering up anything unless Michael really did do it, and he didn't."

Bob heaved a sigh and got up.

"No point talking about it, is there? We're just going around in circles. I'm going to call it a day and take a crack at that Grisham book I've been putting off."

He gave his wife a half smile, as if to say I love you even if I don't understand you, said good night, and took the stairs to their bedroom on the second floor.

CHAPTER 20

It had been Lawrence Finch's habit to join up with several former frat brothers once each year and have a week long 'boys only' get away to some place far from their spouses. This year they had chosen New Orleans. If the truth were known, most of the spouses who had been left behind were delighted with the arrangement. It was not that their marriages were no longer fulfilling, only that they, too, needed a break, a few days to be themselves, not role players in the life they were living.

Sallie Finch was among the wives who had enjoyed the fact that her husband was downing sazeracs on Bourbon Street and otherwise living it up in the Big Easy. She was well aware that living it up might even include a visit to one or more of the city's notorious brothels. She and Larry did not have what is called an open marriage, but they both tolerated the occasional fling. It was part of what made the rough edges of marriage manageable, or so they told themselves. Where Sallie drew the line was on 'affairs,' relationships which threatened to become serious and destroy their marriage. And just such an affair had been brewing on Crooked Lake. The woman was Vivian Neuberger, who had recently moved to the area with her husband, William Neuberger, taken a position as a science teacher at Southport High School, joined the Crooked Lake Birders Club, and carved out a public role for herself as a vigorous critic of that hot new environmental issue, fracking. None of these things bothered Sallie, herself a birder and an environmentalist. What did bother her was that her husband had taken a fancy to Mrs. Neuberger. Moreover, Mrs. Neuberger had reciprocated that fancy. They had both been discreet, but Sallie had a nose for such things and in due course she realized what was going on and where.

She knew that Vivian Neuberger was a formidable adversary. She was relatively young, probably no more than fifty. She was attractive rather than beautiful, taller than Sallie, with fine features and lovely blond hair. She and Larry had invited the Neubergers over for dinner a few months after they had taken up residence on the lake. It had been a thoughtful gesture, and the evening had been pleasant. William, who insisted that he be called Bill, had been good company, but it was Vivian who truly sparked the conversation. She was obviously very smart, but not someone who sought to control the conversation or constantly remind people of her considerable store of knowledge. Both she and Larry had been impressed, but it had been obvious that Larry had also been fascinated. He had hardly taken his eyes off Vivian all evening long, and when the Neubergers left he had talked about her - and never about Bill - for the better part of an hour as they cleaned up and got ready for bed.

Within two weeks, Larry had urged Sallie to invite the Neubergers back. When she had suggested that it might be better to wait until their invitation had been reciprocated, Larry had insisted that that wasn't necessary. They had actually argued about it. Before a month had gone by, Larry had become aware of Vivian's after school habits and managed to have coffee with her on two occasions. Had their schedules been more flexible and the places to indulge their growing interest in each other less public, the matter might have come to a head sooner. As it was, however, it took time for their relationship to mature to the point where Sallie had finally said 'enough'.

That point, somewhat ironically, had come during an outing of the Crooked Lake Birders Club. Larry, who had never been much interested in birds, was not present. But both of the Neubergers were. Agnes McKendrick, the indefatigable leader of the club, had chosen to take this particular hike along the Outlet Trail east of Yates Center. They had paused near a ruined mill along the trail, and Sallie soon found herself talking with Mrs. Neuberger. It had been a strange conversation that began with some generalizations about the compatibility of married couples and then gradually turned to something more personal. Vivian had not said so in so many words, and if challenged would almost certainly have denied it, but it soon became clear to Sallie that what was on her mind was the state of the Finch marriage. That evening, as she recalled the conversation, Sallie decided that her husband had either violated their agreement about extra-marital relationships or was about to. She would no longer tolerate Vivian Neuberger's friendship with her husband.

"Hi," Larry said as he entered the cottage and set down his bag. "How are things on the home front?"

It was almost five o'clock. Sallie greeted him with a kiss, and told him to go ahead and change before they had their usual late afternoon cocktail.

"Hotter than hades down there," he said when he reappeared in a fresh outfit and accepted a gin and tonic. "It's a fun city, but It's a killer in summer."

"Sorry about that. Weather up here has been lovely. So what did you guys do?"

"Most of the time it was just a matter of letting ourselves go and hitting those Bourbon Street restaurants. But the French Quarter isn't all its cracked up to be. You know, nice but overrated. How about you?"

"With one exception, it's just Crooked Lake as usual. I tend to relax when you're away. Sleep late, watch forgettable TV, eat takeout."

"What's the exception?" Larry asked.

"The bird hike last Saturday was a disaster."

"Sorry to hear that. What happened, all the birds gone to Canada?"

"No, Vivian Neuberger got shot up in Anson's Grove. She's dead."

Larry choked on his gin and tonic.

"You can't be serious," he said in a strangled voice.

"I'm afraid I am. Nobody knows who did it. Maybe a hunter, after a deer out of season."

"Good God." Larry Finch tried to find words to express his incomprehension of what he'd heard. He failed and repeated himself. "Good God."

"Needless to say, everybody was in shock. They probably still are. The sheriff's department is working on it. They've been asking dozens of questions of all of us."

Sallie's husband didn't ask her about the questions she'd been asked. Nor did he ask her for details. The news had been shocking. Now he was numb. It was Sallie who would have to do the talking, and she wasn't sure whether she should say something that would tell him that she empathized with his pain or that his little affair with Vivian Neuberger was over. Much as she preferred the latter, she knew it would be cruel, and for some reason she couldn't bring herself to do that. Not yet.

"This is awfully hard, isn't it, Larry?"

"Of course it is. What am I supposed to do?"

"If I were in your shoes, I'd call Bill Neuberger and offer your condolences."

"Are you kidding?" Larry's question was an angry one. "I don't give a shit for Bill."

This was not quite what Sallie had expected to hear. It also made it even clearer that her husband's concern was entirely for Vivian - and for himself.

"Why would it be so hard to get in touch to Bill?" Sallie asked.

"Because he means nothing to me. Nothing at all. It's Viv." Lawrence Finch came very close to breaking down in tears. "I loved her. You must know that. Now what?"

He got up and went to the kitchen for what looked like a very large shot of scotch. Gin and tonic would obviously no longer do. He hesitated in the living room, and then headed for the stairs.

"Forget dinner," he said as started for the second floor bedroom.

"Of course. It will keep. I'm sorry about Vivian, but if it took this to bring you to your senses, I'm glad she's dead."

Larry stopped at the landing and took a tentative step back toward the living room.

"What kind of a monster are you? She's dead and you're glad?"

"Larry, I'm not a monster, I'm your wife. Listen to me! I'm your wife! I refuse to shed tears because another woman in your life is dead. Go ahead and cry your little wounded heart out and then start paying me some attention again."

This battle could have gone on much longer. It could even have turned violent. But it didn't. Larry was sound asleep when Sallie came upstairs an hour later. She washed her face, brushed her teeth, and put on her nightgown. When she turned off the bedside lamp and climbed into bed, she was wearing a satisfied smile.

CHAPTER 21

Jason Eglin's bass fishing boat was barely moving as it edged past the cottages on the bluff side of Crooked Lake's east branch. If he caught a bass or two it would be a bonus, because the reason he was out on the lake had little or nothing to do with the fact that he loved fishing and considered himself to be an accomplished fisherman. He had taken the boat out because he needed to escape from the house and the office and do some serious thinking. And there was much to think about.

He had behaved irresponsibly in barging into Sheriff Kelleher's office and demanding that Officer Jim Barrett be fired. Barrett's job was to keep the county's roads safe from drunken drivers and speeders, not lend his support to the anti-fracking campaign, especially when wearing his uniform. Nonetheless, he knew that he had been out of order when he had so rudely brushed aside the sheriff's secretary and marched into her empty office. He had had, and would again have, occasions to work with the sheriff on matters of mutual interest, and demanding that she sack one of her officers was not the best way to maintain a good relationship.

To his surprise, however, the sheriff had fired Barrett. At least it looked that way. Bill Parsons, another of the sheriff's department officers, had been overheard saying that Barrett had resigned. Which probably meant that the sheriff had given him that face saving option rather than firing him outright. The result he desired had been achieved, if not in the most diplomatic way possible.

Jasper could not understand why fracking was such a hard sell. Signs opposing it could be found at virtually every third cottage and home along the lake. Not that those signs had decided the issue, although they may have influenced the governor's decision to ban fracking. Without question, however, they reflected the view of the summer people, those who didn't have to make their living in Cumberland County. Jasper knew that the influx of seasonal residents was good for the economy, their taxes essential to local economic stability. But they were dead wrong to be so hostile to fracking. It would bring untold numbers of new jobs to the area, a win-win situation for everyone. And it could be done without hurting the environment, as so many were claiming it would. He knew that the companies that did the fracking had done studies and had proved that it was environmentally safe. What was the problem?

He had thought about the issue for years, and he knew where he stood. But there was no silencing the opponents of fracking. Well, that wasn't quite true. One of the most vocal of its critics had been silenced. Vivian Neuberger. Jasper's thoughts turned to Mrs. Neuberger as the bass boat slowly followed the curve of Markham's Point.

He had only met the Neuberger woman on two occasions, both meetings of the local citizenry to debate the fracking issue. She had been a spokesperson to be reckoned with. She wasn't somebody who had heard some Hollywood actor or pop music celebrity denounce fracking and decided that 'if they think it's a bad idea, that's good enough for me.' He had to admit that she was good. Wrong but good. She could make a complicated subject intelligible to the average Joe or Jane. And she was also a high school teacher who seemed to think that it was her job to use her science courses to denounce fracking. He hadn't sat in one of her classes, of course, but he was sure that she had been doing a good job of shaping impressionable minds. Jasper corrected that thought: she had been doing a bad job shaping those minds.

But Vivian Neuberger was dead. She had been killed on a bird hike, of all things. If the local grapevine was to be believed, she might have been shot by one of the people who was taking that hike. In other words, she could have been murdered. Jasper knew nothing about the shooting of this formidable woman. What he did know was that the anti-fracking crowd would find ways to use her death to advance its agenda, whether fracking had anything to do with her death or not. He doubted that it did, but he couldn't shake off a feeling that it might have. The reason for that feeling was a man named Frank Grandi.

Grandi had no roots in the Crooked Lake area, and had moved to Cumberland County only two years earlier. Independently wealthy, he had bought up a number of valuable properties and was rumored to have his eyes on another property whose value was widely regarded as much more doubtful. Jasper knew these things because Grandi was an enthusiastic backer of fracking. The property he was rumored to be interested in had been of no great interest to anyone in many years, but Grandi apparently saw it as the perfect locale for a major hydraulic fracturing project. He hadn't talked about his plans because he didn't want competition. But he had shared his vision with Jasper. What's more, he was convinced that the prospect of unleashing a bonanza of gas from the Marcellus Shale would overwhelm the opposition. The governor may have delayed it, but fracking was coming to Crooked Lake and nothing could stop it. If Jasper's assumption was correct and Frank Grandi had his way, it would come to a desolate piece of real estate whose best known feature went by the name of Anson's Grove.

The problem, other than the possibility that Grandi was overly optimistic, was that he had a terrible temper and a near maniacal contempt for those who crossed him. And one of the people who had crossed him was Vivian Neuberger. It was inconceivable that Grandi had killed her, but Jasper could not get the thought that he might have out of his mind.

When he finally pulled his bass boat onto the shore, he had caught no bass. But he had reached some troubling conclusions about what had been bothering him. In the first place, he would pay Sheriff Carol Kelleher a visit and apologize again for the way he had handled his frustration with Officer Barrett. He would also begin to do what he could to assume a leadership role in the push to bring fracking to Crooked Lake. It was necessary, he decided, to marginalize Frank Grandi. Frank was committed to fracking, but he was also his own worst enemy. Elbowing him aside wouldn't be easy, but somebody had to do it.

CHAPTER 22

Carol had now been sheriff of Cumberland County for ten years, give or take a few weeks. She knew she was older than when she had taken the job. She wasn't sure she was any smarter. Not a year had gone by in which she hadn't faced at least one unusually challenging case. What is more, those cases were invariably very different from each other, a fact which helped to explain why her experience as sheriff had proved to be such a difficult learning curve.

Now, once again, she found herself confronting another strange case which promised to be as different from those other challenging cases as they were from each other. This time it was probable that murder had taken place in perhaps the most ordinary and least threatening of circumstances: the victim, and presumably her killer, had been taking a hike to look for birds.

Carol refocused her attention on the yellow pad in front of her on the desk. It contained a number of names, a few hard to decipher jottings, and several doodles which contributed nothing to an understanding of what those names and jottings were all about. The names were what mattered, and there were four of them: Michael Nagle, Mel Cone, Jason Eglin, and Sharon Lagerfeld. The last of the four names had a big question mark beside it.

They were not the only people she needed to talk with - or talk with again - in her investigation of Vivian Neuberger's death, but for various reasons they were now at the top of her list. Michael Nagle was on her list because there was something about him that both his mother and his neighbor, Jennifer Taggart, seemed determined not to reveal. It might not be important, but Jennifer's husband disagreed and Michael's behavior when he talked with the sheriff supported the suspicion that he might not simply be the typical fifteen year old high school student. Carol had a hard time believing that Michael could have killed Mrs. Neuberger, but until she knew what his problem was she couldn't bring herself to dismiss him as a suspect.

Mel Cone was on her list for a very different reason, thanks to Kevin. He had taken it upon himself to track down a man named Elvis, who might or might not be someone referred to in a notebook one of the birders had left in Anson's Grove. As it turned out, an Elvis Hassett lived on the same street in Yates Center that Cone did. She knew that this didn't prove that the notebook was Cone's, and even if it was it had no obvious relevance to the death of Vivian Neuberger. As a result she had let the matter ride for several days. But it had been impossible to forget about the notebook's cryptic reference to Elvis, and Carol had finally decided to ask a few more questions of the man who had discovered the body of Mrs. Neuberger.

Jasper Eglin's name appeared on the yellow pad because she had recently been talking with her soon to be ex-colleague, Jim Barrett. Carol had no reason to believe that Eglin had anything to do with the Neuberger case. She knew he was an ardent supporter of fracking, which meant that he and Vivian Neuberger held conflicting views on this contentious issue. But he had not been on the bird hike when Mrs. Neuberger had been killed. So why was she interested in him? She couldn't quite explain it to herself, but she knew she would be setting up a meeting with Eglin.

Sharon Lagerfeld was the principal of the Southport High School, and hence had some responsibility for what its teachers were doing. Carol was curious as to whether people had come to Lagerfeld with complaints about Vivian Neuberger. Had the Nagles visited the principal to express their displeasure with what their son was being taught in his science courses? It would not have surprised Carol had they done so. And what had Ms. Lagerfeld told them she would do about it? Carol drew a line through the question mark beside Ms. Lagerfeld's name. She would pay her a visit.

Before making the trip to Southport to see Fran Nagle, Carol swung by the cottage and traded the patrol car for her old Ford. No point in causing anxiety even before she had rung the doorbell. It took several minutes before Michael's mother came to the door. She didn't look pleased to see who was standing on her porch.

"Good morning, sheriff. What brings you here today?"

It was not a welcoming greeting. Nor did she step aside so that Carol could enter.

"I'm sorry to be bothering you today, but I was down in Southport and thought I'd take advantage of it to stop by and ask a couple of questions I didn't get around to the other day when you visited my office. May I come in?"

It was obvious that Mrs. Nagle would have liked to say no, but, as Carol had long ago discovered, people have trouble saying no to an officer of the law.

"Of course." It was a reluctant yes."What is it you want?"

"Do you suppose we could sit down somewhere?"

Mrs. Nagle once again said 'of course,' and then, having conceded the advantage to the sheriff, offered to bring her a cup of coffee.

"That's very kind of you. I won't be needing cream or sugar."

The woman of the house disappeared into the kitchen, leaving Carol to survey the living room. It looked as if it had been furnished by a family with markedly varied tastes. She had no idea how many people lived under the Nagle roof, but all of them appeared to have had a say in furnishing the living room. There was a Danish modern love seat, a heavy, dark couch and chair that looked as if they had been crafted in the late 19th century, and a Mission style cabinet that had seen better days.

Carol had been considering the presence, side by side on the wall behind the couch, of a dime-a-dozen winter snow scene and a knock off of a Braque painting when Mrs. Nagle reappeared with the coffee.

"Many thanks. I thought I'd drop by because I need the answer to a question that I can't seem to get out of my mind. I'm concerned about your son Michael, and I can appreciate it that he's going through a difficult phase. Most teen agers do. But my impression from talking with him is that there's more going on in Michael's life than simply typical teen age problems. Would I be right?"

"What is it you think is wrong with Michael?" Mrs. Nagle asked.

"I don't know, which is why I'm asking you."

"But I don't understand why you need to know more about Michael. He's a 15 year old high school student, and he isn't doing as well in his studies as he should. He doesn't always treat his parents as well as he should either, but like you say, that's typical of kids his age. What more is there to say?"

Carol was reluctant to bring up the Taggarts, but it looked as if she would have to.

"I understand that your neighbors the Taggarts have discussed Michael with you, and that you have shared your concerns about Michael with them. I have the impression that the problem isn't simply that he is uncommunicative and occasionally disrespectful. There's something else that worries you, isn't there?"

Mrs. Nagle had looked impatient with the sheriff's questions. She now looked uneasy. No, that wasn't the right word. She looked afraid.

"What did the Taggarts tell you?" she asked.

They, or rather Mrs. Taggart, hadn't actually told her anything except that they were of two minds on whether to share what they knew with the sheriff. Carol was in no position to make something up.

"Mrs. Taggart seemed to feel it would be a betrayal of trust to share what you had told her. I haven't talked with Mr. Taggart. I am asking you about Michael because I'd prefer not to insist that Mrs. Taggart tell me something that you had asked her not to talk about. I hope you understand my problem. I am not asking you about Michael just because I'm curious. It's important that I get to know as much as I can about the people who were on the bird hike when Mrs. Neuberger was killed."

"But Michael didn't have anything to do with that." This conversation with Mrs. Nagle was sounding more and more like an instant replay of the earlier conversation in Carol's office. It was time to change the subject, or pretend to.

"When we met in my office, Michael said he had had Mrs. Neuberger as a science teacher. Did he ever talk to you about her?"

"He didn't much like to talk about school."

"How did he do in her class? I believe it was biology."

"Not too well, I'm afraid. It wasn't one of his better subjects."

"How about the teacher?"

"About Mrs. Neuberger, you mean?"

This is a conversation in slow motion, Carol thought.

"Yes, that's who I mean. What did Michael think of her?"

Her coffee cup was empty, but Mrs. Nagle raised it to her lips and pretended to take another sip.

"He didn't really say much about her. It was mostly about the things they were studying."

"One of those things was evolution. Mrs. Neuberger would necessarily have spent a fair amount of time on it. Did Michael ever talk with you about that?"

"I know that many people believe in evolution, sheriff. You probably do. But Ralph and I, and Michael too, wish they would give equal time to intelligent design. We just don't believe that God's creatures came about like evolution says. Mrs. Neuberger, she spent a lot of time explaining that we human beings used to be apes. Michael was upset by that. We urged him to do what he had to do to pass the course but not to let it undermine his faith."

Carol doubted that Mrs. Neuberger told her class that humans used to be apes. She experienced a feeling of almost unbearable sadness as she listened to Mrs. Nagle, but this wasn't the time to challenge her beliefs, nor was she the person to do it. Vivian Neuberger had been better qualified, and obviously she had not succeeded.

"So Michael didn't like Mrs. Neuberger." Mrs. Nagle hadn't actually said that, but Carol made it a statement rather than a question, hoping to elicit her agreement.

"I didn't care for all my teachers. I suppose Michael doesn't either. Especially when they give you bad grades or criticize you in class."

"Did Michael say Mrs. Neuberger criticized him in class?"

"Just once, I think," she said, trying to minimize the problem. "I don't think it was important. Something about him not paying attention."

The clock on the mantle struck the hour.

"Oh, my goodness," Mrs. Nagle said. "I wasn't paying attention to the time."

She got to her feet and made a show of being sorry that she'd have to bring their conversation to a close.

"I promised Edie Huntley I'd come by, and I'd forgotten all about it. You'll have to excuse me, sheriff. I don't like to be rude, but - I'm sure you know how it is."

Carol thought she knew how it was.

"Of course. I appreciate you taking the time to talk with me. You go ahead and do what you have to do, and I'll let myself out."

The suddenly busy Fran Nagle said a quick good-bye and Carol made her way back to her car, frustrated that once again she had failed to get an answer to the question of just what was wrong with Michael Nagle. Why this conspiracy of silence? Whatever the reason, she was now absolutely certain that Michael wasn't simply a sullen teenager who was 'going through a phase.'

CHAPTER 23

When Mel Cone answered the phone, his voice betrayed his surprise when the caller identified herself as the sheriff. He devoted a couple of minutes to explaining that he had not been expecting to hear from her and that he had been 'cheating,' having a bit of his wife's Brown Betty before dinner. Considering how surprised he was to get a call from her, Carol was in turn surprised that instead of asking what prompted the call he had chosen to wax enthusiastic about the Brown Betty. For a moment she thought he might be going to give her the recipe.

"Excuse me," he finally said, "I'm just running off at the mouth. What can I do for you?"

"What I hope you can do is agree to meet with me at your early convenience. I'm afraid I don't know anything about your schedule, but I'm flexible."

"You'd like for us to get together again like we did right after that awful accident up in the Grove. Has something come up?"

"Nothing dramatic, but, yes, I would like to talk with you. When might that be possible?"

"It would have to be after work or on a weekend, but I don't have any big obligations other than Friday evenings. That's our bridge night. I know it's already close to five, but I could do it now. But you probably have something on."

"Actually, today would be fine if you don't mind."

"You wouldn't rather I come over to your office?"

"No, no. I have a strong aversion to spending my evenings in the office. How would it be if I stopped by at seven, if you'll be through dinner?"

"Great. We'll save some Brown Betty for you."

Carol was no fan of Brown Betty, and she didn't want to talk with both Mr. and Mrs. Cone. But she'd have some if it would help break the ice and she was confident that she'd be able to get rid of Mel's wife if she had to. Telling Kevin what she'd agreed to do would be a bigger challenge. To her surprise, he readily accepted her explanation for the sudden change of plans.

"The notebook's going to be his, I'm sure," he said. "Even if it isn't, it's time to start pursuing Daddy Bird. I'll hold supper."

Kevin gave her directions to the house on Hollyberry Way he'd discovered earlier in the week.

Carol knew that Mel Cone *could* have killed Vivian Neuberger, but she somehow doubted that he had. Moreover, the notebook could have been left in the Grove by any one of the birders. The reference to Elvis and the fact that a man named Elvis was Cone's neighbor were hardly proof that the notebook belonged to Cone. Even if it did, what was its relevance to the death of Mrs. Neuberger? But Carol had given the puzzling notebook a lot of thought, and her curiosity had finally persuaded her to assume that it was Cone's and that it was time to ask some questions about Elvis and Daddy Bird.

It was only two minutes after seven that Carol pulled up in front of the house on Hollyberry Way. She was greeted by Cone's loquacious wife, who escorted her straight to the kitchen for the promised plate of Brown Betty. Carol had to admit that it was quite good. Fortunately, Penny Cone soon announced that she had things she had to do and left the living room to her husband and the sheriff.

"I don't believe I've had an officer of the law in my home since Donnie was falsely accused of stealing another kid's bike. Turned out to be a big mistake. But you're not here to talk about stolen bikes. How can I help you?"

"I'll get right to the point, Mr. Cone. When you went on the now infamous bird hike, did you happen to leave a notebook back in the Grove? A notebook with a list of the birds you'd seen?"

Carol pulled the notebook out of her pocket and held it in front of her.

The man sitting across from her didn't look surprised, but he briefly closed his eyes and took a deep breath.

"Sheriff, would you like a beer?"

"No thanks, Mr. Cone. If you'd like one, go ahead."

"I think I will."

He got up and went to the kitchen.

So, Carol said to herself, Melvin Cone is the one who left the notebook in the Grove. The one who now needs a few moments to think and decide what he wants to say about it and about such things as Elvis and Daddy Bird. For he would surely know that she hadn't dropped by merely to return his notebook.

"I've been expecting this," he said when he came back with his beer. "I knew your men had been searching the woods. Of course they wouldn't have known what they were looking for, but I figured they'd find the notebook. It didn't have my name in it, but I knew you'd get around to me, whether you guessed it was mine or because you were asking all the birders about it. I thought about it a lot, and I almost came to you to tell you about those weird notes in the back. I wish I had, because now you'll think I was hiding something."

Carol was fascinated. Mel Cone had brought up the 'weird notes' and it looked as if he had decided to explain them.

"Frankly, I didn't know what to think. Nothing in the notebook seemed to have anything to do with the shooting of Mrs. Neuberger. And that's what I've been investigating. Why don't you tell me about what you call your 'weird notes.'"

"I've watched enough cop shows and read enough police procedurals to know that telling the truth is always a good idea. Besides, I haven't done anything illegal."

Mel Cone looked down at his shoes, then leaned back in his chair.

"Are you ready?" he asked. "This will take a while."

"Take your time." Carol wasn't sure what to expect, but she was interested in what Cone would have to say.

"You may think I'm weird, but you've got to understand that I'm not one of those peeping Toms. That's something I would never do. I like to call myself an amateur sociologist. Did you ever study sociology?"

"Not really, but I did take a course or two." An amateur sociologist but not a peeping tom. It wasn't only the notes in the back of the notebook that were weird.

"Well, I didn't study sociology. I was a business major. But a couple of years ago I had a neighbor, Dick Eagen, who always seemed to be coming home at crazy hours. You know, one, two in the morning. I'm not a good sleeper, so there were times when I heard his garage door open and close. Sometimes I'd get up and look out the window, just to see if things were all right. I can't quite explain it, but I got curious about what he was up to. I mean he didn't have a night job, and he did have a wife and kids, so the hours he was keeping seemed kind of strange. I hardly knew him, and I didn't have the nerve to ask what he was doing. Then he moved away. I'd no idea he was leaving, then one day a van pulled up out front and by nightfall he was gone."

Carol couldn't imagine what this had to do with Daddy Bird. Or Elvis, for that matter.

"It was about that time that the Neubergers moved into the neighborhood," Cone said. "Not this street, but Covina, just around the corner and up the block a short way. I doubt I'd ever have met them if it hadn't been that they joined the Crooked Lake Birders Club. Anyway, she seemed like a nice person, although he was kind of stiff, if you know what I mean, plus he was away a lot. This is where it gets weird."

Carol found herself thinking that Cone should get himself a thesaurus and start looking up synonyms for weird.

"I don't want to bother Penny, but if we were up on the second floor I could show you what I mean. You can actually see the Neubergers' place from the back window in my room. It's kind of tall, sort of like a free standing town house. The point is that I'd gotten into the habit of going to the window to see what Eagen was doing, and damned if I didn't start doing it with the Neubergers. Of course I couldn't hear their garage door, but I could see lights on the top floor. Like I said, Mr. Neuberger was gone a lot. But one night when I knew he was away, a light went on up there and I saw Mrs. Neuberger and another man. It's a ways away, but I was sure that the man wasn't her husband. Mr. Neuberger's short, shorter than she is, and the man I saw was much taller, probably over six foot. Naturally, I thought that was interesting, so I decided it'd be a good idea to keep watch on the house."

Of course, Carol thought. It's what peeping Toms do.

Mel picked up his beer glass. It was empty.

"I think I'll have another beer," he said. "Sure you won't join me?"

Carol declined and urged the amateur sociologist to continue his explanation of the mysterious notebook. So far he had explained nothing.

"I had a hard time figuring out who the man was," he said when he returned from the kitchen. "I saw him several times, but the light never stayed on very long. When Mr. Neuberger came back the other man always disappeared and there were never any lights in that upstairs room. But next time Vivian's husband was away, a light would go on again and the tall man was back. Not often, but enough so you'd know something was going on between the two of them. It wasn't until just a few months ago that I realized who the mystery man is. It's Larry Finch, Sallie's husband."

Mel looked pleased with himself.

"How were you able to recognize Mr. Finch?"

"I took a little night walk. I was still dressed, and when the light went out I thought I'd take a little stroll up Covina. He never saw me, but I saw him. And I know the Finches. It was Larry, no question."

"I'm assuming that somehow this explains what you entered on the last page of your notebook. Why don't you tell me about it."

"To tell the truth, I don't remember exactly what I wrote in the notebook. But I carry it around with me in case I see a strange bird. Not many of those, but I did use it to make notes of what was going on in the neighborhood."

"I'm afraid I don't understand your notes. Here, let me show you what you wrote."

Carol handed the notebook to Cone, who read what he had written and nodded his head.

"Yes, that's the way it was. At first I wasn't sure who it was that was visiting Mrs. Neuberger. I can't believe I once thought it could be my neighbor. His name's Elvis Hassett. Anyway, it turned out to be Finch."

"Let me guess. You referred to Daddy Bird when you jotted down the last entry in your notebook, which means that Daddy Bird is Larry Finch. Right?"

"I doubt that he likes to be called that, but it was Paul Raymore's idea."

"I guess he's Bird because his family name is that of a bird. But why Daddy?"

"You'd have to ask Paul. But I assume it's because Larry is Sallie's husband."

"I don't know Raymore. Of course I don't really know any of you. But is it your impression that he meant Daddy Bird to be an affectionate nickname? Or was it his way of ridiculing Mr. Finch?"

Cone considered her question.

"I never thought of it, one way or another. Paul's a funny duck. He's not a particularly friendly person, but he's really into birds. I'm a birder, too, but I'm not in his league. None of us are. Anyway, I have no idea what kind of relationship he has with Larry Finch. Larry's never been a member of the Club."

"If he's not a member of the Birder's Club, how does it happen that you hear all this talk about Daddy Bird? Does Raymore refer to Mr. Finch that way when he's on these bird hikes?"

"Fact is I never heard him talk about Larry. He doesn't talk about much of anything. I'd never heard about Daddy Bird until one day Bill Neuberger used that expression. I told him I didn't know what he was talking about, and he laughed and said that was Raymore's name for Larry Finch. It stuck in my mind because I thought it was kinda funny."

Carol found this conversation interesting, not only because she'd learned who Daddy Bird is but because she was surprised that Mel Cone had been so willing to speak about his life as an 'amateur sociologist.' He hadn't sounded like the man who had pulled a 180 and quickly disappeared when he came upon a sheriff's department car not far from the Grove.

"Tell me, Mr. Cone, why have you decided to share all of this information with me today? You never mentioned it when we met in my office."

"I know, and that's my fault. I should have been more frank when I first met you. But I worried that you'd think I was just telling you stuff so you wouldn't suspect me of having anything to do with what happened to Mrs. Neuberger."

"I see." Carol drew the two words out as if she were savoring the way they sounded. "Why might I not draw the same conclusion today? You could have denied that the notebook was yours."

Or said nothing about Mr. Finch's assignations with Mrs. Neuberger. Carol wondered if what Cone had been telling her was even true.

"I suppose I could have, but my conscience kicked in."

"Did you ever go back to the Grove to search for your notebook?"

He smiled.

"I was going to, but changed my mind. Or perhaps one of your officers changed it for me. I drove over there the day after our bird hike, but a sheriff's department car was parked there and I thought you people would be suspicious, me coming back like that to the place where Vivian was shot."

"Good thinking. We did see you, although we couldn't tell whose car it was that did a quick turn and sped away. I wish you'd had your crisis of conscience a bit sooner. It would have saved me a lot of trouble."

The amateur sociologist looked penitent.

"I guess I owe you an apology, but I think you can see my problem."

Better late than not at all, Carol said to herself. No question about it, Kevin will be very interested in Mel Cone's explanation of the Daddy Bird mystery.

CHAPTER 24

"I made reservations at *The Cedar Post*," Kevin announced when Carol got home.

To his surprise, Carol nixed that idea.

"Normally I'd be delighted to eat out, but not tonight."

Kevin looked surprised, and then worried.

"You're okay, I hope. Not coming down with something?"

"No, nothing like that," she said. "It's late, and my conversation with Mel Cone was unexpectedly interesting. In spite of the fact that *The Post* tends to be noisy, I really don't want to risk being overheard. So if you don't mind, let's eat here where nobody'll hear us except the occasional fly on the wall."

"Very mysterious, aren't you? But of course. Dining out is always a poor second choice if there's breaking news about a case. There may not be much in the fridge, but if you'll give me a few minutes I'll cancel the reservation and whip something up for supper."

"Good. I'm not all that hungry, so don't go to any trouble. Maybe I'll even drink my dinner, so why don't you uncork something."

"That I'll do, but I shall insist on putting some food in our stomachs."

"Of course. I was only kidding. Just don't go to a lot of trouble - I'd rather talk."

It was 8:40 when they poured their wine and went out onto the deck.

"Now, what is the big news?" Kevin asked.

"I don't know whether it's big news. Time will tell. But I think it opens up some interesting possibilities about the Neuberger case. As you suspected, the notebook from Anson's Grove is Cone's. And surprise of surprises, not only didn't he deny it, he seemed pleased to be able to tell me all about it - I mean about Elvis and Daddy Bird. No, I'll take that back. We hardly talked about Elvis - he's yesterday's news. But Daddy Bird is something else."

"So you didn't have to pull it out of him."

"That's an understatement. I not only learned where Daddy Bird comes from, I learned all about Cone's hobbies and habits that led him to Daddy Bird. He calls himself an amateur sociologist, but that's really a euphemism for peeping Tom. He denies it, of course, but he went to great lengths to let me know just how and why he knows so much about his neighbors. Who, by the way, are, in addition to Elvis Hassett, Bill and Vivian Neuberger. And it's with the Neubergers that things get interesting."

"Cone and Neuberger. What's the connection?"

"Let me share the backstory with you. It's not really important, but it was quite an experience to sit there and hear him rattle on about how he came to be spying on the Neubergers."

"He spied on them?" Kevin was obviously intrigued.

"Yes. But to hear him tell it, he got into the habit of spying on his neighbors when a chap living next door kept coming home late at night. It seems that opening and closing his garage doors got Cone's attention and he started looking out his window to see what was going on. Anyway, once addicted to maintaining a nighttime watch on your next door neighbor, it's apparently hard to simply have a good night's sleep when he moves away. The Neubergers moved into the neighborhood not long thereafter, not right next door, but within easy viewing distance up a side street. So Cone started keeping an eye on them. I doubt that you'll be able to guess what he says he saw."

"Maybe if we played 20 questions I could, but I'll let you tell me."

"Larry Finch, Sallie's husband, came to see Mrs. Neuberger when *her* husband was away. Which, I gather, is frequently."

"Cone is sure who was visiting Mrs. Neuberger?"

"He was interested enough in finding out that he made it a point to position himself outside and wait for Vivian's visitor to leave. He seems to know Mr. Finch, says he's the man, all right."

"And I gather that this is the big news, so big you chose not to share it with this evening's crowd at *The Cedar Post*?"

"Maybe not, but inasmuch as it involves a Finch and a Neuberger, and one of them's now dead, I'd say it's important."

"Okay, what do you make of it?" Kevin asked, now as anxious to hear Carol's thoughts on the matter as she was to share them.

"I haven't had time to give it much thought, but I've got a hunch - maybe I should say a hint of a hunch - that Mel Cone's snooping may help me get my first real lead in the Neuberger case. And I do mean *may* help. It's possible that Cone is making all of this up, in which case I will have learned nothing today except that he's a pretty persuasive liar. Or maybe he didn't make it all up, just the business about Larry Finch. Cone may insist that he had nothing to do with Vivian Neuberger's death, but he was much closer to her than anyone else that day, and his story about chasing after some kind of a warbler may be just a convenient excuse. If that's true, why not make up a story that Vivian was two-timing her husband? It might get me to focus on Bill Neuberger as the killer. In any event, I've never met Mr. Finch, and when I do I may want to abandon all the crazy ideas this has set in motion. But for the first time since somebody shot the Neuberger woman, I may have an interesting lead.

"Anyway, I'm making a tentative assumption that Cone is telling me the truth. If he is, it opens up two possibilities in the search for Vivian's killer: she was cheating on her husband, Bill, by having some kind of affair with Finch, and Finch was cheating on his wife, Sallie, by having some kind of an affair with Vivian. Of course Cone never said he saw them in a compromising situation; maybe they were only discussing the migration of whooping cranes. Moreover, Cone only saw them standing up with the lights on, not a promising position for some serious hanky panky. But it strikes me as important that Finch apparently visited Vivian only when her husband was away. At the very least we can make a tentative assumption that what they were up to wouldn't sit well with either Sallie Finch or Bill Neuberger."

"It's a twofer, isn't it?" Kevin said. "Two people could have shot Vivian for a single extra-curricular affair. Bill Neuberger because his wife is carrying on with Mr. Finch, Sallie Finch because her husband is carrying on with Mrs. Neuberger. And both Bill Neuberger and Sallie Finch were not only on the bird hike in Anson's Grove, they both had also left the group with McKendrick and gone off to heaven knows where. Meaning they were in a position to shoot Vivian."

"Interesting, isn't it? If one of them really did kill Neuberger, it says something about how different people react when their spouse is unfaithful. Sallie kills the other woman and Neuberger kills his wife. I wonder if there's any scientific research that makes the point that women are more likely to kill the women who are sleeping with their husband, while men are more likely to kill their wives than the men they're doing it with."

"If there is, I'd like to be part of the control group," Kevin suggested.

"Why are we doing this?" Carol asked. "For all I know, Vivian's death had nothing to do with her infidelity. We don't actually know if she was cheating on her husband, much less whether the other man was Sallie Finch's spouse. Cone strikes me as someone who could very well be unreliable. Besides, young Nagle is still in the picture. And what about Raymore? He may have coined the phrase Daddy Bird, but for all we know he may also have had some grievance against Mrs. Neuberger. It sounds pretty far fetched, but there's also the fracking issue. I know almost nothing about Vivian's relationship with those guys who want to tear up the countryside for some natural gas."

Carol stopped suddenly and hit her forehead with a clenched fist.

"I'd almost forgotten that I've got to start interviewing people to replace Barrett. By now there should be a prospective candidate or two. I don't really have time, but I can't just leave applications sitting in my in-box."

"You've always been a multi-tasker, Carol. I'm sure you'll cope. In the meanwhile, how about supper?"

"It depends on what you found in the fridge."

"Don't gag, but it looks like fruit salad and - sorry, I don't know what this other stuff is."

Carol shoved Kevin aside and looked at a plate containing something she couldn't identify.

"I think fruit salad will suffice," she said.

CHAPTER 25

Paul Raymore stopped at the water's edge and looked across the lake. He had his bathing suit on, but he didn't really feel like taking a swim. His catamaran sat only twenty feet down the beach. He knew it would take less than ten minutes to get it ready to sail, but in spite of a perfect breeze he wasn't in the mood to take it out. Instead of doing either of these things, Paul walked out to the end of the dock, sat down, and put his feet in the water. It was cool but comfortable, and on good days he would have enjoyed it. But this was not a good day. In fact, he could not remember when he had last had a good day.

He had bought the cottage nearly two years ago for two reasons. The first, and as it turned out the least important, was because he had heard, on what he considered to be good authority, that the Finger Lakes were smack in the middle of an excellent flyway for many bird species. Indeed his source had insisted that it was one of the best kept secrets in the eastern United States, the result of an uptick in global warming and the decline of nearby east coast wetlands. But it turned out that his source had been misinformed. The more important reason for buying the cottage was that Vivian Neuberger lived on the same lake. To be more precise, the late Vivian Neuberger. He hadn't regretted spending so much time so far from Fallon, his wife of 23 years. Their relationship had been stable but not exciting, and she didn't seem to mind that he had fallen into the habit of spending more time at the lake than he did at their home in the Hudson Valley. The novelty of 'independent living' and the pleasure he derived from the Hobie Cat compensated for his disappointment in the area's bird life. However, it could never compensate for the failure of his effort to establish a relationship with Vivian Neuberger.

He had talked himself into more frequent trips to one of his favorite hideaways, the Asa Wright Bird Sanctuary in Trinidad. It had long since been overtaken by other places as the go-to spot for bird watching. But he always felt at home there, and had even managed to stake out a relationship with the management which allowed him to give lectures and take guests on some of the sanctuary's favorite walks.

As he moved his feet slowly back and forth through the water at the end of the dock, he focussed on the Asa Wright. His schedule could tolerate a week in Trinidad. Not the ideal time for a Caribbean adventure, but it would be huge improvement over places like Anson's Grove. The only problem was that the people who supposedly maintained law and order in the area might wonder what his motive was for disappearing in the midst of the investigation into Vivian Neuberger's death. Not that Deputy Sheriff Bridges posed much of a threat. Just a plodder, not to mention someone who knew absolutely nothing about birds. The sheriff might be smarter, but he doubted it. People who lived up here the year around couldn't possibly be all that well informed about any form of wild life other than the deer they slaughtered during hunting season and the fish they harvested from the lake. Agnes McKendrick was nothing more than a joke. Even Mel Cone, who liked to think of himself as an expert, was in reality nothing but a bush leaguer. The only person who could challenge his own well deserved status as an authority on birds was Vivian Neuberger, and now she was dead.

That thought brought the hint of a smile to Paul's face. Poor Vivian. She could have been a highly regarded ornithologist. But no, she had settled for teaching science at a local high school. The smile vanished. Vivian had been too busy to parlay her knowledge of birds into a reputation as one of the world's foremost twitchers. But she had found time to create an extra-curricular program devoted to bird life at the school, and word had it that the program was rapidly gaining in popularity. Moreover, she had used her connections with Cornell University's ornithology lab to establish a scholarship, which had gone to one of this year's graduating seniors. And the fact remained that, whatever her reputation among insiders, Vivian knew more about birds than anyone he had ever met.

Paul Raymore would never have characterized himself as a jealous person. But in fact he did possess a jealous streak. And it had everything to do with his obsession with birding. He subscribed to several journals which covered the field, and which periodically found space to report on the arcane subject of who's who among the world's most distinguished birders. He had always harbored a suspicion of such lists; after all, the people on those lists could have cheated. There was no way to verify every bird sighting. He himself had almost yielded to the temptation to claim he'd seen a rare bird when he knew that it wasn't true. Such were the moral hazards of one-upmanship in a highly competitive field. However, it was not until he had met Vivian Neuberger that he had actually become jealous of someone he actually knew.

The sun disappeared behind a cloud which was large enough and dark enough to suggest that a shower was possible. It was suddenly chillier, and Paul decided that it might be wise to push the late Vivian Neuberger out of his mind and act on his decision to call the Asa Wright Sanctuary and make a reservation. He got to his feet, paused for a moment to admire a kingfisher which had just landed on the flag pole at the end of a neighbor's dock, and set off for his cottage.

Anyone entering the Raymore cottage would have instantly been aware that its owner loved birds. A wooden plaque over the door to the porch said it all: Welcome to Bird Land. The living room provided pictorial emphasis. The cottage was not large, but for a place its size it had considerable wall space, and that space was filled with a stunning collection of Robert Bateman prints, all of them depicting birds in their native habitat. To the right were a group of puffins and a lone bald eagle; to the left a great horned owl, a pair of loons, and a cardinal, its red feathers in sharp contrast to a green hedgerow. The city apartment was home to many more Batemans, although he knew that their beauty was largely lost on Fallon. He had brought a few of his favorites to the cottage, leaving his wife with some space for art which she preferred. He had neighbors at the lake, but no friends. Two of them, a young couple whom he had invited over one day to reciprocate their hospitality, had taken to calling his cottage the bird house. The name pleased him.

Paul went on into what the sales brochure had termed a study. While it did contain a desk and chair, the space was largely taken up by wall to wall bookcases that were chock full of books providing pictures and text concerning birds of various regions and countries around the world. Two whole shelves were devoted to birds of North America, and if any of the planet's nearly two hundred countries lacked one or more books showcasing its birds, it was not for lack of shopping for them on Paul's part.

He had not decided whether to make the call to the Asa Wright Sanctuary. There was still the matter of how worried he needed to be about the sheriff's reaction if he were to 'flee the country.' Were he to go to Trinidad, it would not be for a protracted stay. Two weeks at most. But he had no idea how his disappearance would be regarded. The deputy sheriff had been very interested in his disappearance from McKendrick's group of bird watchers in the Grove. But that, of course, merely reflected how little the man knew about the so-called leader of the Crooked Lake Birders Club. Trinidad might be a different story.

In the end, a few minutes of sitting in the study, surrounded by dozens of bird books, had the effect of persuading him to make the call. There was always the possibility that the spartan but comfortable rooms at the sanctuary would all have been booked. But Paul assumed, rightly as it turned out, that the management would gladly 'discover' that they had overbooked, thereby making room for him at the expense of inconveniencing someone else. In fact, to Paul's great pleasure, the woman on the other of the line in Trinidad told him that they would pay for his stay with them if he would give a lecture on birds of the Caribbean. It was a commitment which called for little or no preparation, and he quickly consented.

Having decided that he would disappear for two weeks, he now faced the question of whether he should let the sheriff know what he was up to. He hadn't been told not to leave town, and he certainly felt no obligation to keep local law and order informed of his plans. It was strictly a matter of whether it was to his advantage to contact the sheriff. He thought about it for all of a minute. No, he would not contact her. She knew nothing about him except that his mind was on birds virtually 24/7. It would never occur to her that he had seen Vivian Neuberger as a potential rival. He had never told *anyone* how he felt about her. If Vivian had intuited that he didn't like her and why, it no longer mattered. Vivian was dead.

CHAPTER 26

Sharon Lagerfeld, the principal of Southport High School, was not in the habit of leaving her office until five o'clock or later. But she had to pick up a prescription at the pharmacy on the town square before it closed, so she made Friday an exception, wished her assistant a good weekend, and hurried out to the faculty parking lot. Ten minutes later she was making small talk with the pharmacist while she fumbled in her purse for her credit card.

"Well, hello Sharon. It looks as if we're on similar missions."

The principal turned to find the sheriff standing behind her.

"Carol! I don't believe I've seen you since we hosted the basketball tourney back in March."

"Let's not talk about that. As I remember it, SHS didn't have one of it's better games."

"We stress sportsmanship, even on our off days," Sharon said. "Here, I'm finished. Dan will be glad to relieve you of your money, like he did me."

Carol had made a list of people she wanted to see as the investigation of the Neuberger case progressed, and the school principal was on that list. But speaking with Sharon hadn't seemed particularly urgent, and she hadn't called to make an appointment. The chance meeting provided an opportunity to talk for a few minutes, however, assuming that the woman didn't have some place else where she had to be.

"Funny, running into you like this. I was planning on giving you a call. Do you have a little time now?"

"I always try to make time for our sheriff," Sharon said. "Is it about Vivian Neuberger?"

"More or less. That was a terrible thing, wasn't it? I still can't believe it, and now I'm responsible for trying to apprehend whoever did it."

"Let me call home and tell the kids I'll be delayed a bit. Why not see if a bench is available over in the square?"

A bench was vacant, Sharon made her call, and Carol explained her agenda.

"I'm sure these have been bad days at the school, both for teachers and students."

"Something like this is always a shock. But it's doubly awful when it happens to someone like Vivian. She was such a breath of fresh air in the school. I was convinced we had made one of the best appointments in the our history. She was really the whole package - a beautiful mind, a born teacher, a very special human being. What's worse is that speculation is now running absolutely wild. I don't envy you your job."

"Neither do I. People in my business, unfortunately, are familiar with violence. But this is a special case. Such an innocent event, and such a tragic ending. I hope you won't mind if I ask you a few questions about Mrs. Neuberger. I hate to do this, but we don't really have a lot to go on, which means that I have no choice but to ask questions of everyone who knew the people who were on that bird hike."

"There's been talk that maybe a hunter did it," Sharon said.

"That's possible, but as of today, I don't have a clue as who shot Mrs. Neuberger. In fact, I don't really know much of anything about her. Which is where you come in."

"I'll do what I can to help."

Carol was quite sure that the principal would do what she could to help, but that she wouldn't be comfortable answering all of her questions.

"What you've been telling me is that Vivian was well liked, that she was a very successful teacher. Did you ever hear any negative comments about her, about her classes?"

Sharon hesitated, started to say something, stopped.

"I was going to say no," she finally said, "but I'll be honest with you. There have been a few - *very* few - criticisms. They're what you'd suspect. No names, but there are a couple of families who think she overdoes the section of her biology course on evolution. I'm sure it's a national problem, not just Southport. But it's in the state curriculum, and all Vivian was doing was teaching the accepted scientific case for evolution."

"There's nothing to suggest that she was going out of her way to belittle creation or intelligent design?"

"I'm not sure where you're heading, Carol. Vivian was a good scientist, and it wouldn't surprise me if she pointed out that creationism has nothing to do with science."

"I understand. I ask only because one family I've spoken with seemed to think she was critical of the Bible."

"I guess it goes with the territory. Do you want to tell me the name of this family?"

"If you can assure me you won't share it with anyone, including their son, who's a student at SHS."

"Of course. This is between us."

"Okay. The name is Nagle. The boys' name is Michael. The only reason we are even having this conversation is that Michael was on the bird hike when Vivian Neuberger was killed. When I talked with him and his mother, I got the impression that they were unhappy with the biology class and the emphasis on evolution. They'd have preferred that creationism get equal time in the syllabus."

"Goodness, you don't think Michael Nagle had anything to do with Vivian's death, do you?"

"I have no idea who if any of the 15 or 20 birders who went hiking that day had anything to do with her death. But I have to approach these things with an open mind. And it was clear that Michael didn't like Mrs. Neuberger."

"It would be my guess that Michael didn't like Vivian because he doesn't particularly like any of his teachers. He's a teenager, and like many of his age he's sullen much of the time. He was probably in my office four or five times this past year, and I'm sure it wasn't just Vivian who sent him."

"I expect to be talking further with Michael and his parents. But let's leave him aside for a minute. I've heard of another complaint, and it has to do with fracking. Have you had complaints about Vivian discussing fracking in any of her science classes?"

Sharon made a wry face.

"I've never heard a student mention it. Or a parent, for that matter. But there's one man who has dropped by to complain on a couple of occasions, and what seems to get his dander up is Vivian. He's an ardent supporter of fracking, and Vivian, she was an equally ardent environmentalist who's convinced that fracking could be the death knell of Crooked Lake as we know it. I don't know where he gets his information, because he doesn't have any kids in our school.

But he's convinced that Vivian was out of line to be discussing fracking in a science class. He insists it's a political issue and that she should leave it alone."

"Would this man's name be Grandi?"

"You seem to know the answers to all your own questions, Carol."

"You'd be surprised how often I don't even know what questions to ask. But I'm just trying to put in some kind of perspective Mrs. Neuberger's relationships with people. I feel a bit more secure in what I know and don't know now that we've talked. Your job must consist of a lot of mediation, trying to keep everyone happy when that's inherently impossible."

"I don't think I ever thought of it that way. But principals do have a pretty broad agenda."

"I'm sorry I had to bring up these complaints about Vivian Neuberger, but I appreciate your candor."

The conversation drifted off into pleasanter areas, until finally both Sharon and Carol had to excuse themselves in order to head home. Carol would have liked to subtly inquire as to whether Sharon had any reason to think her recently deceased science teacher might have been cheating on her husband, but she didn't ask the question. Not only was it doubtful that the principal would be aware of her faculty's extracurricular activities; she also knew that even to raise the issue would be tasteless and out of order. Unfortunately, it would be tasteless and out of order to raise it with anybody that she could think of, with the possible exception of Bill Neuberger and the Finches. But if Mel Cone's tale were simply a fabrication, or at best unfounded speculation, raising the subject with them would be unbearably cruel. Yet she knew she was going to have to find a way to learn whether Cone was on to something, for if he was he might have supplied her with the key to the puzzle of Vivian Neuberger's death.

CHAPTER 27

So far there hadn't been many applicants for Jim Barrett's place on the force. Perhaps the problem was that the notices advertising the vacancy hadn't yet received wide enough circulation. Carol rationalized that the explanation was that Jim was still in uniform, still driving around the lake and spreading his good humor among the local residents. One way or another, Jim would be attending his last squad briefing in less than two weeks.

Normally, Carol didn't spend Saturdays at the office. But there were few normal weeks, and this was one of the many that wasn't. She told Kevin that she hoped to be back no later than two o'clock, and set off for interviews with two of the small handful of people who hoped to fill Barrett's shoes in the Cumberland County Sheriff's Department. One of them, due at 10 a.m., was Billy BobTompkins. The other, scheduled to arrive at 11:30, was Erin Dockery.

As she made the drive to her office, Carol wondered about Billy Bob. It wasn't that she had ever met him or even knew of his existence until a few days ago, when JoAnne Franks had ruined her weekend by informing her that two of the applicants could only get away for an interview on Saturday. What raised her eyebrows was the name: Billy Bob. Carol had always assumed that names like Billy Bob were only bestowed on children below the Mason Dixon Line. Way below it, at that. Perhaps this Billy Bob was a Georgian who had chosen to resettle in upstate New York.

Erin Dockery was another story. As with Tompkins, Carol hadn't had time yet to read her letter of application or bio, but she was interested because Erin was obviously a woman and she had already decided she'd like to hire a woman. Of course Erin could turn out to be totally unqualified, but until she discovered that for herself she'd give her every chance to make an impression.

Coffee in hand, Carol had settled down to read what Tompkins and Dockery had to say for themselves. Their backgrounds were as different as night and day. For one thing, Tompkins was older by more than a decade, 33 to Dockery's 22. So, inevitably, was their experience.

Billy Bob, who incidentally had said nothing about hailing from the deep south, was a security guard at a small plastics firm in the western part of the county. His bio sketch revealed little about him, other than his ability to hold a job. He had apparently been with the plastics firm for seven years. The Dockery bio was necessarily brief. She was not long out of high school in Yates Center, and had just finished her third year at Brae Loch College, no major yet declared.

Sam Bridges, who was to participate in the interviews, beat Tompkins by less than two minutes.

"Sorry," he said as he pulled up a chair and sat down. "There was a fender bender down near West Branch, and I was right there so I figured I ought to help out."

"No problem. Probably better we didn't get to talk about this guy before he arrives."

"Why's that? You've already made up your mind?"

"I don't make up my mind about applicants sight unseen."

Sam looked doubtful. He knew that Carol had expressed a desire to hire a woman.

JoAnne called to report that Billy Bob Tompkins had arrived.

The man who walked into the office had chosen to spruce up for his interview. He looked out of place in a blue blazer and poorly knotted tie, and proceeded to ask if they didn't mind if he removed both items.

"Of course," Carol said. "No reason not to be comfortable."

The office was not hot, and Billy Bob was not sweating, but he breathed a sigh of relief as he removed his jacket and tie.

"Thank you. That's much better."

Carol's attention was immediately drawn to Billy Bob's muscular biceps. She guessed that he'd asked to remove his jacket in order to show them off. Probably believes we'll think more highly of his ability to maintain law and order now that we've seen those arms of his, she thought.

"Mr. Tompkins," she said, "thank you applying for a position with the force. How do you think you can help us?"

Tompkins seemed puzzled by the question.

"How can I help? Why, I thought you had a vacancy, and, well - I've been in the security business and sort of figured what you do would be right up my alley."

"Tell us, what was the nature of your work with *Cramer's Plastics?"*

"Security. You know, like any company would, they needed somebody who'd make sure the place was secure."

"You mean locked up after hours, things like that?"

"Sure. There's always somebody wants to steal company secrets."

"You're talking about the competition," Carol suggested.

"Yes, that's it," Tompkins said, his smile suggesting that he now understood what the sheriff had in mind.

"If you were working for us, what would you like to be doing?"

"What your men in uniform do. Arresting speeders, breaking up fights, things like that."

"Have you ever had any run ins with the law around here?"

"No, ma'am. I'm what people call a straight arrow." Then a smile broke out on Billy Bob's face. "Sorry, I just remembered, I did get in trouble once back a few years. Nothing big, but I'm sure you want your officers to tell it like it is."

"We do, and they do. What was your problem?"

"Like I said, it was nothing big. Just a bunch of the guys having some fun after a few too many."

It looked as if Billy Bob wanted them to know that, just like lots of guys, he'd pushed the envelope on occasion but was basically a good citizen.

"Let me guess. Mr. Tompkins." It was Deputy Sheriff Bridges, joining the conversation for the first time. "You got yourself a DWI, right?"

"I thinks that's what it was. Just that once, though. I'd have sworn I was way under the limit."

"We appreciate you being up front with us," Sam said. "The sheriff and I, we always check the records."

Tompkins smiled. It was a weak smile.

The interview lasted another twenty minutes, focussing mostly on the responsibilities of sheriff's department officers, some of which differed considerably from Billy Bob's expectations. There was also the usual talk about hours, pay, benefits, and the like. By the time they had covered the bases, Tompkins seemed both slightly less sure of himself and slightly less interested in abandoning what was apparently a cushy job at *Cramer's Plastics*.

"Well, what do you make of Mr. Billy Bob?" Carol asked when the man with muscular biceps and a DWI had left the building.

"For one thing, he hadn't really done his homework," Sam said. "Security work indeed."

"I think he's better suited for work as a bouncer at a nightclub. Unfortunately, we don't have that kind of nightclubs around here."

"Which means that our woman applicant has the inside track, right?"

"Hardly, Sam. My being interested in having a woman on the force doesn't mean I'm ready to give the job to someone who's under qualified just because she's been known to wear a skirt. Besides, JoAnne says we've got three more interviews next week. Hopefully, there may be others by Monday."

"The Dockery woman is due at, what, 11:30? Think I'll go see what's on my desk."

Sam went back to his own office and Carol was left with forty five minutes to consider how best to approach the woman applicant who was barely more than a girl.

When Erin Dockery was shown into Carol's office, the sheriff was immediately struck by how diminutive she was. So much for a decision not to require job applicants to specify their height and weight. It was doubtful that the Dockery woman was more than five foot two, and if she tipped the scale at more than one hundred pounds Carol would have been surprised. The result was to make her look even younger than 22. She was wearing no makeup and wore her dark hair in a ponytail. Otherwise, she was well dressed but had made no effort to look like anything but a college girl.

"Hello, Miss Dockery," Carol said as she shook hands. "This is Deputy Sheriff Bridges. Please have a seat. I understand that you have just finished your junior year at Brae Loch, and I don't see anything on your application that says anything about what you are hoping to do with your life. You've applied for a position with us, of course, but you haven't even declared a major or indicated what you would like to be doing in, say, another five or ten years."

"What I'd like to do is be in law enforcement. But Brae Loch doesn't have a program in it, and Mom's not well and I can't be away where I could get that kind of degree. I thought I could get some OJT right here. You know, on job training. People I talked to said your department's a good one, that it could be a good experience. Anyway, I didn't want to sound like I was just using you until I could transfer."

The girl had gotten quickly to the point.

"What is your interest in law enforcement?"

"Not everyone lives the way he should. My Dad didn't, and he got into trouble and then he died too young. I don't want other people to do that. I think I could help. Maybe it wouldn't work out, but right now it looks like a way I could make things better. I know I must sound like maybe I'm just making it up because I'd like a good job. But I've thought a lot about it, and I think I'm ready to learn police work. It sounds kinda corny, but I'd like to change the world. Do you know what I mean?"

"Tell me, Miss Dockery, do you know people - or know about people - whom you really admire, people you believe have changed the world?"

"My all time favorite person would be Rosa Parks. She's my hero."

Carol was astonished by this reply to her question. Had Erin Dockery been the daughter of one of the small handful of African-American families in Cumberland County, she might not have been surprised. Pleased to hear the choice, but not wholly surprised. And it was obvious that Erin had not named Rosa Parks to impress the sheriff.

Sam had watched the girl, obviously interested in what she'd been saying. But he'd said nothing. He would let Carol question the lone female among the applicants for Barrett's job.

"Very interesting choice, Miss Dockery. Miss Parks was a very courageous person. Let me ask, what if an opportunity comes along to attend a school which offers a major in criminal justice, such as John Jay College down in the city? Suppose they offered you a scholarship. What would you do?"

"To be honest, I don't know. Right now, I couldn't go. Because of Mom. But who knows what's going to happen down the road? What if I got married and had a family and had to quit? But I know you wouldn't refuse me a job because I might get married. They used to do that to young women, didn't they?"

"I'm afraid they did. And I'm not allowed to ask your plans for marriage and children, although I wouldn't ask even if I could."

They talked for another half an hour, the conversation ranging over her mother's health prospects, what she was doing this summer, what courses she had liked at Yates Center and Brae Loch, what her favorite music was, and, in due course, where she might enjoy going to if she had an opportunity to travel abroad. To both Carol's and Sam's surprise, the answer to the last question was Cambodia or Peru. The inevitable question of 'why' she answered by saying she'd heard that both Angkor Wat and Machu Picchu were being endangered by tourism and might have to be closed to the public.

When the youngest of the announced applicants for a position in the Cumberland County Sheriff's Department had left, Carol and Sam looked at each other for what seemed like an eternity before either one of them spoke.

"A penny for your thoughts?" Carol asked.

"An impressive kid, don't you think? Even if she's a she." Sam's face broke into a broad smile. "But seriously, aside from being awfully young, she sounds like she's got a good head on her shoulders. I was going to say she's still an innocent, but she's had to deal with a dad who was a problem and a mother who's been sick, so that's not really fair. Besides, Damoth's only four years older than she is."

"So you haven't ruled her out?"

"I don't think that would be a very smart career move, do you?"

"Go on," Carol said as she stood up. "Get out of here and enjoy what's left of the weekend."

CHAPTER 28

"I'm going over to Dickerson," Kevin said as he poured himself another cup of coffee. "Want to come along?"

"What's the attraction?"

"Hydraulic fracturing. It's been a year or more since I listened to one of those point, counter point debates on environmental issue number one around here. I have a feeling that the conflict may have reached the boiling point by now."

Carol cleared the dishes off the kitchen table and loaded the dishwasher.

"I probably should, but I'm in the mood for some peace and quiet, not listening to my friends and neighbors take pot shots at each other."

"But you told me the fracking issue has even surfaced in the Neuberger case."

"Only because some guy who wants to make a bundle out of it is critical of her using her science class as a soapbox. I may be willing to believe that a birder shot her, but a fracker? Hardly."

"So what do you plan to do with your day?" Kevin asked.

"Absolutely nothing. I've already put in a week and a half, and the county doesn't pay me for overtime."

"The meeting doesn't start for another two hours. Want to take the canoe out?"

"No thanks. Like I said, this is my day to do nothing."

Kevin took his coffee cup out to the deck, which was already bathed in bright morning sunlight. But he was worried. Carol didn't sound like herself. He couldn't remember when she had last sounded so - he was trying to find the word for it, and all he could come up with was blah. She didn't look tired, and normally the suggestion that they take a canoe ride would have produced an enthusiastic thumbs up. Something was bothering her. But there were times when it was okay to ask what the problem is and others when it's better to leave it alone for awhile. This struck him as one of the latter.

When he set off for the 'debate,' or whatever the fracking meeting turned out to be, Carol managed the semblance of a smile and told him she was okay and would see him for lunch, but he wasn't fooled. The drive over to Dickerson did nothing to lift his spirits, and when he arrived at the town hall the room was already filled nearly to capacity, forcing him to take a seat in the back of the room near the door that opened out to the fire escape. He was no longer looking forward to the discussion of fracking.

The meeting was slow to get underway, and Kevin took advantage of the delay to study the crowd. He spotted Officer Barrett, now out of uniform, seated in the front row. He had turned around in his seat and was talking eagerly with two women in the second row. Kevin wondered if one or both of them were part of the organization he was leaving the sheriff's department to join. Several other people in the room were familiar, but none that he knew well. At the moment there was no sign of anger on any of the faces; one could be forgiven for thinking those in the town hall meeting room were simply awaiting the arrival of the entertainment, or perhaps someone who would speak on plans for Crooked Lake's annual Labor Day celebration.

A hush fell over the crowd when some local official rose from his seat at a long table in the front of the room and spoke into a mike, which needed some adjustment to match his considerable height.

"Welcome to our little gathering," he said. "I'm both surprised and delighted at the turnout. We're a good public spirited people here on the lake, aren't we?"

This introduction elicited a few chuckles, but Kevin thought the audience had become more tense.

It was not his intention to make a statement or raise a question, but simply to listen to the colloquy and get a sense of how the wind was blowing on the issue of fracking, now that the governor had chosen to ban it. To his surprise, the discussion was less heated and more civil than he had expected. At least for the first half hour. He heard nothing he had not heard before, although there appeared to be a few outsiders who had been enticed to attend the meeting in order to share their experience of fracking in their own communities in neighboring states and jurisdictions. As the hour wore on, Kevin had the feeling that no one's position had been affected by the governor's decision.

It was not until the 'debate' had gone on for forty minutes and the speakers were beginning to repeat themselves that a man Kevin had never seen before stood up and addressed the crowd in a deep bass voice.

"Most of what I've heard so far is boiler plate nonsense about the need for more environmental studies so our ground water won't smell like crankcase oil and the lake won't turn pea green. Look. Fracking's been going on for years now, and it's been the subject of more studies than those aliens down in Roswell. Name me one case of fracking polluting anybody's water. You people who want more studies of fracking aren't fooling anyone. You'd like to study it to *death.* It's time to say enough to the nay sayers, because fracking is still coming to Crooked Lake, like it or not. It may have received a temporary setback, but it's still not a matter of *if* there'll be fracking in the Southern Tier, but *when.* So let's not just throw up our hands and say it's a dead issue, because it isn't. By extracting natural gas from the shale under our soil we'll give ourselves a new lease on life. The name of the game is still jobs. Do you hear me? Jobs. And if we wait, who do you suppose will get those jobs? I'll tell you who. Places like North Dakota. Do you know why? Because they haven't been sitting around on their duffs, calling for more studies. They know how it's done. They've been doing it! The train is leaving the station, my friends. I'm getting on board."

The room erupted into a a bit of a hubbub. Civility was replaced by verbal finger pointing. In the midst of the confusion, a man stood up at the far left of the crowded room and waved his hands, trying to get attention. It wasn't easy, but eventually the noise subsided.

"How do you propose to do that, Frank?"

The man with the deep bass voice was back on his feet.

"Thank you, Jason. What I *don't* intend to do is wait until the pro-frackers get the upper hand, until the companies that do the fracking come around and start looking for people with promising land to do it on. I intend to get to the head of the line. I've started buying up land, and believe me, I've just started. I know a geologist or two who know the Marcellus Shale formation like the back of their hand. I intend to be the party who negotiates with the frackers."

"Rumor has it that you're planning to take over that area over around Anson's Grove," the man named Jason said. The man named Frank scowled.

"I'm a businessman, Jason. You know that. No point in encouraging the competition. So I don't spread rumors about what I'm up to.

Let's just say that when the day comes I'll be ready to talk to the boys who want to take a crack at all that natural gas we're sitting on."

A woman in the third row joined the conversation The woman was Agnes McKendrick.

"I've heard the rumor about Anson's Grove, too," she said in a stern and disapproving voice. "Have you no shame? That's one of the few undeveloped places around here. We don't need to have it ruined by chainsaws and drilling equipment. The ban was the right call. Tearing up Anson's Grove would be a terrible way to honor the late Vivian Neuberger. She loved the Grove. I'm looking into the possibility of creating a nice burial plot for her up there."

The man with the deep bass voice came out of his chair again and turned to face Agnes.

"There are quite a few cemeteries around the lake, and I'm sure most of them would be happy to make room for Mrs. Neuberger. You could even scatter her ashes over the lake, assuming that our environmental friends didn't regard that as polluting the water. If I were you, I'd forget about Anson's Grove."

It was becoming obvious that the meeting on fracking was fast deteriorating. Kevin had seen something like it happen once or twice at a particularly acrimonious faculty meeting. The afternoon's moderator also took notice of it and sought to restore some semblance of comity. It turned out not to be necessary, because a few people began to vacate their chairs and head for the door. Those few soon became a dozen and within five minutes a mass exodus was underway.

Kevin briefly considered talking with a few of the people he knew, but the person he really wanted to talk with was Carol, so he jogged down the road to where his car was parked and was soon on his way back to Blue Water Point. He hoped that Carol was in better spirits, although he wasn't sure that his report on the fracking meeting would cheer her up.

"I'm home," he called out as he came through the kitchen door. "You okay?"

The question was met by a prolonged silence. Kevin tiptoed through the house to the bedroom, thinking maybe she was taking a nap. She wasn't. It was when he went out onto the deck that he spotted her, sunning herself at the far end of the dock.

"Hi," he said in what he hoped was an upbeat voice as he reached the dock. "This looks like you're having more fun than I've had over in Dickerson."

Carol rolled over and smiled. Whether she was in fact in better spirits, he didn't know yet. But seeing her in her bathing suit gave him a lift. You may now be forty something, he thought, but you look like a million dollars to me.

He leaned down to give her a kiss, and Carol got up onto her knees to reciprocate. If any of the neighbors were watching, they would have nodded their heads in approval.

"I take it the fracking meeting was a washout," she said.

"It depends on what you were expecting. But I'll fill you in in a few minutes. First, what about you? You sounded down in the dumps this morning."

Carol laughed.

"Nothing that bad. I had a bad night - let's say a not particularly restful night, and it wasn't because you pummeled me in your sleep. I simply didn't feel like doing anything when I woke up. You ever had a morning like that?"

"I'll bet it was the Neuberger case. You tend to take it to bed, you know."

"Could be. But I'm a new woman now. See?" As if to illustrate the point, she dove into the lake and proceeded to splash water on Kevin.

"Normally I'd tell you to cut that out until I've changed into my bathing trunks. But maybe the water will wash off some of the unpleasant odor from the meeting. Give me five minutes and I'll join you."

Four short minutes later Kevin did a cannonball into the lake. Ten minutes later they stretched out on the dock and he gave Carol the story of what had happened in the fracking meeting.

"Who was this guy who seems to have broken the meeting up?"

"He never introduced himself, and the moderator didn't really have a chance to do so."

"I'll bet Barrett will know. Sounds like a cocky son of a gun. Why don't you describe him for me and I'll ask Jim who it sounds like."

The rest of the day went smoothly, and Carol wasn't particularly worried about what had happened at the fracking meeting. After all, the governor had spoken. It did not occur to her that this latest discussion of the area's most controversial topic would quickly add a new dimension to the evolving Neuberger case.

CHAPTER 29

Before heading for the office on Monday morning, Carol put in a call to JoAnne and asked her to detain Officer Barrett until she got there. The need to speak with him about the pro-fracking man Kevin couldn't identify reminded her that Jim had only a relatively few days remaining before he said good-bye and became a full time environmentalist. And of the fact that she would be doing some more interviewing that day of prospective candidates to replace him.

As it turned out, Jim hadn't arrived when Carol got there. Probably still grabbing a quick breakfast at the diner down in Southport, she thought. But he appeared at her office door before she had had a chance to do more than pour herself a cup of coffee and skim the resumes of the people she'd be interviewing.

"I understand you need to see me," Jim said. "No problem with the position, I hope."

"Only that we'll almost certainly fill your position, but we won't be replacing you. What's that old cliche? The difficult we do right away; the impossible takes a little longer. Anyway, I need to pick your brain. Kevin was at that fracking meeting over in Dickerson yesterday, and he says he saw you there. But he doesn't know the name of the man who seems to have brought the meeting to an end with a snide remark to Agnes McKendrick, the bird club lady."

"That's no problem. It's Frank Grandi. I think I mentioned him to you awhile back. I don't really know him, but he's obviously still hot to frack, ban or no ban. Word has it that he's difficult to deal with, which I think he demonstrated yesterday. Funny thing, though, I got the impression that our mutual friend Jason Eglin was trying to get Grandi to admit that he's planning to buy up Anson's Grove. Not sure what Eglin's agenda was, but Grandi refused to take the bait."

"So from what you observed, the meeting was much like all the others. I mean no new developments."

"That's true, except for Grandi's suggestion that it might be a good idea to scatter Neuberger's ashes over the lake. That's illegal, isn't it?"

"Good question, and I don't think it's ever come up during my tenure. I'll check on it, but I'll bet it's one of those 'don't ask, don't tell' matters. Anyway, you've answered my question. This is going to be one of your last days on patrol - enjoy it."

After Barrett left, Carol gave some thought to whether it might be wise to locate Frank Grandi and have a chat with him. In the end, however, she dismissed the idea. Fracking was on her mind because Barrett was leaving the force, not because it had anything to do with her principal agenda, the Neuberger case. There was nothing she could or should do to stop Grandi's effort to buy up land in anticipation of what might be a fracking bonanza. Whatever her feelings on the subject, it was not within her jurisdiction.

It was within her responsibility, and at the top of her agenda, to interview the remaining candidates for the position on the force that Barrett was vacating. As had been the case with Billy Bob Tompkins and Erin Dockery on Saturday, Sam would sit in. A substantial portion of the day was consequently devoted to sessions with three young men who fancied themselves as members of the Cumberland County Sheriff's Department. Unfortunately, none of the three made a strong impression on either Sam or Carol. After the final applicant had left the building, Sam shared his disappointment with the sheriff.

"There was a time when I thought this was the kind of job which would attract Crooked Lake's best and brightest."

"It did. You're proof of that, Sam. But we're a long way from the bottom of the barrel, as evidenced by Miss Dockery. What do you say, should I offer her the job?"

"You hoped it would turn out this way, didn't you?"

"Come on, that's not fair. It's just the luck of the draw that the others have serious flaws. Anyway, would you be comfortable having a 22 year woman as a partner?"

Sam gave her what looked like a cautious smile.

"She's green. And I wish she had a few more pounds on her. Can you imagine her running up against a couple of bruisers in a bar brawl?"

"Frankly, I'm more worried that she'll accept a scholarship at some college's criminal justice program and leave us after a year or two. But seriously, I need your honest judgment."

"And you shall have it. Yes, I'd give her a chance. She's smart, and my guess is that she'll learn fast. Besides, I know you've been interested in having a woman on the force for some time, and I respect your judgment. I'm not sure how all the guys would react, but I can't imagine any of them getting really bent out of shape. If it would help, I'll make it my responsibility to teach her the ropes."

"I'd appreciate that, although I expect all the men to play that role. Me, too. I just want it to be clear that if she takes the job she's not going to be assigned the easy stuff. She'd catch on in a flash if she thought we were treating her differently."

"So it's decided?" Sam asked.

"JoAnne and I'll take care of the administrative matters, then I'd like you to give her a thorough orientation. Knowing how the county moves, she won't be on duty for a week or more - if we're lucky - but let's get started. I'll give her a call. Don't say anything to the men until Erin accepts my offer and the personnel office clears it."

"I hope we don't regret this," Sam said as he headed for the door.

"Let's not second guess ourselves."

By mid-afternoon, the process of making Erin Dockery the youngest and smallest officer in the Cumberland County Sheriff's Department was underway and Carol had turned her attention back to the Neuberger case. She closed her office door and picked up a file that contained, among many other things, her ubiquitous yellow pad. She stared at the notes she had made when last she focussed on the shooting in Anson's Grove. There were four names there: Michael Nagle, Mel Cone, Jason Eglin, and Sharon Lagerfeld. Since then she had talked with Cone and Lagerfeld. What she had learned from Cone prompted her to add three more names to her list: Larry Finch, his wife Sallie, and Bill Neuberger. They belonged on the list because of Cone's allegation of an affair between Finch and the late Vivian Neuberger. Unfortunately, she had no proof that there had ever been such an affair, which made discussing it extremely difficult.

She considered Michael Nagle again. The problem in his case was that no one wanted to talk about him. But, no, she thought, that wasn't really true. It wasn't that *no* one wanted to talk about Michael. It was simply that Michael's mother and a neighbor, Jennifer Taggart, didn't want to talk about him. Or at least they didn't want to talk about whatever problem he was experiencing. Carol had never talked with Michael himself, one on one. She had never talked with Bob Taggart, who seemed to disagree with his wife about the wisdom of discussing Michael with the sheriff. For that matter, she had never talked with Michael's father.

Maybe she should devise a strategy for meeting with Michael when his mother was not hovering over him. Maybe she should arrange to see Mr. Taggart. After all, she and Sam had announced their intention to talk with everyone who had been on the bird hike. Mr. Taggart had been on the bird hike, and there was no reason why those conversations had to be couples only affairs.

The alleged affair between Vivian Neuberger and Larry Finch was a different matter, but perhaps there was a way to get closer to the truth without confronting either Bill Neuberger or Sallie Finch with Mel Cone's story. Like Bob Taggart, she had never met Larry Finch. Of course he hadn't been on the bird hike, but it should be relatively easy to use the existence of the birders club and his wife's membership in it to justify a meeting with him. And such a meeting might possibly give her a better picture of the man and his marriage. Nothing ventured, nothing gained.

And then there was Paul Raymore, whose name had also not been on her list. As far as she could tell, there was no problem where he was concerned comparable to the problems involving Michael Nagle, Bill Neuberger, and Sallie Finch. But like Michael, Bill and Sallie, he had been where he could have shot Vivian. He had known Larry Finch and had apparently been responsible for dubbing him Daddy Bird. And she had never met him. Sam had been the one to interview him, and had concluded that he was preoccupied with birds to the exclusion of practically everything else. Much as she trusted Sam's judgment, it just might be worth her while to have a talk with him herself. She added him to her list.

What about Jason Eglin, whose name was just above Sharon Lagerfeld's? She had wanted to speak with Jason because of the unpleasantness over Officer Barrett. But the issue was fracking, which seemed peripheral to the Neuberger case.

Which left Michael Nagle, Bill Neuberger, the Finches, and Paul Raymore. Setting up a meeting with any of them would be difficult, especially when she had to rely on a land line phone call which other family members could answer. On reflection, the easiest of these calls would be to Raymore.

After eight rings, a recording told her that no one was at home but that she could leave a message. Carol was frustrated, but she chose not to leave a call back number. She'd try again on Tuesday.

CHAPTER 30

"I nixed your proposal for dinner at *The Cedar Post* the other day," Carol said when Kevin answered the phone. "Want to make it tonight?"

"Sure. Have you already made a reservation?"

"No, I thought I'd leave that to you. The other night I had too much to tell you after my meeting with Mel Cone. Tonight I have nothing to tell you, except that the name of the man who broke up the fracking meeting is Frank Grandi. So we can share a steak sandwich and talk to our hearts' content without worrying about being overheard. Why don't you make it seven, which will give me a chance to take a brief swim and change clothes."

Two hours later, a good dinner behind them, Carol suggested they take a drive out to the end of the bluff.

"It's only a day or two before full moon," she said. "It'll rise sooner up there than it will from our deck. Okay?"

"Absolutely. 'Moonglow,' one of favorite oldies."

Carol gave him a puzzled look.

"You like 'Moonglow?'"

"Why not? The question you're supposed to ask is whether I prefer the Benny Goodman or the Artie Shaw recording."

"I wouldn't know one from the other. But I remember Dad loved it. He played it a lot, back in the day when everything was on vinyl. But Dad was always a fan of the Big Bands, didn't know a thing about classical music. How come it's one of your favorites?"

"It isn't written anywhere that if you love opera you can't also love jazz and pop. The Beatles and Beethoven have been known to coexist. Just ask me."

"You're full of surprises, aren't you?"

"Probably more than you know. If the piano were at the cottage instead of way down in my apartment, I'd give you my rendition of 'Moonglow.'"

The car was now on the upper bluff road, and Carol was looking pensive.

"Have you ever given any thought to bringing it up to the cottage?"

"The piano?"

"Yes, the piano."

"I'm afraid I can't ship a piano back and forth between the city and the lake on a teacher's salary. And given what I do for a living, I need it down there."

"Have you ever considered buying an upright for the cottage?"

"I have, but it's still a money issue. Tell you what. This fall, when you take a break and come down to see me, I'll play 'Moonglow' for you. Why don't you make up a list of all of your Dad's favorites, and I'll entertain you with a memory lane concert."

"You won't know them all," Carol said.

"Oh, no? Why don't you try me?"

In spite of their announced intention of watching the moon rise, when they got to the tip of the bluff they managed to spend some time talking about the Neuberger case, and even more time smooching like a couple of kids on a date.

On Tuesday morning, Carol tried the Raymore phone number again. Once more, no one answered. Damn! She would have to shift her attention to Michael Nagle. Or perhaps to one of the parties to the alleged Neuberger-Finch affair. And she wasn't quite ready to do either, primarily because she hadn't decided how best to do it. She scanned her roster of the Crooked Lake Birders Club, made a note of Paul Raymore's address, and told JoAnne where she was going. It was close to half an hour later that she approached his lake cottage. The cottage, an attractive building with a yard which looked as if it could use some attention, was down a slope toward the lake, perhaps one hundred feet away. Carol was familiar with Reachers Point, but knew no one who lived there. The odds that Raymore would be at home were small. She didn't know what he did for a living. She wasn't even sure whether he was married. She hoped that he simply had an aversion to answering the phone. It took her less than half a minute to follow the entrance road down to the cottage, where she stopped just in front of the closed door of a one car garage.

It required only a few seconds more to ascertain that the garage was empty. Which meant that it was unlikely that anyone was home.

Nonetheless, she tried what looked like a doorbell and knocked loudly on both front and back doors. No one answered. Carol took out a pad, tore off a sheet of paper, and scribbled a note that asked Paul Raymore to give her a call. She added the office number and stuck the note under the edge of a sign announcing that this was the Raymores' residence.

She was getting into her car when a blond haired, buxom woman in the adjacent cottage waved at her from the neighboring yard.

"Hello, you must be looking for Paul."

"I am, but it appears that he's not at home," Carol said.

"No, he's gone away again. He left yesterday, and didn't come back last night. My guess is he was off to the airport."

Carol stepped out of the car and walked across the yard to where the neighbor was draping some beach towels over a clothes line.

"Did he say where he was going?"

"No. He never does. He keeps to himself."

"Is Mrs. Raymore here?"

The woman laughed.

"She's never here. Well, almost never. I think he comes up to the cottage to get away from her. Or maybe she stays where she can get away from him. I don't think I've seen her more than twice. Funny marriage, if you ask me."

This was interesting, but it didn't help Carol in her quest to have a serious conversation with Paul Raymore.

"What makes you think Mr. Raymore was going to the airport?" Carol asked.

"He had a little suitcase with him," the woman told her, although why that made the airport his probable destination wasn't clear.

It struck Carol that his neighbor paid fairly close attention to the comings and goings of Paul Raymore. Perhaps they were closer than she had let on.

"You say that Mr. Raymore keeps to himself. Do the two of you ever talk?"

"Are you a policeman? I mean, that's what your car says. Has he done something bad and that's why you're looking for him?"

"No, that's not the case." This was no time to spread rumors, and this woman sounded as if she might be capable of spreading rumors. "The fact is, I've never met him, but something came up and I needed to say hello."

"Well, he's a hard one to get much out of. We've been neighbors for almost two years now and I still don't know what he does. It seems to me he's too young to be retired up here on the lake, but maybe he inherited a lot of money. Either that or he and the missus just don't get along."

"Has he ever talked about birds with you?"

"Birds?" The woman came around from behind a beach towel she had just pinned to the clothes line. She looked genuinely puzzled by the question.

"Yes, birds. I've heard that he's an expect on birds."

"You couldn't prove it by me. He's never mentioned birds. Like I said, he's not a talker. I don't even know where he came from when he bought the Stevens' cottage. Maybe Asia"

"He said he's from Asia?" It was Carol's turn to be surprised.

"He said something about it once. But that doesn't make much sense, does it? He doesn't look like an Asian to me."

Carol decided that Paul Raymore's neighbor wasn't likely to be of much more help. She asked for the woman's name, and was informed that it was Muriel Snell.

"Thank you, Ms. Snell. I may be back."

I wonder what she thinks is going on at the Raymore cottage, Carol thought. But, then, so do I.

CHAPTER 31

Just who was Paul Raymore? The more she thought about it, the more Carol realized that she knew less about him than any of the other putative suspects in the death of Vivian Neuberger. Of course most of what she knew about the others who might have been Vivian's killer was mere conjecture. She thought she might know more about Bill Neuberger and Sallie Finch, but that was only because of what Mel Cone had told her about Vivian's alleged affair with Larry Finch. And what did she know about Mel Cone? She thought she knew more about Michael Nagle, but that was only because Mrs. Taggart and Mrs. Nagle had been unwilling to talk frankly about the young man. Why had she been so willing to assume that their reluctance to discuss Michael's 'problem' was somehow germane to the Neuberger case?

Darnn it, she thought. The hard truth of the matter is that I know virtually nothing about *any* of these people. I've never even seen Paul Raymore or Sallie Finch, much less spoken to either of them. I've spoken to Bill Neuberger once, and he seemed a bit full of himself and not all that broken up about losing his wife. But so what? If he had killed her, wouldn't he have been more likely to wear his bereavement on his sleeve? I've also spoken with Michael Nagle, and he had behaved like many a surly teenager, hardly surprising in view of the fact that his obviously unwelcome mother had been hovering beside him during their interview.

Frustrated and temporarily stymied, Carol knew she could not simply put her investigation on hold until Paul Raymore returned from wherever he had gone. She'd have Officer Byrnes track down his wife and make contact with the other half of this apparently estranged couple. But within an hour of her conversation with Raymore's neighbor, Muriel Snell, Carol had decided that she'd promptly put plan B into effect. It involved Larry Finch, who, if Mel Cone were to be believed, had been having an affair with the late Vivian Neuberger.

Officer Byrnes deferred taking action regarding the Raymores, concentrating instead on locating Larry Finch. Rather than call him with a heads up on her intentions, Carol followed Byrnes' instructions and within half an hour was sitting in the Yates Center office of Lawrence J. Finch, Vice President, Beckley Enterprises. Beckley Enterprises was a misleading title for a company that was actually one of the larger of the area's suppliers of agricultural machinery. The woman to whom she had introduced herself had explained that Mr. Finch had someone with him. Carol had explained that she was in no hurry, and the vice president's gatekeeper had retreated to her desk and spent the next ten minutes surreptitiously glancing at the uniformed woman across the room from her.

When the door to the inner sanctum opened, two men emerged. They seemed to be old friends or acquaintances. At least they were smiling and engaged in casual banter. They spotted the sheriff at the same time. The taller of the two suddenly lost his smile. The shorter retained his smile, but cut off whatever it was he was saying mid-sentence.

"Thanks for coming by," the taller man, obviously Finch, said.

"See you soon," his colleague replied, and slipped out the door.

"You look like our sheriff," Finch announced, extending his hand. "What brings you to Beckley today?"

Carol had no intention of answering that question in the outer office.

"We haven't met, and I thought I might come by and introduce myself," she said, edging toward the door to Finch's office.

"Well, of course. Come on in. Would you care for coffee?"

"I'll pass, thank you," Carol said, following him into a room that looked rather small and minimally decorated for a vice president.

"This is a pleasant surprise." The look on Larry Finch's face gave no hint that the surprise was a pleasant one.

"I really should have called, not just popped in unannounced," Carol said. "But I had wanted to meet you and I was in town and thought I'd stop by. I hope that my timing isn't inconvenient."

"No, no, not at all. I'm embarrassed that we haven't met before. I believe you've been sheriff for a few years now."

"It has indeed been awhile, hasn't it? But it's I who should be embarrassed. I'm afraid I tend to meet people who are in some kind of trouble, which would explain our being strangers."

This conversation, which had nothing to do with Carol's mission or Larry Finch's puzzlement, continued for another minute.

Carol brought it to an end with a reference to the recent shooting in Anson's Grove.

"I'm sure you have heard about the recent death of Vivian Neuberger. I assume your wife told you about it, inasmuch as she was on a bird hike with Mrs. Neuberger when it happened."

Carol paused, interested in how Finch would react to this statement of the reason for her visit. She couldn't be sure, but she thought she detected a stiffening of the man's spine, just a hint that the subject was either not what he had expected or just what he had feared.

"Yes, Sallie told me. A terrible story, isn't it? I'd been away. A few of us had gone to New Orleans. It happened while I was away."

It had never occurred to Carol that Finch might have been Vivian's killer. He hadn't even been on the bird hike. Yet he had been quick to let her know that he had been far away from Crooked Lake when it happened. Alibi established, although she couldn't imagine that he needed one.

"I'll have to say that it has been one of the most extraordinary things that's happened here since I became sheriff. One doesn't expect something like this to happen during a pleasant outing like a bird hike. Did your wife - it's Sallie, isn't it? - did she seem to have any idea of how it could have happened?"

How, of course, was by gun shot. But that wasn't what Carol meant by her question. She was genuinely interested in what Sallie Finch had told her husband on his return from New Orleans. She was even more interested in what Finch might say - or not say - about Mel Cone's story that he had been in some kind of relationship with Mrs. Neuberger. She wasn't quite sure how to broach that more important question. She'd play it by ear, see where this conversation would lead.

"Have you talked with my wife?" he asked.

"Not exactly. I haven't, but my deputy sheriff did."

"Well," Larry Finch began tentatively, "she told me about Mrs. Neuberger' being shot during the hike. That's when I first heard about it, when I got back from the trip to New Orleans. It was shocking news. And my wife was right there. It could just as well have been her."

Carol hadn't considered the possibility that someone other than Vivian Neuberger had been the intended victim. She very much doubted it.

"Did your wife give you the impression that she might have been the target?"

"I don't think so, but I can't imagine that someone was deliberately trying to kill Mrs. Neuberger."

It was time to raise the crucial question.

"How well did you know Mrs. Neuberger?" Not did you know her, but how well.

"Not well at all. When the Neubergers moved to the lake, Sallie and I had them over to the house. Sort of a courtesy to new neighbors."

"And did you see them more than that once? I mean, would you describe them as friends?"

Once again Carol thought that Larry Finch's reaction to her question contained just a hint of anxiety.

"I don't think that you'd call us social friends. Pleasant acquaintances perhaps, but nothing more. As you probably know, I'm not a member of the bird club like Sallie is. So she got to know them better than I did."

"In other words, if I wanted to know more about your relationship with the Neubergers I should talk with your wife."

No question this time. Larry Finch definitely looked uncomfortable.

"Because of the birding, Sallie saw them a bit more often, but she didn't really know them. You know how it is, a trip to look for birds every few months or so doesn't really lead to friendships. It's the birds that get all the attention."

Larry Finch's attempt at humor fell flat.

"Did you ever see either Mr. or Mrs. Neuberger again? I mean other than at those 'get to know the newcomers' gatherings?"

"Not that I remember. I may have run into him around town, but I can't recall anything specific."

"How about her? Did you ever run into her?"

If there were any truth to Mel Cone's story, this was the critical question.

"Not that I remember. I've always been pretty busy here at Beckley, and I'm sure she had her hands full at the high school."

It was time to shift the discussion slightly.

"What's your theory as to why she was killed?"

"I don't really have a theory," he said. "I can't imagine it was anything but an accident, somebody who was stalking a deer out of season."

"This only happened recently, so it's too soon for me to pretend I know what happened. But I'm almost certain Mrs. Neuberger wasn't accidentally killed by a hunter. In fact, I very much doubt that her death was an accident."

"But that's terrible. I can't imagine anyone wanting a nice person like her dead. It makes no sense at all."

"Perhaps not, but my officers and I are trying to discover whether it does in fact make sense. And I'm sure that in due course we'll succeed. I don't need to take more of your time, Mr. Finch. I appreciate your willingness to talk with me, and I'll say to you what I've already said to many others. If anything occurs to you that you think might help our investigation, please let me know."

It had been an inconclusive conversation, but that's what she had expected. All in all, Larry Finch had given her no reason to believe that Mel Cone's story was true. His response to her questions had been straight forward. Yes, there had been moments when he had seemed to be on his guard, perhaps a bit nervous about where she had been going with her questions. But why wouldn't he have been? Moreover, he almost certainly would have known, had he been having an affair with Vivian Neuberger, that among the likely suspects in her death would be Vivian's husband and his own wife. Carol found herself wondering whether Sallie Finch had at any time entertained the possibility that her husband was a philanderer. And if so, whether she had any reason, well founded or not, to think that the other woman could be Vivian Neuberger.

CHAPTER 32

Things might have been a lot worse had a young Sonny Parrish not made a dangerous open field tackle and had Southport police officer Lance Kimball not been present. It was a warm sunny day, and the beach at the south end of Crooked Lake was packed with swimmers. Sean Roark was on life guard duty atop his Mendota chair, which gave him a clear view of what was going on up and down the beach and well out into the lake. One of the things that was going on was that a high school aged boy who appeared to be a little younger than Sean was running after another high school aged boy. He had a bottle in his hand. This was definitely contrary to the rules. Signs had been posted which made it clear that glass containers were strictly forbidden on the beach. The boy who was running with the glass bottle had either not read the notices or didn't care. In fact, as he raced past the life guard's stand he smacked the bottle hard against it. The bottle broke and one large jagged piece of it fell onto the shale. Sean Roark immediately put his whistle to his mouth to call attention to this violation of beach policy.

The running boy neither stopped nor looked back. Instead he caught up with the boy he was chasing and lunged at him with what was left of the bottle. At almost that exact moment, Sonny Parrish, alerted to what was going on by the sound of the whistle, dove at the boy with the bottle and, grabbing him around the ankles, brought him to the ground. Most of the crowd on the beach and in the water kept right on doing what they'd been doing. But several people quickly turned their attention to the boys who had fallen to the ground. One of them was Officer Kimball, one of Southport's small police corps. He had seen nothing quite like this in his five years on the local force, but it was obvious that he had to do something about the boy who was bleeding from a gash on the back of his leg and the boy with the bottle who was about to attack his tackler with that same bottle. Kimball caught the bottle wielder by the arm and flipped him onto his back. He got a nearby onlooker to call Chief Bellman and get medical help and, having relieved the attacker of the jagged bottle, he took a good look at the boy he was now sitting on.

"My God," he said, "you're Hank Nagle's son."

The sheriff of Cumberland County heard nothing about this little fracas on the Southport beach until that afternoon, when Officer Damoth called from a gas station just outside of Southport.

"I thought you'd want to hear about this," he said. "I'd just stopped to fill the tank when I overheard somebody report that there's been a stabbing over on the beach in Southport. It seems that that Nagle kid you've been interested in was chasing another boy and slashed him with a broken bottle. I guess he's in custody, although nobody here at the station seems to know exactly what's going on."

"You're sure it was young Nagle?"

"Sounds that way, although there may be more Nagles around here. Do you want me to follow up?"

"No, and thanks. I'll call Bellman."

Carol was both angry and excited. Angry that she hadn't been more forceful in persuading the Nagles and the Taggarts to tell her what Michael Nagle's problem was, excited that it might now be possible to get them to level with her. She put in a call to Bellman.

The Southport Chief of Police picked up promptly.

"Hi, Steve. This is Carol Kelleher. I've just heard that you've had some kind of a crisis down by the beach. The name I hear is Nagle. Would that be Michael Nagle?"

"Hello, Carol. Yes, it's Michael Nagle. He used a broken bottle to cut up another kid, Danny Kuyper. The Kuyper boy's going to be fine, thanks to some quick thinking by my man Kimball. Nagle, he's another story. He's a real piece of work. His parents are worried sick, and I can't say as I blame 'em."

"I don't envy you this one, but that's not why I'm calling. You know about what happened to Vivian Neuberger?"

"Sure do. Now that's a more serious matter, don't you think?"

"The problem is that when she was killed, she was on a bird hike. And the Nagle kid was with her on that hike. It's highly unlikely that Nagle had anything to do with her death, but this news about him turning violent down on the beach has got my attention. I'm going to want to talk with him, and with his parents. What's the situation? Is he locked up? Out on bail?"

"Well, he's a problem, but I can't see him going anywhere. I know his parents, figure they'll take care of him until some decision is reached as to what action to take. Jeezus, the kid's only fifteen. What a mess."

"Okay. Look, I'm not involved in any way in this beach business. But you should know that I'll be talking to him, and to the Nagles. Just didn't want you to think I was horning in on your case."

"Thanks, but to be perfectly honest I'd love to put the whole damn mess in your lap."

"And I'm sure you can understand why I'll take a pass. But let's keep each other posted."

Carol had no sooner rung off than she dashed out to the car and set off for Southport. She hoped that the Nagles would be home. This time she wouldn't be put off.

The Nagles' garage door was up, revealing two cars, which suggested that Mr. Nagle had come home to help his wife cope or perhaps to confront his troubled son.

It was Mr. Nagle who came to the door.

"Yes?" he said when he spotted the sheriff, whom he had never met.

"Hello." Carol did her best not to sound like a prophet of doom. "I'm Sheriff Kelleher. I'd like to talk with you and your wife. May I come in?"

"I suppose that I can't say no," he said, "although we've been having a bad day. Is this about the incident at the beach?"

"Yes and no," Carol said. "But it is about your son Michael."

Mr. Nagle, whose first name Carol still didn't know, reluctantly stepped aside.

"Are you taking charge of this matter?" he asked.

"No. It's Southport police business. By the way, please forgive me, but while I've met your wife, we don't really know each other and I don't even know your name."

"Oh, I'm sorry. It's Hank."

"Thank you. I had hoped to speak with both you and your wife. Is she here?"

"I'm afraid we're all here. The police brought Michael home less than an hour ago. Our doctor gave him a sedative, and I think he's fallen asleep. We still don't know what they're going to do about him. Shall I call Fran down?"

"If you would be so kind." Carol took a seat without having been invited to do so. Hank Nagle went to the foot of the stairs and quietly told his wife that they had a visitor.

Fran Nagle looked as unhappy to see the sheriff as her husband had been.

"I don't understand," she said. "I thought the Southport police were handling this."

"They are. I'm not here because of what happened to Michael this morning." This was not, of course, entirely true, as would become apparent if they ever got around to a discussion of the reason she was sitting in the Nagle's living room.

"Well, then -" Mrs. Nagle apparently thought better of it, and left it at that.

"I shall get right to the point. When we spoke before, Mrs. Nagle, it was about your son, who seemed to be having problems. You said that those problems were typical of boys his age, and that some of them may have had to do with difficulties in school. But what happened this morning doesn't seem to have had anything to do with school. If I'm not misinterpreting what I've heard, it appears that Michael has serious anger management problems. I know that sounds like so much psychological jargon, but I think you'll both agree with me that what Michael did this morning was not simply something that teen age boys do. I have had the impression ever since you and Michael met me in my office that Michael's problems are more than a mere passing phenomenon, that they are really troubling you and that you don't know what to do about them. You chose, Mrs. Nagle, not to talk about them with me. Today I am going to insist that you do so."

The Nagles looked at each other and then back at the sheriff.

"I'm not sure that there's anything I can add to what I told you before," Fran said.

"And I'm sure that there is. Your son is prone to violence. This morning he attacked another boy with a piece of jagged glass. The law does not look kindly on such things, and as an agent of local law enforcement I consider it my business to ask you these questions."

"But when we talked in your office, we were discussing the death of that Neuberger woman. Michael had nothing to with her death. This unfortunate event on the beach is a totally different matter."

"That may be. But my job is to discover who shot and killed Vivian Neuberger. That was certainly an act of violence. So was Michael's attack on that boy this morning. You believe you are protecting your son by withholding information. If you really want to protect him, you will speak candidly about what is bothering him - and bothering you."

Carol chose to rise from her chair.

"I have no idea - none, mind you - who killed Vivian Neuberger. Like a number of other people, Michael theoretically *could* have. I am not a medical doctor, and I am not qualified to speculate on the specific nature of his problem. But it has been very clear to me that something is wrong, and that you are well aware of it. If you want me to deal with facts, not guesswork, you will share your knowledge with me. And seek professional help."

She hoped that her act of standing up had left the impression that if they maintained their silence she would walk out the door and rely henceforth on guesswork. It may have worked.

"Sheriff, could you please bear with us for a moment or two. Please sit down." It was Mr. Nagle who spoke.

"That would depend," Carol said, remaining on her feet.

"There may indeed be something you should know," Hank Nagle continued.

His wife started to say something, then bit her lip.

"I'm listening. What is it?" Carol said.

"Actually, it's something I'd like to show you. It's upstairs. Please wait. I'll be right back."

Mr. Nagle went upstairs. His wife looked as if she were about to cry.

When he came back down he had a some papers in his hand.

"He's still asleep," he said as he placed the papers on the coffee table next to Carol's chair. Then he sat down, offering no further comment.

Tentatively, Carol began to leaf through the papers. There were four of them, all full of drawings which filled most of the page. What she saw were amateurish stick figures, all of them in one kind of trouble or another. Three of the four presented a woman with a sign hanging around her neck. In each case the sign contained the word Darwin, spelled in crude capital letters. One of the drawings showed familiar V-shaped figures of birds diving at the woman. In another, a male stick figure with a bow and arrow had apparently fired an arrow that had penetrated the Darwin sign. The third was, for some reason, the most troubling of the three. In this case, the woman, still wearing her Darwin sign, was suspended from a cross in a crude rendering of the crucifixion.

The Darwin sign board around the woman's neck presumably identified her as Vivian Neuberger. The fourth paper pictured three smaller stick figures, none bearing a sign or other clue as to their identity. The stick figures could be different people; on the other hand, they could all be the same person. One was lying on his back with what might be a long stick rising out of his stomach. The other two were running. The artist was clearly not that accomplished, but in one of the pictures it looked as if the runner was looking behind him. Perhaps he was watching a pursuer, but if so the pursuer was not in the picture.

The Nagles were obviously waiting for the sheriff to comment.

"Does Michael know that you have seen these pictures?" she asked.

"He does," Mr. Nagle said. "He's in the habit of locking himself in his room, and I was concerned about just what he might be doing. One day, when the door was open and he was out, I took a look and saw these pictures on his desk. Three of them, anyway. That's when Fran and I began to really worry about what was going on in his head. We mentioned having seen the pictures and he went ballistic. But it was more about our invading his privacy than it was about the pictures. He dismissed them as just 'fooling around.' Wasn't that the way he put it?"

Mrs. Nagle nodded in agreement.

"He may only have been fooling around," Carol said, "but what I see here isn't ordinary fooling around. Like I said, Michael should be seen by a specialist. I'll see what I can do about getting some names for you, but I think you would be wise to seek help."

"That's what the Taggarts said, but we thought he'd refuse to see someone."

"He probably will resist the idea, Mrs. Nagle, but it's important that you not let him off the hook."

"You really don't think he shot that Neuberger woman, do you?" Fran asked. It was a mother seeking assurance that her son, however troubled, was not a killer.

"It is highly unlikely, but as I have told you, I can't rule it out. These pictures would seem to make it clear that Michael didn't like Mrs. Neuberger. But not liking someone and killing her are very different things."

Carol hoped that she had initiated a process which would provide Michael Nagle with professional help. The Nagles had taken a brave step in finally sharing with her this evidence that their son's problem might indeed be serious. Now there was but one additional question to ask.

"I understand that you have a gun collection, Mr. Nagle. Are all of the guns in that collection where they should be? Where you traditionally keep them?"

Color began to rise in the man's face.

"I take my responsibility as a gun owner very seriously, sheriff. My guns are all under lock and key, and Michael does not have a key. Besides, I have been very conscientious about teaching him gun safety."

"That's good. But have you had any occasion when you've noticed that one of your guns is missing or not where it should be?"

"You do think Michael might have killed that woman, don't you?"

"I have tried to explain my position, Mr. Nagle. Mrs. Neuberger is dead and someone shot her, almost certainly someone on that bird hike. There were nearly 20 people on the hike, and I'm interested in all of them - their relationship with Mrs. Neuberger, their guns, *everything* that would help me to identify the person who killed her. Or, just as important, to eliminate them as suspects. So, please, try to answer my question."

"No, I can't recall any occasion when one of my guns was missing."

"Thank you. I know this has been very difficult for you, and I appreciate your help. I suspect that Michael needs your support more right now than at just about any other time in his young life. Take good care of him."

CHAPTER 33

Agnes McKendrick had always been a relatively self confident woman. She was pleased with the life she had led, and she harbored very few regrets about things she had done or not gotten around to doing. But now, in the wake of Vivian Neuberger's tragic death, she had to admit that her self confidence was on the wane. It wasn't that she sorely missed Vivian and worried that her death might cost the Crooked Lake Birders Club some of its members, or even, heaven forbid, its very existence. Vivian was a relative latecomer to the club and had not become more than a casual acquaintance. They had never developed a social relationship, and although she would never admit it to anyone else, she was somewhat wary of Vivian's considerable knowledge of birds. Not that the high school science teacher had ever flaunted her ornithological bona fides. But she did know her birds, and Agnes couldn't get it out of her mind that if she were ever to make a wrong identification Vivian would be aware of it, even if she never corrected her. Still, the woman would be missed.

As for the future of the birders club, there might initially be some reluctance to go about business as usual. Some would find it unseemly, and they might actually finesse the next scheduled outing. But the club would soldier on because most of its members found pleasure in getting together to traipse through the woods or canoe through the lake's outlets. Indeed, it was almost certain that someone would speak up and insist that Vivian would want the club to thrive. There would always be a Crooked Lake Birders Club because it would be a way of honoring Vivian.

Nonetheless, Agnes was doing more worrying than was her wont. And she knew why. Two things bothered her. The first was that someone in the club, someone whom she had considered either a friend or at least a person who shared her love of birds, had deliberately killed a fellow birder. Of course there were those who thought the shooter had been a hunter, but Agnes was certain that that was not the case. She was confident that the sheriff shared her opinion. She had thought about it for several days, and had always come to the same conclusion: the killer was one of her own. Unfortunately, she found no solace in that conclusion. It meant that unless the killer was unmasked and dealt with severely, she would be looking forward to future bird hikes with a murderer in their midst.

The other thing that bothered her was the problematic future of Anson's Grove. She loved the Grove. She had rescued it from neglect and she thought she was responsible for turning it into one of the area's premier retreats from the encroachment of greedy developers. It held the promise of relative pristine wilderness for years, hopefully decades, to come. And if her plans came to fruition, it could be the setting for a memorial to Vivian Neuberger. Agnes had not devoted much thought to that possibility, but once the idea had come to mind it rapidly became something of an obsession. Vivian may not have needed such a memorial, but the Crooked Lake Birders Club did, and Agnes was prepared to fight for it. But now a man named Grandi had come into the picture, and he had both the money and the clout to threaten her plan for the memorial and her vision of the Grove's future.

She had just finished her second cup of morning coffee when her growing anxiety about the future of Anson's Grove led to a decision to pay it a visit. Agnes recognized the impulse as nothing more than a way to stoke her anxiety. But it might also strengthen her resolve to do something about Grandi, not that she could think of anything she would be able to do. He had not made a public announcement of his intention to acquire the Grove, but she had convinced herself that that was what he planned to do. His performance at the fracking discussion in Dickerson had only increased her certainty that Anson's Grove was in jeopardy.

As she climbed the hill from the road to the Grove, she actually felt a surge of her old self confidence. The sight of the wooded area where she had so recently led a bird hike made Grandi's threat seem less urgent. When she got to the Grove, she found a nearby spot which was cool and sat down, her back against a lofty red oak. She had been there less than a minute when she heard someone.

"Well, well, what have we here?"

Agnes half rose to her knees and looked in the direction from which the voice had come. There, standing not ten feet from her, was Frank Grandi. He was dressed in a pair of tan shorts, a black T-shirt, and sturdy sandals. Her first thought was one of vulnerability. She was alone, a long way from help, and facing a man she distrusted, a man she suddenly feared. Agnes scrambled to her feet and backed toward what she thought of as the greater safety of the woods.

"Please, Mrs. McKendrick. I'm harmless. Just look at me." He held his open hands out in front of him, then proceeded to turn the pockets of his shorts inside out. "See? No gun. Like you, I thought it would be a good idea to take a walk in the woods."

Agnes braced herself against the tree. She realized that she was overreacting. This was a man who might take possession of Anson's Grove in order to turn it into a fracking site; he was not a man who was likely to be contemplating rape.

"What are you doing here?" she demanded.

"It's like I said, I'm taking a walk. Nice day for it, don't you think? When I saw you coming up through the vineyard I thought 'how nice, I'll have company.'"

"I prefer to walk alone," she said.

"Really? I thought you usually led a pack of bird watchers. Where are they today? Perhaps Mrs. Neuberger's unfortunate death has convinced them that bird hikes aren't quite the lark they're cracked up to be. Oh, sorry, that's a pretty bad pun."

Grandi wore a smile that Agnes regarded as calculatedly diabolical. He's toying with me, she thought.

"I had hoped to have the Grove to myself today," she said. "I wanted to think about the memorial to Vivian Neuberger."

"Oh, yes, the memorial. A nice idea. But like I said the other day, it might be a better idea to scatter her ashes over Crooked Lake. More appropriate symbolism, don't you think?"

"Mr. Grandi, I'm not in the mood to discuss funeral arrangements for Vivian Neuberger with you. If you don't mind, I shall be going back to my car and leave you to your morning constitutional."

She set off through the vineyard.

"I'm sorry you have to go," he called after her, "but you should know that this is not what I'd call a constitutional. I prefer to think of it as research."

Back in her car, Agnes took a few deep breaths and then pulled out her cell phone. It still contained the number of the sheriff's office, and she quickly dialed it.

After identifying herself, she asked if it might be possible to see the sheriff. It's very important, she told Ms. Franks, and said that it would be best if she could meet with her today. It was arranged that the sheriff could see her at 11:30.

It was only five after ten, and Agnes was already in Cumberland, nearly an hour and a half before her appointment. She was too eager to share her news with the sheriff to do anything else; in any event, there was not enough time to do any serious shopping. As a result she drove into the parking lot of the sheriff's department, climbed the stairs to her office, and advised Ms. Franks that she knew she was early but was quite happy to wait.

Carol was surprised to hear that Mrs. McKendrick had already arrived. Curious as to what it was that had prompted such an early arrival, she stepped out into the waiting room and greeted the leader of the Crooked Lake Birders Club with a cheery hello.

"I want to apologize for breaking into your schedule on such short notice," Agnes said to the sheriff. "But I think you'll agree it's important. Please go ahead and finish what you are doing. I'll be right here."

Carol was busy, but not too busy to keep Mrs. McKendrick waiting until 11:30.

"Give me three minutes, and we'll talk," she said and gave JoAnne a thumbs up sign as she went back to her desk. Exactly three minutes later she reappeared at the door and motioned for Agnes to come in.

"Care for coffee?" she asked her visitor.

"That's nice of you. Could I have two teaspoons of sugar?"

"As you like it." She buzzed JoAnne with the order.

"Now, let's hear what it is that brings you to my office today."

Agnes McKendrick wasted no time on preliminaries.

"I have just come from Anson's Grove, where I ran into Frank Grandi. He's the one who shot Vivian Neuberger."

This was obviously not what the sheriff had expected to hear.

"Frank Grandi?"

"Yes. You may not know him, but he's the man who's going to buy up the Grove in order to be in on the ground floor when they start fracking around here."

Carol had heard that Grandi was an advocate of fracking, not to mention a man of considerable wealth. And Kevin had reported Grandi's exchange with Agnes about Anson's Grove at the meeting in Dickerson. But even more important was Agnes's assertion that

Grandi, a man who had not been on the bird hike in the Grove, was responsible for Vivian's death. That Grandi might be contemplating buying up the Grove was certainly possible, although she had heard nothing official to that effect. As far as his responsibility for killing Vivian, her skepticism immediately kicked in.

"Let's back up a minute, Mrs. McKendrick. How do you know that he killed Mrs. Neuberger?"

"It has to be him. He's hell bent on controlling fracking around the lake, and Vivian was his most respected and outspoken opponent. She'd have stood in his way both on the fracking issue generally and on the Grove deal in particular. Now she's dead, and he's up there in the Grove casing the area for when fracking gets a green light. It looks pretty obvious."

"But our governor has banned fracking."

"That ban won't last, sheriff. Mark my word."

Carol knew there was no point in arguing the matter, so she turned her attention to the more immediately important subject.

"But Mr. Grandi surely didn't tell you that he had killed Mrs. Neuberger, did he?"

"Oh, of course not. He's not that dumb. But he's so cocksure of himself, you can just about tell what's going on his head."

"Did he ever say anything about being around the Grove when Vivian was shot?"

Agnes began to look a bit unsettled by the sheriff's questions. There seemed to be some doubt about her news regarding Grandi.

"I know I don't have what I think they call a slam dunk on Grandi's guilt. But that's why I came to you. You'll know how to corner him, get him to confess. What I know is what comes across when I talk with him. It isn't what he says, it's the vibes he gives off. I figured if you would spend some time with him, you'd see what I mean."

This is going to require tact, Carol thought. There may be something in what she says. Very probably not, but I can't simply dismiss her theory of the murder.

"Mrs. McKendrick, I'm very grateful to you for sharing this with me. I shall certainly make it a point to question him, both about his plans for the Grove and about Vivian Neuberger. It is bound to be sensitive. We can't come right out and accuse him of anything, but we have an obligation to ask hard questions. It would help us if you refrained from talking to other people about Mr. Grandi, even close friends of yours. Word would be sure to get back to him, and then he could well clam up. Do we understand each other?"

"We do, and thanks for hearing me out."

"May I ask if you have any plans for another outing for the club? I've been afraid that it might be difficult to get your people interested in another hike so soon after this tragedy."

Carol thought the question would demonstrate her sympathy, and hopefully atone for the fact that she hadn't immediately embraced Agnes's theory that Grandi had murdered Neuberger.

"I haven't decided on next steps," she replied. "I'll have to sound out some of the regulars."

"That sounds like a good idea. I suspect that Vivian would have wanted you to carry on."

"I like to think so," Agnes said as she walked out of Carol's office.

CHAPTER 34

Larry Finch celebrated his 57th birthday all by himself, sitting at the counter of the Yates Diner and trying to convince himself that the meatloaf and mashed potatoes were as good as the waitress had promised. It had been a very difficult two weeks. The good mood that he had brought back from New Orleans had vanished the moment Sallie reported that Vivian Neuberger was dead. The news had been so devastating that he hadn't even made an effort to feign mild regret or, at the very least, indifference. Instead he had wallowed in self pity, admitting to his wife what she obviously already knew, that he had been in love with Vivian. The result, quite predictably, was that he had not only lost Vivian but Sallie as well. Not that their relationship had been particularly close. But they had settled into a reasonably comfortable middle-of-life relationship soon after their marriage that might have survived his affair with Vivian Neuberger if he had been a bit more discrete and hadn't gone to pieces with the news of her death.

He and Sallie still slept in the same bed, but they didn't talk a lot. She had done something special for his birthday each year since their marriage - something like a weekend trip to the Jersey Shore, tickets to a Yankees game. Not this time. There had been no hint that she remembered the date. That morning she had announced over breakfast that she and a few woman friends were getting together for supper and an amateur theatre production in nearby Watkins. It hadn't been necessary for her to express regrets that he'd have to shift for himself that evening; her announcement of her plans was made without apology.

He was annoyed with himself that he had done nothing to snap out of his funk. While it was true that he had handled a meeting with the sheriff without giving her a hint that his life had fallen apart, he wasn't, on reflection, that pleased with their conversation. It would have been foolish, of course to confess to her that he had been having an affair with Vivian. In retrospect, however, he regretted that he had not asked the sheriff more questions, had not tried to tease out of her more information about her investigation.

He took a sip of coffee and found himself wondering whether Bill Neuberger might have been aware that his wife had been having an affair. He quickly brushed the thought aside. How could Bill have known? Larry had been extremely careful. He had visited Vivian only late in the evening, well after dark, and *never* when Bill was around. In fact, he had always made sure that no one else was around. He had made it a practice never to depart the Neuberger house until he could see no car on the road, no late night walker in the neighborhood. He had even gone so far as to insist that he and Vivian never make use of the Neubergers' bedroom, thereby avoiding the remote possibility that they would leave some small clue to what was going on. No, he thought, Bill could not have known of Vivian's unfaithfulness unless she herself had carelessly said something which planted a seed of doubt, and he could not imagine that she would have done that.

It was not until he had finished the meatloaf and was sampling the diner's apple pie that something else occurred to him. Something he should have thought of before, something that figuratively sent a chill down his spine and literally caused him to drop his fork on the diner's linoleum floor. If Bill Neuberger could not have known that his wife had been having an extra-marital affair and hence could not have killed her, there was someone who did know about the affair - his own wife. Sallie had obviously not killed her wayward spouse. But was it possible that she had killed the other woman? Why had that possibility not come to his mind earlier, even on the day she had told him about Vivian's death and the fact that she had known for some time about his affair with her?

Sallie had never said anything that could be construed as a hint that it was she who had fired the fatal shot in Anson's Grove. Larry thought he knew his wife pretty well, and he found it very difficult to imagine her as a killer. Or was it simply that he had never before done something which might have led her to become one? This was not something that could be contemplated in the Yates Diner over a piece of apple pie.

Larry paid his check and walked the short block to where he had parked his car. He sat behind the wheel for several minutes, trying to decide where to go and what to do. He didn't really wish to go home. The house had become as unwelcoming as had Sallie, and he was becoming adept at finding excuses to leave it early and return to it late. But if he were to confront his wife and ask her point blank whether she had killed Vivian, he could think of no place better suited to do it than in their own home for the last five years. He assumed that Sallie would be back sometime around ten o'clock, although it was possible that she would kill more time in the hope that he would already be asleep when she got home.

Posing the question of whether she had killed Vivian would require more than Larry's normal quotient of courage, so when he arrived home he went straight to their liquor cabinet for what would prove to be the first of three glasses of Scotch. He spent the first twenty minutes pacing the floor and practicing what he thought would be the best way to raise the issue. Unfortunately, nothing sounded right to him, so that when Sallie walked in the front door he still had no good idea of just what he was going to say. For a brief moment he almost lost his nerve altogether. But her withering comment that she hoped his evening had been fun snapped him out of it.

"I'd like to talk with you," he said, motioning to the vacant couch. "I'm having Scotch. How about you?"

"There's nothing to talk about, Larry. I'd rather catch the ten o'clock news, and I can do it without Scotch."

"What I have to say trumps the ten o'clock news, Sallie. So let's sit down. You caught me off guard with your story of Vivian's death when I got back from New Orleans. I failed to ask a question I should have raised at the time. I'd like to do it now."

He took a seat across from the couch.

"Please sit down."

It was curiosity, not a desire to do what her husband ordered, that persuaded Sallie to take a seat.

"Here's my question. And I'd appreciate an honest answer. Did you kill Vivian Neuberger?"

Although this was almost certainly not the question Sallie had expected, she didn't bat an eye.

"I'm sure you do not want me to say that it was I who killed dear Vivian. So I shall put your mind at rest and tell you it wasn't I. If I had been of a mind to kill someone for this extra-curricular fling of yours, that someone would have been you, not Vivian. So please continue to grieve for her, but don't make matters worse by blaming me for your sorrow."

"You swear that you had nothing whatsoever to do with her death?"

"Larry, let's not become melodramatic. I'm a woman, remember? A member of the weaker sex, and a very small one at that. What is more, I do not own a gun. And inasmuch as you aren't a hunter, I couldn't very well have borrowed your gun to get rid of poor Vivian. Have you ever known me to hurt anybody? Why, I've never hurt a bird. I've even been known to go out of my way to avoid stepping on a wooly bear caterpillar. Now is there anything else you'd like to ask me, because I would like to take my shoes off and rest my tired feet."

Sallie had said just what he had expected her to say, but he wasn't satisfied. While it was possible that Vivian's killer was someone he didn't even know, including a careless hunter, the most logical candidates were her husband and his own wife. He knew this, but it was doubtful that the sheriff did. He did not believe that Bill Neuberger was aware that Vivian had been unfaithful, but he had to concede that he might be wrong. Sallie, on the other hand, was well aware that Vivian had strayed from the marriage bed and who had led her astray. Larry's problem was that he wanted Vivian's killer to pay for taking her life, yet he did not want to be dragged into the investigation of her death. He would have to speak with the sheriff again, but he had no idea what he would say to her. Perhaps it was already too late to undo the damage his impetuous affair with Vivian had set in motion.

CHAPTER 35

They had not even had the farewell party for Jim Barrett, but Erin Dockery was already on board. At least she was wrapping up the paper work and other steps necessary to put on a uniform and start patrolling. Carol had introduced her to the other officers and debated how she would break her in. The latter was also high on Erin's agenda. Now Erin was at Carol's door, ready for her marching orders.

"I had't imagined there'd be so much to do before I went on duty," she said.

"Oh, yes, we are very bureaucratic. We don't want anything falling between the cracks. But our agenda right now is to let you see what it's like to be part of Cumberland County's law enforcement team. You'll get started partnering with Officer Parsons. He's usually out patrolling the lake, but he offered to take you under his wing."

"I'm not sure I can remember everyone, but isn't he the older man, the one with that little mustache?"

"You're very observant. But I wouldn't want you to think of him as 'the older man.' He's still a long way from retirement, and I doubt that he wants to be known as our senior citizen. You did talk with Officer Barrett, didn't you? He's the man you're replacing."

"Yes, I did. He's very nice. He told me all about the problem of fracking. It seems to be a big issue around here, and he thinks it's a bad idea."

"Well, it's one issue this department normally has nothing to do with. But it's an issue that has cropped up in a case we're investigating right now. You won't be involved in the Neuberger case, at least not directly, but it happens to be our biggest problem at the moment, so it's probably a good idea to give you some idea what it's about."

"Two or three of the officers mentioned it. Especially your deputy sheriff. Do you think he has a problem with me coming on the force?"

Carol was surprised by the question.

"I don't think so, but why do you ask?"

"It wasn't anything he said, and I'm probably imagining it. But I thought he looked sort of - I don't know, maybe stern. Like he wasn't sure whether I'd fit in."

"I'm sure you will, Erin. Sam's a former marine, likes to do things by the book. The fact is we haven't had any change in personnel in quite a few years, and he hasn't had any experience working with a woman. Other than me, that is, and we get along just fine. He was in complete agreement that you were the applicant we should hire, so I'm sure you misread him."

"I'm glad to hear that," Erin said. She sounded genuinely relieved.

"Okay, now how about a little background on the Neuberger case. It's mostly Sam and I that have been dealing with it, but all the officers are familiar with what happened and more or less where we stand. You ought to know what they know."

Carol proceeded to give Erin a quick report on the case, not expecting her to ask any questions. To her surprise she did.

"I don't mean to interrupt, but what you said about rumors that this woman was having a relationship with one of the bird watchers' husbands is interesting. It reminds me of what happened in a book I read recently. Of course it wasn't about bird hikes or things like that, but this woman in the book killed the woman her husband was doing it with. You'd think a woman would be maddest at her own husband, but in the book she went after the other woman. Just a coincidence, I suppose."

Carol reminded Erin that they had no proof that Vivian Neuberger had been having an affair with Sallie Finch's husband, much less any evidence that Sallie had shot Vivian. But she was interested in her comment.

"Was this book you're describing a work of fiction?"

"No. It was a translation of a book in French about a national scandal in France. I can't think of the name, but I'll check it out and let you know the title and the author."

"I'd appreciate that." Carol was interested in Erin's reading habits. She also realized that she'd had few if any conversations recently with young women about sex and sexual relationships. Today's crop of millennials was undoubtedly more sophisticated, or at least more aware about such things than her own generation had been.

When Carol left Erin in the hands of Bill Parsons, she found herself thinking hard about this new recruit. She had known that she was young, and she had looked it in her interview. Somehow, however, she now looked even younger in her uniform. She had been well dressed when she showed up for the interview, but her outfit had been that of a college student. For some reason the uniform made her look smaller even if it was a good fit. Carol had wanted to hire a woman, and she had. What is more, she had wanted to hire this woman. But for the first time she was just the least bit worried that there might be men out there, men that Erin would encounter while on patrol, who would see her as a pushover.

She set aside those thoughts and turned her attention to the Neuberger case. The last person she had discussed it with, other than Erin Dockery, had been Agnes McKendrick, and Agnes had apparently become obsessed with the idea that Frank Grandi was the one who had killed Vivian. She was sure that Agnes was dead wrong, but she had already given some thought to talking with Grandi and perhaps it was time to do so. With Officer Byrnes help, she located him and had JoAnne put a call through. Not unexpectedly, he was not at home. Her message was brief and said nothing about her agenda. In fact, she wasn't sure she had an agenda. She simply indicated that she would appreciate it if he would call her back so that they could discuss a mutually agreeable time to get together. If by some odd chance Agnes was on to something, he would have a very good idea what was on the sheriff's mind. If not, he might wonder, but in all likelihood he would return her call and agree to a meeting.

Thinking about Frank Grandi as a hypothetical suspect in the Neuberger case led her to some thoughts about the shooting, which in turn prompted the question as to why she had received no forensic ballistics report. One thing led to another, and Carol was soon busily reflecting on her own feelings about guns. She and Kevin had debated the issue from time to time. Like many big city dwellers, he was of the opinion that there were too many guns in too many hands, and too few restrictions on how they could be purchased and where they could be carried. Carol, a long time resident of a much less thickly populated part of the country with a far larger number of hunters per capita, had never given the issue as much thought as he had. There had been exceptions, of course. She had been as horrified as Kevin had by the horrific shootings in Newtown, Aurora, and other places, and disappointed that the Congress had not found the courage to address the problem. But now she was confronted with her own indefensible case of gun violence. Somebody had had a grievance with Vivian Neuberger and had taken it upon himself - or was it herself? - to use a gun to solve the problem. The NRA's mantra that the way to deal with bad guys carrying guns was for more good guys to carry more guns would have been no help to Vivian.

Carol refocussed on the problem of why she had heard nothing regarding what had been learned about the gun that had killed Vivian. She was about to reach for the phone, when JoAnne called and reported that she had a visitor.

"Who is it?" Carol didn't want to talk with 'a visitor.'

"He's one of those people who were looking for birds. His name is Peter Hornaday."

Carol tried to remember what a man named Hornaday looked like, but was unsuccessful. Probably one of the people Sam had interviewed. She had other things on her mind, but she knew that she shouldn't turn away anybody connected in any way to the Neuberger case.

"Okay, send him in."

CHAPTER 36

The man who entered the sheriff's office was tall and thin and white haired. Carol had never seen him before.

"Good morning, Mr. Hornaday. I'm afraid we haven't met."

"That's right. You and that deputy sheriff of yours must have divided us up and I got him as my interrogator."

Carol knew that Sam liked to treat these interviews as interrogations. She wondered if he had told Mr. Hornaday that he was being interrogated.

"Just chance that it was Officer Bridges you talked with. I'm glad to meet you. What is it that brings you here today?"

"It has to do with the question your deputy didn't ask me the other day. I thought maybe you'd want to know about it, and I was in Cumberland to do some shopping. So here I am."

The way he said it suggested that Mr. Hornaday just might be critical of Sam and wanted the sheriff to know it.

"I'm glad you stopped by," Carol said. "Why don't you tell me what the question is that Officer Bridges didn't ask you."

"It didn't come to me until the other day when I was talking with Agnes McKendrick. She was trying to get a sense of whether we're all interested in planning another birding trip. She wants to honor Vivian Neuberger by keeping the club going. You know, it's that old carry-on spirit. Anyway, that's not why I'm here. Agnes was going on about how she'd talked with you at some length, mostly about those of our members who wandered off on their own during the hike. It's pretty obvious what's on her mind. She figures that whoever shot Vivian was one of the ones who didn't stick with the group. Unless, of course, you believe that some fool of a hunter did it, and I'm willing to bet you don't buy that. Agnes is a worrier. She worries about most everything. And one of the things that's worrying her is that while she knows who went wandering off during the hike, she doesn't know when they left and where they went. Of course that's because she's always out in front of us, leading the pack, eyes on the treetops. But I not only know who left the group, I know where they went. All except Sallie Finch, that is. Officer Bridges didn't ask, but I think you ought to know."

It was clear that Peter Hornaday had spoken with Mrs. McKendrick before her meeting with Frank Grandi had changed her mind and convinced her that he was Vivian's killer. If he really knew where the wandering birders had gone, Carol certainly wanted him to share that information with her. But she was surprised that he would know such a thing. Had they confided in him? It seemed unlikely.

"This is interesting, Mr. Hornaday, and it could be very important. Let's take them one at a time. How about Mr. Raymore?"

"He didn't leave right away," Hornaday said. "But he has no patience with Agnes. He knows much more about birds than she does. When he left, he didn't try to hide what he was up to. He just slipped off up the hill towards the west side of the Grove. Didn't say anything to anyone, just set off as if he was going to walk to Cumberland."

"Where was he going? To Cumberland?"

Hornaday laughed.

"Oh, no. Cumberland must be fifteen, maybe twenty miles away from the Grove."

"So where was he going?"

"I can't say. But he was heading up the hill, away from the rest of us, farther away from the cars."

"But you said you knew where the birders went. He didn't tell you where he was going?"

"Raymore never tells anyone anything. He's a law unto himself."

"Let me make sure I understand you. You don't know where Mr. Raymore was going?"

"I'm afraid not. Like I said, I know where he went but not where he was going. He went up and over the hill. That's important, don't you think? It was the opposite direction form where Mrs. Neuberger went, so it's unlikely he was her killer."

Carol now realized that Peter Hornaday's information, while possibly important, was a far cry from vital to her investigation. Raymore's going 'up and over the hill' didn't mean that he hadn't later reversed course and headed back toward the vineyard.

"So what you're telling me is that you only know in which direction Agnes's wanderers went when they left the group."

"Yes, but that would seem to be critical. Remember, Mrs. Neuberger was killed down hill from the Grove, down in the vineyard."

"Okay," Carol said, deciding not to sound dismissive of Hornaday's logic. "Tell me about where Mrs. Neuberger went."

"She was the first one to take off. She left only about twenty minutes after we started the hike. And she headed in the opposite direction from the one Raymore took. I know it sounds melodramatic, but she looked like she was off to the vineyard and her rendezvous with death."

Carol didn't know anything about Peter Hornaday, but she wondered if his 'rendezvous with death' line meant that he read poetry.

"How about her husband?"

"Now that was interesting. She had only been gone about five minutes when he, too, decided to leave the rest of us. When he passed by me, unlike the others, he leaned over and whispered 'gotta take a leak - too much coffee.' I thought it was kind of funny, not at all like him. But what's important, he never came back."

Hornaday hadn't said in what direction Bill Neuberger had gone to relieve himself, so Carol asked.

"Like Raymore, he went away from the vineyard." In this case, however, Hornaday did not choose to absolve him of responsibility for Vivian's murder. Carol wondered why, but chose to press on to the other wandering birders.

"You say you don't know where Sallie Finch went. Why not?"

"We came across some strange looking mushrooms, got to talking about 'em, and she decided to take a rest. We left her sitting under a tree, so I never saw her again during the hike."

"Which leaves young Nagle."

"Right. Nagle and Cone. Don't forget him. The Nagle kid was obviously bored, but he stuck it out until not long before the time we heard Mel hollering to get our attention. I think he figured he'd beat everyone back to the cars. Anyway, that's where he seemed to be heading."

"What about Cone? I think he's the only other birder who didn't stay with Agnes."

"He decided to take a walk not long after Raymore did, and he set off straight for the Vineyard. Which I thought was strange. He'd told me he'd read something somewhere about an unusually late migration of warblers, but you see warblers in the woods, not in an open field. Anyway, he's supposedly an expert, so I took his word for it."

"Do you make it a habit to keep an eye on what your fellow birders are doing?" Carol asked. She wasn't sure whether Hornaday would interpret the question as a subtle criticism. But he didn't.

"When I join one of Agnes's hikes, I do it because I need exercise. I'm one of the club's senior citizens, as you may have learned, so you won't find me leading the pack." He chuckled. "I guess it's because I bring up the rear that I'm able to see what my colleagues are doing."

"I appreciate you sharing this information with me, Mr. Hornaday. Let me ask if you yourself have any ideas about what happened to Vivian Neuberger. Our investigation is in high gear, but we always like to consider what other interested parties think, and all of you birders are certainly interested parties."

"Oh, absolutely. It's all most of us talk about. There's been some speculation, but I think people are afraid that naming names will just lead to trouble in the ranks. But you asked, so let me take a guess - just so you don't tell. I've got a hunch it'll be either Finch or Cone. Pure guesswork in Finch's case. With Cone, it's because he was obviously the closest to her when she was shot. Frankly, I can't imagine that either of them did it, but once you eliminate the others, who's left?"

Carol found it interesting that Hornaday had eliminated the others. And that he had included Sallie Finch.

"Any reason to suspect Finch other than that you didn't see her leave?"

"No." But then he had a second thought. "Well, there's the fact that I don't much like her. Sorry, that's no reason to finger her, is it?"

"And why don't you like Mrs. Finch?"

"Good question, sheriff, because I'm not sure that I have a good answer."

When Carol later reflected on this strange meeting with Peter Hornaday, she wasn't quite sure what had been the most important thing she had learned. But she found it interesting that he had come to her office to offer his unsolicited thoughts on who might have killed Vivian Neuberger.

CHAPTER 37

When Hornaday left, Carol assumed that she would have some time to deal with the problem of the missing report from forensic ballistics. Once again, however, her agenda was put on hold, this time by a call from Jason Eglin. He had indicated earlier that he would like to sit down with her to apologize for the way he had treated both Officer Barrett and JoAnne Franks. But from her point of view the matter was not urgent. Cooler heads had already put the subject in proper perspective, and Carol had more important business on her plate. But courtesy and the need to keep open lines to town officials required that she agree to meet with Eglin, with the result that the two of them were at the Southport diner for lunch just an hour and twenty minutes later.

The sheriff had already taken a place in a booth when the commissioner walked in. He spotted her quickly, shook hands, and slid into the seat across from her.

"Glad you could make the time," he said. "From what I hear, your days are pretty much taken up by that terrible shooting of the school teacher."

"You're right about that. Who would ever have thought that someone would gun down someone like Vivian Neuberger? We've had our share of problems recently, but this one is really beyond the pale. But let's not get into that. How are things in your bailiwick?"

"All things considered, not bad. The usual problems of under-funded this and that, complaints about assessments, you know. But I needn't pretend that we have it worse than you."

"Before we get serious about anything, why don't we put our orders in. I'm looking forward to something edible for a change - too many days of take out in the office."

They studied their menus, made their decisions, and turned their attention to Eglin's reason for seeking the meeting.

"In the first place, I've never given you a proper apology for the way I came barging into your office about your man Barrett. Bad judgment on my part."

"It's history, Jason. No need to apologize." Actually, Carol was grateful for the apology, even if the issue had become moot.

"I guess I was also too hard on Officer Barrett. It's a shame, isn't it, how this fracking business gets under our skin? You didn't need to let Barrett go."

"If it will make you feel better, Jason, I didn't let him go. He's been one of my best officers. He resigned to take a job with an environmental organization. He'll probably continue to be an opponent of fracking, although we had a frank conversation about it and he really believes that fracking would be a good idea if only there were guarantees that it was environmentally safe."

Eglin gave the sheriff a smile and shrugged his shoulders.

"I'm glad to hear that. It's been on my conscience that he was sacked. But what I really wanted to get together to talk about is Frank Grandi, not Barrett."

"Grandi? That's interesting. Agnes McKendrick and I were discussing him just the other day. He's supposed to be pro-fracking, but you already know that."

"That's the problem. I think he's right, of course, but Frank is a hot head, and, well, to be perfectly honest, I think he hurts the cause more than he helps it. I know you don't agree with me about fracking, which is why it's rather awkward to ask for your help. But I've been wondering if you could find a way to speak to him."

Carol was surprised. Jason Eglin had a different agenda than she had assumed.

"What is it you'd like me to talk with him about?"

The arrival of lunch interrupted their conversation momentarily.

"It has to do with Vivian Neuberger, the woman who was shot up in Anson's Grove."

Eglin paused, as if he were trying to decide just how to phrase what he wanted to say.

"Grandi has never come right out and said he wants to buy that property, but I'm sure he does. Unfortunately, he also goes around poor mouthing the Neuberger woman. She was anti-fracking, as you probably know. She was also well liked, apparently an excellent teacher. But she made her position on fracking clear in her science classes, and that really irked Grandi. He saw her as the leader of the opposition, and when she died he was practically gloating. It's beginning to look to me as if he's actually hurting his - or should I say our

- cause more than he's helping it. You can't go around disparaging the Neuberger woman without making her a martyr, and that's what I'm afraid he's doing."

"You're probably right, but what is it that you think I can do about it?" Carol asked.

"I don't pretend to know anything about your investigation of the shooting in the Grove, but common sense tells me that what happened up there gives you a reason to remain interested in the place. In other words, you won't want Grandi to be taking over your crime scene. Am I right?"

"I doubt that I'd have put it that way, but you're right that my office is still very much interested in the Grove. As far as Grandi buying it, if that's your worry, I frankly don't even know who owns title to that property."

"I'd bet that Grandi knows. And he's not going to tell. I've done a little research, and from what I've discovered it's a very complicated matter, not just something you can go to the courthouse and look up in a few minutes. I was hoping that you could use your investigation to put a lid on the possibility of a preemptive move by Grandi."

"That sounds like a pretty dicey scenario. If I were to raise the issue of title to the Grove, wouldn't he just be encouraged to move faster? Frankly, I don't know that I have authority to prevent a real estate transaction in a case like this. Nothing like it has come up in my years as sheriff."

"What about McKendrick's idea of creating a Neuberger memorial grave site in the Grove? Is that possible?"

It was dawning on Carol that Jason Eglin was doing his best to draw her into an intramural contest for leadership of the local pro-fracking community. If she were to have a conversation with Grandi, she had assumed it would have to do with Vivian's shooting and the possibility that he might have been the guilty party. It had never occurred to her that she would be encouraged to find a way to block Grandi from taking over Anson's Grove.

When they had settled the bill and gone their separate ways, Carol remained undecided as to whether she would seek a meeting with Frank Grandi. What she *had* decided was that she had to find out who in fact owned title to Anson's Grove. It wasn't until she walked out of the diner into the town square that she remembered that she was only a few short blocks from the Nagle residence. She decided to see how Michael was doing.

It was an obviously tired Fran Nagle who came to the door.

"Hello, sheriff. Come on in." There was no smile, but there was no sign that her visitor was not welcome.

"I promise to be brief, but I was in Southport and thought I'd see how Michael is doing."

"We wish we knew. Dr. Benjamin has been talking with a specialist he knows, and we're trying to set up a time to take Michael up to Rochester to see him. I think it's going to be Friday. Chief Bellman has been a prince about this. The Kuypers, they're not happy, as you can imagine, but we're lucky. Their boy didn't get cut as badly as we first feared, and if this specialist can help as much as Benjamin thinks he can, my guess is that they'll not press charges, just settle for us paying doctor's bills."

"It sounds like busy days around here."

"You can't imagine. The best news is that Michael seems to have calmed down. I mean he knows he's in trouble and he's sort of laying low. Spends almost all of his time in his room."

"Do you think it would be all right if I said hello?"

Fran Nagle looked doubtful.

"He sees you and he'll start thinking again about Mrs. Neuberger and that shooting business. There's no special reason why you have to see him, is there?"

"No, I was just anxious to let him know I'm concerned."

"I can tell him you asked about him, but I don't want to get him all riled up again."

"Okay, let's do it your way. If something comes up that I need to see him about, I'll call ahead. In the meanwhile, best wishes with the specialist. You'll be taking the drawings along when you see him, won't you?"

"Dr. Benjamin says we have to."

"Good. And thank you for the update."

When Carol left the Nagle house she didn't look back. But she had the feeling that Fran Nagle was watching her down the front walk to her car.

CHAPTER 38

Carol had long been interested in - and skeptical of - coincidences. She and Kevin had discussed the subject many times over the years while she had served as sheriff of Cumberland County. It was later in the day of her strange lunch with Jason Eglin that something occurred to her which started her thinking once more about coincidences.

She had been reflecting on the Neuberger case and the cast of characters it had brought to her attention. Crooked Lake and its environs had what Carol had always thought of as a stable population. Summer vacationers came and went, of course, but the overwhelming majority of year around residents came from families which had lived on or close to the lake for many years. Their grandparents, even their great grandparents, had experienced the impact of prohibition on the area's wineries and had seen cars displace horse drawn carriages on the streets of Southport.

But as Carol thought about the people she had been interviewing and thinking about in her effort to identify Vivian Neuberger's killer, she realized that several of those she was coming to think of as persons of interest in the case had actually moved to Crooked Lake fairly recently. The Neubergers had made it their home for only a little more than two years, Paul Raymore for half a year less. Somebody had said something about Sallie Finch also being a relatively late arrival, although Carol knew less about her than she did about the others. And now the latest entry on her roster of persons of interest, Frank Grandi, had been spoken of by both Jim Barrett and Jason Eglin as yet another newcomer to the shores of Crooked Lake.

Was it, as seemed most likely, simply a coincidence? Or had some of them known each other somewhere else, and had that relationship had something to do with the death of Vivian Neuberger? Carol was sitting behind the wheel of her car at the intersection of Market and Vine Streets, waiting for the light to change. She took advantage of the moment to peer into the mirror and take a good look at herself. The face that looked back at her was that of a sensible woman. Carol decided to dismiss this latest flight of fancy. After all, the odds that Paul Raymore or Sallie Finch or Frank Grandi had known Vivian Neuberger prior to moving to the lake were so long that there was no point in wasting time contemplating the possibility. Whatever it was that had led to Vivian's death had germinated right here in Cumberland County. An affair between Vivian and Larry Finch? A mentally disturbed student's hatred for his teacher? An overwrought fracking supporter's frustration with the leader of the opposition? And nothing had emerged to suggest that Raymore had any reason to shoot Vivian; Carol doubted that anything would emerge. But if it did, it would almost certainly have developed right here on Crooked Lake, not in some other place, at some other time.

By the time that she got back to the office, Carol had convinced herself that it was indeed but a coincidence that so many of the people involved in the Neuberger case had only recently become denizens of Crooked Lake. She had made up her mind to focus instead on the puzzling absence of a report from ballistics.

"You're a very popular person," JoAnne told the sheriff as she passed her desk.

"Oh, how so?"

"Three calls, everyone says it's urgent."

"Well, they're going to have to wait. Right now I've got to spend some time on the missing ballistics report."

"That's one of the three calls. It's Dr. Crawford. Do you want me to call him back, say you're here?"

Carol knew that Doc wasn't a ballistics expert, but he would have to have collaborated with someone who was. She told JoAnne to get him on the phone.

"On second thought," Carol said, "see if he can come over here sometime this afternoon."

"I think that's his plan. I figured you'd want to see him, but I didn't know when you'd be back."

"Well, I'm back. By the way, you said three urgent calls. Who are the others?"

"One was someone named Frank Grandi. He said you'd know what's on his mind. And Mr. Neuberger. He didn't say why he was calling, but he acted as if you'd be glad to talk with him."

"He's right, but Doc Crawford comes first. Let's see when he can make it, then we'll schedule Neuberger and Grandi."

Carol busied herself neatening up her desk. Not that Doc would care, but she did. She had always worried that something important - small but important - would get buried under a mountain of papers and forms, only to turn up too late to help her solve some problem. She was also aware that she was filling time, waiting impatiently for word from JoAnne that Doc would be along shortly. She hoped it would be soon.

It turned out that Doc would be along in half an hour, which wasn't bad considering where his cottage was located. It gave Carol time for a candy bar and a cup of coffee.

"Doc, you're looking great. What's your secret?"

"Your daddy would be disappointed in you, Carol, fibbing like that." He smiled, but it was at best a weak smile. "We both know that even fair to middling would be stretching the truth. But I appreciate the compliment. My barber was more honest, even if it cost him a better tip. What's the good word with you and the professor?"

"Fine. Just fine. But much as I love to talk about Kevin, I'm hoping you're here to tell me what killed Vivian Neuberger."

"Of course. But I'll bring you up to date on Mrs. Neuberger on one condition - that you agree to join me at my place for dinner. I'll let you pick the date, but I'm hoping it can be soon. Are we on?"

"That's a wonderful idea, and the answer is yes. Just don't do anything fancy."

"I was planning on roast pheasant, but I can do hot dogs if you'd rather."

"Tell you what. I'll talk with Kevin tonight and then get back to you about a date."

"Good. This is an invitation that's way overdue. Now, about that poor Neuberger woman. Somebody shot her, but you know that, so the question is who and with what. I did the autopsy, and with Freddy Reichler's help we can tell you just about everything except who did it. First things first. Whoever shot her, didn't do it at close range. I wish I could tell you how far the shot travelled, but once you get beyond two feet, maybe three, it's impossible to tell. Anyway, there was no gunpowder stippling or soot deposit, which makes it clear that the shooter wasn't right next to her."

Carol interrupted.

"We know the victim was out in the open, some distance down hill from the grove of trees where we think the shooter was standing."

"So it looks like we're on the same page," Crawford said. "The bullet was a hollow point, and it came from a handgun, a pistol or a semi-automatic, not a rifle. It didn't fragment within the body, so there wasn't a lot of tissue damage, which pretty much rules out a rifle."

Doc Crawford had been leaning forward in his chair, as if to emphasize every word. Now, having told his story, he sat back.

"So what are we looking for?"

"A .40-caliber, let's say a Glock, maybe a Ruger. Something like that. By the way, handguns aren't as reliable as rifles. Reichler tells me they wouldn't be much good over forty yards, fifty if the shooter is a real good marksman."

Carol sighed.

"All of the birders were frisked before we let them go. None of them had a gun. Which I suppose doesn't mean a thing. I can't picture people on a bird hike carrying a gun with them, but I'm sure there are people who carry one wherever they go. Sam says most of the birders had a back pack or something in which to carry binoculars, a thermos, chapstick, you name it. Even a gun. Now you're saying the weapon was a handgun, which means that the shooter didn't have to assemble and then take apart a rifle. In any event, we've been assuming that the shooter ditched the gun somewhere."

"And you haven't found it." It was a statement, not a question.

"And probably never will."

"Carol, you may have wondered why it's taken me so long to report on a simple autopsy. I should apologize, except that I haven't been in control of my schedule lately. I'm afraid that I've done my last autopsy for you. You're looking at a sick man, not someone who's even in fair to middling health. It's been one test after another, a second opinion, even a third, but I'm too old and too smart to deny the obvious. I'm a cancer patient. My oncologist is guardedly optimistic, but he can't fool me."

Carol was shocked with this explanation of why there had been no report on ballistics.

"Oh, Doc. No. Say it isn't so."

Crawford smiled, and this time it was the real thing.

"I've run a pretty good race, don't you think? And I think I've done you some good. But - well, you know all the old cliches as well as I do. Anyway, it's time to read a few books, sit on the porch and not feel guilty. Time to put on a meal for you and your Kevin. You will get back to me about a date, won't you?"

"Absolutely. I'll call tonight. And please, don't do something like pheasant. Hot dogs or burgers sound much more like us."

She was trying to lighten up the conversation, but tears were welling up in Carol's eyes as she said it.

CHAPTER 39

Doc Crawford's news had been much like a blow to the solar plexus. Carol had know Doc for many years, and they had enjoyed a friendly, good humored relationship, in spite of the fact that they saw each other primarily when a case required an autopsy. That he was very ill was inconceivable. And ironic. His professional role for many years had been to examine the dead, and by doing so to determine the cause of their death. He had performed that service for Carol many times since she had abandoned the practice of law and become sheriff of Cumberland County. But now he had done it for the last time.

It took her the better part of an hour to do some anticipatory grieving. Sam had come by, as had JoAnne and Officer Byrnes. Each time she had said 'later' and closed the door. It was mid-afternoon when she took a deep breath and sent word for JoAnne to get in touch with Bill Neuberger. There was work to be done, and she had decided that she'd prefer to be talking with Neuberger than Grandi.

Her reason for preferring to see Vivian's husband rather than the wealthy fracking enthusiast was that he was a much more likely suspect in the Anson's Grove shooting and it had been too long since they had spoken. Both common courtesy and curiosity dictated that she should return his call.

"Sheriff!" The way he said it made it sound as if he were greeting a long lost friend. "Thank you for getting back to me. We need to talk. What does your calendar look like?"

"In my profession, I find that I can always take time to see people who have something to do with an investigation. And it has been quite awhile, hasn't it?" It suddenly occurred to Carol that she had to meet Neuberger at his home, not at her office. "Is later this afternoon possible? I could stop by and see you on my way home. Any time after five, as long as it's convenient for you."

"Why sure, that would be fine. It isn't out of your way, I hope."

It was quite definitely out of her way.

"Not at all," Carol told him. "Just tell me when would be a good time."

"5:45? That's the hour when Viv and I always invited friends in for a drink."

"Then 5:45 it shall be."

Carol's sudden decision to hold the meeting at the Neuberger house was due to the fact that she wanted to see where Mel Cone claimed to have seen Larry Finch visiting Vivian Neuberger. She doubted that it would be possible to see the third floor room where those assignations allegedly took place, but she would at least be able to get a fix on the neighborhood. Moreover, it sounded as if Mr. Neuberger might be planning to offer her a 'cocktail hour' drink like he and Vivian had done with their friends. Had the Finches been friends? Had they shared a drink with the Neubergers at 5:45 on Covina Street in Yates Center?

The prospect of seeing Bill Neuberger had the effect of temporarily taking Carol's mind off Doc Crawford's news. By five o'clock she had made arrangements to see Frank Grandi the following morning and called Kevin to report that she'd be late for supper. How late? She didn't know. But she found herself hoping that it would be later than usual.

On her visit to Mel Cone's home, she hadn't bothered to case the neighborhood. She remedied that bit of oversight by slowly driving around it this time. The neighbors might wonder what the police car was doing, but Bill Neuberger hadn't seemed to mind. There was plenty of street parking available, and Carol found a place right in front of the tall, three story house where he lived.

"Welcome to my humble abode," he said as he opened the door. "Please come in. As you'll soon see, the place now lacks a woman's touch."

Carol had never cared for that expression, but let it pass this time.

"I hope your neighbors won't be wondering about your choice of company tonight."

"They all know about Viv by now, and they've been very thoughtful. Nobody's been badgering me with questions, and a couple of the neighbors have brought me a casserole. They probably don't know that I'm a pretty good cook."

So, he cooks but doesn't pick up after himself. Carol considered these attempts by Bill Neuberger to define himself as she followed him into the living room. For some reason, she didn't think it necessary to repeat her words of sympathy when first they met.

"It looks like we're in for a heat wave, doesn't it?" It was hardly an original conversational gambit, but in fact it had been a hot day.

"Oh, please forgive me, sheriff. Viv didn't like to keep the air conditioner on. You're welcome to shed your jacket."

"I'll be fine, and I agree that we overdo air conditioning. Like a lot of other things."

Carol wasn't sure what she meant by 'a lot of other things' or why she'd said it. Better to shut up and let Neuberger do the talking. After all, it was his agenda that had brought her to the house on Covina Street.

"Here, have a seat," Bill said, motioning to what looked as if it were his favorite recliner. "What would you like to drink? Scotch? Bourbon? Gin and tonic?"

Carol would have preferred wine, but said that the gin and tonic would be fine.

Preliminaries out of the way, they sat facing each other in a living room bathed in afternoon sun streaming through floor to ceiling windows along the west wall.

Mr. Neuberger had seized control of the conversation in their first meeting in her office. Today he seemed willing to let her take the lead. She was willing to do it, but he was the one who had requested the meeting, and she would like to hear what he had on his mind.

"You tell me you need to talk with me. As you can see, I'm here, and I'm interested in what you want to tell me. Or is it ask me? So why don't you go ahead."

"What I want to tell you is that I regret the way I approached our meeting back in your office. You were interviewing me, like you were everyone else who'd been on that bird hike, yet I kind of took over. I'm afraid I must have sounded like a know it all. I don't have a transcript of what I said, but I suspect that you thought I was telling you how to conduct your investigation. That's not like me. It had been a terrible couple of days. Viv dead, my world suddenly all askew. I guess I was handling things badly. Can you understand?"

"Please don't be hard on yourself, Mr. Neuberger. Losing a spouse like that has to be one of the toughest things to cope with. I certainly didn't think you were telling me how to run my investigation."

Actually, that's how it had seemed, but she appreciated it that he was offering an apology.

"Anyway, that's what I wanted to tell you. But I do need to ask you a question, too. You won't be surprised, I'm sure, that I'm anxious about how your investigation is going. I'd expected - no, let's say I had hoped - to have heard from you before this. Some word about how things look now that the confusion of those first few days had settled down. I want to know what you can tell me about Viv's death."

Was this the reason for their meeting? So that he could apologize for the aggressive way in which he had handed the interview and press her for a progress report on the investigation? Somehow she had expected something more specific.

"You might be surprised, Mr. Neuberger, that investigations like this rarely produce results quickly. Gathering useful information takes time. We learn things and then we learn that what we've learned is irrelevant. Different people have different impressions of what they've seen and heard. And it goes without saying that the person who could be most helpful, the person who committed the crime - the person who shot your wife - is the person who has the greatest incentive to lie, to spread misinformation, to direct attention away from himself. Or herself, as the case may be. I never expected that it would be easy to discover who shot your wife or why."

"I suppose I knew this is what you'd tell me. But she was my wife, for God's sake. This not knowing is driving me up the wall. A guy needs closure. Until then I expect I'll wake up every night and never get back to sleep."

Carol hated the invocation of the word 'closure.' It had become a cliche, and she very much doubted that Bill Neuberger would experience closure when his wife's killer had been identified, tried, and given a long jail sentence. What was more troubling, his little speech had sounded rehearsed. And he wasn't through.

"Agnes McKendrick stopped by just yesterday to see if I thought planning another hike would be a thoughtless thing to do or an appropriate memorial gesture. I practically kicked her out of the house. Can you imagine going on another hike when one of the birders, maybe the one right next to you, is the one who shot and killed your wife?"

No, Carol thought, I can't imagine such a thing. And I'm sorry that I can't hurry things up. But then, she said to herself, maybe I can.

"I may not be able to complete this investigation as fast as either you or I would like, but now that I'm here, how would it be if I asked a few questions? Maybe you can help me."

Neuberger looked and sounded uncertain.

"I don't see how I can help. I've told you all I know."

"Experience has taught me that all of us know more than we think we know about many things. Why not let me test your memory?"

"If you think it will help."

"Let's say it *may* help. What about the other members of the Crooked Lake Birders Club? Did you and your wife count any of them among your friends?"

"You asked me about this when first we met, sheriff. The answer is still no."

"I know. Maybe friends is too strong a word. How about people whose company you enjoyed from time to time?"

"You don't really enjoy anybody's company on a bird hike. All people talk about is birds."

"Did any of the other birders invite you and your wife to join them for drinks or even for dinner? Sometimes people try to welcome newcomers with an invitation like that."

"Now that you mention it, we were invited to dinner by the Finches. She was in the birders club, he wasn't."

"When was that?"

"If I remember correctly, it was a year ago this spring, not long after our first outing with the Club."

"Did you get together with the Finches again?"

"We probably should have, but it never happened. Probably because I'm down in the city a lot." Neuberger smiled a rueful smile. "No, that's just an excuse. We just never got around to it."

What else could she ask without implying that there was more to the relationship between the Neubergers and the Finches than Mr. Neuberger had admitted?

"You may not have known the Finches well, but it seems that you might have known them better than any of the other birders."

"As I mentioned, Mr. Finch wasn't a member of the birders club. But you're probably right, that we knew them better than the others. At least we were in their house, so I suppose we have some sense of their tastes. Frankly, she isn't a very good cook, although maybe she was just having an off night. He was more interesting than she was. At least he seemed to have more varied interests. Sallie's conversational repertoire seemed pretty much limited to birds. Of course Viv knew a lot about birds, too, but I think, like me, she got tired of Sallie."

"What is your opinion of Mr. Finch?"

"Remember, I only saw him once, and that was over a year ago. Opinion? Hard to say. If it's positive, it's only because I have a pretty poor opinion of Sallie. Maybe he's as boring as she is. I wouldn't really know."

Carol decided to risk it.

"Did you observe anything that evening that suggested Mr. Finch might be interested in your wife?"

Bill Neuberger smiled.

"How interesting. May I infer that someone told you that he was?"

Carol was debating with herself how to answer the question when Neuberger beat her to the punch.

"It would have been Paul Raymore, wouldn't it? Not only is he Crooked Lake's self styled expert on birds, he's also an irresponsible gossip. I have no idea whether Mr. Finch was interested in Viv. If he was, I suppose I should say that he has good taste."

"Actually, Mr. Raymore never said anything to me about Larry Finch."

"Really? May I ask who told you about his interest in my wife?"

"You know how it is. Somebody plants a rumor, it starts circulating, sooner or later it comes to my attention."

"You'd rather not share your source with me?"

"I think it would be prudent not to feed the rumor mill."

"Fair enough." Neuberger rose from his chair and looked at his watch. "Look, I have things I have to do. Things that Viv would be doing if she were with us. I'm sure I will be one of the first people you contact when you finally figure out who killed her."

He walked Carol to the door and flashed his patented smile as he said good-bye.

"Of course," Carol said. "I promise to stay in touch."

CHAPTER 40

Had Bill Neuberger been too quick to dismiss the rumor that Vivian had been having an affair with Larry Finch? And why had he claimed that Paul Raymore had been the source of that rumor? Carol had not expected him to admit knowledge of his wife's alleged infidelity, and she had not wanted to cause trouble for Mel Cone by reporting that he had been her source. But an impression lingered that Mr. Neuberger had not been entirely straight forward with her. She was aware, however, that that impression may have been due to what Cone had told her, in which case all she was doing was giving more credence to Cone's story than to how Neuberger had responded to her questions.

She replayed her conversation with Bill Neuberger over and over in her mind on her way home at the end of the day. In the end all it did was to remind her that she needed to have a similar conversation with Sallie Finch. By the time she pulled in behind the cottage, however, she had decided that, while she hadn't really learned anything, she had at least broken the ice. It should now be easier to question Sallie about Larry's interest in Vivian. Or was it Vivian's interest in Larry?

"I'm bored," were Kevin's first words when Carol found him on the deck, staring off into space.

This was not his customary greeting, and it took her by surprise.

"You're bored?"

"That's what I said."

"What's the problem?"

"You won't like this, but the fact is that you and I seem to be leading parallel lives recently. I sit around at home, you're preoccupied with the Neuberger case. Frankly, I miss you."

Carol was alarmed.

"But I'm right here. See?" She leaned over him and gave him a big kiss.

"I know. And I know you can't help it if you're working full time while I'm at loose ends. But we're becoming like ships that pass in the night."

Carol decided to sit down rather than change out of her uniform.

"Come on, it isn't that bad. Just the other evening we had supper at *The Cedar Post* and took a nice drive out on the bluff to see the moon rise. I thought it was fun, and I thought you did, too."

"It was, but it was almost a week ago. We don't even talk much these days."

"It's this damned Neuberger case, isn't it?" They had been there before when she'd been caught up in an investigation which didn't seem to be going anywhere. "I'm stymied and you feel left out."

She got to her feet.

"Let me get us something to drink and we'll talk about what we can do about it."

When Carol came back with two glasses of Chardonnay, she handed him his and resumed her seat.

"Don't worry. I'm not going to suggest that you cope with boredom by getting busy on that article you're writing. That's between you and your dean. Your problem, in my humble opinion, is that you want to have a role in nailing Vivian Neuberger's killer. Initially, you thought you had a role, thanks to being on the bird hike when Vivian was shot. And then you became interested in Mel Cone's notebook and Elvis and Daddy Bird. Voila! Now you've got yourself a mission. Unfortunately, that's not the way the Cumberland County Sheriff's Department works. It's not like the Hawk's Nest case, when it made sense for you to go over to Albany to see what was up with your former student. Or when my budget problems necessitated sending you back to Albany to help me solve that Welcome Inn tragedy. There's no reason why I should ask you to do what Bridges or Parsons or one of my other officers can do. Do you see my problem?"

"I understand, but it seems to me that I've had some useful ideas in almost all of your cases. Why is this one so different?"

"Do me a favor, will you? Let me change out of this uniform, then let's take the canoe out and talk about the dearth of useful leads in the Neuberger case that's driving me crazy. I promise to listen."

"The canoe is a good idea. I hope we have a few more before we get back here for supper."

"Good. Now let me change."

Half an hour later, they had paddled half a mile up toward West Branch and then out to the middle of the lake. Because it was the dinner hour, the lake was almost entirely devoid of boat traffic. The wind had died down, and they had stowed their paddles, allowing the canoe to drift slowly towards the far shore.

"I think I feel better already," Kevin said. "But you promised to talk about what I can do to move the Neuberger case along, so why don't you give me a quick update on where things stand with your suspects."

"Part of my problem is that I'm still not sure just who is a suspect and who isn't. But I'll try."

Carol proceeded to give him a short sketch of where things stood with each one of the birders who had wandered away from their leader during the hike in Anson's Grove. It quickly became apparent that he already knew much of what she was telling him. And that he had no idea how he could 'move things along,' even if she were willing to give him more of a role in the investigation.

"The only other possible suspect," she added, "would seem to be Frank Grandi. You saw him in action at that fracking meeting. Frankly, I have trouble with the idea that he might have killed Vivian. But Agnes McKendrick seems to think he did it, based, I guess, on what she sees as his determination to buy up the Grove and the surrounding acres. I have an appointment to see him tomorrow, and I'm having trouble figuring what to ask him. 'Did you kill Mrs. Neuberger?' is surely a non-starter."

"I'm not sure what the problem is. McKendrick's never going to outbid him for the Grove. By the way, who owns the Grove? It looks like no man's land to me."

"I don't know. But I'm sure Grandi does."

"Well, that's a question to ask him. Maybe the owner hates fracking. Or maybe he's itching to unload a piece of property that's nothing but an albatross."

"Very good, Kevin. Another bird connection."

Kevin laughed.

"Thanks, but I wasn't trying to be clever."

"But maybe Grandi and the Grove would be a good assignment for you. As far as I'm concerned, who killed Vivian Neuberger and who owns Anson's Grove are two unrelated matters. The first one is my responsibility. The second is none of my business, at least as far as I know. Personally, I think fracking is nothing but a red herring. For all I know, Grandi's interest in the Grove is just a figment of McKendrick's imagination. Or maybe it's a rumor Grandi himself likes to encourage to distract attention from what may be his real plans."

"So why might it be a good assignment for me? I want to help nail the Neuberger killer, not solve a real estate problem."

"There's nothing in my department's regs that mentions fracking. So there's no reason why I should assign any of my men to it just because Agnes McKendrick has a vivid imagination. On the other hand, what if there is a connection and I missed it?"

"You don't want to live with a bored husband, so you're going to palm off Grandi and the Grove issue on me. Is that it?"

"You can't believe I'd do something like that, can you?"

Kevin slapped his paddle on the water, splashing Carol in the process.

"I can, but I'll take the assignment anyway. Kevin Whitman, undercover agent back in harness. At a minimum, I'll learn whom Grandi will be buying from, assuming that he wants to buy the Grove."

"You do understand, I hope, that I intend to keep my appointment with him tomorrow. He'd smell a rat if a certain professor of music showed up at his door in lieu of the sheriff."

"I know better than to push my luck, Carol. Let's head back to the cottage and have some supper."

"And another glass of Chardonnay to toast with?"

"I insist on it."

CHAPTER 41

It turned out that Frank Grandi's sizable fortune hadn't led him to buy one of Crooked Lake's more impressive summer homes. Instead, Carol found herself parking in front of fairly large but decidedly ordinary house on the Clemson Road. The Clemson Road lay some distance from the lake, and its most distinctive feature was the number of Amish horse-drawn buggies that used it on the average week day.

The car in the driveway, a jet black Jaguar, was more stylish than the house itself. To Carol's surprise, a man was seated behind the wheel and the driver's door was open.

"Good morning, sheriff," he addressed her in a deep bass voice as he stepped out of the Jaguar. The dark haired man who looked to be in good shape extended his hand.

"Mr. Grandi? You look as if you were getting ready to go somewhere."

"That is true. I was getting ready to go into the house to put on some coffee in anticipation of my meeting with you. I've been out for a morning drive, but I wouldn't have missed meeting you for love nor money."

For no reason she could think of, Carol didn't believe him. She was sure he had been about to drive off, which he might well have done if she had not been five minutes early.

"Come along. I've been looking forward to this."

Carol followed Grandi across the back yard and into the house. En route she ran her hand quickly across the hood of the Jaguar. It was cold. Frank Grandi had not been out for a morning drive.

"Please go on in and make yourself at home while I get the coffee started. Right through the door there. My apologies for not picking up the paper. I'm not exactly one of the neatest people I know."

Carol took a seat in a chair which had seen better days. So had the rest of the living room. The only item of interest in the spacious room was a very large piece of expressionist art. She thought she recognized the artist, but could not think of his name. The room lacked a bookcase; there was not a book in sight. Perhaps there were books in a den or study elsewhere in the house. Although what she had heard about Grandi suggested that he might not be a reader, even non-readers usually had a few books lying around.

"Well, now, why don't you tell me why I'm to have the privilege of your company this morning," Grandi said as he set a cup of coffee before the sheriff.

"It's like I said when I called. I need to talk with you about the late Vivian Neuberger."

"Yes, of course. But why me?"

"We're investigating her death, which means that we need to talk with everyone who knew her."

Carol took a sip of her coffee. It was not fresh, but had been warmed over.

"I didn't know her," Grandi said. "I doubt that I ever spoke to her, and I'm not sure I would recognize her if I ran into her on the street."

"It's more than a matter of people knowing her. How about knowing *about* her? Your name has come up several times during conversations about Mrs. Neuberger, suggesting that your life and hers might have intersected in some way."

"My life and hers intersected? I'm not sure what that means."

"Did you and she have mutual interests? Or perhaps conflicting interests that might have led people to mention both of you? Over the last few weeks my officers and I have had interviews with many people who knew something about Mrs. Neuberger. We're doing just what we always do in cases like this. So what can you tell me about Vivian Neuberger?"

"I suppose I could say that the answer to your question is nothing, nothing at all. But that isn't what you want to hear, and I assume that you already know the answer to your question. You must have heard that the late Mrs. Neuberger and I had our disagreements about fracking. But there are hundreds of people around the lake who disagree with me about fracking. You see their placards along the road everywhere. I'm sure you aren't interviewing every resident of the area who disagrees with me. So why are we talking today about my relationship with Mrs. Neuberger?"

It was beginning to look as if Carol would have to acknowledge the rumor that Grandi had been the one who had killed Vivian.

"I suppose it's that while many people around here oppose fracking, Mrs. Neuberger was more than just an opponent. She seems to have taken the lead in local efforts to make sure that it doesn't happen. Did that have any bearing on how you felt about her?"

"What I think you are driving at, sheriff, is a rumor that I may be the one who shot her the other day when she was on a bird hike. You are welcome to ask me if there's any truth to that rumor, and I'm sure my answer won't surprise you. So let's dispense with the games. There's talk that a hunter did it. I hunt, but I never hunt in June and I am much too good a hunter to mistake a woman for a deer. What's more, don't you think a disagreement about fracking is a pretty ridiculous reason for killing someone? I'm really disappointed. If you think there's anything to the rumor that silly woman is spreading, it seems to me that the local citizenry should be looking for a new sheriff."

The word that Frank Grandi was an unpleasant man with a bad temper was proving correct.

"I'm afraid I'm not aware that somebody you call a silly woman is spreading a rumor that you killed Mrs. Neuberger."

"How could you not be aware?" Grandi said. "If I didn't have such a thick hide, I'd be tempted to sue her for libel."

"She's published this charge? Where?" Carol was sure the woman was McKendrick.

"All right, score one for the sheriff. I meant slander."

"Do you mind telling me who is spreading this rumor?"

"You know damn well it's Agnes McKendrick."

Carol had no intention of becoming involved in a discussion of the woman who was leader of the Crooked Lake Birders Club. She changed the subject.

"I was initially surprised that you and I had never met. But I've learned that you only moved to this area recently. Where was home before you came here?"

The question seemed to puzzle Grandi.

"Scranton," he finally said. "Ever been there?"

"Once, and sorry to say I was just driving through. As I remember, it's kind of a twin city with some place called Wilkes-Barre."

"Good memory."

Carol, with Officer Byrnes's help, had done a bit of research on fracking sites. Scranton was close to a major one in Pennsylvania. It made sense. But Carol had been careful not to make fracking the central issue in their discussion. It was Grandi who had brought it up. And she had said nothing about Anson's Grove and his reputed interest in it. That was to be Kevin's piece of the puzzle, although she still suspected that it would turn out to be irrelevant.

Before she left the house on the Clemson Road, Carol considered asking if the Neubergers, Paul Raymore, or any of the other relative newcomers to Crooked Lake who were persons of interest in Vivian's death had recently lived in the Scranton area. But she had already told herself that this was not a promising line of questioning, and in the end she chose not to bring it up.

Carol had plenty of time on her trip back to her office in Cumberland to weigh her impression of Frank Grandi. His reputation as a man of money had not been confirmed. There had, of course, been the Jaguar and the expressionist painting - why couldn't she remember the name of the artist? - but otherwise there was nothing about the house on the Clemson Road to suggest that the owner was one of the area's wealthiest men. Nor had his reputation as a hot head been on display during their conversation. Yes, he had made it clear that he thought Agnes McKendrick was a silly woman and even that Carol herself might be over her head in her role as the county's sheriff. But he had said these things matter of factly, his voice always under control. He was obviously a man of strong views, but some of those views were reasonable enough, such as his observation that a disagreement about fracking was a pretty ridiculous reason for killing someone.

The bottom line, she thought, was that the ardent champion of fracking was not a particularly likeable person, but that he was a prohibitively long shot to be Vivian Neuberger's killer.

CHAPTER 42

The sign on the door informed Kevin that the person he wanted to talk with was ill and that she hoped to be back in the office by Thursday. In a busier jurisdiction than Cumberland County, such an office would never be closed on a weekday; the staff would be larger, and someone would be on duty to answer Kevin's questions. But not in Cumberland, and not today. He shrugged his shoulders, managed a 'why should I be surprised' smile, and climbed back into the Camry. What now? His assignment to gather information as to whom Frank Grandi would be buying Anson's Grove from would have to be put on hold, at least until Thursday. Kevin started the engine but let the car idle while he argued with himself about whether he was up to another day fighting writer's block in his effort to produce a paper for the annual Mozart conference. With nothing better to do, he decided to return to the cottage and give it a try.

It took him only half an hour staring at his computer to realize that, whatever he did with the rest of the day, it would not be writing his paper. He got a glass of iced coffee and went out onto the deck. It was a beautiful day. He found himself thinking about Anson's Grove and what he had hoped to accomplish had the woman not been ill. It was then that he remembered something Agnes McKendrick, the leader of the Crooked Lake Birders Club, had told him about the Grove. Actually, what she had told him was not, strictly speaking, about the Grove, but about the empty corner of the county in which the Grove was the principal feature. She had mentioned that a house, now long abandoned, sat in a swale at the far end of Benson Road. He didn't recall any specific mention of how far it was from the Grove, but he had a general impression that it was no more than a few miles. Suddenly he knew what he was going to do with the rest of his day.

Kevin made himself a ham and cheese sandwich and stuffed it into his back pack along with an apple and a small thermos of more iced coffee. It was close to half an hour later that he pulled off the county highway and onto Benson Road, the wretched washboard that ran past Anson's Grove and set off in the direction of the deserted house. Agnes had claimed that it could not be missed. Just keep going until the road runs out, she had said.

He could have driven to the end of the road, but he was in no hurry. Even here, far above the lake, he felt a cool breeze. And he knew the walk would do him good. Besides, it was an adventure. He hadn't visited an old deserted house since he was in junior high school. Now one of them lay dead ahead of him.

Kevin's guess that the old house was no further than two miles from where he had parked the car turned out to be fairly accurate. He didn't have an odometer, but he'd taken long walks often enough to be confident that he'd come at least a mile and a half when he spotted the house. As he closed the distance to it it became obvious that it was a house only in the most generous sense of the word. Cabin was more accurate, and it, too, might be an exaggeration. Not only was it small, it was also in an advanced state of ruin. It had not totally collapsed. The cinder blocks on which it rested were still visible, but the roof had caved in, all of its windows had been broken out, and the door was little more than a splintered slab of wood. If anyone had lived in it since the first world war, Kevin would have been surprised.

He had approached to within a dozen yards of this cabin when he spotted a car on a weed choked patch of gravel beside the shattered door. It was not that old a car, but a fairly recent model black BMW with a New York license plate. Its owner had made no effort to keep it tidy. While it had obviously been washed on the outside fairly recently, the interior looked as if it had served as the driver's office. It reminded Kevin of a number of his faculty colleagues. They dressed well, but heir desks were disaster areas.

His curiosity aroused, he walked over to the house and began peering through the broken windows.

"What do you think you're doing?" The voice came from off to his right. The man standing there was wearing camouflage fatigues and a New York Mets baseball cap. And he was pointing a shotgun directly at him.

Kevin reflexively raised his arms, then slowly lowered them.

"Just looking around," he said, trying not to sound as frightened as he actually had been when he first saw the gun. "Could you please lower that gun?"

"No, I couldn't. Who are you?"

"That's what I was going to ask you," Kevin said. "It's my understanding that this place is deserted and has been for many years."

"As you can see, it's not deserted. What are you doing poking around where it's none of your business?"

Kevin sensed that he should reconsider his decision to explore the deserted house. The man who was aiming the shotgun at him could not be the owner of the place, and had no more right to be there than he did. But this did not look like the time or place to invoke whatever law applied to such situations.

"I'm just out taking a walk. Nice day for it, don't you think? I'd heard there was an old house down here, thought I'd see what it looked like."

"Okay, now you've seen what it looks like."

The shotgun swung away from his chest and toward the ground. The shot exploded with a noise so sharp Kevin had the momentary sensation he'd been hit.

"Don't you fuck with me," the man said. "Next time I won't be aiming at these damned weeds."

Kevin doubted that the man would shoot him, but he knew better than to challenge somebody who had both a gun and an unpleasant disposition. He tried to look nonchalant as he turned to walk back toward the Grove, but he didn't think the man with the shotgun had been fooled. Only once did he look back. The man still stood in front of the crumbling house. The gun was still pointed at him.

He walked slowly, but his mind was in overdrive. The man who clearly didn't want him lingering around the decrepit and empty house was definitely not Frank Grandi. He'd seen Grandi at the fracking forum in Dickerson. But the man was also not simply a vagrant who'd found a place to sleep at the end of the old Benson road. The black BMW said otherwise, as did the shotgun and the crisp well pressed fatigues. Could he be a friend of Grandi's, someone the fracking advocate had deputized to keep an eye on Anson's Grove for him? It was certainly possible, but the more he thought about it the less likely it seemed. What would Grandi be accomplishing by such a strategy? Kevin could think of nothing that made any sense, unless, of course, there was something about the abandoned dwelling below the Grove that he was unaware of. And was likely to be unaware of until Thursday.

One thing Kevin did know, however, was that the man with the gun who didn't want him hanging around the ruined house drove a BMW with a New York license plate number SXP-3982.

He climbed into the Camry and affected a turn about similar to the one he and Carol had watched Mel Cone make the day after Vivian Neuberger had been shot. Kevin's thoughts immediately turned to Vivian' death and the question of who might have killed her. Carol had developed a list of suspects, even if officially she still called them persons of interest. The list contained anywhere from four to six names, depending on when you asked her. It would have contained seven, the seventh nameless, had she been willing to include a hunter. But they had agreed that a hunter was extremely unlikely for any number of reasons. It was at that moment that it occurred to him that a seventh suspect didn't have to be a hunter, anxious to kill himself a deer, indifferent to the fact that it wasn't hunting season, and unable to distinguish Vivian Neuberger from a deer, but a man who drove a black BMW and had a strong proprietary interest in a long abandoned house at the end of Benson Road.

Kevin was not ready to seize this idea and run with it. He was too rational, too logical - or so he told himself - to embrace such a patently far fetched scenario and offer it to Carol as a promising explanation for Vivian Neuberger's violent death. After all, a handgun, not a shotgun, had been the weapon of choice in the Neuberger shooting. Moreover, he knew absolutely nothing to suggest that the man in the fatigues and a Met's cap even knew Vivian, much less wanted her dead.

Nonetheless, he intended to report on his little morning adventure to Carol as soon as he got back to the cottage. A quick call to the MVA should be able to tell them who owned the BMW.

CHAPTER 43

Carol had told Officer Byrnes that the task of discovering where the birders who had only recently moved to Crooked Lake had come from was not urgent. But it was the kind of assignment Tommy liked, so when he had some time he busied himself with the issue of where the Neubergers and Paul Raymore had come from. Carol had already learned that Frank Grandi, the only non-birder among her persons of interest, had recently arrived from northeastern Pennsylvania.

The sheriff's reason for her interest in where the birders had come from had to do with the possibility that some of them might have known each other prior to moving to the lake. By the time Tommy had finished his initial inquiries, it was apparent that if they did, it was not because they had lived near each other. The Neubergers had lived for years in Suffolk County on the eastern end of Long Island. Paul Raymore had also come from the metropolitan New York area, but well north of the city on the Hudson and therefore a very long and hard drive from the Neubergers. He had also checked on Sally Finch, and he had discovered that hers was a different and more interesting story. It had taken him somewhat longer to track down the pertinent information.

Tommy shared with the sheriff what he knew about the Neubergers and Paul Raymore before turning to Sallie Finch.

"Would you like to hear about the Finch woman?"

"Why, does she turn out to be another recent arrival?"

"Not exactly," Tommy said. "Her husband worked for the Treasury Department down in Washington until he had a stroke, which led him to early retirement and a move to Crooked Lake. She entered the picture more recently. Close to five years ago, to be more precise. That's when she married Finch and joined him up here."

Carol was disappointed in herself. She could have learned this by the simple act of asking more questions when interviewing her. The story of Sallie's marriage to Larry Finch would certainly have been common knowledge around the lake.

"Were you able to find out where she came from?"

"Springfield, Virginia. She had apparently lived there for many years and divorced her first husband not long before she married Finch. Seems she had known Finch since they attended the Fletcher School at Tufts University many years ago."

"Well, it looks like you've been on a wild goose chase. Thanks, anyway, Tommy. We never know until we ask."

"There's one other thing," Byrnes added. "Can't see what it has to do with anything, but an old neighbor of Mrs. Finch volunteered the information that she worked for the CIA. I think this neighbor was trying to explain the breakup of her first marriage. Seems like the husband, a man named Palmer, was tired of living with a spook. Sorry, that's my term, not hers. Anyway, CIA people aren't supposed to tell anybody anything about what they're doing, and hubby number one had finally had enough of that kind of life."

Carol found all of this interesting but irrelevant to the Neuberger case. It looked as if Palmer had finally shed Sallie because of her CIA connection and Sallie had then cut her ties to the agency and moved to Crooked Lake to start a new life with someone she'd known since college. If Mel Cone was to be believed, this new life was now in trouble. Or was it? Perhaps Larry had been chastened by Vivian's death and had decided henceforth to honor his marriage vows. Or maybe Larry Finch and Vivian Neuberger had, contrary to Cone, never been having an extra-marital fling.

"Thanks, Tommy. I think we can stop worrying about past lives of our birders. By the way, how do you find all of these people, like the neighbor down in Virginia?"

"Perseverance, Carol. One thing leads to another. You know how it is."

She wasn't sure that one thing always leads to another. Sometimes it ends up in a cul de sac.

Over lunch that day Carol made a snap decision to call Sallie Finch. It wasn't that what Bridges had told her about his interview with Sallie needed further investigation, or that Byrnes' report opened a new line of inquiry. It was that she realized that she had never actually met this woman. She had given Cone's story enough credence to have a follow-up conversation with Bill Neuberger. What about Sallie Finch? If Cone were to be believed, Sallie was as likely a suspect in Vivian's death as Bill Neuberger was. She recalled Kevin's remark after she had shared Cone's allegation with him: it's a twofer, isn't it? The same extramarital affair could have turned either Bill or Sallie into a killer.

Carol didn't ask JoAnne to place the call. She picked up the phone and did it herself.

The small woman who had been compared to a bird by both Sam Bridges and her own husband answered the phone.

"This is the Finch residence. What may I do for you?"

"Hello, Mrs. Finch. This is Sheriff Kelleher. I realize that I haven't met you, and I thought it was time to remedy that."

"Strange thing," was Sallie's reply. "I've been contemplating calling you. Curiosity, you know. Just wondering how your investigation is going. I'm sure if there'd been an arrest of Mrs. Neuberger's killer, we'd all have heard about it."

"That's probably true. There's been no arrest. As I said, I'm calling because we haven't met and I think we should. Do you suppose we can find a time soon when I could drop by?"

It was a confident Sallie Finch who answered the question.

"Of course. You name it. I've just returned from visiting some old friends in Virginia, and my calendar is wide open."'

It turned out that Sallie's calendar wasn't quite as open as she had thought. Carol's suggestion that they get together for lunch led to an apology.

"Oh, I'm sorry. I'm always over promising. Can it be later in the day? I volunteer at the hospital in Yates Center, and they're counting on me until three."

"What about four?"

"Perfect. I'm looking forward to it."

Carol had no idea whether Sallie - or any of the other birders, for that matter - looked forward to a meeting with the sheriff. At least she had sounded more welcoming than Carol had expected.

The woman who greeted her that afternoon at four o'clock looked less like a bird than Sam had said she would. Small, yes; nose a bit beak-like perhaps, especially when viewed in profile. But her blouse and slacks were of a colorful pattern that reminded Carol of no bird she had ever seen.

It was obvious that Sallie Finch was also sizing the sheriff up.

"My goodness," she said. "I'm not sure what I expected, but you look more like one of those morning TV cookies than a sheriff. I'm glad to see that the good looking ones do sometimes handle the tough jobs that keep our society functioning."

Carol wasn't quite sure how to respond to this unusual compliment.

"We try," she said.

"Well, come on in." Mrs. Finch stepped aside and Carol entered a spacious living room. The sheriff had long been of the opinion that pictures and art objects can offer a useful clue to the background as well as the interests of people. In this case they suggested time spent in the Middle East. Three prints by David Roberts adorned the wall opposite the entrance, one of which she thought she remembered from a college course as the portico of some Egyptian temple. Several brass urns and two beautiful samovars occupied niches in a book case and the mantle over the fireplace. Might as well take advantage of the decor to learn a bit about Mrs. Finch, she thought.

"I always admire a room that creates a nice sense of place," she said as she paused before the bookcase. It contained a substantial library of books about Saudi Arabia and the Islamic world more generally, with emphasis on history and culture. "You and your husband must have spent some time in the Levant. Or was it Turkey, or perhaps Iran?"

Sallie laughed.

"I'm afraid Larry doesn't share my fondness for that part of the world. But I certainly wasn't going to put things in storage when I moved here, and he graciously agreed that I could refurnish this room. So I'll have to confess that this is my space. I don't even allow Lettie to touch it. Lettie, she's our housekeeper. The second floor is another story."

Meaning, Carol assumed, that Sallie's husband's tastes were better reflected in a 'man cave' somewhere upstairs.

"You moved here recently?" Carol asked, feigning surprise.

"Just a few years ago. It was a second marriage for both of us. Larry because he'd lost Jeannette to cancer, me because Jared and I had come to realize we didn't have a lot in common."

"So you'd lived somewhere in the Middle East?"

"Visited, not lived. It's a fascinating culture. Actually, it embraces several cultures. They share many things, but they get along today about as well as they did in Lawrence of Arabia's time. Remember that film? I fell in love with Omar Sharif the minute I saw him emerge from the desert heat on his camel. Are you married?"

Surely you know by now that I'm married to one of your fellow birders, Carol thought.

"You met my husband," she said. "He was with you in Anson's Grove the day Vivian Neuberger was killed."

"Oh, of course. Mr. Whitman. Charming man. Where are my manners? Have a seat and I'll rustle up some coffee, unless you'd prefer tea. The Arabs serve it from one of those lovely pots, but I think I'll stick to something that's easier to wash up."

"Coffee will be just fine. Black, no sugar, if you please."

"Of course. We aren't really a tea culture, are we? Not yet, anyway."

What that was supposed to mean, Sallie did not say. She disappeared down a hall, leaving Carol to pick a seat.

"Here we are," she said moments later as she set down Carol's coffee mug on a small table next to her chair. "Now, you were going to tell me how your search for Mrs. Neuberger's killer is going."

Carol's agenda had more to do with questions she wanted to ask than it did reporting on an investigation that had been going nowhere fast. Her most important question, of course, was the one suggested by Mel Cone's story that Sallie's husband had been having an affair with Vivian Neuberger. But she thought it best to raise other, less critical questions, first, thereby preserving the fiction that this was really just a get acquainted meeting.

"Do you have a family?"

"No. I never really wanted children. That was a part of my problem with Jared. In a way it's surprising that we didn't call it quits a long time ago. Kids don't fit well with some lines of work."

This sounded like an invitation to talk about what Sallie did for a living.

"That suggests you work outside of the home."

"I did. Now I'm just a happily retired woman who goes on bird hikes."

"I think I heard somewhere that you might have worked for the CIA."

That comment elicited another laugh.

"Sounds romantic, doesn't it? You must have been doing your homework on us birders. Well, what you heard is true, although I haven't made it a practice to discuss my professional life. The agency frowns on it. It's really not as fascinating as all those spy novels and movies would have you believe. Anyway, there's not much for people with my training to do on Crooked Lake. When I left Virginia, I walked away from my job, too."

Carol guessed that Sallie's work for the CIA must have taken her to the Middle East on occasions, but saw no reason to inquire about it. It would only lead to a conversational dead end with nothing to do with the Neuberger case.

They talked for another half an hour, covering a fair amount of ground, including the status of her investigation. It was following a question by Sallie about whether the sheriff had found the members of the Crooked Lake Birders Club cooperative that Carol raised the subject that was the reason for her visit.

"How well did you know the Neubergers?"

Sallie did not react as if she were surprised by the question.

"Not well. They were even newer to the area than I was. We tried to help welcome them to the lake by inviting them to dinner. I assumed that they'd invite us back, but it never happened. So other than that one evening we had no relationship with them at all. Except for the bird hikes, and I don't think there were more than three or four of those."

"It's my impression that Mrs. Neuberger was quite knowledgeable about birds."

"Oh, no question about it. The club is really an odd group. Most of us are in it either for the exercise or because we think of the birds as our fine feathered friends. Then there are those who take it seriously - one might even say too seriously. People like Paul Raymore and Mel Cone. I'd put Vivian Neuberger in that category, although to be honest she was closer to a professional than simply an avocational birder."

"How about yourself?"

"I'm no expert, but I guess I'm one of those people who tend to store away useless knowledge. Show me a bird, tell me it's a hooded merganser, and I'll file that information away somewhere up here."

Sallie tapped her forehead.

"I mentioned hearing the rumor that you were with the CIA. Another rumor is that Vivian Neuberger might have had - how should I say this? - an inappropriate interest in your husband."

Sallie's face betrayed not the slightest hint of anger or anxiety. Or of surprise. But she didn't seem to be in any hurry to comment on the rumor.

"I have no idea whether Mrs. Neuberger had what you call an inappropriate interest in Larry," she finally said, her voice low, her words measured. "I never asked her, and she's currently in no position to speak for herself. I suspect your source is someone who knows nothing but delights in making trouble for others. I also assume that the rumor is not about whether Mrs. Neuberger had an interest in my husband, but whether such an interest had blossomed into an affair. That, as they say, would be a horse of another color. If you believe that the matter merits your attention, I'd suggest that you consider speaking about it with Mr. Neuberger."

"I share your attitude toward rumors, Mrs. Finch. But I also have had experience with rumors which have been critical to the resolution of a case. I think you can appreciate why I'm in no position to dismiss this rumor as simply malicious and unfounded gossip. After all, if by any chance it happens to be true, it might explain why Mrs. Neuberger was shot."

"And lead you to the guilty party," Sallie added. She didn't need the sheriff to spell it out for her. "I'll be only too happy to help you by asking Larry if there's any truth to the rumor. I can assure you that it's very hard to fool someone with my training and experience."

"I shall probably be talking with your husband myself," Carol said, "and, as you have suggested, with Mr. Neuberger." She didn't add that she had already done so in both cases. "I suspect that this rumor may simply be a nasty way to tarnish the late Mrs. Neuberger's reputation. Or to embarrass Mr. Neuberger or you and your husband. It may be a way for someone to shift suspicion from himself to others. For all of the these reasons, I have no choice but to treat the rumor as a part of my investigation. I hope you understand."

"Of course. It's your job." Mrs. Finch chuckled. "I'll bet you've heard that one before."

CHAPTER 44

Kevin had considered that his experience at the ruined house was so bizarre that he should immediately notify Carol. In fact, he had driven half way to Cumberland before he thought better of it. He knew that his assignment had been to research the matter of the title to Anson's Grrove, and decided that bursting in on Carol and regaling her with his close encounter with a shotgun might only reflect badly on his own judgment.

Instead, in a major effort to demonstrate to himself and his wife that he still had command of his priorities, Kevin took a deep breath and tackled the Mozart paper again. To his surprise, inspiration came to his rescue, and while he didn't add many pages to his draft, he did make a significant dent in what he had been coming to believe was an impossible task. Pleased with himself, he set off down the lake in the canoe just before five, expecting to be back at the cottage before Carol arrived home.

As luck would have it, or more accurately as Carol's conversation with Sallie Finch would have it, she got to the cottage earlier than usual, anxious to share with Kevin the news that she had just been interrogating a CIA officer. Her 'hi, I'm home' elicited no answer, and it was almost half an hour later that she finally saw him. He was beaching the canoe.

"Cheers," she called out, raising her wine glass in a toast as he stowed the paddle.

"You're drinking alone," Kevin said as he climbed the steps to the deck. "Always a bad habit."

"Yes, and you're canoeing alone. Get yourself up here. I've got something to tell you."

Carol's account of her meeting with Sallie Finch had the effect of reviving Kevin's interest in Mel Cone's 'sociological experiment.'

"So who's your guilty party now, Vivian's husband or our birdlike Mrs. Finch?"

Carol frowned.

"I don't think you've been paying attention. You're supposed to tell me what you make of Sallie's career as a spy."

"We don't know that she was a spy," Kevin said. "Maybe she just had some kind of desk job. The real spy was Cone - he admits he spied on Vivian and Larry Finch, carrying on up there in the attic. I'm interested in who killed her. It couldn't have been both Neuberger and Finch, so my question is which of the two strikes you as the liar."

Carol was disappointed. She had hoped that Kevin would be excited to hear that one of her suspects was a spook.

"I take it that you don't see Sallie's career in the CIA as potentially relevant to my case."

"How could it be?" Kevin asked. "It's possible, I suppose, that Vivian was a double agent, passing secrets to the Taliban, and Sallie took her out in the interest of national security. But I'm sure you don't believe that, and neither do I. It might make a good John LeCarre novel, but we're dealing with a case of marital infidelity, not espionage."

"Okay, okay. I get the point." Carol sounded frustrated. "And don't forget that we have no evidence that Vivian died because she was cheating on her husband."

Before exhausting the subject, Carol had to confess that neither Bill Neuberger nor Sallie Finch had said anything that made one of them a more likely killer of Vivian than the other. And Kevin had to admit that he really did find Sallie's CIA background fascinating, even if it had nothing to do with Vivian's death.

It was Carol who suggested that they should probably have supper before Kevin shared his news of the day.

"I don't think so," he said. "I almost got shot today, and I'm sure you'll want to hear all about it."

"What are you talking about?" Carol wasn't sure whether Kevin was putting her on or had had some kind of accident.

"It's true, although I doubt that I was ever in real danger. I decided not to risk it."

"Risk what?"

"Getting shot."

"Kevin, sit back down." He had gotten up to refill his wine glass.

"I thought I'd like a refill. How about you?"

"Yes, and then I'd like you to tell me what this is all about. From the beginning."

He completed his 'more wine' mission, and then told her what had happened after his discovery that the person responsible for records of county properties was ill.

"That's pretty much all of it," he concluded. "The guy looked tough, and he's obviously had some practice intimidating people."

"I wish you had called me as soon as you got back to the cottage. That way we'd have his name - or at least the name of the car's owner. I don't like the sound of this. I'm 99 percent sure this guy has no right to be camping down there in that abandoned house. And I'm 100 percent sure he has no right to be threatening you with a shotgun. Or anything else, for that matter."

"I'm not sure I handled it very well," Kevin said.

"On the contrary," Carol said, her voice much sterner than usual, "you did the right thing by not challenging him. I don't want to lose my husband of just four years to a gunslinger with an itchy finger. So don't you ever go macho on me."

"Maybe the guy was just casing the place, thinking about buying it."

"Oh sure, and scaring off other potential buyers. The guy who's probably thinking of buying property up that way is Frank Grandi. That's what Jason Eglin thinks. McKendrick, too. I'll make you a bet the guy with the shotgun is working for Grandi with instructions to keep everyone else away."

Carol paused, thinking about what she had just said.

"What if this guy you met there was in the area when the bird hike took place? Grandi tells him to chase intruders away and he did it by shooting Vivian Neuberger."

"Something like that occurred to me, too," Kevin said. "But Vivian wasn't an intruder. She was on a bird hike with almost twenty other people."

"I know, but remember she'd wandered off from the group. She could have looked like an intruder. Grandi's got a mean reputation, and a lot of people seem to think he's got an eye on the Grove, which could well mean that whole area. Look, I don't know who it was that was threatening you or whether he works for Grandi. But I'm going to find out. Tomorrow."

"You aren't planning on going down to that abandoned house are you?"

"I'll start by checking the plate with MVA. If I have to take it a step further, Sam and some of the boys will be with me. Don't worry, there won't be any shootout, OK Corral style."

It was sometime later, after a pickup supper and a scrabble game that Carol, for the first time since they had gotten married, won handily, that they retired. Five minutes later, still wide awake and thinking about the CIA and shotguns, Kevin rolled over and got Carol's attention.

"I don't think the guy in the BMW could have killed Mrs. Neuberger. Crawford says it was a handgun that did it. Our BMW friend was wielding a shotgun."

Carol didn't sound interested.

"He's probably got a whole arsenal of guns, Kevin. A Glock one day, a Remington the next. Now go to sleep."

CHAPTER 45

It was Erin Dockery's second day on patrol by herself. She was thrilled to be behind the wheel of a car which told the world that she was an officer of the law. She was also nervous. Officer Parsons had been a friendly mentor, offering helpful tips on how to cope with situations she was likely to encounter, but never sounding the least bit patronizing. In her days with him he had issued only two tickets. He was obviously of the school that believed a warning was usually a more effective way to change bad habits. But now Parsons was back on water duty and she had her own car. She herself would have to decide how to handle the law breakers. She hoped that they would be few and far between.

On her very first day on highway patrol Erin had learned about one of the rituals which helped to explain the department's easy camaraderie. Officer Parsons had driven only a few miles before he pulled off the road at a *Dunkin' Donuts*. Two other official cars were already there, and when they went in they were greeted by two officers she had met but didn't yet know well. It was her introduction to the morning roadside coffee stop. She remembered her first reaction: they were all supposed to be on duty, but here they were, consuming coffee and calories and talking about things that had little or nothing to do with law and order. By the end of her first week she had decided that the loss of fifteen minutes was a small price to pay for the pleasure of working for the Cumberland County Sheriff's Department.

On this, her second day of driving solo, she ordered coffee, resisted the temptation to indulge in a donut, and mostly listened to her 'veteran' colleagues, some of them no more than five years her senior. For a change, the conversation focussed on the Neuberger case, a subject which had come up at squad meeting. It wasn't the first time since the sheriff had briefed her on it that there had been talk about the shooting and the ensuing investigation. But it was the first time she had heard any of her colleagues venture an opinion on the case.

"Can you believe it, we're investigating a CIA operative." It was Officer Grieves.

"And a woman at that," Officer Damoth observed. He realized immediately that he had committed a faux pas. "Oh, I shouldn't have said that. Sorry, Erin. I guess I thought it was a men only agency."

Erin had seen or heard nothing to suggest that the other officers in the department either resented her presence or doubted her ability. Her instinct was to laugh off Damoth's comment.

"No problem," she said. "We're known for our spying skills."

It hadn't been a particularly clever remark, but it seemed to have defused an awkward moment. When she vacated the table to return to her car, she gave the men a warm smile.

It was an uneventful day. Until 4:00 pm, that is. There had been a scary moment near Franklin that morning when two young boys playing catch had chased an errant throw into the street. The car that might have hit one of them had not been speeding, and the boys had the good sense to abandon their chase until it had passed. There had been no need to stop, but Erin had pulled over and politely urged them to move their game further back into their yard. Other than that, Cumberland County's citizens seemed to have been on their best behavior.

The trouble arrived just as Erin came to a rural intersection north of Dickerson. There were no stop signs, nor did there appear to be a need for them. Traffic was light and visibility was good in all directions. Erin slowed down to allow a car approaching the intersection from her right to pass. The clock on the dash had just turned over to four when the red Lexus roared past her at what she guessed was at least 75 miles per hour. I'm not sure what Officer Parsons would do with this one, she said to herself, but I'm going to issue my first ticket.

She swung sharply to the left and soon the patrol car was going faster than any car she had driven since getting her driving license. At first it looked as if the driver of the Lexus had no intention of slowing down, but fortunately he thought better of what he was doing and pulled off on the shoulder about a mile and a half down the road.

Erin's nerves began to act up again as she caught up with the Lexus and pulled up a car length and a half behind it. There's a first time for everything, she thought as she stepped onto the pavement.

The man sitting behind the steering wheel was bald but didn't look older than her father. He did, however, look angry.

"Do you know why I pulled you over?" Erin asked. Parsons had suggested that it was a good way to begin a conversation with someone you were about to ticket.

"I presume you have a quota, and I'm going to be part of it." The man's face was florid. "And what, pray tell, is someone of your tender age doing out here playing gotcha on our highways?"

Erin knew that she was not going to be drawn into a conversation like this.

"Let me see your driver's license."

"I was trying to strike up a conversation, young woman."

"Your license, please."

"I see. A one way conversation. Manners weren't part of your training program, I see."

"I'm going to have to insist that you hand me your driver's license."

The driver of the Lexus, apparently temporarily out of repartee, fumbled for his wallet, discovered that he couldn't extract it from his pocket while wearing his seat belt, and proceeded to make a production of unbuckling and producing the wallet.

"There," he said, handing it over to Erin. "Are you satisfied?"

Erin studied the license. She was immediately aware that the name was a familiar one. William R. Neuberger. It was familiar because she had heard the sheriff and a couple of her colleagues refer to a Vivian Neuberger, the victim of a shooting which was topic number one around the office. There might be a number of Neubergers in Cumberland County, but Erin doubted it. She was sure she was talking to Vivian Neuberger's husband.

She quickly suppressed the temptation to let Mr. Neuberger know that she knew who he was. It had nothing to do with the fact that he was speeding, and she didn't want to give him an opening to assert that his wife's death was responsible for his irresponsibile behavior.

"Mr. Neuberger, I want you to step outside." It was time to determine whether he was driving under the influence.

"If you think I'm drunk, you had better have another think."

"We shall see."

Neuberger continued to grouse, but he also demonstrated an ability to walk a straight line with such ease that she chose not to subject him to a breathalyzer test.

He pocketed the ticket, buckled up in a way that called attention to the fact that he was complying with the law, and eased slowly onto the road.

"Quota filled?" he said as he pulled away. There was something else, but Erin didn't hear him. Probably just as well.

Erin was pleased to find the sheriff at the department at day's end. She wasn't looking for praise for how she had handled the Neuberger situation, but she thought that the sheriff would be interested in what had happened. Needless to say, Carol was.

"Your first speeding ticket, and it goes to one of my persons of interest. Sorry, Erin. We try to be careful calling a person a suspect in a murder investigation. You say he gave you some lip?"

"I'm afraid he did," the young officer said. "He obviously thought I was too young to be doing this. He knew he'd been speeding. Never tried to argue he wasn't. But he was clearly trying to make me uncomfortable, get me to say something I shouldn't."

"Interesting," Carol said. "Considering that he's been questioned about his wife's death, you'd think he'd be more cautious, not say things that could irritate me. Of course he might not have expected you to be having this conversation with me, but I doubt it. It sounds like he was either so annoyed at being pulled over that he wasn't using his head, or he was trying to gain some advantage by the way he handled what happened. But I can't imagine what that could be. It's obvious that I'm going to have to have a chat with him."

Erin asked a question that had been on her mind ever since she'd ticketed Neuberger.

"Do you suppose he's the one who killed is wife?"

Carol smiled.

"I have no idea who killed Mrs. Neuberger. As I said, he's a person of interest, but so are several other people. I believe you suggested that Mrs. Neuberger's killer might have been the woman whose husband was having an affair with her."

"Oh, yes, but that was just because of a book I was reading."

Erin looked embarrassed.

"I'd like to read that book. Why don't you give me the name?"

"Right now I don't remember, but I'll check up on it for you if you'd like."

"I'd like. Now about Mr. Neuberger. It sounds as if you handled a difficult situation very well. I normally don't have any problem with my officers discussing things with their colleagues. Same in this case. But I'd appreciate it if you don't mention ticketing Mr. Neuberger until I've had a chance to talk with him, and I propose to do that tomorrow."

Carol looked at Erin to see if she understood her reasoning. If she didn't, she didn't say so. Instead she looked as if she had been admitted to the club.

After Erin left for the day, Carol put a call through to Bill Neuberger. He was at home and he answered on the fifth ring.

"It's the sheriff, Mr. Neuberger. I'm sure you've been expecting to hear from me."

"Well, yes, I was, but I must say I didn't expect it to be so soon." The man coughed, apologized, and proceeded to offer what sounded like a half hearted mea culpa. "You do understand, I hope, that I had not been drinking. I know it isn't fashionable these days, but I'm a teetotaler, have been all my life. It was just one of those cases where you're on a straight away, almost no cars in sight, and next thing you know you're going a bit too fast. I've already written the check."

"What I called about was that I'd like to see you. The phone isn't the ideal way to discuss things like this. I'd like to do it tomorrow morning before you get wrapped up in whatever's on your agenda. Is that acceptable?"

"It doesn't sound as if you're giving me any choice. So of course, I'm at your disposal. At your office?"

"No, why don't I meet you at your house. As I recall, it's just south of Yates Center. How about nine?"

"That will be fine." He didn't sound nearly as fired up as he had when Erin pulled him over.

Carol, in turn, found herself wondering just what she expected to learn from their meeting.

CHAPTER 46

The thunderstorm hadn't been predicted, and when it struck at around one a.m. it jarred both Carol and Kevin awake. He reached over to turn on the lamp on the bedside table. It had no sooner flickered on than it went out.

"Damn." Their area rarely had a power failure, but they faced one now. Carol prowled around until she found a flashlight, and within a few minutes they had located candles and retreated to the living room, where they watched the occasional lightning bolt and listened to the thunder, which seemed to be concentrated on the bluff directly across from the cottage.

"What did we do to deserve this?" Kevin asked.

"Let's not complain," Carol said. "I like it for a change. Reminds us that Mother Nature lives by her own rules."

"Where do you suppose the idea that it's *Mother* Nature came from?"

"You'd rather it were Father Nature?" Carol sounded surprised that Kevin might actually think so.

"It's just as logical."

"No it isn't. We may have to put up with patriarchies when it comes to politics, but nature is another story. Nature is about fertility, about creation. No question about it, it's Mother Nature."

"Carol, it's the middle of the night. We're having a thunderstorm. Can't we leave it at that?"

"Of course, dear. But need I remind you that you're the one who brought up this nonsense about Father Nature."

"I think I'm ready to go back to bed," Kevin said, suddenly interested in changing the subject. "Let's blow out the candles and snuggle."

"Great idea," Carol said, taking his hand and following him back to the bedroom.

The alarm reminded both of them it was seven o'clock. Kevin shut it off and pulled Carol to him.

"How about some more thunder and lightening?" he said in a sleepy voice.

"I would never be able to explain to Mr. Neuberger why I missed our appointment," she said as they nuzzled.

"I'm sure you'd think of something," he said.

"Like a date with Mother Nature," Carol said, as she pushed off the covers and sat up in bed. "I'd love to stay right here all day, but no can do. Duty calls. And take a look - skies have cleared."

"Power on?"

Carol got up and tested the lights.

"All's well," she said as she flipped her bedside switch.

"Sorry to hear it. I prefer candles."

"Personally, I'm a fan of lights out. Sleep on if you can; I'm taking a shower." She disappeared down the hall to the bathroom.

———

As she drove to Yates Center for her meeting with Mr. Neuberger, Carol found herself wondering if he and Vivian had had a relationship as satisfying as hers and Kevin's. Or had the fire gone out. Had Vivian shifted her amatory interests to Larry Finch? And had Bill retaliated by killing her? Whether these thoughts had anything to do with his treatment of Officer Dockery the previous day she had no idea. But she would be looking for clues that might contribute to an understanding of what had happened in Anson's Grove.

Whatever Bill Neuberger had to say for himself, he had taken the trouble to be ready for the sheriff. He was well dressed, as if to counter Erin's report with evidence that he was a man of the world. He had a pot of coffee ready, and a plate of tempting looking scones on the table next to her seat in a neat and tidy living room. Everything suggested that he was planning to be on his best behavior.

"This is a pleasure. It's not often that I get to enjoy breakfast with important personages."

Why the stilted 'important personages', Carol didn't know. But she was more interested in his reference to breakfast.

"I certainly didn't intend to interrupt your breakfast hour," she said.

"You haven't. I'm a light eater. Coffee and scones, that will do it for me. What about you? Cream and sugar?"

“Black, unsweetened, thank you. I do appreciate it that you are willing to begin your day with me.”

“No problem at all. And let me repeat my apology of yesterday. I am not an habitual speeder.”

“I’m sure you’re not. But I haven’t come to discuss the ticket, Mr. Neuberger. I wanted to say something about the way you treated my officer. You may have been annoyed, but there was no reason to berate her as you did. She was only doing her job.”

“I may have been out of order, sheriff, but frankly I’m used to dealing with adults. Vivian and I never had children. It was a shock when this little girl began telling me what to do. I never expected to see one so young playing policeman. I suppose it’s hard in an area like this to recruit experienced people.”

“Actually, I like to think my officers are pretty well qualified to do what they do.”

“Of course. I’m not being critical. It’s just that I’m used to the way things are down in the Hamptons.”

Intentionally or otherwise, Bill Neuberger was reverting to the persona she had observed when she first interviewed him. Let him think what he will, she thought.

“You remind me of a question I had meant to ask. What brought you from the Hamptons to Crooked Lake?”

“Birds. I can do what I do pretty much anywhere. Vivian wanted to be nearer the Cornell Ornithology Lab - she has some close friends there and it had become her personal philanthropy. Birds, I can take ’em or leave ’em, but not Viv.”

“Are you planning on moving back downstate?”

“Could be. I’m not exactly in a hurry. I haven’t even buried Vivian yet. Speaking of which, why haven’t you released her body? I want to hold a little memorial service.”

Carol had been wondering about this, too, inasmuch as she didn’t have the authority to release it. After all, it had been a month.

“It always takes more time when foul play is an issue,” she said. “My guess is that you can begin planning the service, just don’t lock in a date yet.”

“To be honest, I haven’t been in any great hurry. I’m sure I’d have to come up with some music featuring birds. Viv had a whole library of classical stuff with bird motifs. She played something about a swan a lot, can’t remember who wrote it.”

Not that planning a memorial service was any of her business, but she knew she'd be asking Kevin if he had any ideas about bird music. Something else that wasn't strictly speaking any of her business came to mind. She decided to say something.

"The way you tell it, you and Vivian had different interests. But it sounds as if your marriage worked for both of you." She wasn't sure what Bill would think of this invitation to talk about his marriage.

At first he said nothing. When he finally did, he surprised her.

"You've probably been wondering why I don't seem to have the proverbial broken heart. I'm sure others have also been wondering. That McKendrick woman actually asked me about it. Let's just say I'm not the demonstrative type. None of my family was. But I loved her in my way. I don't suppose I ever asked her if she loved me, and it didn't really matter. The fact is the marriage worked, and I shall miss her."

This is not the kind of confession, Carol thought, for which there is anything one can say without feeling somewhat foolish. But she wanted to say something kind. It would simply be a conversation filler if Bill knew nothing about his wife's alleged affair with Larry Finch. If he was aware of such an affair, however, he might well suspect that Carol knew about it, too.

"No two marriages are ever exactly alike." she said.

She hadn't expected Neuberger to comment, and he didn't. What he did do was ask the sheriff if she'd like a second cup of coffee. It was obvious that he wasn't encouraging her to say yes, but inviting her to use the offer as an excuse to say she had to be going.

"Thank you for your time," she said as she got up. "Just remember to be polite if and when you encounter Officer Dockery again. She's new on her job, but she's a smart one."

After Carol had left, Neuberger poured another cup of coffee and helped himself to a scone. He was thinking about the sheriff's department. He was annoyed that he'd had to apologize for the way he had spoken to the young woman officer, but it was a minor thing. After all, the talent pool in Cumberland County would be shallow, and hiring competent people had to be a perennial challenge. There were exceptions, of course. He was one of them, and there were always a few even in the remotest backwaters. The sheriff was obviously a cut above average, but he was convinced that she, too, wasn't the brightest bulb in her line of work. How could she be if this was the best professional niche she could find?

He smiled at the relative ineptitude of local law and order. It offended his sense of order and efficiency. But then, he said to himself, in the circumstances, why should I complain?

CHAPTER 47

Carol was at the other end of the lake from Southport, but she had no appointments on her calendar until that afternoon. Impulsively, she decided to drive down the lake and pay a visit to Michael Nagle. Unless he had himself a summer job, he would probably sleep in like other teen agers and thus be on hand when she arrived. If he wasn't there, she would not have wasted much time. And she was anxious to see Michael without having forewarned either him or his chronically worried mother.

She was circling the town square and about to turn once more onto the street shared by the Nagles and the Taggarts, when she spotted one of her department's patrol cars on the side of the road, its driver frantically waving out his window at her. Parking was a bit of a problem, but she found a place and headed across the square to where her colleague was waiting. It was Tommy Byrnes.

She leaned in the open window and asked him what the problem was.

"No problem, just a heads up and when I saw you I thought I'd pass it on now rather than wait until we're back at the office."

"I'm all ears."

"JoAnne says a call came in this morning from a Muriel Snell. She says you'll know who she is. Anyway, she called to say that Paul Raymore is back."

"Well, what do you know. The mysterious bird expert decides to return to the nest. Did she offer any details?"

"No, just that she thought you'd like to know."

"She's right about that. He's the only one of the people who wandered away from Agnes McKendrick on that bird hike that I haven't met. I think I'm going to change my plans."

"Change your plans?"

"Right. I was on my way to the Nagles to see how young Michael is doing. But he'll keep, while Raymore might just take off again."

"Want me to do something about him?"

"No, you do whatever brings you to Southport."

Tommy looked momentarily disappointed. But then he shrugged.

"The truth is I have an appointment with my dentist in another ten minutes."

"Nothing serious, I hope."

"That's what I'll be finding out," he said.

Carol wished him good luck and went back to her car and the trip to Reachers Point.

The drive took her back up the road toward Yates Center. This time there was no sign of Mrs. Snell but, more importantly, there was a car parked outside the Raymore garage.

Carol rapped sharply on the back door. And waited. Approximately two minutes passed, and she found herself thinking that perhaps the man was sleeping off jet lag.

But then he appeared. He looked confused, as well he might, considering that he faced a woman in a police uniform whom he'd never seen before.

"Yes?" And then almost immediately, recognition. "Oh, you must be the sheriff."

"Yes, I am. Sheriff Kelleher. And you are Paul Raymore. I had expected to meet with you before this, but I've been busy and I believe you've been out of town. May I come in?"

"As long as you don't mind the condition of the place. I just got back from a trip last night, and you know how it is."

If Mr. Raymore was alarmed to find the sheriff at his door, he didn't act it. Other than the fact that he looked tired, there was something vaguely *GQ* about him. A reasonably handsome man, he obviously hadn't shaved since his return and he sported a tan that became him. He was wearing shorts and sandals, and a brightly colored summer shirt that had not been buttoned. He had a hairy chest.

Carol was immediately struck by the profusion of bird prints.

"Who is the artist?" she asked. "He - or is it a she? - does beautiful work."

"Indeed he does. It's Robert Bateman. Here, why don't you take a seat while I get you some coffee. Okay?"

"Thanks but no thanks. I've had my quota." She took a seat and resumed her inspection of the room. "I've heard that you are our lake's number one birder, and this confirms it."

She nodded in the direction of the wall opposite them.

"I'm not sure about number one, but I guess you could say I'm slightly bird crazy. It's one of the reasons why I bought this cottage."

This information surprised Carol.

"I think we have our share of birds, but I wasn't aware that it was anything special."

Raymore smiled.

"I was looking for a get away place, and a chap I know told me he'd heard that the Finger Lakes might interest a birder like me. I think he just happened to catch a lot of migrating birds one time in the Montezuma marsh area over near Auburn. But it's still a nice place to relax, even if birding here is not top drawer."

"But you did join the Crooked Lake Birders Club."

"I suppose that's what you've come to talk with me about." Raymore laughed. "By the way, I'm just back from a trip where I saw quite a few more birds than you'll find around here."

"Really? Where to?"

"Trinidad, down in the southern Caribbean. There's a place there called the Asa Wright Nature Center which I visit from time to time."

Carol remembered thinking Raymore's neighbor had said he might have gone to Asia. It had been Asa.

"I hope it was a good trip."

"Yes and no," he replied. "I saw some bellbirds, a few toucans, all kinds of hummingbirds. Even gave a lecture. But I've been there a dozen times. It was sort of like feeding an addiction. So I cut the trip short and here I am."

"Well, I'm glad we finally caught up with each other. Let's talk about that tragic bird hike when Vivian Neuberger was killed."

"That was indeed a tragedy, wasn't it?"

"Did you know Mrs. Neuberger well?"

"I wish I'd known her better. She was a real authority. But no, I only knew her from the few hikes we took with McKendrick's club."

"What was your impression of her?"

"You don't form much of an impression when you're tramping through the woods or canoeing up a lake inlet. But she was a professional. I like to think I know a lot about birds, but she beats me, hands down."

It sounded to Carol more like a competition than a hobby.

"I suppose different birders have different specialties," she said.

"That may be, but Mrs. Neuberger knew it all."

Did he mean that literally?

"That's not kind," Raymore corrected himself. "Anyway, she never put the other birders down by showing off her knowledge."

"Do you have any idea who might have killed Mrs. Neuberger?" Carol asked.

"Absolutely none. It makes no sense, does it?"

"Do you know the Finches well?" she asked, changing the subject.

"Sallie Finch?"

"Sallie and Larry."

"Only Sallie. Larry wasn't part of the club."

"I ask only because a couple of people have called Larry Finch Daddy Bird, and when I asked where that name came from they said it was you."

"Oh, that." Paul Raymore looked uncomfortable. "Just a poor joke."

"People don't usually use nicknames when referring to people they don't know, but you seem to have coined the name Daddy Bird for Larry Finch."

"I can't imagine why. I'm not sure I'd recognize the man if I ran into him on the street."

"Back to the fatal hike. I'm told you left the group that day."

"I'll have to plead guilty. My guess is you'd have done the same if you'd been with us."

"Where did you go?"

"Your deputy sheriff asked me the same question. You might say I went off to where I could hear the birds, not McKendrick."

"But you had no special agenda?"

"No, and it certainly wasn't my agenda to waylay Mrs. Neuberger and kill her. Of course that's what everyone will have told you. In my case it happens to be the truth."

"Do you own guns?" Carol asked.

"Bridges, I think his name is - he also asked me that. Weeks ago. I'm surprised he didn't tell you that the answer is no."

"Actually he did," Carol said, allowing herself a small smile.

By the time Carol left the cottage with all the Bateman prints, she still lacked a good sense of where Paul Raymore stood among her persons of interest, much less her suspects, in the Neuberger murder case. He hadn't said so, of course, but there had been just a hint that he might have envied Vivian her position as a rival in the hierarchy of Crooked Lake birders. That this might have constituted a motive for murder struck her as ludicrous. But she was not a birder, and she had no way of knowing how seriously some of them might take such a seemingly benign avocation.

CHAPTER 48

Deputy Sheriff Sam Bridges had discussed his mission with Carol the previous day. They had, he thought, covered every possible angle. But for some reason, Sam was uneasy. It wasn't that he was concerned that the man would pull a gun on him. Unlike Kevin, who was unarmed and had been taken by surprise, Sam was both armed and forewarned. Moreover, he knew that the man had no legal explanation for his presence at the long abandoned house. So he would simply tell him to pack up his belongings, if there were any, and move along. There would be no argument. Why, then, this feeling that his meeting with Mr. Campbell would not go well?

He had never heard of Garth Campbell until MVA records identified him as the owner of the black BMW with New York license plate SXP-3982. Now he knew that Campbell lived down in the Catskills in Monticello, worked for a firm that specialized in kitchens and baths, and like Frank Grandi, was a vocal advocate of fracking. There was no proof that he knew Grandi, but for obvious reasons it seemed likely that he did. Was it because Campbell could be working for Grandi that Sam was anxious? After all, Grandi had a reputation as a trouble maker. Perhaps he recruited people like himself, men who were single minded, ornery, willing to test the limits to have their way. Sam was speculating about such things and their possible consequences for his unscheduled meeting with Campbell when he reached the turn off towards Anson's Grove.

He guided his patrol car onto the Benson Road and immediately slowed down, the better to withstand the punishment it meted out to the rare driver foolish enough to venture onto it. He had never driven to the end of this road, never seen the abandoned house which was reported to be at its terminus. Sam could not understand why anyone would choose to risk damage to his car once he became aware of how poorly the road had been maintained. That thought prompted a quiet laugh. The Benson Road had not been poorly maintained. As he had discovered the day Vivian Neuberger had been shot, no effort had been made to maintain it at all, much less to improve it in a great many years.

At a speed of no more than ten miles per hour, it took Sam almost that many minutes to reach the point below the Grove where he had parked and met the birders. It took him the better part of another half hour before he reached his destination. The Grove was now well out of sight behind him, and the derelict house, overgrown by vines and surrounded by maple trees, was barely visible. One thing was clear, however. There was no car parked beside it.

Sam had given no thought to the possibility that the car might be gone, but of course he should have. Perhaps its owner had not been using the derelict house for some nefarious purpose, as they had assumed. Perhaps he had only been there the once, on a day when Carol's husband had also traveled to the end of Benson Road. But that seemed unlikely. According to Kevin, the BMW's driver's behavior had not been that of someone who had just happened on the old ruined house. He had obviously felt a proprietary interest in it. Which meant that in all likelihood he would return.

Only with some difficulty did Sam maneuver the patrol car so that it faced back up the Benson Road. If it became necessary to leave the swale in a hurry, he didn't want to be facing the wrong way. The car positioned as he thought prudent, he shut off the engine and stepped out to take a better look at the house he had heard so much about but never seen.

It looked very much as Kevin had described it, right down to the rotting porch and the empty windows. The vicissitudes of nature could have been responsible for the missing windows, but Sam had a feeling that at the some time in the past young boys had had some fun breaking them and, no doubt, using them as a means of access to the abandoned dwelling. Sam might be able to squeeze through one of the windows, but he intended to try the door first. That the lock could still be intact after all these years was doubtful. It was as he had expected. The door swung open with a bit of reluctant groaning, but posed no problem. It was little more than a few shoves away from collapsing.

Little effort had been made to make the interior livable. The cabin - for it was much too primitive to be called a house - was for all practical purposes empty. There were only two rooms, one apparently a combination living room/bedroom, although it contained neither a chair nor a bed. The other and smaller of the two rooms might have been a kitchen, although the only evidence that that had been its purpose was an old fashioned sink with a rusted pump and a small open hearth which accounted for the cabin's chimney. Whoever had lived here had obviously made do without electricity and had drawn his water from a well. Someone who knew more about such things might be able to hazard an intelligent guess as to when the cabin had been built, but Sam was reasonably certain that it was back in the 19th century. Why, he wondered, had the builder, presumably the hermit Anson, gone to such trouble in such an inhospitable setting to carve out such a pathetic place to live. Sam tried to imagine the magnitude of the task of digging the well, cutting and shaping floors and walls and roofing, and turning this god-forsaken pocket of the wilderness into something he presumably called home.

The larger room contained no furniture, but it did possess two items which attested to the recent presence of Garth Campbell. One was a sleeping bag, which had been rolled up, tied, and left against a wall near the door. It was not brand new, but it looked to be in good shape. Next to it rested a navy blue back pack. Sam turned it upside down and shook it until its few belongings fell to the floor. A half full bottle of spring water; two candy bars; a deck of cards held together by a rubber band; a small bottle of pills, the label of which identified them as xanax; an oddly shaped tool whose purpose Sam couldn't imagine; a faded polo shirt with the words Hurley's Hut across the chest. Sam picked up the polo shirt. It looked as if Campbell had used it as a rag rather than as an article of clothing.

No clue there to the man who had pointed a shotgun at the sheriff's husband. Unless possibly the pills said something about his physical condition. Sam had never heard of xanax. For the first time since he had entered the cabin, he thought he detected a familiar odor. He went from one room to the other, sniffing, trying to recall what he was smelling. It came to him when he reconsidered the polo shirt. It was the smell of sweat, sweetened by something else. Perhaps sun tan lotion, or some kind of after shave. Sam saw no need to pick up the contents of the back pack. Better to use his time exploring the grounds around the cabin. There should be a privy somewhere, but he saw no sign of one when he stepped outside. There was just a hint of a path until it disappeared altogether in a dense thicket of trees. Pushing the vines out of his way as he entered the woods, Sam came to what was obviously the ruins of an old outhouse. It was in no condition to provide privacy when nature called. Garth Campbell must have relieved himself somewhere in these woods, but this was not a problem Sam felt any need to solve. He turned and headed back to the cabin.

He had almost reached it when he heard a car. It was coming down the Benson Road, much as he had nearly an hour earlier. Campbell! Sam had been studying the man's hideaway, but had almost forgotten the man himself. Well, he thought, this is why I'm here. He stepped around the rotting porch and stood there at the foot of the road, watching a black car approaching slowly. It wasn't until it as only a few car lengths away that he realized it was not a BMW he was staring at, but a Jaguar.

The Jaguar rolled to a stop directly in front of the patrol car, so close that the hood ornaments were practically touching. The man who emerged from the Jaguar looked nothing like the description he had been given of Garth Campbell.

"Good morning, officer. What brings you to this woe begotten corner of Cumberland County?"

The words were pleasant enough, but the voice that spoke them had a sharper edge.

"That's what I was going to ask you," Sam said.

"No secret. I was in the mood for a drive, and this is where I ended up. Pretty rough road, wouldn't you say?"

"Which is why I asked what brings you here. Wouldn't think you'd want to drive a nice car like yours on a road like that."

"Slow and easy, that's my motto. But tell me, what on earth are you doing down here? Somehow I don't think you'll be issuing many speeding tickets on this road."

It was obvious that the driver of the Jaguar had no intention of explaining himself. Sam was equally certain that the man had been here before. His name may not be Campbell, but Sam was willing to bet that he knew Campbell.

"I'm here because we heard that someone was staying in this cabin. It doesn't make sense. Like you said, this is woe begotten country. Who'd want to hole up down here? We made a few inquiries and found out his name's Campbell, Garth Campbell. You know him?"

"Never heard of him," came the laconic answer. Sam didn't believe him. He'd never met Grandi, but he was almost certain that the man he was talking to was Frank Grandi. Two men driving fancy cars and subjecting them to the wretched Benson Road. Two men who were known to be strong advocates of fracking. He didn't know what they were up to, but instinct told him that they were in it together.

"You're Frank Grandi, aren't you?"

The driver of the Jaguar was too smart to deny that he was Grandi. He'd known that the officer would already have memorized his license plate number. Moreover, the officer worked for the county sheriff, and the two of them would compare notes and know that they had met and talked with the same man.

"Yes, I'm Grandi," he said. "But what it this about somebody named Campbell?"

"Like I said, he's been staying in that old run down shack behind me. Sure you don't know him? Drives a black car like yours, only it's a BMW."

"Sorry I can't help you, but I don't know any Campbells. You ask me, he's crazy."

Sam very much doubted that Garth Campbell was crazy. And why would Grandi deny that he knew him? And claim he'd just happened to be on the Benson Road this morning? Wasn't it far more likely that he knew Campbell, knew he was using the old cabin, and had come to meet him there?

"Whether he's crazy or not, I came down here to evict him. As you can see, he's not here, which means I may have to make another trip down that damn road."

"What are you going to do about him?" Grandi's question may simply have been a conversational gambit, but Sam thought he was genuinely curious.

"I'm going to remove the stuff he left here, put up a no trespassing sign."

"Isn't that a bit excessive? Poor guy's not hurting anybody but himself."

"Public safety issue, Mr. Grandi. We try to discourage people putting themselves in harm's way. It was less than a year ago when a couple of kids were poking around in an old deserted barn and the floor gave way. One of them broke his collar bone and got a nasty cut on his head."

"If it was me, I'd say it was their fault for doing something stupid."

"Maybe so, but it's my job, so if you'll excuse me -"

Sam opened the trunk of the patrol car and brought out a printed sign, a long board, a heavy duty hammer, and a box of large nails.

While Grandi watched he reloaded the back pack and put it and the sleeping bag in the trunk and then nailed the board across the the door and posted the no trespassing sign. It wouldn't keep out anybody who was determined to enter the cabin, but it might give the casual visitor - perhaps even Campbell - something to think about.

Sam had hoped that Grandi would get the message and leave, but he seemed more interested in watching the county's law and order official do his thing. Which meant that Sam would have to ask him to leave, for there was no way that he could make it out of the cul de sac with the Jaguar blocking his path.

"You can tell people you've seen me earn my pay," he said, "but I've got other things to do and that means I'll have to ask you to move your car."

"Oh, of course." Grandi went through an elaborate pantomime of apology. It was soon apparent that merely turning the Jaguar around and pulling it as far to the right as possible might not provide Sam with room enough to leave. Grandi would also have to go back up to where Benson Road met the nearest county highway.

When the two vehicles reached the intersection, Grandi got out of the Jaguar and walked back to the patrol car.

"This has been an interesting morning, officer," he said when Sam rolled his window down. "Proves that there's always something new under the sun. Anyway, I hope you run into this Cambell fellow. He'll probably want his back pack back."

"I'm sure we'll find him in due course. Meanwhile, I'd keep that Jag off the Benson Road if it were mine."

Sam was willing to bet that Grandi would not keep his Jag off the Benson Road. He wouldn't drive back to the abandoned cabin right now. Probably not even today. But someday he would be paying another visit to Garth Campbell or whomever would be the next inhabitant of that derelict dwelling.

CHAPTER 49

The sheriff's unfinished business included a call on Michael Nagle. She also needed to talk with his parents, and, more importantly, his doctor, provided they could find a way to deal with the confidentiality issue. But she wanted to see for herself whether young Michael was less belligerent, more willing to talk about his demons. Since the episode in the waterfront park he had apparently not been working. It was Carol's understanding that the doctor up in Rochester had put him on a regimen of drugs and insisted that he 'take it easy' for a few more weeks.

As had been her plan the day before, Carol did not make an appointment.

"Good morning, Mrs. Nagle," she announced when the chronically anxious mother opened the door. Fran Nagle's face reflected the fact that she wasn't happy to see her.

"Hello, sheriff. I wasn't expecting you today."

"If my life had not been so busy, I would have stopped by sooner. But I'm concerned about Michael. How is he doing?"

Mrs. Nagle looked puzzled, as if she had been asked a trick question.

"How's he doing?"

"We know he's being treated by a doctor. I've been wondering if he's - shall we say calmer?"

"Calmer." It was as if saying the word had a similar effect on Michael's mother. "He stays in his room most of the time. That's what Dr. Boylan expected him to do, although it's kind of strange. I haven't seen him so lethargic since the year he had all those children's diseases."

"I'm glad to hear it," Carol said. "It sounds as if he has some of his impulsive behavior under control."

"Dr. Boylan says he can go back to work in another week. It'll be a relief to see him doing something for a change. It doesn't seem natural, lying around like he does."

"What is it that Michael will be doing?"

"He's a bagger down at the grocery store. They were very understanding about the time off. Hank told them he'd had a hernia."

Carol wasn't sure the Nagles should have made up such an excuse for Michael. She wondered how he'd handle it. But she wasn't surprised that they had wished to conceal the fact that the real reason for his absence was that a psychiatrist had insisted upon it. Mental health was still a difficult subject for many to deal with.

"I'd like to talk with him," she said.

A familiar look of something approaching panic crossed Mrs. Nagle's face.

"I don't think that would be a good idea," she said.

"Did Dr. Boylan say something about Michael not having company?"

"It's not exactly that. But if you were to talk to him, it'd get him thinking about Mrs. Neuberger and that would get him all upset."

"I hadn't planned on talking about Mrs. Neuberger. I would simply like to see how he's doing."

"I know, and that's nice of you. But Michael, all he knows about you is that you're looking for whomever killed that woman. What if seeing you gets him worked up again about something he didn't do?"

It was obvious that the Nagles, or at least Mrs. Nagle, remained convinced that their son was completely innocent of the tragedy in Anson's Grove. It would do no good for her to tell Michael's mother that neither she nor her husband knew that for a certainty.

"Has Dr. Boylan talked with you about those pictures that Michael drew?"

For a fleeting few seconds Carol thought that Mrs. Nagle was going to ask what pictures she was referring to.

"We haven't really discussed the pictures," Fran finally said.

Carol wasn't surprised. Psychiatrists typically treated conversations with their patients as privileged communications. Dr. Boylan would surely be aware that bringing Michael's mother into the picture at this stage would not only be unprofessional but unwise.

Carol would have preferred a few minutes alone with Michael, but she made a suggestion which she knew Mrs. Nagle would prefer.

"Let's go, let me say hello. I promise not to mention the bird hike."

She got up, assuming correctly that Michael's mother would not protest further.

Michael looked like a different person than she had remembered. She wasn't quite sure just what the difference was. Was he more subdued? Yes, but it was more than that. Was he half asleep? Perhaps, but that could have been an act of will. Was he simply indifferent? Carol could understand it where his mother was concerned. She presumably popped into his room frequently, and just as frequently he probably tuned her out. But Carol had assumed that her presence would produce a different reaction. It hadn't.

"Hello, Michael. I've been worried about you, and thought it was time I stopped by to see how you're doing."

"I'm doing fine." He showed no sign of saying more.

"I hope you and Dr. Boylan are getting along okay."

As soon as she had said it, Carol regretted doing so. Unless Boylan were a magician, she doubted that he and Michael would have bonded.

"He's okay. Asks too many questions, but I guess that's what shrinks do."

Carol's initial reaction to Michael calling the psychiatrist a shrink was one of surprise. But she knew she shouldn't have been surprised. He might not be doing that well in school, but Michael, like most teenagers, would already have a good vernacular vocabulary where such things were concerned.

"I'll bet you're looking forward to going back to work."

"Not really."

"Oh, why's that?"

"It's boring."

Michael was not in an expansive mood, which made conversation difficult.

"Is there some course you're taking this fall that you're looking forward to?" It would not have surprised her if he gave her another laconic answer, such as 'no.'

Michael's answer was characteristically laconic, but it wasn't 'no.'

"I haven't registered. It sure won't be science."

Mrs. Nagle, who had been sitting uncomfortably at the bottom of the bed, stood up. Carol assumed that she thought the conversation was heading for dangerous waters.

"Maybe we should let Michael sleep," his mother said.

"I don't want to sleep," he said. Carol wasn't surprised to hear him say it, but she felt somewhat encouraged that it was said without obvious animus.

"No, of course not," she said, "but I should be going anyway. It was good to talk with you, Michael. Take care of yourself."

She preceded Mrs. Nagle out the door and down the stairs. There was no point in extending this brief meeting longer. She had no sense of what was going on in Michael's mind. What she did have, however, was a picture of what he had been doing with his time alone in his room. In addition to a laptop that she couldn't read, the surface of the big work table contained a sketch pad and other drawing supplies, plus several interesting drawings. She had been conscious of the drawings ever since entering Michael's room. As she left, she had made a point of taking a closer look at them. They were all efforts to capture what could be seen out the large picture window behind the work table: trees in bloom, clouds in a blue sky, a church steeple in the background, and, attached to the window, a large bird feeder.

The drawings were obviously the work of an amateur. But they weren't bad. They were considerably better than Michael's angry picture of birds attacking a woman who was obviously his science teacher, Vivian Neuberger. Some of the birds at the window feeder in these new drawings were actually recognizable. Two were clearly intended to be woodpeckers. More importantly, all of the drawings on the work table could be described as peaceful.

CHAPTER 50

Carol stood at the back of the stage surveying the high school auditorium. She was surprised that Bill Neuberger had chosen it for this wife's memorial service. Perhaps the Neubergers had not been affiliated with any church. Perhaps Sharon Lagerfeld, the principal, had persuaded Bill to have the service at the school. After all, there were not many logical settings for such a service in Southport, and Vivian had been best known since moving to the lake for her role as the high school science teacher.

The seats in the auditorium were largely empty, but the stage was crowded. The number of students in the crowd were a testament to Vivian's popularity. Not surprisingly, Michael Nagle was not among them. Many, perhaps most, of the teachers were there. Carol looked for members of the Crooked Lake Birders Club. A few of them she hadn't met and couldn't vouch for their presence, but she recognized all of the those she had interviewed. Unless Vivian's killer turned out to be a hunter or Agnes McKendrick's candidate, Frank Grandi, he (or she) was very definitely among those who had come to pay their last respects to her. Carol thought that Bill Neuberger looked as if he would rather be somewhere else, and she wasn't sure she could blame him. He seemed to be engaged in conversation with Sallie Finch, although the 'bird-like' woman seemed to be doing all the talking. Once more the sheriff found herself wondering whether either of them knew what Mel Cone had said about their spouses. Or, more importantly, whether there was any truth to his allegation.

With the exception of some of the students and several members of the faculty, she thought she knew everyone on the stage. Everyone, that is, other than a casually dressed woman with a short pixie haircut who appeared to be looking for someone. Carol decided to introduce herself. She slipped through the crowd, nodding hello as she worked her way toward the stranger.

"Hello," she said as she reached her side. "I don't believe we've met. I'm Carol Kelleher. A terrible tragedy, Mrs. Neuberger's death."

"It certainly is. How did you know her?"

Carol had been hoping to finesse this question, but knew it would probably be impossible.

"I guess you could say that I'm in charge of the investigation into her death. I'm the sheriff of Cumberland County. It wasn't appropriate to come to the memorial service in uniform. What was your relationship to her?"

"The fact is I hardly knew her. In person, that is. But she was a major supporter of Cornell's Ornithology Lab. I work there, and I'm here to represent the Lab on this sad occasion. I don't envy you your job, but I hope you'll catch whoever did this terrible thing soon. Or perhaps you already have, and word just hasn't reached us over at Sapsucker Woods."

"I'm afraid not. Everyone says such nice things about Vivian, but I never had a chance to meet her. Sorry, I didn't catch your name."

"I don't think I introduced myself, sheriff. It's Naomi Sager."

"I'm just now in the process of learning about Vivian. I know she was an authority on birds. Perhaps I should say an accomplished scientist. What was her connection with Cornell?"

"She's a benefactor of the Ornithology Lab, not to mention a major contributor to our publications." Ms. Sager closed her eyes and took a deep breath. "I haven't acquired the habit of using the past tense, have I?"

"It's going to be hard for a lot of people. I assume you heard that this happened on a bird hike."

"Yes. My picture of Vivian is of someone who always wanted to be out in the field. I'm sure she was invaluable to your birders club."

"That's what I've been hearing. Most of the birders over here aren't what you'd call experts. I don't know much about the club, but it's been my impression that Vivian was one of only two or three who really was an authority."

"Just a guess, but would one of the others be someone named Raymore?"

"You know Mr. Raymore?"

"No, never met him, but we've talked on the phone a couple of times. I mention his name because when he called he was asking about Mrs. Neuberger."

"Really. That's interesting. He lives on Crooked Lake, and he was on the bird hike when someone shot Vivian. You say he has been asking about her. What was his interest?"

"I'm not really sure. His name just came to mind as we were talking. For people in the know, Raymore is considered one of the top birders in North America. I took a call from him a couple of years ago. He was of the impression that Mrs. Neuberger was somehow affiliated with the Ornithology Lab, and wondered if she lived in Ithaca. I knew she had moved to Crooked Lake, and told him so. I remember that he called back some time later to tell me that he appreciated my information, and that he, too, had chosen to move there. A case, I guess, of some serious birders getting together."

Paul Raymore had never mentioned this to Carol, which she found interesting. It sounded to her as if Raymore might have moved from the metropolitan area to the lake because he'd discovered that the Neubergers now lived there. Unfortunately, this was not the time or place to pursue the matter. She'd find a way to bring it up when next she talked with Raymore.

"By the way, if you'd like to meet Mr. Raymore, he's right over there." Carol looked off in the middle distance to her right and nodded in that direction.

"Why, yes, that would be nice. I'm sure he's grieving, just as I am."

Carol took Naomi Sager's elbow and steered their way through the crowd to where Raymore was talking with his bete noir, Agnes McKendrick.

"Mr. Raymore, may I interrupt and introduce you to someone. I'm sorry, Agnes, I should include you, too. This is Naomi Sager of Cornell's Ornithology Lab. Paul Raymore, and this is Agnes McKendrick."

It was obvious that Paul did not recognize Sager's name. He shook hands, as did McKendrick,

"Do I know you?" he asked.

"We've spoken on the phone, Mr. Raymore. About Mrs. Neuberger. But it was quite a long time ago."

"Oh, of course." Raymore had made the connection, and it made him uncomfortable. Carol guessed that he would not want Ms. Sager to launch into a trip down memory lane which would reveal more about his interest in Vivian Neuberger than he was willing to share. He shifted the subject.

"How are things at Sapsucker Woods? I'll bet that the Lab's staff loves to have that as an address."

"It is distinctive, don't you think?"

Carol would have loved to listen in on a frank discussion of Paul Raymore's interest in Vivian Neuberger, but it was obvious that he was not going to allow it. She would have to pursue the matter herself, and if he were not forthcoming, she might be having another conversation with Naomi Sager. In fact, she was confidant that she would be having another conversation with Ms. Sager.

"What do you say we let these people play catch up, Agnes." Carol proceeded to steer the leader of the Crooked Lake Birders Club towards what looked like a podium. The timing was perfect. Someone got the attention of the crowd by cueing up the audio of Ralph Vaughan Williams's 'The Lark Ascending.' The memorial service for Vivian Neuberger was underway.

CHAPTER 51

The memorial service for Vivian Neuberger left Carol with mixed feelings. Those who had been called on to speak about her life had uniformly praised her intelligence, her love of nature, and the many ways in which her coming to Crooked Lake had enriched all their lives. But Vivian had been a neighbor for such a comparatively short time that these eulogies invariably felt incomplete. Had she had a sense of humor? Did she have a charm which wasn't easily captured by a recitation of her accomplishments? Carol, after all, had never met her, and when the last speaker had spoken and the crowd had begun to drift off to the school parking lot, she realized that she still did not really know the woman.

There were still a few people clustered around Bill Neuberger. One of them was a man she had decided she needed to talk with. Mel Cone. She went over to where they were standing and hung back, waiting until the others had expressed their condolences or best wishes to Bill. She herself spoke briefly, both because she sensed that Bill was anxious to leave and because she wanted to catch Mel before he got away.

"Mr. Cone," she said as she caught up with him at the door. He turned and, recognizing the sheriff, stopped and smiled.

"What did you think of that affair?" he asked as she joined him.

He hadn't said so, but the way he had said it left the impression that he didn't care for memorial services generally or thought this one had been disappointing.

"I'd call it sad, wouldn't you? Not like what we think of as an occasion to get beyond sorrow and focus on a life well lived."

"I don't think anyone really did justice to Vivian," Mel said. "But then she hadn't really been here all that long."

"Are you in a hurry to be somewhere? I'd like to talk with you, if you can spare me ten minutes or so."

"Why, of course. There's a bench over there," he said, pointing. "Is that good enough?"

"Sure, but let's wait until the last few 'friends of Vivian' have left."

"Which means that you don't want to be interrupted? Or overheard?"

"I'm not contemplating anything secret. I just need some information."

They had the parking lot to themselves when Carol broached the subject that had been on her mind.

"You're a hunter. And a gun collector. Am I right?"

"That's right. It's like I already told you, or maybe it was your deputy. Is there a problem?"

"No. I'm just fishing for some information, and it's because you do own guns that I thought you might be able to help."

It was obvious that Mel didn't know what was on the sheriff's mind.

"I'll do my best," he said in something less than a convincing voice.

"I want to ask what you can tell me about whether any of your fellow birders are gun owners. I figured that people who have guns would be most likely to know whether any of their acquaintances also have them."

"Does this mean that whoever did your ballistics work has identified what it was that shot Vivian?"

Yes, Carol thought, but I'm not ready to divulge that information.

"We're getting there," she said. "Now, do you happen to know if any of the people on the bird hike own guns?"

"I thought your people asked that question of everyone that day in the grove."

"We did, but let's think about it. What if somebody had a gun, shot Vivian, and then ditched the gun. After all, it appears that none of the hikers had a gun on them when they were searched. Officers Bridges and Byrnes are certain about that. But that doesn't mean that none of the birders on the hike owned a gun, does it?"

His wrinkled brow suggested that Mel was thinking about it.

"Frankly, most of the talk on those hikes is about birds, not guns. Unfortunately, I don't think I can be of much help. The only person who ever said anything about guns was Hornaday. He's a funny duck. He never said anything about owning 'em, but he seemed interested in the fact that hunters were responsible for the extinction of the passenger pigeon. He'd read something about it, thought it was amazing that a bird that once flew in flocks of billions could have been wiped out by hunters."

"I think I've read something about that myself. Apparently there's talk of trying to bring the species back to life, using what we know about DNA, cloning, things like that."

"It's all talk," Cone said. "If it were up to me, I'd rather try to recreate the woolly mammoth."

"And that's it as far as the birders club is concerned?"

"I'm afraid so. For all I know, I'm the only member of the birders club who actually collects guns. Which probably makes me suspect number one." Mel laughed at the thought. And then an idea came to his mind.

"Wait a minute," he said. "There's one other thing, although I doubt it has anything to do with what happened to Vivian. I think Bill Neuberger has a gun. At least he did."

This news was more interesting to Carol than the story about Hornaday and passenger pigeons. Bill had been quite clear in his assertion that he was not a gun owner.

"Let's hear it," she said.

"It was back when the Neubergers hadn't been here that long. I barely knew him, but we had a conversation about crime in this area. Seems his house down where they'd come from had been broken into, and he'd bought himself a pistol for protection. He wanted to know if break ins up here were common. I remember laughing, telling him that nobody I knew even locked his door."

"Does he still have that pistol?"

"I have no idea. Probably does. It's easier to get yourself a gun than it is to get rid of it, unless of course you simply throw it in the lake, which doesn't strike me as something somebody like Neuberger would do."

"You're probably right about that," Carol said. "Anyway, you don't think Bill was a hunter?"

"We never discussed it, but he sure doesn't look like one to me. Wouldn't you agree?"

"I'm not sure hunters have a distinct appearance."

"It doesn't look like I've been very helpful. But like I said, I hope that my being a hunter doesn't make me the prime candidate for Vivian's killer."

"If you were to be a prime candidate, it would have more to do with the fact that you were closest to her when she was shot than because you're a hunter."

Carol had smiled as she said it, but Mel didn't take it lightly.

"You aren't serious, are you?"

"If I thought you were Vivian's killer, do you suppose I would have sought you out for information about who's who among gun owners in the Crooked Lake Birders Club?"

"No, I don't suppose so," he said. But when they broke off their little tete a tete on the bench, he wasn't so sure. Perhaps the sheriff had been giving him another chance to divert attention away from himself. If that had been her intention, she would seem to have succeeded.

CHAPTER 52

Carol was comparing notes with Kevin while dinner simmered on the stove. His news was disappointingly thin. The county official with whom he wished to speak was still stick. A note on the door in the county office building told him so. Kevin wondered if there were filing dates that had been missed, and if so whether there was a clause somewhere in the regs that provided for exemptions.

As for Carol, she shared her feelings about the sad memorial for Vivian Neuberger and reported on her meeting with Mel Cone.

"According to Mel, it looks as if more of the birders have guns in their possession than they have heretofore let on," she said.

"How would Mel know something like that?"

"He's a collector, and I thought he might be familiar with others who share his interest in guns. Turns out that Bill Neuberger is a gun owner, contrary to what he's told us."

"Neuberger admits it?"

"No, nothing like that. The Neuberger home down on Long Island had been burglarized, and according to Mel Bill bought himself a gun to protect them from further break-ins. I guess Cone was sharing the local wisdom that crime is a rarity up here, everyone leaves the door unlocked."

"Crime a rarity?" Kevin guffawed. "How about murder?"

"I know, but that wasn't what was on Neuberger's mind."

"So, according to Cone, the husband of our most recent murder victim didn't get rid of his Long Island security blanket?"

"I don't think he knows what Bill did with his pistol, but he seems to believe he still has it."

"Does he have any ideas about the others, like Raymore, or Finch? I mean they also claim not to own guns."

"If he does, he didn't say. And I think he would have if he knew."

"Funny thing. I didn't think of it until just this minute. It concerns our ex-CIA suspect, Finch. Why wouldn't she have a gun?"

"She says she doesn't."

"So does Neuberger. Besides, why wouldn't she have one? Or more than one, for that matter? People in her profession carry them."

"You don't know that," Carol said, disapprovingly.

"Well, there's 007."

"Oh, come on. He's a figment of Ian Fleming's imagination."

"But he's in the same business, spying for king and country."

"If I remember correctly, Bond works for MI6, not the CIA."

"No matter. I'll bet that CIA officers carry fire arms. Maybe we could check it out on Wikipedia."

"This isn't a very productive conversation. Let's eat," she said. "What I should be doing isn't trying to find out if more birders have guns, but seeing if Bill Neuberger still has one."

"Probably a good idea, but I'm betting that Sallie Finch has a gun. Chances are her husband doesn't know it, but I'll bet his predecessor does."

"Even if husband number one could tell us whether she used to have a gun, there's no way he'd know whether she has one now."

Carol got up and headed for the kitchen.

The first thing the sheriff did after squad meeting the next morning was to call Bill Neuberger. She was willing to run the risk that he had slept late.

"Good morning. This is Sheriff Kelleher, and I hope I didn't wake you up."

"I'm not sleeping well these days. You caught me having my second cup of coffee."

"Good. We need to talk. Would it be okay if I came around sometime this morning?"

"As you must know by now, I'm always at your disposal. How is 10:30?"

"I'll be there."

Neuberger was still drinking coffee when Carol arrived. She figured it had to be at least his third, perhaps his fourth.

"I don't like to say it," Carol said, "but I thought the memorial service was almost cruel. For you, I mean. There were nice things said about Vivian, of course, but I had the feeling that it was a drain on you."

"I could have done without it," he replied, "but everyone felt it had to be, so what could I say? Thank goodness, it was mercifully brief."

Carol had been of the impression that, if anything, it dragged on a bit too long.

"I hope you were able to get away fairly quickly after the service."

"Thanks for your solicitude, but I don't believe you have come over to talk about the memorial service. What is it that I can do for you?"

"It shouldn't take long, but something has come to my attention which I'd like to share with you."

He remembered his manners and offered her both a seat and a cup of coffee, which she accepted with alacrity.

"It has to do with guns," she said. "It is essential that we know who among the members of the bird club possessed a gun at the time of the hike in Anson's Grove. All of you were searched at the time, and none of you had a gun on your person. We subsequently asked each of the birders if they owned guns, and only three said they did. You were among those who said that they did not. I'm sorry to be repeating all this, but I want to be sure that we are in agreement."

"Well, yes, what you're telling me sounds right. What is the problem?"

"The problem is that I have heard that you do in fact have a gun."

"That's a lie!" Neuberger was irate. "Who told you I have a gun?"

Carol preferred to avoid implicating Mel Cone if she possibly could.

"The way I heard it, someone had broken into your home and you acquired a gun for your own protection."

"It's that bastard Cone, isn't it?"

"All he did, Mr. Neuberger, was tell me what you had told him. And he didn't volunteer the information, he mentioned it only when I pushed him to tell me if he knew of any of his fellow birders who might own a gun."

Neuberger relaxed somewhat in his chair. But his voice was still strained.

"He had no business telling you I had a gun. The fact of the matter is that when we moved to the lake home I got rid of the gun. I did it because Cone himself told me that break-ins are practically unheard of around the lake. He claims he never locks his door."

"How did you get rid of your gun?"

"For God's sake, what is this? Are you doubting my word?"

"No," Carol said, trying to keep the conversation civil and low keyed. "It's just that it's a well known fact that guns have a way of landing in the wrong hands. I'd feel better if I were sure that it couldn't have happened with yours."

"If it will make you feel better, I got a reasonable price for it from a gun shop in Elmira. I can't remember the name of the place off hand, but I'll see what I can do to locate the receipt."

"I'd appreciate that," she said.

Neuberger looked at the sheriff as if she expected her to charge him with something else.

"Is that all?" he asked.

"Unless there's something else you want to tell me."

"Actually, there is. It hadn't occurred to me that you'd be interested, or that I should say anything about it until you sprang this story of Cone's on me. But it would appear that things have changed, so if you have a few more minutes -"

He left it at that, whatever he planned to say unsaid, waiting for the sheriff to say something.

"I have no urgent appointments. If you have something you'd like to share with me, please go ahead."

A small hint of a smile appeared on Bill's lips.

"This may take a few minutes, so how about we have another coffee."

"No thanks, I've had my quota for the morning."

"As you please, but I'm an addict. Be right back."

It took a bit longer than it had the first time, but Neuberger was soon back in his chair, another steaming cup of coffee in hand.

"Have you ever been aware that someone has an inappropriate interest in your spouse?"

Carol could not believe what she had just heard. Bill Neuberger was about to lay to rest any doubt that Mel Cone had been correct. Vivian had been having an affair with Larry Finch, and her husband had known all about it.

"No, I don't believe I have," Carol said, choosing not to mention the episode of Kevin's teaching assistant. This was not about her; it was about Bill.

"Well, I have. And it was brought to my attention by my wife. The man who seems to have been enamored of her was our friend Mel Cone."

Neuberger paused to admire the shock on the sheriff's face. To say that Carol was stunned would be an understatement. So much for Larry Finch.

"Yes, Mel Cone," Bill continued. "According to Viv, he behaved like a sick puppy when he was around her. She found it amusing, and told him so. If someone told you you were making a fool of yourself, wouldn't you back off? I sure would. But not Mel. It apparently started on our first bird hike with the club, and as far as I know was still going on on the hike when she was killed."

"My God, Bill, why are you just telling me this today? What you're saying makes it sound as if Cone could be your wife's killer."

"Are you kidding? He's a pathetic specimen of the human race, not a killer. I feel sorry for him. Viv did, too."

"But seriously, how can you simply dismiss a man whose advances have not only been rebuffed but who's been laughed at? Not every man would take that kind of blow to his pride so lightly."

"That could be, but Cone isn't every man."

"Just the same, we've talked several times and you've never mentioned this. That strikes me as strange."

"Telling you about it would only have given it an importance it doesn't deserve. It was just a funny, sort of sad, thing that happened. If I'd said something, you'd have focussed on Cone as Viv's killer instead of pursuing the real culprit."

"But you must realize that by telling me of Cone's interest in your wife, you have done just what you didn't want to do earlier. I can hardly ignore what I have learned just because you think Mel is a pathetic innocent."

Neuberger drained his coffee cup and shook his head.

"You will do whatever you feel you must do, sheriff," he said. "All I'm saying is that my neighbor may have been infatuated with my wife, but I'm sure he didn't kill her."

"Who do you think did?" Carol asked.

"You asked me that the first time we met, and I declined to speculate because I didn't know the members of the bird club that well. I shall have to give you the same answer today, and for the same reason. Discounting a few courtesy calls and the memorial service, I haven't seen any of the birders since that dreadful day in Anson's Grove. They are all relative strangers."

As Carol drove back to Cumberland, she was certain of only one thing: contrary to Bill Neuberger's view, Mel Cone would have to be treated as a primary suspect in Vivian's death. For all she knew, that was Bill's intention. But was his story true, or was it simply a spur of the moment ploy to get even with Cone for telling her about his purchase of a gun? She had just recently met with Cone. Now she would have to pay him another visit.

CHAPTER 53

It was a week to the day after Kevin had first sought information about Anson's Grove that he was invited to take a seat in the Cumberland County office which handled property issues. The woman sitting across from him seemed to have made a complete recovery from whatever had sidelined her, although he noticed that there was a box of kleenex close by on her desk.

"I'm sorry to have kept you waiting," she said, which surprised Kevin inasmuch as she had done no such thing. "These summer colds are the absolute worst, don't you think?"

Of course. She was only apologizing for her protracted sick leave.

"They certainly are," he agreed, although he couldn't recall having had a serious summer cold in years. "But I'm here to clarify county policy on abandoned property. Anson's Grove, to be specific. Are you familiar with such a place?"

The woman, who appeared to be in her 40s and whose voice reminded him of a high school history teacher he hadn't particularly cared for, smiled and proceeded to tell him that, of course, she knew all about Anson's Grove.

"What is it you'd like to know?"

"It's my understanding that it's been abandoned for a long time, but I have no idea who, if anyone really owns it, pays the taxes, that kind of thing."

"Are you interested in buying it?" the woman asked.

"Oh, no. Nothing like that." He wasn't about to explain that he was doing some pro bono work for the county sheriff. But he knew he would have to come up with something.

"I'm a writer, and I'm working on a plot which involves an old property which has been vacant for as long as anyone can remember. Then along comes a stranger who lays claim to it, saying his great, great grandfather had farmed it back before the Civil War."

The woman across the desk looked puzzled.

"But you asked about Anson's Grove. What does any of this have to do with Anson's Grove?"

"Well, it doesn't literally have anything to do with it," Kevin said, hoping he hadn't, with the best of intentions, dug a hole for himself. "I was just using Anson's Grove as an example of such a place. That's what writers of fiction do - make up things based upon real people and places. Loosely, of course."

"I'm not sure Anson's Grove is a very good example of what you're getting at. The county can't just let a lot of old abandoned places sit around waiting for squatters to move in. Places like that, after the necessary research, are taken over by the county. After all, we need the revenue."

"But if the county now owns these parcels of land, it can't tax itself, can it?"

The woman behind the desk gave Kevin a tired smile.

"No, of course not. But whoever in due course acquires that land will be taxed."

Kevin had seen where this exchange was going and had chosen to let the woman who reminded him of a former high school teacher win the round. Now it was his turn.

"For a place like Anson's Grove, off in a God-forsaken part of our county, the assessment's not going to amount to much, is it? Not like prime lake front property?"

"Naturally. But even if Anson's is bottom of the barrel, collecting its taxes is better than collecting nothing. That's why we worked so hard to take it over."

"I don't pretend to know much about the place. I've only been there once." Kevin knew that it was a lie. He had visited there not once but three times recently. The woman he had been talking with would never know the truth of the matter. "But isn't Anson's Grove actually two places?" he asked. "One of them is that grove of trees itself and the nearby land where somebody once tried to raise grapes. The other's down in a hollow at the end of that old road. There's allegedly an abandoned, derelict shack down there. Between them they cover a lot of acres. Has the county really treated them as one big plot of land?"

The woman's tired smile gave way to a look of barely concealed annoyance. Just who was this writer and his questions about Anson's Grove?

"Technically, no. The county has the grove and what's left of the vineyard. You'd have to ask someone who knows the details better than I do, but I'm not sure about the rest. It's obviously smaller, presumably less valuable, or so I hear. You're just writing historical fiction, so it can't be that important. Anyway, around here you hear the words Anson's Grove and you're knee deep in local politics."

"By the way," Kevin said, "I hear that people have been using the Grove. Isn't that where that woman was killed recently during a bird hike? And there's talk about it becoming a fracking site."

"The woman's death has come to our attention, yes. There's talk about posting 'No Trespassing' signs. As for fracking, I'm in no position to comment. It's like I said - local politics."

"So what else is new?" Kevin asked, allowing himself to be cynical. His rhetorical question pretty much brought their discussion to an end. It had become obvious that the woman was becoming increasingly worried that she might have already said too much. He could hazard a guess as to what the problem was, but he knew that he was not about to get a lessons on 'local politics.'

When he left, he was well aware that he hadn't learned much, other than that for some reason the derelict shack at the bottom of Benson Road was not legally in the possession of Cumberland County. Thank goodness the woman in the property office hadn't asked him for his name. Had she done so, he would have to hope that she didn't know that the sheriff's husband's name was Whitman. Or that he had made up a pen name on the spur of the moment.

It wasn't much of a report, but Kevin felt obligated to share the county's official position - or perhaps it's semi-official position - with Carol at the earliest possible moment.

"So our fracking friend Grandi would have to buy the Grove before he could sell it to some gas drilling firm. He can't just assert a right of adverse possession. Now that I think about it, he can't claim adverse possession of either area. You can't just take over an old shack for a month or two and claim it's yours because no one has objected."

"They teach you that in law school?" Kevin asked.

"I'm afraid it's not only lawyers who know about it. Besides, it's virtually a matter of common sense."

"What do you make of what I learned?"

"Not much. Well, that's not quite true. It sounds as if the county fathers may be aware of what Grandi may be up to. That's probably where local politics comes in, although I don't understand why they'd be particularly worried about Grandi. McKendrick, yes, but not our leaders over in Cumberland. If Grandi really wants to take a gamble on the future of fracking in the Crooked Lake watershed, he can buy cheap and hope to sell high."

"I shouldn't be admitting this, but I think you'd have gotten more out of talking with the property woman than I did. You're official uniform would have trumped my fiction writer gambit."

"So, it's my uniform that makes the difference?"

"Well, it helps. But seriously, I can't believe she wouldn't have been more willing to share what she knows with the sheriff than with me."

"It could be, but remember, you were anxious for an assignment and I do have a full plate. Let's just say that we know a little bit more than we did yesterday. And that's not a case of damning with faint praise. Take a compliment."

"Should any of this affect what's done with that old cabin where I almost got shot?"

"I think you're over dramatizing your little run-in with Grandi's hired hand. In any event, whether it's county property or not we don't want somebody breaking through rotten floor boards and killing himself."

"I'll drink to that," Kevin said as he headed for the kitchen. "How about some Chardonnay?"

CHAPTER 54

Hank Nagle had been worrying about his guns for weeks, beginning with the shooting death of Vivian Neuberger on the bird hike his son, Michael, had attended. It was not that he thought it necessary to reconsider his life long fascination with guns. The NRA was right: guns don't kill, people do. Some deranged person, probably one of her fellow birders, had shot her. The way to deal with tragedies like this was not to take guns away from law abiding citizens, among whom he included himself. It was to arm the good guys and thereby make it easier for them to protect themselves from the bad guys and those who are mentally ill. Unfortunately, one of the suspects in the Neuberger case was Michael, and Michael was a troubled young man, probably mentally ill, much like the young men who had perpetrated the shootings at places like Newtown, Aurora, Columbine, Virginia Tech, and elsewhere. Hank had done his homework, and he had actually developed a file on such cases, a file both lengthy and disturbing. While Hank was certain that Michael had had nothing to do with Mrs. Neuberger's death, he couldn't shake off the feeling that it wasn't inconceivable that he could have.

It was late in the afternoon. His wife, Fran, was visiting the Taggarts next door. Their older son, Richard, was not home yet from wherever it was that he indulged his love for rugby as a member of a club team with the ominous name the Terminators. The younger son, the troubled Michael, had not yet returned from his first day as a bagger at the local grocery store. Hank was in what he thought of as his den, although a more apt title would have been his gun room. He was standing in front of the wall across from his desk and file cabinet. And he was looking at the contents of a cabinet that occupied much of the wall and stood about seven feet high. Behind large plate glass doors were seven guns, three small chests of dark walnut, a mounted Canada Goose, and, somewhat incongruously, four wooden lobster buoys that had obviously seen service somewhere, although in all likelihood not on Crooked Lake. The cabinet had attractive brass hinges and latches, but they were clearly not designed to provide security for its contents.

Neither were the glass doors. Yet the cabinet had been fitted with a padlock. It would still be easy to gain access, but it would have to be done by breaking the glass.

There was no doubt in Hank's mind that the glass doors to the gun cabinet had never been broken. Unfortunately, and this is what made him very uneasy, he was not nearly so sure that the gun cabinet had never been unlocked without his permission. And he could think of no one who could have done so without first talking with him except Fran, Richard, or Michael. The reason for suspecting that someone else had been into the gun cabinet was something so small and barely noticeable that he had initially dismissed it as a matter of his own carelessness. The padlock had been fastened in such a way that the side with the company's name faced the cabinet and was thus not visible. To most people this would have been a matter of no consequence. But Hank was a creature of habit, so much so that some of his friends actually thought of him as superstitious. He always finished his orange juice before touching his cereal or bacon and eggs. He always put on his left shoe before the right, and, when it was his turn to do up the dishes, he always washed the silver ware before touching a plate or a glass. So it was with the padlock on the gun cabinet. The company's name was of no particular importance to him, but habit decreed that it face outward rather than inward. But for a matter of days - or had it been weeks? - it had faced inward.

He might simply have been annoyed with himself had it not been for the fact that Vivian Neuberger had been shot and killed on the bird hike. The sheriff seemed to be treating Michael as a possible suspect in her death. If, as he was now almost certain, a member of his family had opened the gun cabinet, something he would rather not contemplate was unfortunately possible. Michael might have violated house rules and gotten into the cabinet. Even if the guilty party had instead been his wife or his older son, the cabinet might have been left open and Michael might have availed himself of the opportunity to remove a gun. In either case, Michael could have had a gun with him when he joined the birders club for the trip to Anson's Grove. And given his antipathy for his science teacher and his unbalanced mental condition, he could have killed her.

He had wrestled with the unthinkable for many days. He had taken some comfort from the fact that all of his guns were exactly where he had last placed them. But the more he thought about it, the more convinced he was that this proved nothing. It was one thing for a member of his family to be unfamiliar with the way he always positioned the padlock. It was quite another to leave unmistakable evidence that the guns had been rearranged. His first impulse was to remove the guns and check to see if they had been recently used and not subsequently cleaned. Unfortunately, he had no idea what type of gun had been used in the shooting. He would have to remove and examine all of them, a task that would almost certainly necessitate telling his family why he was doing it. But Hank didn't want the family to know what was on his mind. Not yet, at least. Fran was the least likely to have broken into the gun cabinet, the one most afraid of his wrath were she to have done so. Moreover, if she knew what he suspected she would go to pieces, of that he was absolutely certain.

Michael's reaction was also fairly easy to predict. His lack of respect for his parents was on display almost every day, and could be triggered by almost anything they said to him. He knew the gun rules, but who knew when his demons would override his sense of responsibility? Hank did not want to provoke Michael if he didn't have to. Richard was a different story. Compared with his brother, he was a normal boy on the cusp of manhood and only one year away from high school graduation and departure for college. But to be frank about it, their preoccupation with Michael had come at a cost: neither Hank nor Fran really knew Richard well. They didn't know his friends or his interests, other then rugby. He spent little time in the house, a fact which they attributed to a desire to avoid scenes involving his brother and his parents. How would he deal with questions about the gun cabinet?

Hank had hoped that 'his problem' would be solved by an announcement from the sheriff that an arrest had been made in the Neuberger case. At that point the gun cabinet would cease to be an issue in a felony case and become simply a domestic matter. But the sheriff hadn't tipped her hand, and Hank was becoming more anxious by the day. He didn't think he could live with it any longer. It was at the moment that he heard Richard call out his familiar 'hi, I'm home' that he decided to be proactive. He would talk with his less truculent son.

———

"How'd you do?" Hank asked his son, choosing not to comment on the filthy outfit Richard was wearing.

"Same as usual." His father had no idea what was usual in the Terminators' season.

"Want to talk about what it's like in the trenches?" Hank had heard Richard refer to the trenches, and assumed it was 'rugby talk.'

"Sure. Let me take a shower," his son said as he disappeared up the stairs.

Fifteen minutes later a more presentable high school senior walked into his father's den and plopped down into the recliner near the desk.

"You don't know a thing about rugby, do you?" he asked. "Not to worry. Nobody else does either. You'd have to go to New Zealand to find some one who could discuss it."

"You're right. Do you suppose it'll ever go big time over here?"

"I doubt it. Anyway, you don't want to talk about rugby. What's new with you?"

For a brief moment, Mr. Nagle wasn't quite sure how to respond to a question like that. The gun cabinet issue wasn't new. It had been on his mind for what seemed like forever.

"This is an awkward subject, Richard." Why, he found himself thinking, did his son prefer to be called Richard rather than Dick or Rick or even Richie. "It's been on my mind for some time, and, well, I just haven't wanted to bring it up. But I'm at a point where I don't think I have a choice. I'm not raising it because I'm upset. I'm just worried. Very worried. Do you understand?"

"I don't think so."

"No, probably not. Say, would you like something to drink? Like a coke? I think I'll have one."

Hank got up and headed for the kitchen.

"No thanks," Richard called after him.

That mission taken care of, Hank set his coke on the desk and resumed his seat.

"It's about my guns. I should have talked to you about it a few weeks ago. Actually, it's about more than the guns. It's about the guns and Michael."

Richard's expression made it clear that he finally understood what was on his father's mind. But he didn't say anything.

"I think it's time we talked frankly, son. Somebody has been into my gun cabinet. Was it you?"

"You said this was about your guns and Michael. Why aren't you having this discussion with him, not me?"

"I'm sure you're aware that Michael is in some kind of trouble. It goes back to that shooting that took place on a bird hike. Has he ever talked about it with you?"

Richard laughed.

"Michael never talks to me, except maybe to tell me to get the hell out of the bathroom in the morning. But I know about that bird hike. Everybody knows about it."

"The unpleasant fact is that just about everyone who was on that hike is a suspect. I mean it looks like one of the hikers fired the shot that killed Mrs. Neuberger. And that includes Michael. Your mother and I know that Michael had nothing to do with it, but unfortunately he has made it clear that he didn't like Mrs. Neuberger. And that's why the guns are so important. What if he had access to one of my guns? What if he took it with him on that bird hike?"

"But you asked if *I* broke into the gun cabinet. I don't have a thing about Mrs. Neuberger."

"No, I'm sure you don't." Mr. Nagle downed the remaining coke, crushed the can and tossed it into the waste basket. "Look, Richard, this is very hard for me. For all of us, for that matter. I suppose I've been pretty hard nosed about the cabinet, what with all my rules. But I haven't been as careful as I should have been about the key to the padlock. It's not like I've kept it tucked away in our safe deposit box at the bank. It's never been hard to find, and I've only myself to blame for that. Normally I might be angry that one of you has been in the gun cabinet, but right now I'm not angry, I'm worried. So, please, let's level with each other. Was it you?"

"Fair enough," Richard said. "I've opened the cabinet only once. I don't remember just when it was, but I'm pretty sure I could come up with the date if I talked with Jimmy Lott. Anyway, it was a few weeks back. There was a story going around that raccoons were making themselves at home outside the country club kitchen, getting into the garbage cans, and we decided it'd be fun to see if we could shoot a few. I know, it was a dumb idea. The other guys all had guns, and I didn't want to look - you know, like I was going to chicken out at the last minute. I'm sorry, Dad. You'd think if I was going to break your rules, I'd have a better excuse."

Hank had vowed he would hold his temper if his son admitted to getting into the gun cabinet. It turned out to be easier than he had expected, even if he agreed that shooting raccoons was a dumb idea. But there was still the question of whether Michael had taken advantage of Richard's break-in or pulled a similar stunt himself.

"I appreciate your honesty," he said. "If there's a next time, I trust that you'll ask me before we have a repeat performance. But we must still deal with Michael. How long do you think the cabinet was unlocked?"

"No time at all. I locked it after I took the shotgun out, and I locked it again after I put it back. So it was never unlocked when I wasn't right there."

"And the gun. It was always in your possession? Never lying around the house?"

"Absolutely. I understand you're concerned about Michael getting his hands on it, but it would have been impossible. His bird hike was in the morning. I took the gun out of the cabinet late one evening, and put it back not that long after midnight."

Mr. Nagle impulsively stood up and went over to the recliner and gave his older son a big hug.

"This really is important to you, isn't it?" Richard said, coming up for air.

"Yes it is," Hank said, "but for some reason I don't think we're out of the woods yet."

"You think Michael broke into the cabinet, too." It might have been a question, but it sounded very much like a statement of fact. Hank Nagle felt the same way, and he knew that in all probability he would shortly be raising the same issue with Michael. He was sure, however, that it would not be anywhere near as civil a conversation as the one he had just had with Richard.

Later that evening, while he was fighting insomnia, it also occurred to Hank that if Michael were to break into the cabinet it would not be to retrieve a shotgun. He still didn't know what kind of gun had been used to kill Vivian Neuberger, but his own experience and common sense told him it was probably not a shotgun.

CHAPTER 55

A stiff breeze was responsible for the white capped waves on Crooked Lake that were pushing the catamaran rapidly in the direction of the bluff. Paul Raymore was at the tiller, and in spite of his worries he was enjoying the ride. Thirty, maybe forty more yards and he'd come about. When he did, he saw for the first time that the sheriff's patrol boat was crossing his wake in the distance. It was not one of the noisier boats on the lake, and he hadn't even heard it over the sound of the wind whistling through his sail. Whoever was at the wheel of the patrol boat waved hello, and Paul responded dutifully. The men had not been close enough to exchange words, and there had been no evidence that the officers in the boat were interested in him. But the mere fact that he had been reminded of the sheriff's department served to spoil his day.

The encounter with the sheriff at Vivian Neuberger's memorial service had been unsettling. She now knew that he had inquired of the Cornell Ornithology Lab about Vivian before he had moved to Crooked Lake. It was likely that she had drawn the conclusion that his presence on the lake had something to do with the fact that Vivian also lived there. Raymore wondered what the sheriff knew about birds. Did she know enough to wonder why someone alleged to be a birding expert would have moved to the lake even if its bird life, while interesting, was hardly unusual? He hardly knew the sheriff, but he was willing to bet that she regarded Vivian, not local bird life, as his reason for shifting his domicile from the Hudson Valley to Crooked Lake.

It had occurred to him that the sheriff would be calling on him one day soon. Whether merely to satisfy her curiosity or because she found his interest in Vivian suspicious, he did not know. Would it be better to beat her to it and make the first move? He toyed with that idea all the way back to his lake home, first embracing it as a way to deal preemptively with his anxiety, then rejecting it for fear it would look as if he were eager to divert her attention from his interest in Vivian. And of course he was eager to do just exactly that. By the time he had beached the Hobie Cat and lowered the sail, he had made up his mind to call the sheriff and arrange a meeting, preferably at his home, not her office, and at a time of his choosing, not hers.

But Paul had also decided that he would not side step what was sure to be the sheriff's main interest. Quite the contrary, he would tell her a long and sad tale about his relationship with Vivian Neuberger.

Ms. Franks took his call and did what she did when the caller was a 'person of interest' in a murder case. She promptly put Raymore through to the sheriff.

"Good morning, Mr. Raymore." Carol used her cheery voice. "What can I do for you?"

"I'm calling because I'd like to talk with you. I didn't really have a chance to do so at Mrs. Neuberger's memorial service. I have no idea what your schedule is like, but might it be possible for you to come by my place this afternoon? I'm in the middle of a project, and am expecting some calls. So I'd prefer to see you over here if you don't mind."

Carol wondered why Raymore would want to see her when he was in the middle of a project and so soon after their meeting at the memorial service, but she was intrigued by the call and there was no reason she couldn't get away from the office early.

"No problem. I can do it on my way home. How about five?" Actually, the Raymore cottage was not on her way home, but what would an extra half hour matter?

"That's very nice of you," he said. "It would be while you're off duty, wouldn't it? Maybe I could entice you to join me in a glass of sherry."

Carol didn't much care for sherry, but she mumbled something that he would interpret as a 'thank you.'

And so it was that the sheriff paid another visit to 'Bird Land' en route home to Kevin and their cottage on Blue Water Point. She even had an opportunity to say hello again to Raymore's neighbor, Mrs. Snell, who was shaking out a small throw rug.

Carol had decided to accept the sherry. It gave her an opportunity to study the Bateman prints while Raymore was playing host. He reappeared shortly with the sherry (too sweet for her taste) and a small tray of crackers and cheese.

Inevitably, they exchanged a few words about the memorial service, which both agreed had not been as saccharine as they had feared it would be.

"Terrible thing, though, saying good-bye to someone so young," Raymore said. "And so talented. I hardly knew her. How about you?"

"I'd never met her," Carol told him, "although I'd heard nothing but good things about her."

Carol was tempted to take the initiative and raise the obvious question about Raymore's calls to the Cornell Ornithology Lab about Vivian. But he was the one who had asked for the meeting. She'd let him raise the subject if he wanted to. If he didn't, she would get around to it by the second glass of sherry.

As it happened, they wouldn't have to wait for a refill.

"I'm sure you're interested in the fact that I was in touch with the Cornell people about Vivian."

Paul waited for the sheriff to say that she was indeed interested. Carol decided not to.

"Is there some reason why I should be interested?" she asked.

This was clearly not what he had expected.

"Well," he began, "it seemed like maybe you'd wonder why I'd be making inquiries about Mrs. Neuberger."

"I think you asked me over for a glass of sherry so you could tell me why you called the Ornithology Lab about her. So why don't we forget about what is going on in my mind. I'd like to hear what's on yours."

"You're probably right. If I were in your shoes, I'd want to learn as much as I could about Vivian's relationships with the other members of the birders club. So I guess I've tried to put myself in your shoes, tried to think like you would. The other day you learned that I had spoken about Vivian with somebody at Cornell. If you want to know as much as you can about my relationship with her, and I assume that you do, you now know something about that relationship that you didn't know before. Am I right?"

Carol smiled.

"You're quite right. I had no idea that you knew of Mrs. Neuberger before you moved to Crooked Lake, or that you were making inquiries about her from people at Cornell. Presumably you are now worried that I will draw the wrong conclusions from what I have just learned. We're having this conversation because you want to disabuse me of those wrong conclusions. You want me to know how it happens that you and Vivian did have some kind of a relationship. Well, here we are, and I'd very much like to hear about it. I don't often ask my host if I may have a second drink, but I suspect that it may take some time for you to tell me all about you and Vivian, so perhaps you'll excuse my manners and pour me another sherry."

"Of course." He collected the bottle from the sideboard and refilled both of their glasses.

"As you may assume, this all has something to do with birds," Raymore said as he resumed his seat. "I'm a serious birder. Lots of people like birds. They put out feeders. They take occasional bird hikes, which usually means that they have a bird book or two around the house as well as field glasses to help spot and identify birds they see. But, to be perfectly frank - you would probably say I'm immodest - I take the birding business to an entirely different level. And I suppose I'm pretty obvious about it. The record will show that I am among the world's foremost birders. And this isn't just my opinion. There are publications that keep track of such things, publications that will tell you all about twitchers like Nigel Carcross. And me."

Paul took a sip of his sherry.

"And then there is Vivian Neuberger. Unlike most birders, she is a professional ornithologist. Bu unlike most ornithologists, she is also a world class birder. She doesn't toot her own horn like Nigel and I do. Which is why I never knew about her until relatively recently. Vivian first came to my attention when I happened to be reading a journal article on hawks. It was some time ago, let's say about two years. Vivian was the author. It was a brilliant piece, the work of an ornithologist who knew her field. But it was also the finest wedding of academic writing and sophisticated commentary on birding I've ever read. I figured she must hold a chair at some prestigious university, but it turned out that that wasn't so. Her credentials were impeccable, but she seemed to be a free lancer. I checked her out on the internet and came across references to the Cornell Ornithology Lab. It was then that I had a brainstorm. I got the idea that she and I might get together and write the bird book to beat all bird books. It would have her professional erudition and my world class understanding of birding. The fact that she also knows a lot about birding would guarantee that the book wouldn't be simply a scissors and paste job. Do you get the picture?"

"I think so. And you're going to tell me that you liked the idea so much that you decided to move to where Vivian lived so that you could work collaboratively on the book."

"Well, that's true, but you have to remember that I'd never met her and had no idea whether she'd be interested in such a project. I figured that a phone call from out of the blue wouldn't do it. After all, she didn't know me either. The better strategy, I thought, was to find out where she lived, take up a residence there, and - how shall I put this? - insinuate myself into her life. Let her get to know me, to know that co-authoring a book with me was not just a hare-brained idea by a guy who happens to like birds."

"And so you called Cornell?"

"Exactly. I remembered those references to the Ornithology Lab and assumed she had some connection there. The person I spoke with - it was apparently the woman you introduced me to yesterday - was obviously someone with great respect for Vivian. She was eager to do whatever she could to put me in touch with her. Vivian didn't actually work at the lab, so she said she'd do some checking and call me back. By this time I'd become so obsessed with my idea I guess I was impatient. I called again before she had a chance to get back to me. That's when I learned that Vivian now lived on Crooked Lake. Frankly, I'd never heard of it, but as you know it's not far west of Cayuga Lake where Cornell is. I asked around, and a friend of mine told me he'd heard it was a good area for observing bird migration."

Paul laughed.

"He was wrong, and I didn't do much research on the subject. Not that it mattered. I can do what I do professionally from almost anywhere, and if I feel the urge to see some exotic birds it's as easy to get to Brazil or wherever from here as it was from the Hudson Valley. It was Vivian that mattered, and she was here. So I moved."

"Did you ever contact her before moving here?"

Another laugh, this one slightly bitter.

"I should have. Fact of the matter is that I never talked to her about my idea. I'm not what you'd call shy. But I worried that she'd just brush me off, that it'd be better to move to the lake and establish some kind of relationship first. Which I suppose I did, more or less, thanks to those damned bird hikes."

Raymore went silent. It looked to Carol a if he were thinking about the relationship he'd never really established with Vivian Neuberger.

"I know you haven't lived here long, Mr. Raymore, but surely you've had plenty of opportunities to broach the subject of a jointly authored book. How come you never discussed it with her?'

"It's hard to explain. I never got to know her really well, but it didn't take long before I realized it would never work."

"You realized that without ever bringing the subject up?"

"Sometimes you just know. It was better to admit to myself that it was a bad idea than to listen to her tell me she wasn't interested."

"So how would you describe your relationship with Mrs. Neuberger?" Carol asked. She was finding it hard to believe that Raymore, after all the trouble he had gone to, had simply dropped the idea without ever mentioning it to Vivian.

"That's easy. There wasn't any, other than the bird hikes, and fortunately there weren't many of those."

"You were never in each other's homes?"

"Never. I'm not what you'd call a gregarious person. The Neubergers, as far as I could tell, weren't either. Her husband was away a fair bit, and I considered taking advantage of the situation to visit her. But she'd have misunderstood my motive."

Raymore made a face. It wasn't pleasant.

Carol had just about decided that Raymore's long story had come to an unexpected dead end when he made the comment about Vivian misunderstanding his motive.

"You were going to call on her but changed your mind because she'd misunderstand. Forgive me, but now I'm the one who doesn't understand."

"Sheriff, it's not my place to complicate your investigation of Vivian's death. Or to speak ill of the dead. But it really isn't very complicated. Mrs. Neuberger was an attractive woman, a fact that did not go unnoticed by a number of members of the Crooked Lake community. When you have spent as much of your life as I have paying attention to the ways of small birds, it is no great challenge to be aware of the ways of one's fellow humans. I had wanted to persuade Vivian to join me in what I hoped would be a rewarding literary adventure. I did not wish to become another of the moths circling her incandescent light. It did not take me long to discover that that was the fate that awaited me if we were to collaborate on a book. She would be the author. My name, if it weren't relegated to the end notes, would have been in very small type - 'with the assistance of Paul Raymore.' No thank you."

In due course this strange conversation came to an end, leaving Carol puzzled about what she had learned. About Vivian Neuberger. And, more importantly, about Paul Raymore. Vivian had fared very well in Paul's account until the very end, at which point he had changed his tune and presented her in a very different light. Why? Why had he chosen to dismiss her as a consummate egotist, in love with herself and her capacity to manipulate - and emasculate? - men? And why had he done so without supplying a shred of evidence?

Carol had expected Raymore to tell her things about his relationship with Vivian which would demonstrate that he had no motive for killing her. Was that the message in his strange story about the ill-fated book project? If so, it was not entirely convincing. For that matter, had Raymore ever actually contemplated such a book project, or had he simply made it all up? And if so, why?

CHAPTER 56

When Carol arrived home, she promptly gave Kevin an account of Paul Raymore's strange story of his 'relationship' with Vivian Neuberger. Not surprisingly, Kevin's eyes lit up and he jumped into the conversation with suggestions of what Raymond was up to.

"I wouldn't believe a word of it," he said. "Excepting, of course, the phone calls to the Ornithology Lab. He couldn't very well deny that. But the rest of the story could easily be a complete fabrication. Who's to know?"

"I'm suspicious, too. But what if he did have such an idea and what if he did talk with her about it? Then it's possible she mentioned it to her husband. At least it's worth asking him if she'd ever brought up such a plan. Somehow I doubt that Raymore discussed the idea with other birders."

"Raymore had plenty of time to cook up a story that would make his call to the Lab look innocent. It's still possible that he and Vivian go back a lot further than he's admitted."

"It sounds to me as if we're trying to prove he's guilty of shooting Vivian, yet where's the motive? And the gun? I feel like I've got a headache coming on. Let's have something to eat, and then I'll arrange a meeting with Bill Neuberger for tomorrow."

Before Carol had a chance to meet with Neuberger, she had both an unexpected call and an unexpected visitor the following morning. The call was from Doc Crawford.

"Oh, Doc. I've owed you a call for the better part of two week, and now it's you who's on the phone. How are you doing?"

"Not bad. Some days the chemo wears me out, but as they say, all things considered. Anyway, you must remember that I'd promised you and your lucky man a dinner sometime soon. I woke up this morning feeling that this could be the day. Or maybe tomorrow. How's your schedule?"

"That's sweet of you, but you don't need to do this. Not now. Why not wait until you feel better."

"If you're afraid I'll be slaving over a hot stove all day, forget it. I know I promised pheasant under glass or something like that, but let me make a different proposal. The moon is full, or close enough to it so you'd never know the difference. What would you say we enjoy it - nothing fancy, just some bourbon to toast the moon with and maybe some strawberry shortcake."

"Forgive me, but I'm not following you."

"No, of course not," Crawford said. "I just splurged and bought myself a party boat. It's second hand, but it's in good shape, and I decided I needed something to perk me up. So how about we take a boat ride out to where we can see the moon rise over the bluff."

"I can't believe this. You bought a party boat?"

"Why not? And I'd love to have you on my inaugural cruise. So what will it be, tonight or tomorrow? The weather report says clear skies, not a drop of rain in the forecast."

"Tonight," she said. "You name the time."

"I'll be at your dock by eight."

"Anything I should bring?"

"Just Kevin."

Carol had just gotten off the phone, having told Kevin of the evening's plan, when Jim Barrett walked into the office.

"Excuse the unannounced entrance, Carol, but I had to see you before I punched in for the day. How are things around here?"

"Pretty much the same," she answered, coming around the desk to shake hands. "But you look like environmentalism is agreeing with you."

"It is. What's the word on Miss Dockery?"

"She's doing just fine, which isn't to say we don't miss you. Come on, have a seat."

"Love to, but I can't stay. I'm here because there's something you ought to know. Maybe you've already heard, but I'm guessing we got the news first. It's about our friend Frank Grandi."

"Ah, your bete noir. I think you can spare five minutes, so have a seat and tell me about him."

Jim sat, somewhat tentatively, on the edge of the chair across the desk from his old boss.

"He's gone back to Scranton, and I suspect he wasn't anxious to do so."

"You're right - I hadn't heard about this. What do you know about it?"

"Not much," Jim said, "but what I hear is that he's in some trouble down there. One of our people hails from that area, and he reports that the local paper ran a piece on him. He's alleged to be the landlord for a lot of properties that aren't up to code, not to mention the fact that he's a tax delinquent. In other words, he's the kind of dishonest businessman we don't need around Crooked Lake."

"You say he's back in Scranton?"

"That's what I'm told. It's not my impression that he's moved - this happened just a couple of days ago. But I guess it's serious enough that he figured he'd better go back and fight the charges, try to clear his name, whatever he had to do. It may not amount to much, but I thought you'd be interested. Who knows, it might even take his mind off fracking on our watershed."

"Interesting." Carol was inclined to treat Grandi as a marginal figure in the Neuberger case, but she appreciated the heads-up. She'd do some checking into who's who in Scranton and put in a call or two.

"Like I said, I can't stay. Got to drive over to Canandaigua."

"Of course, so get going. But thanks a lot."

"Place looks neat," Barrett said as he headed for the door. "Probably Dockery's influence."

It was mid-morning when Carol parked outside the Neuberger house at the top of the east lake road, just south of Yates Center. What, she wondered, did all these Crooked Lake birders tell their neighbors about the recurrent visits of members of the sheriff's department? All of them might find it annoying. For one of them it might lead to chronic anxiety and sleepless nights.

She never knew what to expect from Bill Neuberger. He had been self assured, he had been opaque. He had been relaxed, he had been tense. He had never been diffident. This morning he had chosen to be annoyed. Mildly annoyed, but annoyed nonetheless.

"As you requested, sheriff, here I am," he said as he ushered her into the house, "ready for my latest interrogation. I would have thought that by this time you would have learned everything that I might have to tell you. But no, you have thought of something else. Would you prefer to discuss it over coffee?"

It was not exactly a warm, welcoming offer.

"That would be very nice. Black, please."

Neuberger took a pass on coffee. Either he had already had his fill or he was simply anxious to get down to business and keep it brief.

"Now what brings you here again?" he asked after handing her her coffee.

"As far as I can tell, there were only three people on the hike when your wife was shot who could be called expert birders: Mel Cone, Paul Raymond, and Mrs. Neuberger. You have told me something about Vivian's feelings about Mr. Cone. How about Mr. Raymore? Did she ever share her impressions of him?"

"Just what are you getting at?" Her question had only made him more annoyed.

"Your wife and Raymore would have been quick to recognize that they were more knowledgeable about birds than the others. It would have been natural for them to gravitate to each other. All of us like to talk with people who share our interests. What about Mr. Raymore and Vivian?"

"What are you implying?"

"I'm not implying anything. I'm only asking if Vivian ever talked to you about another expert birder, Paul Raymore."

"Their relationship was in no way intimate, if that's what you mean."

"I wasn't suggesting that it was. I only hoped you might tell me what she had to say about him."

"I don't recall that she said much of anything about him other than that he knew a lot about birds."

It was apparent that if she wanted to find out whether Vivian had ever said anything about a joint book project with Raymore, she'd have to ask her question outright.

"I have heard," Carol said, "that Paul Raymore was at one time interested in co-authoring a book about birds and birding with Vivian. Did she ever say anything about it to you?"

"That strikes me as a strange idea. In any event, if she and Raymore ever talked about it, she never mentioned it to me."

"And Raymore. Did *he* by chance mention it?"

"No, and I can't imagine why he would. Frankly, the very idea doesn't sound at all like Viv. She and I didn't talk much about what she was writing, but I'm sure she never wrote something with somebody else."

Carol thanked him for listening to her and answering her questions to the best of his ability. She was about to leave, when Bill posed a question which suggested that he might be more interested in what his wife had been up to than he had let on.

"Who was it that told you about Viv and Raymore?" Not who had told her about the book idea, but about his wife and the birders club's top birder.

"I'm not at liberty to say," Carol said, "considering that it was only a rumor."

"Don't you think I have the right to press this rumor monger for his source?"

"For the time being, perhaps it's better to assume that your wife would have told you if there's any truth to the rumor."

Bill's reply to that was a derisive snort. Apparently Vivian couldn't be counted on to share with her husband everything she was doing.

CHAPTER 57

Carol both looked forward to the moonlight ride on the party boat and dreaded it. She wanted to see Doc again, yet she knew that he wouldn't look like himself. Chemotherapy typically did that to people, and it was always a reminder of how fragile life can be. Doc would joke about it. He'd claim he'd been looking for an excuse to treat himself to a party boat and with it a regular rendezvous with each full moon. But he wouldn't fool her. She wasn't in the habit of thinking of him as an old man. He had aged gracefully, never complained about life's vicissitudes, and seemed to charm everyone he met, from toddlers to the most senior of Crooked Lake's senior citizens. But now he was in trouble. If it were otherwise, he would not have announced that he had performed his last autopsy for her.

Doc would not want her and Kevin to bring him anything. It was his party, and he would be showing off his new toy and reveling in the opportunity to give them a ringside seat at the rising of the moon. But for some reason, Carol had to take him something, something special. And that something would be Doc's favorite, peanut brittle. She had long ago discovered a place which not only sold it but made it right there on its own premises in Yates Center. Everybody raved about it, including Doc, so she'd stop at *Granny's Kitchen* on the way home from a late afternoon meeting with Mel Cone. Or, to be more honest with herself, she would stop by at the Cone residence on her way home from shopping for peanut brittle at *Granny's Kitchen.*

Cone could have waited another day, but she really did need to talk with him. He was the man who had told her that Vivian Neuberger had been cheating on her husband. And now that husband was claiming that Cone himself had been making passes - at least verbally - at Vivian. It occurred to Carol that some critic would soon be comparing Crooked Lake with Peyton Place.

The woman who opened the door was the creator of the Brown Betty.

"On, my. It's the sheriff. What's Mel been up to now?" It was a poor attempt to make light of the fact that a uniformed officer of the law was standing on the door step.

"I need to talk with your husband," Carol said. "Is he at home?"

"Yes, of course. Right down the hall to the left." She raised her voice to let Mel know that he had a caller. "It's the sheriff."

"What does she want?"

"I'll only take a few minutes, Mr. Cone," Carol called out.

"I'll be right there."

Right there turned out to be three minutes, which Carol spent leafing through a magazine on the coffee table.

"Sorry to keep you waiting. Problem was somebody was keeping *me* waiting. What can I do for you this time?"

"It's about Mrs. Neuberger," she said. "Again."

"Let me guess," he said. "You want to know if she owns guns."

"No, I want you to tell me how you'd describe your relationship with her."

Mel Cone's face, already tan from the summer sun, seemed a shade darker.

"I'm afraid I don't understand. We had no relationship other than the bird hikes."

"I'm under the impression that you paid a great deal of attention to her after hours affair with Larry Finch."

"Well, yes, but you asked about *my* relationship with her."

"So I did. I guess I was wondering if, like Mr. Finch, you were also interested in her."

"That's outrageous." Mel stood up, as if he were about to leave the room. Carol was sure that he was debating with himself whether to ask her to get out of his house.

"You may be right. Vivian Neuberger's death seems to have spawned more than a few rumors, and I suspect that some of them are indeed outrageous. If you'll sit back down, I'll tell you about this rumor and we can talk about it."

Cone considered her suggestion, took a deep breath, and resumed his seat.

"I promise that I won't mince words," Carol began. "But I have been told that you had taken a fancy to Vivian, that you were, shall we say, pursuing her."

"That is sheer hogwash," he said, his anger barely under control. "I'm surprised - no, actually I'm deeply disappointed - that you should even give such a blatant piece of nonsense a second thought."

"But you asked me to accept your charge that Larry and Vivian were having an affair. I suspect that Larry would call *that* a blatant piece of nonsense. And we don't know what Vivian would have to say about either Larry or you because she is now dead."

"Yes, but I saw Vivian and Larry together with my own eyes. Nobody saw Vivian and me together."

It didn't occur to Mel until he had said it that 'nobody saw Vivian and me together' could easily be misconstrued. In any event, he chose not to retract the statement.

"One other important point," Carol said. "The person who reported that you were anxious to have an affair with Vivian also claims that it was Vivian who told him about it. For what it's worth, my source also claims that Vivian rejected your advances. She seems to have used the word 'pathetic' to describe you."

"Based on what you have told me, your source for this nonsense about Vivian and me has to be Bill Neuberger. I would have to assume that he fed you this fictional tale because he thinks it makes his marriage look like a match made in heaven. Beautiful Vivian rejects suitors in favor of good old faithful Bill. Ergo, Bill has no motive for killing her. I'd give him credit for a great story if it weren't for one thing: Vivian's affair was with Larry Finch."

Mel stood up again. It was obvious that their conversation was at an end. But then he had another thought.

"Let's make that a great story except for two things."

"What's the other one?" Carol asked.

"To make it believable he had to accuse me of something I didn't do."

When she set off for home, a box of peanut brittle tucked under her arm, Carol had no idea whether to believe Bill Neuberger or Mel Cone. For that matter, she had her doubts about the veracity of a number of the other members of the Crooked Lake Birders Club, including Paul Raymore and Sallie Finch. An evening with Doc Crawford promised to be a welcome change of pace.

CHAPTER 58

It was almost 8:10 when the party boat pulled up at the end of the dock. Kevin was on his feet and looped the rope Crawford had handed him around a cleat.

"No need to climb out of the boat," Carol said. "We're all ready and raring to go."

"Thanks, but if you don't mind I'd like to make one last pit stop in your restroom before we set off."

"Sure. Let me give you a hand," Kevin said.

"I may have seen better days, but I'm still perfectly able to climb out of this boat by myself."

"He just doesn't want to have to fish you out of the lake," Carol said.

"I haven't fallen into the lake in years, Carol, and I'm not about to do it now."

It was only a few minutes later that they pushed off, Doc Crawford at the wheel and Carol and Kevin relaxing in the cushioned seats on either side of him.

"What do you think?" It was still light enough that they could see Doc's familiar mischievous grin.

"Smooth ride," Kevin said.

"And comfortable," Carol added. "I haven't been in a party boat in years. You surprise me, though. How come?"

"I like to get out on the water, and the fishing isn't what it used to be. So what were my options? It was relaxation or speed, and when have I ever been in a hurry. A neighbor told me he'd seen one of these things for sale over on Three Mile Point, and damned if it didn't look tempting. But the truth is that my favorite sport is moon watching, and there's no better way to do it than from the middle of the lake, where you can sit right in the middle of its reflection on the water. You'll see."

Doc had picked a good night, one with a cloudless sky and the moon close enough to full that if it wasn't no one would know for sure. The sky over the bluff always acquired a foreshadowing of moonlight just before the moon itself came into view. While they waited, the boat circled lazily in the calm waters and they each enjoyed a piece of Doc's strawberry shortcake.

"I'd hazard a guess that she'll make her appearance in about five minutes," he said. "That's when lake ritual calls for a small dollop of bourbon."

"Lake ritual?" Carol asked. "You just bought the boat. How do you know there's any such thing?"

"It begins tonight. Here, hold your glasses up."

Of course Carol and Kevin had watched the moon rise over the bluff many times from their seats on the deck or the dock, not to mention a few times from the canoe. But when it appeared that night, they had to agree that it was special.

"Come on, bottoms up," Doc admonished them.

They watched in silence as the moon slowly rose above the crest of the bluff.

It was Crawford himself who broke the silence.

"That was nice, don't you think?"

"No question about it," Carol said. "Much better than our usual nightly complaint that the Neuberger case isn't going any place very fast."

"I was going to bring that up," Doc said. "Just not before moon rise. We haven't talked since I gave you my autopsy report, and I think you owe me a progress report on your investigation. I assume there's been no arrest, or word would have gotten out."

"You're right - no arrest. My list of suspects is long enough to keep me busy, but no smoking gun as yet."

"Or maybe too many smoking guns," Kevin suggested. "Figuratively, of course."

"Interesting. Back when I completed the autopsy, I'd have been willing to bet that your killer would turn out to be whoever among those birders was the best marksman."

"Care to explain?" Carol asked.

"Sure. The fatal shot came from a handgun, and they don't have as stable a shooting platform as a rifle. Hence less accuracy. The shooter was standing at a distance from the victim; you weren't sure how far away he was, but the greater the distance the greater the negative effect on accuracy. All of which means that a good marksman had the best chance of getting in a fatal shot."

"But it doesn't mean that the killer *had* to be a good marksman. He could have been lucky."

"I thought we'd agreed that the killer couldn't count on luck," Kevin said.

"He couldn't," Carol agreed. "But that doesn't mean that he wasn't lucky."

"Don't misunderstand me," Crawford said. "I'm not saying that the killer was a good marksman. I'm only saying that the odds would have favored a good marksman, so that's who I'd be looking for first."

"Frankly, Doc, it hasn't been easy to get a good picture of who among the birders own guns, much less who among them is a good marksman."

The three occupants of the party boat debated the subject for the better part of half an hour as the moon rose higher in the sky. Eventually the conversation turned to the doctor's health.

"I know you've said you've performed your last autopsy," Carol said, "but I'd feel a lot better if you were to tell us you were just kidding."

"It's a day to day thing," Crawford replied. "Why don't you make it easier for me by promising that there won't be any more murders around here."

"Would that I could. But seriously, you're sounding pretty chipper tonight, not like somebody who's ready to retire."

"You and Kevin have that effect on me, but tomorrow's always another day. We'll just have to see how the rest of my chemotherapy regimen goes."

"I've got a little something for you. It's been known to guarantee that chemo works." Carol dug into the back pack she'd brought with her and pulled out the box of peanut brittle.

"Here," she said, handing him the box. "As you can see, I'm not above a little bribery."

Doc got out of his seat and gave Carol a big kiss.

"You're much too sweet," he said. "The moon put on a good show, but I should be getting home and I have to drop you two off first. Okay?"

"Of course. It's been fun."

After wishing Doc well, Carol and Kevin indulged themselves for another twenty minutes on the deck.

"How do you think he's doing?"she asked.

"It's been a siege, but I suspect our boat ride was almost as good therapy for him as chemo. You know him better than I do. What's your opinion?"

"Doc's always been strong, but he's worried. I guess any of us would be."

"Strange, isn't it, that somebody as full of life as he is would make his living carving up the dead."

"You really have a way with words, Kevin."

"I know. Anyway, it's been a nice evening. And Doc did push us to think about what kind of marksmen our birders are. I'd start with Mrs. Finch. I can't believe the CIA would let any of its agents go on a mission unless they could nail a terrorist with a BB gun at 100 yards."

"You don't know anything about the CIA. Unless there's an opera where the tenor is one of their agents."

"Okay, you've got me there. But I'd recommend we call the CIA and ask a few questions about their gun policies."

"Good. You do it. I'll bet they hang up on you, and maybe start tapping your phone. As for me, I'm going to hit the sack."

CHAPTER 59

In spite of her best efforts to forget about Doc Crawford's comments about the importance of marksmanship and Kevin's interest in the CIA's gun policies, Carol had trouble falling asleep. Just as it's not a good idea to hit the bottle just before bedtime, experience had told her that late evening conversations about her latest murder investigation were likely to be a recipe for insomnia. Sheer will power kept her from sneaking a peek at the time on her bedside alarm clock, but it didn't put her to sleep.

Inevitably, Carol did doze off from time to time, but she was wide awake again shortly after six the next morning. Kevin was obviously not sharing her problem. She decided to get up and start the coffee.

By 7:45 she had showered, dressed, and eaten breakfast. Kevin was still fast asleep. Reluctantly she wrote a short note to him, tucked it under the sugar bowl on the kitchen table, and slipped out the back door. It was not yet 8:15 when she pulled into the sheriff's space in the Cumberland parking lot. Carol now knew what she was going to do with her day, but it was too early to do it. She stifled a yawn and made herself another cup of coffee.

When the squad meeting was over, Carol's impatience grew by the minute. She kept looking at her watch and went through the motions of being busy. She had two phone calls she wanted to make, but she didn't want to make them when the people she wanted to talk with were still in bed. When her watch told her it was 9:15, she decided to make the first call whether the other party was ready or not.

Officer Byrnes' notes told her that Sallie Finch's first husband's name was Jared Palmer. She wasn't surprised that he wasn't at home. She was surprised, however, that his present wife seemed to be interested that a sheriff from some place in upstate New York was inquiring about his first wife. Not only interested, but anxious to make sure that this officer of the law get in touch with her husband a.s.a.p.

"Jared is semi-retired," she said. "You just happened to call on one of those days when he's at the office. He's a dermatologist, or perhaps you already know that. He sees patients at his old firm from time to time. What seems to be the problem?"

"It's not really about Dr. Palmer," Carol said, "but rather his first wife. I need some information, and I believe that he can help me. Perhaps you have his office number."

"I'm sure that Jared would prefer to take the call here rather than at the office. He's usually home on Thursdays by one o'clock."

Carol assumed that Mrs. Palmer would like to be where she could overhear at least one end of the conversation between the sheriff and her husband.

"If he can call me back by one or close to it, that would be fine." She gave Mrs. Palmer her phone number.

"Could you give me some idea what this is about? Jared is sure to want a heads up in case he has to put together some information for you."

"Just tell him that it's about what his first wife did for a living." Carol knew that this would not satisfy Mrs. Palmer, but she had no intention of providing more details.

Inasmuch as the other call she planned to make was to Sallie Finch, and inasmuch as she needed to talk with Jared Palmer before she spoke with Sallie, Carol was temporarily stymied. Rather than spin her wheels at her desk for several hours, she decided to drive down to the Southport grocery store and pick up some staples she knew were in short supply at the cottage. It would prove an unexpectedly productive use of her time.

When she climbed out of her car in the grocery's parking lot, the first person she saw was Michael Nagle. She had forgotten that he had started work as a bagger there. He was apparently taking a break, and was doing his best to look cool, leaning against an advertisement for local sweet corn and inhaling deeply on a cigarette. Michael didn't see her at first, and when he did, he almost choked on his cigarette.

He tossed it to the pavement and crushed it with his foot.

"Hello, sheriff. I didn't know you were looking for me."

"Hello, Michael. I haven't been looking for you. I think I was as surprised to see you here as you were to see me. But I'm glad to see you up and about. You must be happy to be out of the house for a change."

"I guess. It's kinda boring."

Carol was doing her best to avoid asking the questions that were on her mind. Questions that might turn him into the sullen, even angry, young man she remembered from their early encounters. The problem was that she didn't know anything about his mental state after weeks under the care of Dr. Boylan. At the moment he seemed normal, and she had been encouraged by the placid sketches of birds she had seen on his desk the last time she had been in the Nagle home. But she doubted that he had been 'healed.' She wasn't even sure that someone with his problems could ever be completely healed. She wished that she could have a candid conversation with the doctor.

To her surprise, Michael was the one who asked the next question.

"Did Dad tell you about the gun locker?"

Carol wasn't sure what he was referring to, but the mention of guns put her on alert.

"What is this about a gun locker?"

"It's where he keeps his guns. You must have seen it. Anyway, it was Richard, not me."

"I guess the answer to your question is that, no, your father didn't tell me about it. What did you think he might have told me?"

"That it was my brother who broke into the locker. Dad suspected me, but it was Richard."

Carol wasn't sure which was most interesting, the fact that the gun cabinet had been opened without permission or that Michael had decided to tell her about it. Why hadn't Mr. Nagle told her about the break in? The answer, obviously, was that he suspected Michael and worried that his son, now possibly in possession of a gun, could have used it to kill Vivian Neuberger. She could imagine the man's relief when he learned that it was his other son who was guilty of breaking into the gun case.

"How did you learn that your brother had done this?"

"He told me himself. When he told Dad the truth, he figured he'd be furious. But that's the funny thing - Dad wasn't furious. Richard said he actually seemed to be relieved."

Of course he was relieved, Carol thought. Now it was all but certain that Michael would no longer be a suspect in Vivian's death. And Michael would know this, which would explain why he was willing to speak so candidly to the sheriff about it.

"Do you and Richard get along well?" she asked.

"Not too bad. He's tried to be a big brother, keep me out of trouble. But it hasn't been the same recently. He's got a steady girl friend, he's started thinking about college. I suppose you'd say we aren't exactly the buddies we were a year or two ago."

No, probably not, Carol said to herself. Michael hadn't said so, but in all likelihood his own problems had intensified as he reached adolescence, making it harder for Richard to be a mentor.

CHAPTER 60

Jared Palmer called Sheriff Kelleher at 1:07 pm that afternoon, confirming his wife's opinion that he would indeed be anxious to hear what was on the sheriff's mind.

"Regina says you were calling about Sallie."

"Yes, and I'm interested in her professional life, not your marriage to her. I understand that you knew she was with the CIA."

"That's true. She used to joke about the fact that the agency - that's what she called it - didn't want its employees to admit what they did for a living. Of course she never said she was one of its employees. It was a strange kind of wink-wink affair, if you know what I mean, and I played along. Until I decided enough was enough, that is. It's weird, isn't it, never being able to ask your wife 'what did you do today?' If she hadn't had a good sense of humor I'd have bailed out of that marriage long before I did."

Carol had made it clear, or tried to, that she wasn't interested in Palmer's marriage to Sallie, but she made no attempt to cut him off as he explained his growing frustration with his role as an agency spouse.

"Aside from what you refer to as a wink-wink relationship, were there any tangible clues as to what Sallie did when she left home?"

"Oh, sure, although none of them by themselves were what you'd call proof of a CIA connection. I mean she also spoke Arabic and Turkish, even some other Middle Eastern language. Farsi, I think. If she were a Syrian or an Iranian, that's understandable, but Sallie came from old New England stock. Her language skills obviously helped her when she went to the Middle East, and that's something she did a lot. Sometimes for a week, sometimes for a month of more. I never cared much for foreign travel, so I wasn't going to begrudge her time in a part of the world whose culture she loved. She spoke about free lance travel pieces she was writing, but I figured it was a CIA cover. The only time we ever really discussed it was after 9/11 when the media was full of talk about Arab terrorists. I suggested she ought to postpone a trip she was planning until things had calmed down. She just laughed and told me she'd be safer than she'd be in our nation's capital. Maybe she believed it. She also collected stuff from the Middle East - art objects, things like that. Maybe they came from galleries in New York, but she could just as well have found them in Beirut or Istanbul. Like I said, she was in places like that a lot."

"For what it's worth, Sallie doesn't make much of an effort now that she's retired to deny a CIA connection. One other question, if I may," Carol added, turning to the primary reason for her call to Mr. Palmer. "Did Sallie ever own a gun?"

"She did, although once again I have no evidence that it had anything to do with the CIA. It was a pistol or revolver or whatever you'd call a handgun. She wasn't a hunter, and neither am I. Of course a lot of people here in Virginia own guns. Carry them concealed, too, I imagine. This is a state that's pretty gung-ho when it comes to guns."

Palmer laughed.

"I guess I should say gun-ho. Anyway this part of the state includes a lot of military types, what with the Pentagon and a lot of those beltway bandits with their military contracts."

Carol couldn't help but add intelligence types, what with Langley right there in the backyard.

"I'm just wondering whether Sallie may have had a gun because CIA personnel are required to carry them," she said.

"I wouldn't know about that. But Sallie loved to go down to a target range not far from here. She didn't talk about it a lot, but it was always clear that she was proud of her marksmanship."

And so, it turned out, it didn't really matter whether the CIA required its agents to carry a gun. What mattered was that Sallie Finch had a history of gun ownership and she worked diligently to maintain her skill on a firing range.

Carol was in the process of bringing this conversation to a close when Palmer asked the question she had expected him to ask as soon as he called.

"What is it that Sallie has done which prompts all of these questions?"

Carol had no intention of planting in his mind a suspicion that his former wife might be a killer. That could be unfair to Sallie, and, for all she knew, it might make the current Mrs. Palmer unnecessarily nervous.

"Very probably nothing," Carol said, anxious to defuse any worry she may have created by making this particular phone call. "It may be a problem that's of interest to the CIA only because of its preoccupation with secrecy."

Palmer seemed interested in pursuing the matter a bit further, but Carol pleaded the urgency of an incoming call and, thanking the Palmers for their help, she hung up the phone.

Armed with the knowledge that Sallie Finch had spent many hours at a firing range to preserve her marksmanship skills, the sheriff immediately placed a call to the Finch residence. Happily, Sallie was at home.

"Mrs. Finch, I fear I'm making a nuisance of myself, but I'd like very much to have another talk with you. Is it possible we could do it this afternoon?"

"You know I'm always at your disposal, sheriff. I presume it's about the Neuberger case."

"Actually it's about the CIA."

"Really? If you know anything about the CIA, you'll be aware of the fact that they're security conscious. With good reason, I suppose, but it means that I must be more careful about what I say than is really necessary. But I shall do my best to be helpful. Where do you propose we meet - here or there?"

"As is often the case, I'm always looking for an excuse to get out of my claustrophobic office. So how about your place?"

"Of course. Time?"

"What about three?"

"Three it is."

When three o'clock rolled around, Carol was once more in the midst of evidence that Sallie Finch had an abiding interest in the Middle East. The Roberts prints, the collection of books on the region's history and cultures, the art objects. Once again she found herself wondering just exactly what was the original purpose of the urn in the alcove across the room from the couch.

Sallie set down two glasses of iced tea and took a seat at the other end of the couch.

"Okay, so it's the CIA we're to talk about."

"Yes, and I'm a complete novice when it comes to the US intelligence community. I realize that this is a sensitive subject, but

I hope you can be of some help. Does the CIA expect its agents to carry guns?"

Sallie smiled, but Carol thought she had detected a moment's hesitation first.

"I see. You are discussing the Neuberger case after all, aren't you? Your question, if I may translate, is 'do I own a gun, courtesy of the agency, with which I might have shot Mrs. Neuberger.' Let me first repeat myself, sheriff. I did not shoot Vivian. But to get back to the question you asked. Of course the CIA wants its agents to protect themselves, and so like a great many Americans we do carry a gun. In my case, I should use the past tense. I did carry a gun, but it didn't accompany me into retirement."

"What is the CIA policy regarding guns after retirement?"

"This is getting rather personal, isn't it? After all, I believe I'm the only member of the Crooked Lake Birders Club who once worked for the agency. In any event, it's a simple matter. We are US citizens and therefore we have a 2nd amendment right to remain armed. If we own a gun which the agency has issued, we are expected to turn it in, after which we can stop by the nearest gun shop and purchase a replacement. I have already explained that, unlike what I assume to be the case with the majority of former agents, I do not own a gun. I do not hunt, and I have no one I need to protect myself from. I did, of course, have a gun, and if you have the time and are interested, I could tell you something of its life span after the CIA and I parted ways."

It was obvious that Sallie Finch was now enjoying herself. She may have been momentarily disturbed when she realized what was on the sheriff's mind, but she had recovered nicely and was acting as if she were in control of the situation.

"I'd love to hear about it," Carol said.

"I rather thought you would. A refill on the iced tea?"

"No thanks."

"Okay." Sallie tucked her legs under her on the couch, and launched into her story.

"In what could be called my professional life, I got to meet a lot of interesting people. Among them were members of the Saudi Arabian royal family. The country is not just Arabia, it is *Saudi* Arabia. In other words, it is ruled by the house of Saud, which is a very large house indeed. I could draw you a map, sort of like those charts of British dynasties you see in history books. But it would be a bore, so let's just say that the king has many relations, thousands of them. I got to know quite a few of them, one of them very well. He was young and charming and, most important, not guilty of taking himself too seriously. Of course no woman in his country could aspire to do what I was doing, which seemed to make me of considerable interest to Sherif Ali. That was what I called him, Sherif Ali, after Omar Sharif's great film role. He found it amusing. I liked to rib him about the way the Saudis treated women, and he always claimed that it should be blamed on Wahhabism, not the royal family. You don't need to get me started on that subject. Anyway, I was in Riyadh for the last time before I left the agency when I decided I'd like to give him a going away present. As you may have guessed, it was my revolver. It would be a reminder that there are ways to protect women other than wrapping them up like mummies."

Sallie paused, apparently to give the sheriff a chance to comment on this recital of her contribution to cross-cultural relations. It occurred to Carol that honoring the principal of gender equality could be a tricky proposition for her own government's foreign policy. She said as much, only to be reminded that the United States itself hardly had an impeccable record. Sallie seemed ready to elaborate on the subject when she realized that it wasn't the point of her story.

"Sorry. I'm wandering," she said. "But back to my friend in the royal family. One day I came across a press release in an Arab language paper I subscribe to. My favorite member of the Saudi royal family had been killed when his motorcycle crashed. It was a sad ending to a charmed life. At the time I never gave the gun a thought. It wasn't until you asked me about CIA gun policy that I remembered that when I lost my old friend I also lost my gun. I wonder what kind of diplomatic incident we'd have on our hands if I were to try to locate that revolver today."

"It's an interesting story," Carol said.

"And what irony, his losing his life that way. We used to talk about his motorcycle and the fact that I wouldn't be allowed to ride one over there. What a country!"

"I get the impression that in spite of its problems, you actually liked Saudi Arabia."

"I didn't mean to leave that impression, sheriff. One doesn't like or dislike Saudi Arabia so much as marvel that it exists. If oil were not needed, no one would give a damn about it."

Carol had heard Kevin say very much the same thing. She wondered what he would think of Sallie's story of the CIA gun. A gun that could not have been used to kill Vivian Neuberger if, as Sallie tells it, it now lies somewhere in the vast reaches of that oil rich country. Riyadh? Mecca? The Empty Quarter?

"Thanks for your help, Mrs. Finch," Carol said as she got up to leave. "Let's stay in touch."

It was a silly parting remark. Of course they would stay in touch. But neither of them had any idea that they would be in touch with each other again the very next day.

CHAPTER 61

"There's a message here for you," JoAnne called out as Carol climbed the stairs to her office. "Officer Barrett. I think he's lost some weight."

Carol had seen Jim just a few days earlier, and hadn't been aware of any weight loss.

"It's probably because he doesn't get to have those big breakfasts at the Southport diner," her assistant continued.

"What's the message?"

"I left it on your desk. Something about that man Grandi."

The message told her that the person she should contact at Scranton's *The Times-Tribune* was Suzanne Koslowski. She apparently worked at the city desk and had done the piece on Frank Grandi's troubles. Unfortunately, Ms. Koslowski was away from her desk on assignment. Carol left her name and number but made no mention of Grandi, assuming that the fact the call had come from a sheriff in western New York would result in a puzzled but quick call back.

She was about to sort through her in-box when Sam Bridges tapped on her door and pushed it open.

"Hi, Sam, what's up?"

"Nothing much. Just thought I'd let you know where I'm off to - that shack down below Anson's Grove where one of Grandi's men was hanging out."

"Well, we're on the same page. I've been trying to reach the woman at the Scranton paper that tells us Grandi's facing some potentially serious allegations."

"Glad to hear it. All I'll be doing is seeing if anybody's been back in the cabin. My 'no trespassing' measures weren't all that difficult to overcome."

"I've got no gripe against Scranton or Lackawanna County, but I hope Grandi stays over there for a few months. Maybe permanently."

"You don't sound as if he's a prime suspect in Mrs. Neuberger's death."

"I'm not sure I ever thought he was. Somehow I doubt that somebody with fracking at the top of his agenda is going to be deterred by a high school science teacher. Anyway, have a good trip."

"I'll survive it. I'm not sure about the patrol car."

It turned out to be an uneventful trip, although Sam did his share of cursing as the car bounced up and down on the road to what was left of the cabin. There had been no break-in, or if there had been, evidence of it had been carefully erased. There was nothing for Sam to do, but he was not anxious to take the drive back up the Benson road, so he spent the next fifteen minutes exploring the area, looking for some sign that others had visited the cabin since he had last been there.

That sign took the form of half a dozen cigarette butts that had not been there when he had had his little confrontation with Grandi. Six cigarettes told him that someone had been there and that he had stayed for at lest half an hour. Two of the butts were beside the porch, suggesting that the smoker had sat there, debating with himself what he should do. Three were back toward the makeshift toilet in the woods. The sixth was in the car turn-around area he and Grandi had used. Presumably the visitor had gotten back into his car, sat there while he took one more smoke, and finally jettisoned the cigarette and driven away from the hollow.

As to who the visitor was, Sam had no tangible clue, only an understandable hunch: Garth Campbell. The sheriff had just conveyed to him the news that Frank Grandi was in Scranton. Of course he could have paid his visit to the cabin before leaving Crooked Lake, but from what Sam knew of Grandi, the man was not one to be intimated by a 'no trespassing' sign. Campbell, however, and in spite of the fact that he had threatened Kevin with a gun, was but a bit player in this charade who was much less likely to challenge local authority. But Sam knew that this was just a hunch. They did not even know for sure that Campbell was Grandi's pawn.

He considered picking up the cigarette butts, but quickly dismissed that impulse and set off back to Cumberland. All he had accomplished was to subject the patrol car to another grueling trip over the Benson Road.

Suzanne Koslowski returned the sheriff's call shortly before 11:00. Carol explained who she was and why she was calling.

"You know something about Mr. Grandi?" Koslowski asked.

"I know nothing about Mr. Grandi's problems with the law in Scranton. I am calling because he is a person of interest in a matter over here in the Finger Lakes. A former member of my staff recently told me about a piece which *The Times-Tribune* had published, a piece which I understand you wrote. I'm afraid I can't help you with your coverage of your Grandi story, but I think you may be able to help me with my case. Okay?"

Carol was confident that Ms. Koslowski would take the time to talk with her. She would be curious about Grandi's 'other story,' and it was possible that there'd be something in it that would make reading about his troubles with the law in Scranton more enticing. The phone conversation lasted for nearly 25 minutes, during which time Carol learned more about Grandi's role as a landlord and his tendency to evade his responsibilities as a citizen.

Necessarily, Carol was careful not to suggest that Grandi might have done anything unlawful. She herself thought it highly unlikely that he had been Vivian Neuberger's killer, and she realized that if she were to mention that case it would soon be a subject of discussion in Scranton. Better to emphasize Grandi's interest in fracking and buying up property around Crooked Lake and to seek more details about what it was that had caused him to hurry back to Pennsylvania.

By the time she had thanked the reporter and hung up the phone, Carol was convinced of two things. One was that Frank Grandi was a despicable specimen of humanity. The other was that she had learned nothing that was relevant to her efforts to bring the Neuberger case to closure. Perhaps, confronted with problems of his own, he would abandon plans to pursue fracking in the Crooked Lake area. It was then that for the first time in weeks she recalled her conversation with Jasper Eglin and his quest for help in dealing with Grandi, a fellow pro-fracker. She decided to call Eglin. She hadn't tried to persuade Grandi to soft-pedal his advocacy of fracking. But she suspected that Eglin would be grateful for the news that Grandi had, at least temporarily, become preoccupied with something else.

CHAPTER 62

That evening at the cottage on Blue Water Point began with a glass of Chardonnay and a report to Kevin on Frank Grandi's troubles.

"I've just about come to the conclusion that we should discount Grandi as a possible suspect in Vivian's death," Carol said.

"I knew it," he said. "Grandi and fracking were to be my contribution to the solution of your case, and now I'm informed that I've been wasting my time."

"I'm sorry, and what's more I may be wrong. But we never really believed that someone other than a member of the Crooked Lake Birders Club killed Vivian. We were just touching all the bases."

"Well, don't you think that if we're to start drawing lines through our roster of suspects we ought to take stock of who's left before we run out of suspects."

"We're a long way from running out of suspects, Kevin. But yes, I'm all for taking stock. If you'll pour us another glass of the lake's finest, I'll check my briefcase. There's bound to be a yellow pad in there with a few of my doodles and fugitive thoughts on the case. By the way, what's for dinner?"

"You want to eat first?"

"No. I just want to know whether what you've planned will keep while we discuss murder."

"I didn't feel like cooking, so I went the deli route. Which means ham sandwiches and salad."

"Sounds like what I had for lunch, but so what," Carol said and set off for the bedroom and her briefcase.

When they had settled down on the deck for a serious discussion of who was most likely to have been Vivian Neuberger's killer, neither was very sanguine that it would be a fruitful conversation. Virtually every new development in the case had raised more questions than it had answered. The cast of characters they had come to know over the weeks since Vivian's death seemed frustratingly unable to provide information which could lead to a breakthrough in the investigation, yet remarkably able to offer information which could not be verified.

It was obvious to the sheriff that some members of the birders club had declined to tell her all they knew, and that others had chosen to tell her things that were almost certainly untrue or at least misleading.

"So where do we start?" Kevin asked.

"How about motives? I know we've been there before, but maybe it's time to take another stab at identifying what might have prompted these people to take the risk of shooting a colleague in the middle of a bird hike."

Kevin looked pensive.

"I know I asked you," he said, "but what would you say to starting with guns."

"Guns?"

"Yes, guns," Kevin said. "There's an element of guessing in ascribing motives to these people we don't really know that well. But we know who has guns and what kind of guns. Why not work our way back to motives?"

"What do you have in mind?" Carol looked doubtful.

"Remember what Doc Crawford said about looking for the best marksman among the suspects. Mrs. Neuberger was shot by a handgun, and they're less reliable than rifles and shotguns. Whoever shot her had to be pretty damned good to hit her square in the middle of the back. So why don't we start by checking off everyone's guns and what we know about their skills, and then see if that may help us get a picture of what happened up in the Grove."

"I seem to be spinning my wheels, so maybe I should do it your way." She looked at her yellow pad and proceeded to run down what they knew about the key birders and guns.

"Mel Cone has guns, including handguns, all properly registered. Paul Raymore has no guns, at least none registered. Sallie Finch's situation is the same as Raymore's. Bill Neuberger has no guns registered, but may have an unregistered handgun - the one he bought to protect his home down in the Hamptons. Young Nagle's too young to have a registered gun, but his father has them, including a handgun. And then there's Frank Grandi, who has a whole armory of guns, all registered. That covers everyone we've been worried about. But there's no guarantee that having no registered guns means they don't have any. So Sallie Finch, for example, may secretly have a whole hoard of them, including handguns."

"That's a good beginning, although we know it's probably not a complete picture. Your data shows that Cone, Grandi, and the Nagle family have handguns. Let's assume that Neuberger does, too. That leaves Finch and Raymore as unknowns; if they do own handguns, they are in violation of state law in not having them registered."

"So where does this leave us?" Carol asked, still looking skeptical.

"I'd say it brings us to the question of marksmanship. Who among them is good enough to have brought down Vivian Neuberger with a handgun at a considerable distance during the bird hike. What do you think?"

"What I think is that there's still too much we don't know. We know Sallie Finch is a good marksman, but she doesn't have a handgun any more. We have no idea whether Raymore owns a gun, much less whether he qualifies as a skilled marksman."

"I know. But here's where we have to make a few educated guesses. You've talked with them and I haven't. What do you think about Finch and Raymore? How likely is it that either one of them owns an unregistered handgun?"

"Sallie says that she gave her government issue handgun to a Saudi Arabian prince and that she has no need for a gun now that she's retired. As for Raymore, he -"

Kevin interrupted.

"I was asking for an educated guess. Do you believe Finch?"

Carol gave the question some thought. Kevin interpreted it as a 'no.'

"So you don't trust her. Why not?"

"I'm not sure. For one thing, I find it hard to believe that after carrying a gun for years she could just walk away from the gun culture. More importantly, I guess it's because her story about this Saudi friend she gave her gun to is - let's just say it seems unlikely. At the time it seemed pretty straight forward, not at all rehearsed. But the more I think about it the more it doesn't quite ring true. After all, the CIA policy seems to be that weapons it issues have to be turned in when someone leaves the agency. I'd have thought that the CIA, of all employers, wouldn't have let a friendship with a foreign national override agency policy."

"Especially when the foreign national is from the ever unpredictable Middle East?"

"For all I know it happened just like she said it did. Maybe the agency is still pursuing the matter privately."

"Somehow I don't think the CIA negotiates such matters privately. Anyway, you were going to give me an educated guess, and I have a hunch that Sallie Finch, good marksman that she is, is still a suspect in Vivian Neuberger's death. How about Raymore?"

"We know nothing about his marksmanship. Sam doubts that he's ever owned a gun. I wouldn't know about that, but he just isn't a gun owner type."

"What's a gun owner type?" Kevin wanted to know.

"Hey, I'm the one with experience as a cross examiner. It's hard to define, but you know one when you see one. Moreover, don't you find it difficult to imagine a birder with Raymore's standing as someone who's also a lover of guns? You wanted my educated guess, and you have it. Paul Raymore doesn't have a secret stash of guns somewhere."

"So, Finch should still be treated as a suspect, Raymore should not. How about our border-line case, Bill Neuberger?"

"He claims he sold his gun, but as of this evening we have no proof of that claim. I believe he intended to get rid of it but just hasn't gotten around to it. Mel Cone thinks Bill is unduly influenced by his experience down on Long Island, thinks he's equivocating, waiting for a media report of some catastrophic break-in right here on Crooked Lake."

"And your educated guess?"

"It's like Raymore. Guns have never been a part of his life or experience, and that's not going to suddenly change now."

Carol scanned her yellow pad and shook her head.

"That just leaves Cone and Nagle," she said.

"Oh, yes, the man who introduced us to Daddy Bird."

"At first I didn't take Cone that seriously, but now that he's shared his voyeuristic findings with us and been accused of an unhealthy interest of his own in Vivian, I'm afraid that he'll have to stay on my list. He's a weaselly kind of guy, don't you think?"

"That's one way of putting it. But common sense says to treat him as a suspect. After all, he'll always be the birder who was closest to Vivian when she was shot."

"I've no idea how good a marksman he is, but he owns a lot of guns and by his own admission uses them a lot, so I'd bet he's not a bad shot."

"And then there's Nagle, our troubled teen ager."

"I've worried more about him than any of the others," Carol, said, "hoping he wouldn't turn out to be the killer. Can you imagine how terrible that would be? Fortunately, I don't think he needs a lot of our attention. We know the family has guns galore, but I had an unexpected run-in with Michael the other day and I think our youngest birder can be taken off our list."

"Why's that?"

"Apparently his brother, Richard, did break into their gun cabinet, but he confessed to their father what he'd done. That got me thinking, and my educated guess is that we've been wasting our time on Michael as a suspect. I'm 99 per cent sure he didn't know Vivian would be on the hike, and even if he did and had a gun with him up in the Grove, he'd have to have been lucky to hit her smack in the middle of her back. After all, he's just 15 years old."

"I hope you're right. Boys that age have been known to do some pretty awful things."

"It's my impression that he's on a regimen of meds that's doing him a world of good. We can always put him back on the list of suspects if we have to. But we haven't said anything yet about Grandi. Do you want another educated guess?"

"You're going to take him off the list, too?"

"For the time being. Like Nagle, I doubt very much that he knew Vivian would be taking a hike in Anson's Grove that morning. And I think he's too smart to risk his interest in fracking here by killing an outspoken high school teacher. In any event, he's currently preoccupied with legal problems down in Scranton."

"Remarkable! Our sheriff has just reduced the roster of suspects in the latest Crooked Lake murder to two. Sallie Finch and Melvin Cone."

"If you tell that to anyone in the media, I'm getting a divorce. Let's take a break and have that ham sandwich."

CHAPTER 63

The ham sandwich, apple pie, and an unexpected phone call from Gretchen Ziegler, Carol's old friend in Albany, meant that they didn't get around to considering the issue of motivation for the shooting of Vivian Neuberger until it was getting dark.

"Let's put it off until tomorrow," Kevin suggested.

"No way. We were making some real headway, and I don't want to lose our momentum."

"I know, but I'm running out of steam."

"Tell you what," Carol said. "Let's take a quick swim. That'll wake you up."

"But it's almost dark."

"I don't know about you, but I remember after dark swims as the most fun."

"I'll bet you used to go skinny dipping," Kevin said, a smile spreading across his face.

"I did, and I'm sure you did, too. If I offered to make this one a skinny dip, would you go along?"

"Okay, let's take a swim. But I'd rather wear my bathing suit. I think they have company at the Brocks, and I don't want to be surprised if someone turns on the porch lights."

As Carol had predicted, a dip in the lake proved refreshing. It also generated further talk about trying it sans bathing suits at some future time. By the time they had toweled off, it was closer to ten than nine.

"You wanted to tackle peoples' motives for killing Vivian," Kevin said, "so why don't you lead off."

"I've been giving the subject some thought, and maybe a better approach would be to look at motives more generally, not just for wanting Vivian dead. I mean, what led Cone to spy on her? What's the real reason for Raymore's precipitous move to the lake? And for his not sharing his joint book authorship idea with her? You see what I mean?"

"Sure, so go ahead."

"Let me start with the business of Cone spying on Vivian. After all, that's what really moved this investigation into high gear. Do you believe that he's simply a chronic voyeur? Remember, he said he'd been watching his next door neighbor, and that when the neighbor moved away he simply transferred his attention to the Neuberger house."

"I thought we'd agreed that it's a toss up, could go either way. He either saw what he said he saw or he made it all up."

"That's true, but it gives us two questions. If he did see Vivian with Larry Finch, why was he watching her house? On the other hand, if he didn't see Vivian with Larry, why did he want us to think that he had?"

"If Cone made the whole thing up," Kevin said, "I'd say it was because he wanted to steer your attention away from him. Which he did. We started thinking about Bill Neuberger and Sallie Finch as suspects, both with a reason to kill Vivian - infidelity."

"But that's also true if he actually saw Vivian and Larry together up in that attic room. Then the question becomes why was he watching that room. One explanation is that Mel is simply a voyeur; he's always peeking into nearby windows. Isn't there another, even better explanation? Of course there is. He *himself* was interested in Vivian. Remember, Bill Neuberger told us so, said Mel was virtually panting after her and that she rebuffed him."

"But it's possible that Bill was lying," Kevin argued, "maybe just getting even with Mel for telling you about Bill having a gun. Vivian isn't around to verify Bill's charge, and Mel's denial would be suspect."

"That's the problem with practically everything these birders say," Carol said. "But I suspect Mel and Bill were both telling the truth. Vivian was a very attractive woman, and at least one of her colleagues in the birders club is of the opinion that she was both very much aware of it and enjoyed using it."

"Who's that?"

"Paul Raymore. He claims that he had gotten to know Mrs. Neuberger well enough to realize that she was quite capable of manipulating men. Emasculating them is the way he put it, and he obviously didn't relish the idea of her emasculating him."

"So," Kevin said, "the victim of the Anson's Grove murder isn't the perfect woman we've been hearing about."

"I, for one, have never thought of her as a perfect woman," Carol said. "That's asking too much of all women - and, I'm quite sure, of all men. But I'd also rather not jump on the bandwagon of her detractors. I feel reasonably confident that Sharon Lagerfeld's assessment of Vivian will be closest to the mark in the end."

"Lagerfeld? She's the school principal, right?"

"She is, and I do value her opinion more than I do that of most of McKendrick's flock, including Raymore."

"Now that we've brought Raymore into the picture, what's the motivation issue where he's concerned?"

"There's a lot of them," Carol said. "Why the move to our lake? Why the story about his plan for doing a book with Vivian? Why his decision to scrap that idea? I'm talking about both his reason for doing these things and his reason for telling us about the book project in such exquisite detail."

"I thought the reason for the move to Crooked Lake was obvious - Vivian Neuberger."

"Except for the fact that he initially stressed the advice of a friend who said it was a great area for birding. Raymore is one helluva smart birder, someone who would know full well that that isn't true. Why would he find it necessary to give me such a patently false story?"

"Because he didn't want to talk about Vivian," Kevin suggested.

"Yes, of course, but I guess I'm offended to think he had such a low opinion of my intelligence that he thought he could sell me on the idea that we're in bird heaven. And frankly, I'm not ready to buy the business of his needing to be on the lake to sell Vivian on the book project. It's purely guesswork, but I think he made it all up."

"You think Cone and Neuberger are on the up and up, but Raymore isn't?" Kevin asked.

"What we're looking for is motivation for what they've been saying and doing. Something about Raymore doesn't ring true. I'm willing to concede that Vivian fits in there somewhere, but writing the greatest bird book since Audubon? I don't buy it. If it weren't for Raymore and the book, I'd be telling you that the biggest cock and bull story is Sallie Finch's about her friendship with a charming young Saudi Arabian."

"You aren't in the trusting mood tonight, are you?"

"Well, what do you think? Mrs. Finch doesn't have a gun any more because she gave it to a member of the Saudi royal family, after which he conveniently died in a motorcycle accident. Ergo, there's simply no way of tracing the gun. It's possible, I suppose, but I'm more inclined to say it belongs in a modern day Arabian Nights tale. I wish I knew a lot more about her connection to the CIA. She wouldn't quit the agency to save her first marriage, but she did retire at a relatively early age to move to Crooked Lake to marry Larry Finch. Go figure."

"You're still puzzled by all these birders moving to the lake recently, aren't you?"

"Indeed I am," Carol said. "At first I thought it might have something to do with the fact that some of these people had known each other somewhere else and moved here because of it. That doesn't seem to be true, but it still strikes me as strange that people from Virginia, the Hamptons, the Hudson Valley - even Scranton - arrived just in time for another summer of murder on Crooked Lake."

"You haven't mentioned Michael Nagle, or isn't he still a suspect?"

"It isn't Michael, it's his family whose motives puzzle me. If he'd been your son, don't you think you'd have taken steps to deal with his problems long ago? Instead, the Nagles resisted doing anything until he cut that other boy down at the Southport beach park. How do you explain that?"

"Not easily. What about Grandi?"

"It's like I said, he's not a first tier candidate. I'll be only too happy to change my mind if something new surfaces, but for now I'd prefer to concentrate my energies elsewhere."

"It sounds to me as if you're ready to wrap this discussion up."

"I am. We haven't solved Vivian's murder, but I think we've done a pretty good job of identifying the big questions. I'm ready for one last dip in the lake and then to bed. How about you?"

"We're still in our bathing suits, so why not?"

"Good. I'll be in the water before you get as far as the dock," she called back to Kevin as she left the deck and sprinted across the lawn.

CHAPTER 64

Darren Patrick parked his delivery truck and set off for the front door at 307 Ridge Road in Yates Center, a small package tucked under his arm. Erin Dockery obeyed the stop sign at the southern end of Ridge Road, and then slowly followed a somewhat beat up old Chevy toward the edge of town. It was when she was almost abreast the UPS truck that she was aware that the driver was waving frantically at her patrol car. Erin pulled over to the curb and leaned out the window.

"You have a problem?" she asked the man in the brown uniform who was standing on the stoop.

"He's fallen down." Erin, of course, had no idea what the UPS driver was referring to.

"What seems to be the trouble?"

"Something's wrong here. The man in there is lying down and he isn't moving."

Erin climbed out of the patrol car and walked up the flagstone path to where her interlocutor was now peering through the large glass window in the front door.

"In there," he repeated.

He stepped aside so that Erin could see what he was talking about.

An inner door was ajar, and some distance behind it, where the entrance hall gave way to a room off to the right, a man's body lay on a parqueted floor, face down, one arm under him, the other stretched out ahead of him. A large object that looked like an strangely shaped metal basket stood upside down beside him. She thought that he had either tripped over it or knocked it down.

"Give me a minute," she said to the UPS man, and pushed the glass door open.

"Hello. Are you all right?" she called out. It was obvious that he wasn't all right, and she went on in and over to where he was lying. There, in addition to the 'metal basket,' was a revolver, just under a yard away from his outstretched hand.

It took no time at all to ascertain that the man was dead. Erin hadn't previously encountered a dead body in her life, discounting those that reclined in a casket. But her training, brief as it was, had been sufficient to tell her that this man had taken his last breath. Of course it wasn't up to her to make that finding. She took out her cell and called 911.

Once the para-medics had been contacted, Erin asked the UPS man for the name on the package which he was carrying.

"Finch," he replied. "Lawrence H. Finch."

She had not been involved in the Neuberger murder case, but she did remember the name Finch, with the result that she was immediately on the phone to the sheriff's office. The sheriff was in, and three minutes later she was on her way to Ridge Road in Yates Center.

"When the paramedics arrive," Carol instructed Erin, "don't let them move the body until I arrive. Has the gun been fired?"

"I can't be sure, but I doubt it. The gun is cold. What's more, I can't see anything that tells me the victim's been shot. Should I dismiss the UPS delivery man?"

"Let him go, but get his name and phone number. And stay alert."

Erin couldn't remember a time when she had been more alert. She immediately turned her attention to the gun. She wasn't sure what she should do with it, but she was sure that she shouldn't leave it on the floor by the body where the para-medics would be working. She'd just told the sheriff that the gun couldn't have been fired because it was cold. But she had no idea when the man had collapsed to the floor. For all she knew it had been hours ago, in which case the revolver might still have been used to kill him. Or, another thought struck her, it might be the dead man's and he had tried unsuccessfully to use it to defend himself.

She realized that all of this was nothing but uninformed speculation. Better that she wait for the paramedics and the sheriff.

"The sheriff says to go on along," she said to the UPS man. "Just let me have your name and a number where we can reach you if necessary."

Erin found a powder room and in it a box of kleenex. She pulled out several tissues and took them back to the living room, where she knelt beside the gun and carefully wrapped them around it before putting it in her jacket pocket. She was anxious to mark the spot on the floor where it had been lying, but couldn't find anything to do the trick.

"Do you happen to have any tape on the truck, Mr. Patrick?" she asked the driver as she read his name from the card he handed her.

"Sure. It comes in handy sometimes."

"Good. Do me a favor, and bring me some before you leave."

The UPS man gave Erin a small role of tape and she saw him off on his rounds just before the para-medic team arrived. Erin tore off a piece of the tape and stuck it to the floor where the gun had been. She was back on her feet again when a short, stocky man with salt and pepper colored hair and a bushy beard and mustache preceded his two colleagues into the house.

He seemed surprised to see the police officer.

"That was fast," he said. "How's it happen that you got here before we did?"

"I'm the one who called 911," Erin said, introducing herself and explaining how it was that she had arrived at the Finch house so quickly. "He's back there on the floor, right where I found him. The sheriff is on her way."

She stepped aside, and the three para-medics took up positions around the dead man. The short man with abundant facial hair was obviously the team leader, and he set right to work feeling for a pulse and other signs of life. Erin chose not to mention the gun. If they found evidence that the man had been shot, she would let them know what she had done with it and why. Her own examination of the man on the floor had been brief and cursory, but she doubted that he had been shot. She hoped that the sheriff would not be critical of her decision to pocket the gun.

It didn't take the para-medics long to reach the same conclusion she had: the man was indeed dead. It took them only a bit longer to come to a tentative conclusion as to what had killed him. There was no evidence that he had been shot, or had been dispatched by a knife or some other weapon. The older and more experienced para-medic closely examined the man's face, sniffing around his mouth and pulling back his eye lids.

"It doesn't look like he's been poisoned," he said to his colleagues. "It must have been a heart attack, maybe a stroke, and if that didn't do the trick the fall did."

It was while the para-medics were discussing the situation, with the team leader expressing his feeling that the victim may have suffered a massive cerebral hemorrhage, that the sheriff arrived, accompanied by Officer Byrnes. Facial hair waved a quick hello to them, but turned his attention immediately back to his colleagues.

Erin looked at her boss with something approaching awe.

"Unbelievable!" she said. "You must have broken the speed limit."

"I took a shortcut," Carol said. Byrnes rolled his eyes. "What's the preliminary verdict?"

"They've been too busy to talk to me, but I think I heard something about a cerebral hemorrhage. He was definitely not shot."

Carol stood in the doorway, looking at the scene on the floor ahead of her.

"But you said there was a gun near his body."

"I did, and there was. I was afraid that the para-medics would move it out of the way or, you know, accidentally knock it aside, so I put it in my pocket for safe keeping."

Her tone of voice made it clear that she was hopeful that the sheriff would not upbraid her for this bit of preemptive action.

Carol studied her youngest and newest officer for what seemed to Erin like an eternity.

"Erin, let's step out of here for a minute," she finally said, taking her by the elbow and steering her away from the little gathering in the living room.

The para-medics had been paying no attention to them, but now they were definitely out of hearing range.

"Do they know anything about there being a gun by the body?"

"I'm afraid I never mentioned it."

"What about when you called 911?"

"No, should I have?"

"What about that UPS Man who was at the door? Did he talk about the gun?"

"You mean in front of the para-medics?"

"That's exactly what I mean. In other words, is there *any* way they would know that there had been a gun on the floor, a gun that had disappeared before they got to work on the body?"

"I don't see how."

"Good. And we're not going to mention it. If it's clear that he wasn't shot, it's irrelevant that there was a gun by his body. At least it's irrelevant as far as the para-medics are concerned. We're another story. So let's leave it that way. Not a word about a gun. By the way, I hope you didn't pick it up with your bare hands."

Erin was both relieved by what she was hearing and mildly irritated that the sheriff might think she'd handle the gun so carelessly.

"I know I'm new here, but I do know we have to be extra careful about handling evidence."

"Yes, Erin, you've done very well. What do you say we have a word with the para-medics."

CHAPTER 65

Carol had never expected that there would be another death in the Neuberger case, and she had no evidence that Larry Finch's demise was in any way related to that of Vivian Neuberger. It might well be a simple coincidence. But if there were any truth in Mel Cone's story of an affair between Vivian and Larry, both had paid the ultimate price for cheating on their spouses.

By the time that the para-medics had completed their work, Larry Finch's body had been removed, and Officer Byrnes had paid the necessary visits to the curious neighbors, Carol was left with the question of what to do about the missing Sallie Finch. Nobody in the neighborhood seemed to know exactly where she had gone and when she might be back, but there was a rough consensus that she hadn't gone out of town and should be back "before too long,' whatever that meant.

For all of them simply to leave the house on Ridge Road and resume their normal routines was out of the question. In the end, Carol let Tommy Byrnes take her car and go back to Cumberland. She herself wanted to be present when Sallie got back, and she chose to let Erin stay with her. After all, for all practical purposes it had been Erin who discovered Larry's body, and, as their newest recruit, might benefit most from watching the impact of what had happened on the man's wife.

The living room, with its collection of Middle Eastern art and art objects, now looked much as it had when Carol had previously visited it. With one obvious exception. The large urn, which Erin had first thought of as an oddly shaped metal basket, was still standing upside down beneath the shelf from which it had been dislodged, presumably by Larry when he had fallen to the parquet floor. Tommy had taken lots of pictures, thereby capturing the way the room had looked at the time of Larry Finch's death, so there was no danger that restoring the urn to the shelf would deprive them of 'a scene of the crime.' But Carol was thinking of what she wanted Sallie to see. And why.

She was determined not to put the gun back where it was, and Larry would not be returning to his place on the floor. If she righted the urn and placed it on its shelf there would be nothing to suggest what had happened in the living room. No, Carol thought, she would leave the urn where it had fallen. It would be the first thing Sallie would notice, one less thing for her to describe to the new widow. And it would start Sallie thinking. About what, Carol didn't know, but she hoped that it might lead to something that would help clear up the mystery of the Neuberger case.

"What are we going to do about that thing?" Erin said, pointing to the urn.

"That's what I've been thinking about, and I've decided to leave it just like it is."

"Do you think Mrs. Finch had something to do with what happened to Mr. Finch?"

Carol shook her head.

"Nothing surprises me anymore, but I'm pretty sure that Mr. Finch was alive and well when his wife left the house this morning. To be honest, I have no idea what Mrs. Finch's reaction will be when she sees that the urn has been knocked onto the floor. Or how she reacts to the really big news that her husband is dead."

Carol was beginning to worry about just how long they would be engaged in such idle speculation when Erin gestured toward the window across from the dislodged urn.

"A car just pulled into the driveway," she said. "I'll bet it's her."

It was immediately apparent that Sallie was aware that something was wrong. A neighbor had probably said something to her as she left her car. She spotted the two officers of the law as soon as she reached the glass door.

"What is this?" she asked, her voice reflecting surprise but also just a hint of annoyance. "My God, what have you done to my urn?"

Sallie had seen the displaced urn. She rushed past them to examine one of her favorite *objets d'art*.

"Who did this?" It was an accusatory question.

"Mrs. Finch, do you suppose we might find a place to sit down and I'll explain everything."

Well, not everything, she thought to herself.

The change that came over Sallie was so abrupt that it was as if she were suddenly a different person. It had nothing to do with what she said. She actually said nothing. But something had come to her mind, something so important that it drained the color from her face, something that caused her to grab the back of a chair for support. She recovered quickly, but it was obvious that it would henceforth be more difficult for her to concentrate on what the sheriff was about to tell her. In fact, it looked as if Sallie Finch wasn't sure she wanted to hear what the sheriff wanted to tell her.

"Sheriff, I'm not feeling very well. Whatever it is came over me while I was driving home. I'd like to lie down for a bit. Can you just give me the gist of what you have to tell me? Then we can get together for a longer conversation later, even this afternoon. But I really need to lie down."

Carol didn't know what Sallie's problem was, but she was pretty sure it wasn't that she needed to lie down.

"Of course we can postpone our talk until later, but there's something you need to know. I'm sorry, but it really can't wait. Your husband is dead. We don't know exactly what caused his death, but it looks as if he had a heart attack or a serious stroke. It apparently happened right here in the living room, and when he fell into the wall here and knocked your urn to the floor. I'm so sorry to have bad news for you. We found him because a UPS driver was trying to deliver a package, and my colleague - this is Erin Dockery - was nearby and took charge. A para-medic team came promptly; they only left a little over half an hour ago. Mr. Finch's body was taken to the local hospital. That's only temporarily, of course, but there may have to be an autopsy."

Sallie had sat down. Carol reached over and patted her hand. She really did feel for the poor woman, even as she was conscious of strongly mixed feelings about her.

"Is there something I can do for you?" Carol asked. She could not imagine what that something could be.

The bereaved woman hadn't said a word as she listened to the bad news. She still looked almost chalk white, and she hadn't relaxed her grip on the back of her chair. Carol wished she knew what was bothering Sallie - something that had been bothering her even before she had been told of Larry's death.

"I regret that I had to be the one to share this terrible news with you," Carol said, and repeated her offer of help, not that she expected Sallie to seek it. Whatever her problem was, Carol was almost certain it wasn't that she had just lost her husband.

Sallie Finch eventually managed to politely ask her and the other officer to please leave.

"There must have been something wrong with the cassoulet I had for lunch. If you don't mind, could you please leave. I'm sure I'll be okay, but not now. Thank you."

She moved to the door, opened it, and waited patiently while Carol and Erin said their good-byes and wished her well.

Neither Carol nor Erin had anything to say until they left town and headed for Cumberland. It was then that the sheriff put a question to her young officer.

"Did you notice anything unusual back there?"

Erin looked away from the sheriff and out over the lake, the better to hide what she was sure was a trace of anxiety on her face. Was the sheriff testing her?

"I'm not sure," she answered, somewhat tentatively. "I expected her to say something about her husband being dead, but all she talked about was how she felt. Not about her husband, but about food poisoning or whatever was bothering her.That seemed kinda strange."

"I thought so, too," Carol said. "Her mind was on something else before I told her her husband was dead, but I thought she'd forget about it and react to my news. She never did. No questions. No tears. She didn't seem to be stunned to hear that she'd just lost him. Most people would sound shocked, even if their marriage was on the rocks when they got the news."

"Why do you suppose she didn't? Sound shocked, I mean."

"This is strictly a guess, Erin. But I'm betting it was because when she walked into the house she realized that something was missing, and that that something was momentarily far more important to her than everything else. And that includes her husband's death."

"I'd never been inside that house before, so I wouldn't have any idea whether something was missing. The only things missing that had been there when I arrived were Mr. Finch's body and the gun, but they wouldn't have been there when she left home this morning. I'm confused."

"You aren't alone. But I have a hunch - just a hunch, mind you - of what's bothering Mrs. Finch. If I'm right, the Neuberger case may be coming to an end."

CHAPTER 66

Carol's first order of business upon arriving back at the office was to buzz Officer Byrnes.

"Hi, Tommy," she said, relieved that he hadn't already gone back on highway patrol. "I want to take a look at the pictures you took back at the Finch house. When will they be available?"

"How about now," he said. "Normally I'd have weeded them out, but I could tell that this wasn't any routine matter. So they're all there. I started going through the lot, but frankly it's boring. Want to take a look?"

"I do."

"Okay, just give me a minute."

While she was waiting, Carol and Erin exchanged a few words before the rookie officer hit the road.

"I'll be needing that gun you've tucked away in your jacket pocket," Carol said.

"Of course. I intended to hand it over before I left. I'm still not sure whether removing the gun from the floor was the right thing to do."

"As things turned out, it was definitely the right thing to do, no question about it. We learned some things we wouldn't have learned if it had still been where you found it when Mrs. Finch got home."

"We did?" Erin looked and sounded puzzled.

"Let's say I'm almost certain that we did. I need to take a look at Tommy's photos, do some heavy thinking, but I think we may be much closer to wrapping up this case than we were when I came to work this morning. I'll fill you and the men in after I've given Mr. Finch's death some more thought."

Three minutes later Carol had scanned the first several dozen shots. They all showed the urn which had been knocked over, and they showed it from every possible perspective. They easily confirmed what she knew to be the case, that the urn was upside down. More importantly, they confirmed what she *thought* was the case, that the urn was resting on the floor at an angle. This latter fact had not seemed to be that important when they had been standing in the Finch's living room. But the more she had worried about Sallie's behavior while she and Erin were driving back to Cumberland, the more she had become fixated on the question of whether the urn had landed squarely or at an angle. It might not have made any difference. On the other hand, it might have made all the difference in the world.

Rather than ponder the implications of the urn resting on an angle on the Finch's living room floor, Carol turned her attention to an autopsy. She called Doc Crawford. She wanted to call him. She dreaded calling him.

"It's my favorite sheriff," he answered promptly. "What will it be - another boat ride, another autopsy?"

"Hello, Doc, you sound in good spirits."

"All things considered, I guess I am. At least my oncologist says I'm holding my own."

"Does that mean that you're willing to take a request for an autopsy under advisement?"

"And to think that I had assumed my days as a pathologist were behind me. I should have known better. If it were anybody else, I'm sure I could think of a reason to say 'no thanks.' It may depend on when you'll be needing my help."

"It's that case of murder on a bird hike, remember? You autopsied the woman who was killed, Vivian Neuberger, said she was shot by a handgun."

Carol suddenly realized that what she was telling Doc was misleading. It could even be irrelevant.

"Wait a minute, Doc. Let's start over. We don't need another autopsy on Mrs. Neuberger. It's on a man named Larry Finch who is alleged to have been having an affair with the Neuberger woman. He died this morning, and it looks like a fatal coronary or a stroke. No evidence of foul play. So forget what I said about murder and a bird hike."

"Are you sure these two deaths aren't related? Two people having an affair, both now dead, all in the course of a typically lovely Crooked Lake summer."

"Look, Doc, this is a bit tricky. Like I said, Finch's death doesn't look suspicious. I have no idea what if any medical problems he may have had. If he and Mrs. Neuberger weren't having an affair, and there is no proof that they were, only an allegation by a local voyeur, we wouldn't be having this conversation. But you're right, given the circumstances I'd feel a lot better about things if I had an autopsy on Finch."

"You do have a problem, don't you? You may have told me this before, but if so I've forgotten. Were either the Neuberger woman or this guy who turned up dead this morning married?"

"They were. And you should know that I consider both Mr. Finch's wife and Mrs. Neuberger's husband suspects in her death. If so, why couldn't they be suspects in Mr. Finch's death as well?"

"By the way," Doc asked, "where's the body right now?"

"The coroner was understanding - we couldn't just leave Finch's body lying where we found it. We had no idea where Mrs. Finch was and when she'd be back, and as luck would have it her husband's doctor happened to be out of town. Given the para-medic team's opinion, the best we had at the moment, the body was moved to the morgue at the hospital in Yates Center."

"Well, you say there's no evidence of foul play, so whether an autopsy is in order will probably depend on what Finch's physician has to say when he gets back. Otherwise, it would be up to the next of kin, and that'd be the wife. Of course if you could nail Mrs. Finch for the shooting death of Mrs. Neuberger, that would make an autopsy of her husband's body an easy call."

Carol laughed.

"Don't hold your breath. What I think you're telling me is that I'll have to sweet talk Sallie Finch into okaying an autopsy on her late husband. I'm going to have to talk to the man who worked with you on the Neuberger shooting. It's Fred Reichler, isn't it?"

"Right, only he prefers to be called Freddy."

"I have a question to put to him which may be more important than the autopsy. We found a handgun next to Mr. Finch's body, and it's a Glock. I'd like to have Reichler examine it, tell me if he can whether it could be the same gun that fired the bullet that killed Mrs. Neuberger."

"Sounds like a good idea. If you'll hold for a minute, I'll give you his number."

Carol waited for what seemed like an unusually long time, and it was a winded Doc Crawford who returned to the phone with the number.

"It's not my business to tell you how to take care of yourself, Doc, but you sound as if you should take it easy."

"I'm an authority on taking it easy, Carol," he said. "Unfortunately, Freddy's number wasn't where it's supposed to be. What I'm not an authority on is maintaining an organized desk."

"I'm familiar with that problem. Anyway, thanks for Reichler's number. And speaking of thanks, Kevin and I really loved the party boat ride, moon and all."

"You already thanked me for that," Doc said, "but you're welcome to repeat yourselves. I had fun, too. Just let me know if you'll be needing an autopsy."

Carol replaced the phone and settled back in her chair to consider what had happened in the Finches' living room earlier that morning.

CHAPTER 67

When Carol arrived home that evening, Kevin was immediately aware of two things and proceeded to comment on both of them. One was that his wife looked exhausted. The other was that she sounded excited.

"I am exhausted," she said. "This was one of those days that makes you feel like you've aged by ten years. Maybe more. But it's also one that makes you feel like you've won the jackpot. Does that sound like a contradiction?"

"It sure does, but for what it's worth you don't look at all like you've aged ten years. Maybe a week, but that strikes me as acceptable if the jackpot's big enough."

"I don't want to get too excited, but I think I've solved the Neuberger case. And I'd call that a pretty big jackpot."

"Well, congratulations!" Kevin took two big steps and wrapped his arms around her.

"Let's not overdo it," she said, backing away. "If I'm wrong, we'll be facing one huge let down."

"It won't happen. You're the pessimist. When you say you've solved a case, I always know it's in the bag. Anyway, I want to hear all about it. Why don't you give me a quick overview, then let's head out to *The Cedar Post* to celebrate. I'll get the wine, you find a seat on the deck."

"Do I get to shed the uniform?"

"Whatever you wish. I'd listen if you only were wearing your birthday suit."

Carol ignored this and hurried down the hall to change.

When she reappeared, the wine had been poured and the reservation made.

"I've left you time for half an hour's worth of the headlines," Kevin said.

"You understand, don't you, that I won't be able to walk you through everything at *The Post*? I'm not ready to treat our conversation as a press release, which it would be if I shared it with all the tipplers out there."

"I know, which is why I'm suggesting that you leave out the exhausting stuff and concentrate on the happy ending. Like who killed Vivian."

"Unfortunately, who killed Vivian - or why I think I know who killed Vivian - makes no sense unless you know the whole story. And it all began this morning when my most recently minted officer, Erin Dockery, called me from Yates Center to report that she was dealing with a death in a house owned by people named Finch."

"That would be Sallie Finch, right? How'd it happen that Dockery was there?"

"Yes, it was Sallie's house, although the person who died was her husband. And Erin was at the house because a UPS driver was delivering something and motioned for her to help him. Complicated, isn't it?"

"Let me guess. Something Dockery saw or heard proves that Sallie killed her husband. Hence case closed."

"I'm afraid it wasn't that simple. In the first place, the paramedics on the scene think Mr. Finch had died of natural causes, like a heart attack or brain hemorrhage. It looked as if he simply collapsed, and in doing so he knocked over one of Sallie's oriental urns. That's where it gets interesting. The urn landed upside down, but at an angle which meant that a handgun we found on the floor could have slid out from under the urn when it hit the floor."

"There was a gun in the urn?" Kevin asked, trying to make sense of Carol's report.

"That's what I think. Remember that both Sallie and her husband had each sworn that they didn't own a gun. Yet there was one on their living room floor, right next to the body. Where did it come from? This is where your wife's 'brain in overdrive' comes into the picture. How about the urn? Sallie had made it clear to me that the living room, with all its Middle Eastern memorabilia, was her space, out of bounds to her less cultured spouse. I hadn't been impressed by her story of what had happened to her CIA issued handgun. The more I thought about it - and I thought a lot about it today - the more it seemed possible that she had kept the gun and tucked it away for safe keeping. Why not in the urn? Who was to know? And who would have expected that Larry would choose the area next to the urn to take his fatal dive?"

"And I'll bet you've already done some research on the gun and know it was the one that shot Vivian Neuberger. Right?"

"Not quite. I got in touch with a ballistics expert, the one who helped Doc Crawford in his autopsy on Vivian, and he now has the gun. He expects to be back to me in a couple of days, but I think there's a pretty good chance that the gun in the urn is the one that was used to kill Vivian. Ergo, Sallie Finch is Vivian's killer."

"So you aren't one hundred per cent sure."

"Come on, Kevin, don't be a wet blanket. The evidence it's Sallie is mounting up pretty fast, don't you think?"

"But Sallie hasn't confessed, has she?"

"She wasn't even there when first Erin and then Tommy Byrnes and I got to the Finch house. When she did arrive, the body had been removed, and so had the gun. That's when Sallie practically gave herself away. She was nervous, couldn't stop looking around as if something were missing. And what would have been missing? How about the gun? She could see it wasn't under the urn or on the floor, which would have told her we'd beaten her to it. Which is exactly what happened. She'll have had a tough day, trying to figure out what we know and deciding what her story is going to be this time."

"You think that what happened today rules out all of your other suspects?"

"I thought we'd already decided that Sallie was among the most likely suspects. Of course something unbelievable could happen, even today, like Paul Raymore admitting killing Vivian because she refused to co-author that bird book. Or Mel Cone and Bill Neuberger confessing that they plotted the whole thing together and were tired of waiting for me to catch on."

"Okay, I see your point. But it all seems to have come together so suddenly. Almost too easily, if you know what I mean. It's the best case of *deus ex machina* since Euripides."

"What *are* you talking about?"

"Sorry. I guess I'm just showing off my erudition. Let's head for *The Cedar Post*."

"First you explain this latest display of your erudition."

"It's nothing, really, just an old phrase explaining how logic gets set aside at the end of a play by some dramatic last minute intervention. It happened a lot in the Greek tragedies. Just when a resolution of the plot looks hopeless, the Gods step in and put everything in order. At least for Euripides it was the Gods. In the Neuberger case, it was Larry Finch, who showed up in the right place at the right time, to demonstrate that the murderer - or murderess - was his wife. Isn't it remarkable that he collapsed in the living room, not in the bathroom? Or that it didn't happen when Sallie was at home?"

"I hope you're not telling me that this *deus ex something or other* bailed me out of a dilemma I couldn't solve."

"Heavens, no," Kevin assured her. "You'd have brought her to justice one way or another, even if her husband had taken a vacation in Nepal. It's just that the way it happened reminded me of how Euripides and those Greek tragedians used to do it."

"Good. Now let's get something to eat," Carol said. "Just please remember that we're not to share my good news with everyone over dinner. Word might get back to Sallie before I have a chance to read her her rights."

CHAPTER 68

Kevin and Carol had themselves a good dinner at *The Cedar Post,* during which they had said nothing about Vivian Neuberger's murder which might have reached Sallie Finch. Unfortunately, Sallie had not spent the day waiting for the sheriff's next move.

The sheriff and the young officer who was with her had finally paid their respects and left Sallie alone in her empty house with a load of anxiety. News that Larry had died while she was out had, of course, come as a shock. But the knowledge that her husband was dead had been overtaken by even worse news: her gun was now almost certainly in the possession of the sheriff. Losing a spouse was one thing. Losing the weapon with which she had killed Vivian Neuberger was something else, a far more serious blow to her peace of mind.

Sallie stood by the porch door, watching as the sheriff and her companion drove off in their patrol car. The moment they disappeared around the corner, she hastened back to the living room and the now empty shelf which had held her favorite urn ever since she had moved to the house in Yates Center. The urn was still there, of course, but it was now on the floor, leaning against the wall. And it was upside down, just as she knew it would be. That would have been bad enough had it been more or less perpendicular. But it wasn't. The open top of the inverted urn was not flush with the floor. To Sallie it looked like a wide open mouth, a mouth that had spat out her gun when the urn fell to the floor. She got down on her knees for a closer inspection of the problem. It wasn't quite as bad as she thought it would be, but the gap between the urn and the floor was still a good four to five inches wide, more than ample space for the urn to give up the gun when it landed.

There was no point in trying to imagine exactly what had happened. Larry had obviously crashed to the floor, involuntarily reaching out with one or both of his arms as he fell. Whether he had dislodged the urn with his ams or his body didn't matter. One thing was certain. The picture that was now confronting her was the same one the sheriff would have seen when she entered the living room hours earlier, other than that Larry's body and her handgun had been removed.

She climbed to her feet and carefully lifted the urn, turned it right side up, and eased it back onto the shelf were it had spent so much time before today's debacle. Leaning over the urn, she reached inside and probed the bottom. It was empty, as she had been sure it would be. The gun would have been somewhere on the floor, near Larry's body.

Sallie retreated to the kitchen, where she warmed up what was left of the morning's coffee. She would have liked to make a fresh pot, but she needed it now, not in another fifteen minutes. She needed it now because she had some hard thinking to do, and she had always regarded strong coffee as conducive to hard thinking.

The scene which greeted her when she took her coffee back to the living room was too depressing, so she returned to the kitchen, cleared the breakfast dishes off the table, and took a seat. The sheriff had a temporary advantage. By this time she would have put the old CIA Glock in the hands of whoever handled ballistics for her. That person would already have learned enough from his examination of Vivian Neuberger's body to know what he'd be looking for in a gun. It wouldn't take him long to conclude that the gun which had been recovered from her apartment was the gun which had killed Vivian. Or if he could not swear with absolute certainty that it was *the* gun, the odds were close enough that the sheriff could now proceed on the assumption that she, Sallie Finch, had been Vivian's killer.

Well, the sheriff's advantage had to be temporary, and that would be the case only if she took action promptly. It would be the second time during the summer she had had to face the need to act promptly. The first was when she finally realized that Larry was having an affair with Vivian. Sallie had not divorced her first husband, left the CIA, moved to Crooked Lake, and married her old flame from college days only to tolerate his affair with a high school science teacher. She had decided to punish him by killing the object of his affection. She had decided to let him live with the knowledge that he had forever lost the love of his life. She had planned it so carefully, executed it so perfectly, that she had actually enjoyed watching Larry suffer.

That strange interlude in her life had now come to an end. Larry was gone, and Crooked Lake would soon have to follow. She had no desire to pay him - or what was left of him - one last visit. Somebody would step up and take care of his body and his estate. She had been wise to insist on maintaining separate incomes and, for all practical purposes, separate lives. Which made the first step in her disengagement from life in upstate New York a trip to the bank. She finished her coffee, peered out the windows to see whether any of her neighbors were out and about, and learning that none were, quickly got into her car and set off to make a very large withdrawal from Citizens North.

The rest of the afternoon was spent selecting clothes she expected to need in the near future. There was no reason to pack now for all seasons or for all situations. She would shed no tears for the wardrobe she was leaving behind. Saying good-bye to the paintings, the art objects, the collection of books about the Middle East - that was much more difficult, but it couldn't be helped. She made a hasty search through the library shelves, picked out three books which had long been favorites, and tossed them into the little blue suitcase along with her clothes, none of which had been carefully folded. It was fairly late in the afternoon when Sallie set off on a final walk through of the house. She added another pair of earrings and a bracelet to the suitcase, said farewell to a favorite silk areca palm in the second floor corridor, and found room in her purse for a small framed photo of herself on a camel by the pyramids. It was an old picture, and not a particularly flattering one. But it reminded her of another place and another time. It made her smile.

The fridge was well stocked, but she wasn't hungry. She settled for a V8 juice and a peanut butter sandwich.

"Okay, time to go," she said to the empty kitchen as from habit she picked up after herself. Fifteen minutes later she was out of town and heading south. An hour later she was on Route 15 and on her way towards Washington, some 300 miles away.

The road was but lightly traveled, and she was making good time. But she had not made up her mind as to where she would spend the night. Perhaps as soon as Williamsport, maybe Harrisburg. Or if she were still wide awake and willing to spend a few more hours behind the wheel, perhaps somewhere in northern Virginia, not too far from Dulles Airport. Because that was her interim destination. There would be a non-stop flight the next day to Istanbul, and Sallie intended to be on it.

She had made no plans, if one were to discount the steps needed to close and lock the door to the house at 307 Ridge Road and leave

Yates Center before Sheriff Kelleher paid her another visit. She had feigned an upset stomach that afternoon to get the officers of the law out of the house, and they had been sympathetic. They would probably have left soon anyway to give her some time for grieving. But she was sure that they wouldn't be away for long. The clock on the dash told her that it was now 7:29. For all she knew, the sheriff had already tried to contact her. If she hadn't done so today, she would surely be at her door tomorrow.

Well, Sallie said to herself, tomorrow I shall be en route to Istanbul. How long will I be there? I have no idea. I will need to size up the situation, locate old contacts, travel around the region a bit. The one thing I do know is that I have taken my last bird hike.

Sallie had always found the question of when dusk turns to dark a really hard one to answer. By the time she was well into Maryland, the few cars she met all had their lights on, and she had caught a glimpse of a bright moon in the eastern sky. She felt relaxed for the first time since leaving Crooked Lake, and she was at last prepared to concede that it really was dark. Her thoughts turned again to the Middle East and to a line from some book she had read or some play she had seen: the past is another country. She had no intention of ever revisiting the past she had left behind only five hours earlier. It would soon be simply another country. She would, however, soon be revisiting a past she thought she had left behind when she resigned from the CIA. She hoped that it would not seem like another country.

With any luck, Sherif Ali would be there.

CHAPTER 69

The phone rang ten times before Carol heard a recorded message. 'Neither Sallie nor Larry is available. Please leave your name and phone number and we will get back to you as soon as possible. Have a nice day.'

This was bad news and it almost certainly guaranteed that she would not have a nice day. She had obviously miscalculated badly. She would drive over to Yates Center and see for herself what was going on at the house on Ridge Road, but she had no illusions about what she would discover. The odds that Sallie was anywhere near Crooked Lake were somewhere between unlikely and nil.

As she had expected, the house was locked and Sallie's car was gone. She walked around the house, peering in the windows, looking for some sign of life. What she saw told her that Sallie had righted the urn which Larry had knocked over. It told her nothing else.

"Good morning."

Carol turned away from the living room window to see who was there. It was a youngish woman, still in a housecoat, standing on the neighboring porch.

"You must be looking for Mrs. Finch," the woman said. "I think I saw you here yesterday. But Mrs. Finch isn't here. I don't know where she was going, but she left early last evening. She had a little blue suitcase with her."

The odds had just been reduced to nil. Carol sighed. It was a sigh of resignation.

With the help of Yates Center's finest, she gained access to the Finch house, only to find no clue as to where Sallie had gone.

Kevin wasn't at the cottage when she called with the bad news. Her message for him was brief and to the point.

'Not only is Daddy Bird dead; the other Finch has flown the coop. I'm afraid I'm going to need a lot of TLC.'

It was a tired sheriff who walked through the back door of the Blue Water Point cottage that evening.

But contrary to her expectations, Kevin wasn't wearing a long face. He looked positively cheerful.

When he released her from a welcome home hug that momentarily took her breath away, she stepped back and shook her head.

"You didn't check your messages, did you?" she said. "You don't know what happened."

"I think I do, but that's not what we need to talk about after you shed your uniform. We're going to strategize. Okay? Come on, get yourself into something more comfortable while I pour the wine."

"You did get my message?" Carol sounded doubtful.

"I did, and I'm understandably anxious to hear about it. But then we're going to turn our attention to what I assume is the case of the missing Finch. We don't just dress our wounds with TLC around here. We catch criminals."

Carol, somewhat confused by Kevin's mood, nonetheless did what he had asked. Ten minutes later she reappeared on the deck, sans gun and uniform.

"Here," he said, handing her a glass of wine. "Now do you suppose you could give me an abbreviated account of just what happened today. Your message made it sound as if Sallie Finch killed her husband and then took off for parts unknown."

"Correction. I'm sure the para-medics were right - Larry Finch died of natural causes, but Sallie *did* take off for parts unknown because she had become convinced I knew she'd shot Vivian Neuberger. Which means that we had our killer but then let her slip right through our fingers."

"How would Larry's death have convinced her that you knew she was guilty in the Neuberger case?"

"Because of the gun. It's like I told you last night. The minute Sallie saw the overturned urn a look of panic came across her face. Something was missing, and that something was the gun. She knew the gun had been in the urn and would almost certainly have been dislodged when the urn toppled. But where was it? Well, where could it be? In my hands. She had assured me that she no longer had a gun, and that had now been disclosed as a lie. And why had she lied about it? Because she had used the gun to kill Vivian Neuberger."

It didn't take more than ten more minutes for Carol to explain for Kevin's benefit just what had happened at the Finch house.

"And then I blew it," she said. "I should have assigned a couple of my men to keep a close watch on her, to make sure she didn't hit the road. How could I have been so stupid? She's smart. CIA smart. There I was, waiting for a conclusive ballistics report, waiting for her to cook up yet another story about the gun. She's gone, heaven knows where to."

"You mean you don't know where she is tonight. That doesn't mean she's in some alternate universe. We can find her."

"How do you propose to do that?"

"Why not start in the most logical places. How about down around Washington and Langley? That's where she lived most of her professional life. I'd be in touch with her first husband. He'd know who her friends were. He'd know something about her extended family. Or what about the Middle East? That's where she played spook, collected art objects, cultivated relationships with guys like Sherif Ali."

"I'm not exactly Crooked Lake's number one doofus, Kevin. I've already tried to reach Palmer, the ex-husband, and I'll keep trying. But I'm not optimistic. She'll know it's the first place I'd think of, a good reason to go someplace else. Even if that's where she headed, she's not going to go running back to Palmer and it's unlikely that Sallie would have shared much of her private life with him. Like I said, she's CIA smart. As for the Middle East, that's the world's number one black hole. How do you track down a small American woman who could be anywhere from Beirut to Dubai, almost certainly with a name other than Finch? And don't tell me the agency is going to help me find her. They'd rather let a murderer get away scott free than jeopardize the secrecy of their operations."

"I'm not saying it'll be easy, but I am saying that it's way too soon to assume that the Neuberger case is at a dead end. There's your man Byrnes' reputation for tracking down information on the internet. There are airline flights to check."

"I've already started that search, but it's a needle in a haystack exercise when we don't know where she might have been going or what name she was using. I'm a realist, Kevin."

He refilled their glasses and gave his wife a kiss before resuming his seat of the deck.

"All right, let's assume the worst. Our bird-like lady has escaped justice. Bad news, of course, but not the end of the world. If I were your Doctor Watson, I'd have chronicled one success after another when it comes to maintaining law and order on Crooked Lake. I very much doubt that every sheriff wins them all. Even Holmes had a bad day or two. Remember Irene Adler? Or should I refer to her as 'the woman?' In any event, you don't have a cold case on your hands."

"Thanks for the Holmes comparison, but I should remind you that we live in the real world, not fictional Victorian London. Besides, you don't score many points for knowing whodunnit if the culprit lives happily ever after."

"Which means that we're still going to do our best to nail the elusive Mrs. Finch. Right? Let's look at it positively. Maybe doing it will necessitate a trip to some exotic far off place where she's holed up."

The expression on Carol's face said 'no way,' but she managed a smile.

"You know, you're the best thing that ever happened to me. It's hard to get into a funk when you're around to cheer me up with crazy ideas like that. Why don't we shelve Sallie and the Neuberger case for tonight and see about dinner."

"Now that *is* a good idea. Mrs. Finch will keep. After all, tomorrow's another day."

Carol groaned at the throw away Scarlett O'Hara line. Kevin headed for the kitchen.

CPSIA information can be obtained at www.ICGtesting.com
Printed in the USA
BVOW06s0026230615

405651BV00003B/3/P